He was a black Marine Corporal, accused of a crime he did not commit.

He was trapped, desperate, and afraid.

He found the one person who could help him—he read her name in a newspaper article—and sent her an impassioned letter asking for a chance to be heard:

"I would not jeopardize my life, my marriage, or my career to such horrendous actions. I have come this far being very cooperative and patient, by trusting and keeping my faith in the Lord, the help of my wife, family, and friends. I implore you to come to my aid in this time of need."

Activist Lori Jackson believed in Scott's innocence, and she devoted herself to overturning an unjust sentence and freeing an innocent man. In the case of the United States vs. Corporal Lindsey Scott, Lori Jackson was a relentless warrior who fought to see justice served—and won. This is the remarkable true story of a crime, a conviction, and a landmark case in the fight for racial justice.

DANGEROUS
EVIDE

DANGEROUS EVIDENCE

ELLIS A. COHEN

WITH

MILTON J. SHAPIRO

BERKLEY BOOKS, NEW YORK

DANGEROUS EVIDENCE

A Berkley Book / published by arrangement with
Hennessey Entertainment Ltd.

PRINTING HISTORY
Berkley edition / May 1995

ISBN: 0-425-14725-8

BERKLEY®
Berkley Books are published by The Berkley Publishing Group,
200 Madison Avenue, New York, New York 10016.
BERKLEY and the "B" design
are trademarks belonging to Berkley Publishing Corporation.

PRINTED IN THE UNITED STATES OF AMERICA

10 9 8 7 6 5 4 3 2 1

For Lori

I think that if I was the defense counselor, and had (this) case, I would rip the prosecution to shreds.

—MAJ. DONALD THOMSON, USMC,
  former lead prosecutor,
  United States v. *Cpl. Scott*

ACKNOWLEDGMENTS

Being involved in anything for a decade is a long time in anyone's lifetime. Being involved with *Dangerous Evidence*, at times, seemed like a lifetime.

There were many times that I was among masses of people, and there were those many other times that, for better or worse, I was very much alone. But throughout these years there was always an end in sight. And, if I've learned anything from pursuing this story it is what my parents have preached to me over and over again, "You've gotta believe . . ."

Obviously, there are so many people I would like to thank for their tremendous support. Without their support, there would have been no end in sight.

In first position (always) are my dear parents, Leonard and Selma, who were like magicians and did the impossible over and over again: They continued to pull "rabbits" out of some magical hat, which helped me to continue to make this important project a reality. Their love and their many, many personal sacrifices kept me going during some very tough, lonely, and even dangerous moments. I am blessed to have parents who are also my best friends and who always believe in me one hundred percent. I try to replicate their best qualities (and there are many) every day as my show of thanks to them for my being so very fortunate to have them as parents.

Without Lori Jackson, there would have been no end to this book. Without Lori Jackson, Corporal Lindsey Scott would still be serving a thirty-year prison sentence at Leavenworth. And without Lori Jackson, I and so many other people would never have learned the ultimate meaning of believing and sacrificing, or what a guardian angel is really all about. She was a lot of things to a lot of people, but, to me, she was my very special friend. She taught me more about life in five years than all the textbooks I read growing up. *Dangerous Evidence*, which I dedicate to Lori, is meant as the ultimate Valentine to one of the world's best people. Rest in peace!

To John Leino, a lawyer's lawyer, my friend for life: thanks for standing by me over the many years and never wavering in your support and friendship, no matter which way this project turned. Your sincere loyalty, as well as all the time you gave to the research of this book, is deeply appreciated. Again, thank-you for being *semper fi*.

Thanks to Susan Allison, my editor, for her belief and guidance in bringing this book to fruition. Her knowledge of life and her editing skills added immeasurably to the depth and clarity in my finished book.

Thanks to Jennifer Lata, assistant to Susan, for her tremendous help throughout the entire process.

Thanks to Milt Shapiro for seeing and believing in my vision. His many years of writing impressively shows throughout the book. It was a pleasure to have worked with him.

And thanks to Bernard Kurman for selling the book to The Berkley Publishing Group.

From the very early days of this project, there were many other important and significant people who played a vital part in my investigation of the truth about this incredible story:

I thank Joe Wershba, former senior producer of *60 Minutes*, who first hinted that there was an important story within *his* story. Without his tip, there would have been no *Dangerous Evidence*.

Thanks to some wonderful former colleagues of CBS Entertainment, who believed in my long-range vision of this story long before it became a huge national phenomenon: Bob Silberling, Steve Mills, Sid Lyons, Kim LeMasters, Jane Rosenthal, John Kander, Bill Wells, Maddie Horne, Adele O'Dutton, Larry Strykman, Lynne Fields, Norman Powell, Elsie Walton, Richard Katz,

Jonathan Levin, Susan Holliday, Mary Mazur, Pat Guy, Lo Gorious, Elizabeth Masterton, and Ken Stowe.

Thanks to some very special people: Gary and Sheila Lattin, Jean and Dave Caplan, Suzanne M. Ford, Betty Gomes, Roseanne Hartman, Fran Needle (rest in peace!), Dorothy Moen, and my brother Jerry. Without their support, there would be no finished book.

Thanks to some of the important *real* people of this story for their cooperation throughout the years: Gary R. Myers (who became a very special friend); Laurie Tag-Myers (Gary's devoted wife); Patty Leino (John's devoted wife and very special friend to this project); Paul Jackson (Lori's devoted husband); Lori's seven children; Lindsey, Lola and Latavia Scott; James and Mildred Scott (Lindsey's parents); James "Tommy" and Jewell Howard (Lola's parents); Lieutenant Colonel Richard Thomas Harry, USMC (Ret.), and Francis Scott (Lola's friend-in-need).

Thanks to some of the Marines who assisted me throughout the years by answering my many questions and by furnishing me with many vital documents and opening some normally closed doors: Major Ron McNeil (someone I immensely respect and am proud to call my friend. And a special "thanks" to Ron's wife, Dale, for her cooperation in assisting me when I had to track down her husband); Lieutenant Colonel John Shotwell; Major Kathy Robbs; Lieutenant Colonel Fred Peck; Lieutenant Colonel David Tomsky; Lieutenant Colonel Rick Stepien; Lieutenant Colonel Bobbi Weinberger; W.O. Bill Henderson; W.O. Randy Gado; Lieutenant Colonel Jim Messer; Captain Brennan Lynch; Major Frank Pote; 1st Lieutenant Margaret Kuhn; Corporal Tony Garcia; 1st Lieutenant Suzanne Brown; Commander David Larson; Major Jerry Broeckert; Lieutenant James Brooks; Major Alan Roach; Captain Steve Hinkle; Judge Adkins; Judge Clark; Commanding General Frank Petersen; Gunnery Sergeant Paul Gasparotti; and a *special* thanks to Major Donald Thomson for sharing the government's secrets.

Thanks to some additional people and organizations that were associated with this story, who were either interviewed or added some assistance in other ways: NIS agents who allowed me some time and some insight into their world—Agents Lindner, Wardman, Rivers, Martin, and the Public Affairs Officers; Ervan Kuhnke; Ruby Hills; Judy Connors; Nellie McLeod; M. Morgan Cherry; Dave Lagerveld and other members of the Prince William County Police Department; members of the Criminal Investigation Division of Security Battalion, USMC (Quantico); members of the Department of the Navy; members of the FBI; members of the United States Marshals; and members of SAVAS, Inc. (Sexual Assault Victims' Advocacy Service).

Thanks to some of the many reporters (electronic and print) and sketch artists that I shared many questions, answers, notes, and gossip and rumors: Lee Hockstader (*The Washington Post*); Jim Clarke (WJLA-TV / ABC-TV, Washington, D.C.); Gary Craig (*Potomac News* / Associated Press); Mike Brown (*The Courier-Journal*); Joe Johns (WRC-TV / NBC-TV, Washington, D.C.); Julie Brienza (United Press International); Renée Pullum (WUSA-TV/CBS-TV, Washington, D.C.); Ron Sauder (*Richmond Times-Dispatch*); Elaine Lipe (WHAS-TV / CBS-TV, Louisville, Kentucky); Clinton Schemmer (*Potomac News*); Carolyn Landon (Courtroom Sketch Artist); Eileen Mead (*Potomac News*); Nancy Cook (*The Free Lance-Star*); Judy Lineberger (Courtroom Sketch Artist); John McGrath (WHAS-TV / CBS-TV, Louisville, Kentucky); Everett Mitchell, II (*The Courier-Journal*); Karen Gummick (Courtroom Sketch Artist); Lynda Richardson (*The Washington Post*); Richard Cohen (*The Washington Post Magazine*); Dana Verkouteren (Courtroom Sketch Artist); John Hannerhand (WTTG-TV / FOX-TV, Washington, D.C.); and various stringers for CNN.

Finally, thank-you to some very special friends: Ellen Muir, New York City's number-one event-maker, who has been a supportive colleague for more than twenty years and who will succeed one day in convincing me to relocate back to The Big Apple; "Big George" Roberson, who always defines what a friend for life is all about; Lisa Mackey-Ferrell, one of the best professional makeup artists in the USA, who is a caring friend and cheerleader; Steve Yeager, a very accomplished writer-producer-director, who's been advising me for thirty years; Jana Gladstone, who was with me when I first got hooked on this story, and remains one of my good-luck charms; Lee Kappelman, my wonderful TV-motion picture agent, who brings some real excitement and sanity to my day-to-day business; Linda Lichter, my entertainment attorney, who keeps a great legal eye on my company's business; Sue Kanta and Michelle Druckart-Branco, two of the most seasoned supervisors with United Airlines Premier Executive division, who have helped me countless times in my coast-to-coast commutes; Eve Lapolla, my good-buddy, who never quits trying to find the right "Ohio" film project for me; John Moore and James Barnett, my friends at the U.S. Post Office, who always give my mail special handling; and "the little boy," who always keeps my family smiling.

—Ellis A. Cohen

PROLOGUE

"Targets of the Naval Investigative Service (from admirals to seamen to enlisted Marines) complain that NIS agents often make up their minds in advance about a person's guilt or innocence, then build a case to support their theories."

U.S. News & World Report
(cover story, November 9, 1992)

It was the most brutal and sensational crime in memory at Quantico, the primary base of the United States Marine Corps. On the night of April 20, 1983, a young white woman, the wife of a Military Policeman, had allegedly been kidnapped on government grounds by a black assailant, raped, sodomized, and then stabbed in the neck and left for dead. Based solely on the victim's hazy identification—and *no* other direct evidence—a Marine, Corporal Lindsey Scott, the only black MP in the elite Quantico Criminal Investigation Division, was arrested by the NIS, court-martialed, and found guilty of all charges. The Marine was given a lengthy sentence of hard labor at the infamous Leavenworth Prison.

Lori Jackson, a dedicated lifelong civil rights activist—mother of five daughters and two sons, mid-forties, tall, slim, with prominent cheekbones and strawberry-blonde hair, who took pride that she was multiraced: black, white, Cherokee, the product of a turbulent childhood in Alabama where her family had experienced years of discrimination and even death at the hands of the Ku Klux Klan—teamed up with two Washington, D.C., fledgling criminal attornies. Together, they became obsessed with proving the innocence of a man they believed had been "railroaded" and victimized by prejudice. Eventually, civil rights advocates, congressmen, newspaper editorialists, and even CBS-TV's *60 Minutes* joined the cause of justice for the Marine.

This gripping true story—a detective tale and a tense courtroom drama—based on court-martial transcripts, court records, NIS reports, and exclusive on-scene interviews with a compelling cast of characters, will expose the full and shocking truth of how the criminal investigation by the United States government was itself criminal: a combination of bungled investigation, bias, political pressure, suppressed evidence, and a misguided sense of "Semper Fidelis"—the dedication to the Marine mission that in this case resulted in a black eye for the entire military justice system.

> *"If there is any case that encompasses all the elements of faulty police work in the NIS, it is that of Lindsey Scott, a Marine Corporal accused of raping and stabbing a woman on Virginia's Quantico Marine Base in 1983. Scott's lawyers believe the NIS targeted Scott, then built their case against him to fit."*
>
> U.S. News & World Report
> (from the cover story, November 9, 1992)

AUTHORS' NOTE

These are the actual experiences of real people in a very public case. The personalities, events, actions, and conversations portrayed within the story have been reconstructed from extensive research and interviews, utilizing court documents, letters, personal papers, press accounts, on-site observations from the courtroom, personal experiences, and memories of participants.

In an effort to safeguard the privacy of certain individuals, the author has changed their names and, in some cases, altered otherwise identifying characteristics.

All events involving the characters happened as described; only minor details, such as narrative duration, have been altered.

DANGEROUS
EVIDENCE

PART ONE

It is better to risk saving a guilty person
than to condemn an innocent one.

—Voltaire

1

April 20, 1983

They were heading out for an evening on the town, "Mainside" as they called it at the Quantico Marine Base, the huge United States military complex carved out of the forests along the Potomac River thirty-five miles south of Washington. Todd Hamilton, a Navy reservist on two weeks' active duty, had picked up his date, twenty-one-year-old Marine Sergeant Kathleen Brower, at the women's barracks. It was just after 9:30 P.M. as they drove through the dense woods along the main road connecting Quantico's Camp Upshur with the outside world. Suddenly, in the blackness of the pine forest beneath a half-moon, Hamilton's headlights caught the outline of a figure standing in the middle of the road about a hundred yards ahead.

As Hamilton's 1974 Plymouth Valiant topped a rise in the road, he made out the shape of a woman. She was darting left, then right, reminding him of the first time, near his home in Michigan, he'd seen a startled deer caught in his headlights. With one hand the woman was clutching her throat, then she began waving her arms in a strange, frantic way. Hamilton slammed on his brakes. The woman lurched toward the car. Leaning heavily on the hood for support, she made her way to the driver's-side window. As she reached him Hamilton saw that her face and neck were smeared with blood. Blood stained the sleeves of her jacket. Stunned, he rolled down his window, but before he could speak she cried out, "Oh God! Oh God, please help me! . . . He raped me! He cut my throat. . . . I'm dying! I think I'm dying!"

She collapsed onto the backseat as the horrified couple quickly locked the car doors and gave her a wad of napkins to stanch the flow of blood. In the darkness they couldn't see much, but could tell she was young, in her early twenties perhaps, smallish, about five-four. Her short brown hair was matted with blood, her round face frozen in a mask of fear. The woman was close to hysteria, gasping that she couldn't breathe. Hamilton feared for her life. He threw the car into reverse, made a U-turn, and sped back toward the MASH unit at Upshur, about ten minutes away.

The woman sobbed quietly, fighting to catch her breath. Hamilton and Brower figured they had to keep her talking, keep her from slipping away. Brower consoled her, told her she was safe now. Hamilton pushed the old car as hard as he dared, up past seventy miles an hour, trying to concentrate on his driving. He started to pepper her with questions, partly to get her story, partly just to keep her conscious until they could get to the Marine medics.

"Am I going to die?" the woman whimpered.

No, no, they reassured her; her attacker hadn't cut a main artery, Hamilton told her, although, actually, judging from the way she was bleeding and the position of her wounds, he wasn't so sure.

"Who are you?" he asked.

Slowly, haltingly, she sobbed out her answers. "I'm J-Judy . . . Judy C-Connors.*"

"Are you married?"

"Yes . . . my husband is K-Kevin. Corporal Kevin C-Connors.*"

Kathy Brower asked how they could find him to bring him to her. She told them he was a cop, Lance Corporal Kevin Connors, a Marine MP, part of the Security Battalion that policed the giant base.

"Judy, what happened to you?" Hamilton asked.

"He . . . he raped me. He tried . . . tried to strangle me . . . stabbed me and th-then he tried to cut my throat. . . . Oh God, thank you so much for stopping!"

Her voice was fading now and Hamilton felt a wave of panic at the thought that this woman might die right there in the car.

"Who did this to you, Judy?"

"A big black man! He called me . . . said my husband had

---

*Authors' note: Asterisk denotes a fictitious name of a real person.

been in a very bad car accident . . . and he was supposed to take me to him. He raped me! . . . Please, hurry! I can't breathe!"

Between her sobs and moans, her breathing was labored, but Hamilton kept pressing her for details because he had the awful feeling nobody might ever again get the chance to hear her story.

He was flooring the car and in his haste missed the turnoff. He stopped and backed up, silently cursing the delay. Her moaning sounded weaker and she appeared to be losing consciousness.

Finally, after a drive that seemed endless to Hamilton, the inflatable shell of the camp's MASH unit came into view. The car screeched to a halt in the driveway. Brower ran inside to get help and call the MPs while Hamilton gently lifted the small woman from the blood-drenched rear seat and carried her into the makeshift treatment room. The Marine medic needed just one look at the shivering victim to appreciate the emergency. This woman needed a doctor—at once. Quickly the medics bundled her into an ambulance, which roared off to the base regional clinic about five miles away.

Alerted by the MPs, Special Agent James F. Lindner, the investigator on duty that night for the Naval Investigative Service (NIS), was waiting at the first-aid station by the time they wheeled Judy Connors into the emergency room. A former U.S. Army police lieutenant, Lindner had been just eighteen months with the NIS, the agency that investigates felony crimes in the Navy and Marines. Despite his limited experience with the NIS, from the sketchy information shouted over the phone—a white woman, the young wife of a Marine cop, raped and stabbed by a black assailant—Lindner sensed that this could be the most sensational crime to hit the Marine base in many years.

The agent pressed in toward the victim, eager to talk to her. The Navy medics, caught up in the chaos of the emergency room, stopped him, told him he'd have to wait. The victim had lost a lot of blood, her temperature had dropped to ninety-five degrees. She had a deep slash and four puncture wounds near her jugular vein and her trachea.

"Am I going to die? Am I going to die?" Judy Connors moaned. Lindner thought the answer was yes. He was struck by how small and frail she looked. The medics wrapped her in a warming blanket, got her on an IV, and started two units of blood. She was coughing up blood clots and the doctors feared that two of the deeper knife wounds could be life threatening. They decided to transfer her immediately to the Naval Regional Medical Center at Bethesda, the Navy's showcase hospital, famous for treating the presidents of the United States.

Lindner was joined now by NIS agent Claude Rivers and Marine Sergeant Andrew Bryant, who worked with the victim's husband in Quantico's Criminal Investigation Division, the base police force. The three investigators needed desperately to get more details before the victim was taken away. Lindner grabbed her bloodied jacket and blouse to be analyzed for hairs and fibers. He made a mental note to call ahead to Bethesda to make sure the NIS agent there took custody of the rest of her clothes for laboratory analysis. A medical rape examination would also be crucial for the gathering of evidence: pubic hair and semen samples, fingernail scrapings, and any other stray bits of material, no matter how seemingly insignificant or microscopic.

All that would have to wait until the victim got to the hospital. For now, though, Lindner needed more information to get the investigation rolling. They would head out to the crime scene, of course, but first he had to pump the woman for as many details as possible, and as soon as possible, while the attack was still fresh in her mind.

Even as they were wheeling her to the ambulance, Lindner questioned the victim. Dazed, her voice faltering, she gave the agents the outline of her story: her husband, Kevin, had been on night duty and she'd been home alone in her garden apartment, just off the base grounds. Around eight o'clock she'd received a phone call. The man didn't give a name and she hadn't recognized his voice, but he said that her husband had been injured in a terrible automobile accident near Camp Upshur. The caller said they would send someone immediately to pick her up and take her to the base hospital.

Quickly she'd changed her clothes and rushed down the stairs to the parking lot, where she found a car already waiting and backing up toward her. She got in. The man drove her through the woods toward where she thought the hospital was located. However, after a long drive deep into the woods, he pulled to the roadside and stopped the car. He pulled out a knife and forced her to perform oral sex on him. She tried to escape, but he flashed the knife and said, "I wouldn't do that." Then he raped her on the front seat.

Afterward, he ordered her out of the car and marched her into the woods at knifepoint. He made her lie on the ground, then he choked her until she passed out. When she regained consciousness, he was gone and she realized she'd been stabbed in the throat.

Lindner had dozens more questions to ask, but the victim seemed to be fading. He pushed on, however, quietly, getting her to describe the rapist's car, which she thought was tan, or gold, with a dark interior, and she remembered something like a bucket or pail on the backseat because she heard something rattle. She was woozy, but she was able to give the agents a rough image of the man: a big black man, maybe five-eight, with glasses, short hair, and a yellowish or tan jacket.

The medics insisted on lifting her into the ambulance then, and as it raced away the investigators were left with a vague, shadowy outline to go on, a physical description of the man that could fit perhaps hundreds of black men on the sprawling base—and hundreds more off it.

Rivers, nonetheless, reacted swiftly to the woman's description of her assailant. "Sounds like Scotty," he said.

Lindner knew who Rivers meant. True, there were as many as a thousand black men among the nine thousand people who lived and worked at Quantico, and countless other blacks who lived near the Virginia base. The victim had not said a word about her attacker being a military man; nor was there anything else to pinpoint his identity as one—not much, in fact, of a definitive description except that he was black. Yet, within the tightly knit police fraternity, Rivers and Lindner knew only one black man who had reached the ranks of the Criminal Investigation Division, where the victim's husband worked. Only one black man among the hundreds of MPs on the base was now training to join the more elite corps of criminal investigators: Marine Corporal Lindsey Scott.

Lindsey Scott, Marine No. 407-78-9524, was a soft-spoken,

bespectacled college graduate from Louisville, Kentucky. He was twenty-seven years old, had joined the Marines three years earlier after being graduated from Eastern Kentucky University, where he'd studied law enforcement and corrections. He had been a three-sport varsity athlete at DeSales High, an all-white Catholic high school in Louisville, where he was regarded as a serious, if unremarkable student. He had gone on to become the school's first black graduate, much to the proud delight of his parents. Scott was the second youngest among the seven children in a religious, working-class family. His father, James, was an executive chef at a General Electric plant. His mother, Mildred, worked in a factory.

Lindsey Scott professed a strong dedication to the Marines, an admiration for the Corps that was born when he was a little boy watching gung-ho military movies in largely segregated theaters. Clearly the Marines were the best. Young Lindsey wanted to be part of the best. Since boot camp he had progressed steadily: a training stint at Fort McClellan, Alabama, learning to be a military policeman, two promotions, a series of good ratings for conduct and proficiency. Now he was training as an investigator in the Criminal Investigation Division and getting his papers in order to apply for Officers' Candidate School.

Inevitably, Scott stood out sharply as the only black in CID, the only black who worked directly with the base investigators. There was something else distinctive about Corporal Scott, something in his physical appearance. He had a slight trace of a harelip; it gave his speech an occasional lisp. Further, he had a prominent gold tooth in the upper front of his mouth. Because he tended to be a mouth breather, Scott's gold tooth was visible even when he wasn't smiling. Everyone who met him remembered that gold tooth.

On the night of April 20, 1983, as the ambulance bearing Judy Connors sped to the hospital at Bethesda, followed by a military escort, Lindsey Scott was at home, in bed with his wife, Lola, at their off-base apartment. Earlier that evening he had been out shopping for gifts for Lola; the following day was her birthday, and a special one. Lindsey and Lola had known each other since college. Happily married to Lindsey, and after several years trying to conceive following an earlier miscarriage, Lola was now five months' pregnant.

Scott had a clean record as a Marine. He had never been in trouble. When he and Lola turned in for the evening, it was destined to be his last night of peace for a long time to come. Lindsey Scott was about to experience a Kafkaesque nightmare.

2

On the morning following the crime, Agent Lindner drove the forty-five miles from Quantico to the Bethesda Naval Medical Center for the first order of business, getting the victim to put together a facial composite portrait of her attacker. He carried with him the small brown box that contained the "Identi-Kit" marketed by the Smith & Wesson Company and often employed by law-enforcement agencies. Lindner was well trained in the use of the little brown box; he'd used it during dozens of investigations and he knew that obtaining an accurate composite would be crucial to the case.

Back at Quantico, meanwhile, NIS agents would be checking the base vehicle roster to see whether anyone's car matched the description given by Judy Connors. Other agents would be out combing the woods, searching for the crime scene. Lindner shuddered as he pictured the bruised and bloodied face of the victim. Now, as he approached the hospital, he tried to picture the face of her assailant.

"Sounds like Scotty." Claude Rivers's comment flashed through Lindner's mind. He was an experienced enough agent, however, to know that Rivers's knee-jerk suggestion about Lindsey Scott must not influence his handling of the Identi-Kit. Yet Lindner knew Scott, knew his features: slightly chubby for a Marine, thick lips, short hair, glasses, and that little something wrong with his lip. It was a familiar face, after all, because until recently, when Scott moved, the two men had lived in the same apartment complex—Spanish Gardens. Judy Connors, too, lived at Spanish Gardens, where, on several occasions, she had seen Lindsey Scott.

Most law-enforcement agencies, as a matter of course, do not allow an investigator to direct a case in which he knew both suspect and victim. Personal knowledge—perhaps even prejudice—could color the investigator's perceptions and judgment, influence his handling of the unfolding evidence. But in the insular world of the Naval Investigative Service, this potential complication was ignored. NIS Agent Lindner was on the case. That the NIS would overlook this problem, arguably a conflict of interest, was not surprising; historically, the agency was not famous for consistent, meticulous attention to detail.

Lindner knew the Identi-Kit would be difficult; it was so under the best of circumstances. Now, as he observed Judy Connors's puffy eyes, her bandaged face and neck, he wondered how sharp she would be. Pulling a chair up to her bedside, he began to walk her through the Identi-Kit process: using clear plastic sheets in a ring binder to select various facial features, choosing from among hundreds of lips, noses, eyes, chins, and hairstyles. Only Lindner and the victim were present in the hospital room as they tried to assemble the face of the rapist. Sensing Judy's fragility, the agent spoke slowly, his voice gentle.

Working from her description—a black male, about twenty-five years old, medium height, medium-to-husky build—Lindner assembled the corresponding plastic sheets. Then, following the kit's instructions, he began to overlay the clear plastic sheets that would add specific characteristics to the face.

He started with Chin 03, and referring to the charts for assembling a black male face, he added Nose 21 and Lips 23. The Smith & Wesson chart suggested Eyes 25. A broad-nosed, thick-lipped face began to take shape, a face with cold, empty eyes.

Judy Connors had said her assailant wore squarish, black-framed glasses. Lindner added those, then began working on the hair, which he knew was usually the toughest aspect of an ID. This was the only section of the Identi-Kit where the investigator was instructed to begin by showing the various choices to the subject; hairstyles are too numerous for reliance on an accurate verbal description, and hair is often a person's most distinctive characteristic.

Lindner asked her to look at all the hairstyles. She chose Number 136, a shortish mass of tight curls.

He added 136 to the binder and showed her the half-formed face.

"Too short . . . longer," she said, gesturing toward the chin. Lindner moved the plastic sheet by one notch, sliding the chin downward to lengthen the face. He showed it to her again.

"Um . . . lips. The lips are too thick."

He switched Lips 23 to Lips 22 and showed the face to her once more. Still too thick, so he tried Lips 21.

"Okay, Judy," he said softly, "I'm going to show you the face again and please tell me, is there anything wrong with the picture?"

She squinted at the face and furrowed her brow. "The glasses are still wrong." They weren't square enough, she said. So Lindner substituted a pair that was a bit more squarish, Number 15.

"There's still something wrong with the hair," she said.

Lindner showed her the book and, again, following procedure, allowed her to pick out the hairstyle herself. She chose 133 this time, but when he added it to the composite, she shook her head in disappointment. It was still all wrong. Somehow, the shape didn't work. Too long on top. This did not look like the man.

The hair, as usual, was the problem, Lindner realized. She wanted shorter hair, but the Identi-Kit didn't have anything shorter. Improvising, he took Number 136, the original style she'd chosen, and dropped the whole head of hair down by one notch to make it look more closely cropped. Then he turned the binder once again to show her.

Judy Connors's eyes widened, and she paled. Her hands came up to her mouth and she began to sob, shaking her head violently.

"That's him," she said. She closed her eyes for a long moment, opened them again, stared at the composite. "That looks like the man."

Lindner looked at her then back at the Identi-Kit. The face that he had assembled was the face of Lindsey Scott. He left the kit at her bedside and walked out into the hall to find a telephone.

*   *   *

It was a bright spring morning at Quantico. Corporal Lindsey Scott, wearing his best "dress blues," was enjoying a rare day off, watching a military parade on the broad, manicured lawn of the base drill field. He snapped to attention and saluted the passing color guard just as his superior, Sergeant David Martin, pulled up in a Jeep. "Hop in, Scotty," Martin said pleasantly, patting the empty seat beside him. As they drove off, Martin asked, casually, if he'd heard the news. Scott appeared puzzled—what news?—then horrified as the sergeant began unfolding the grisly story that occurred the previous night in the woods near Camp Upshur.

Martin said it was the worst crime on the base in living memory and the victim was Kevin Connors's wife. Scott, who had trained with Connors and at times carpooled with him, expressed his shock and sympathy.

Sergeant Martin might have allowed Scott a few minutes to stop and change his uniform; instead he drove him directly toward Camp Upshur to join in the search for the crime scene.

When the Jeep pulled to a stop off the road among the thick woods, Scott heard the barking of police bloodhounds and could see dozens of men from Security Battalion walking the bumpy road and scouring the underbrush. All the Marines were wearing their "cammies," camouflage uniforms. Conspicuous enough as the only black in his unit, Scott now felt distinctly out of place in his dress blues. What he didn't know, of course, but later believed, was that this was part of a calculated tactic by the NIS to single him out. (Scott and his lawyers would later be convinced.) They wanted to see how he would react at the scene of the crime.

As a member of the Criminal Investigation Division and an investigator-in-training, Scott had never participated in a serious case of this nature. Thus, over the next hour or so, as the search for the crime scene continued, he asked questions of various colleagues: how was such an investigation carried out, how was evidence obtained, how long would a semen sample remain detectable—and so on. The responses were curt, brusque, and to Scott it seemed that the eyes of his colleagues lingered on him, their glances questioning. Perhaps, the thought occurred to him, he was being too inquisitive. Still, he was studying to become a criminal investigator, and he recalled that his commanding officer had explicitly told him, "You never learn if you don't ask questions."

By midafternoon, with nothing discovered, not even certain they'd searched anywhere near the right place, Scott's unit motored back to their base of operations, the Provost Marshal's Office (PMO).

Their failure to pin down the crime scene posed frustrating problems for the investigators, for surely it would yield important clues, forensic evidence. They would try again, and yet again, if necessary. Meanwhile PMO was buzzing with talk about the rape case. Scott sensed that when he talked to his colleagues about it, there was something indefinably strange about their responses, a coldness, a withdrawal. He was being treated differently. He wasn't sure why, until suddenly it dawned on him, and he began to sweat under the hot glare of suspicion.

By day's end, gnawing anxiety became stark fear. Two investigators, including Rivers, the man who had initially targeted him, told him he was wanted at NIS headquarters. "When we get you over there," Rivers said ominously, "we're going to make a deal with you." Escorted to the grim red-brick building, deposited alone in an empty office, Scott fought to control his rising panic.

More than most Marines, Scott knew enough to be particularly frightened of the NIS. He'd heard how they worked and he knew that for whatever reason, once they targeted you, you were finished.

They kept him waiting in that cheerless room, alone—standard psychological pressure—until finally NIS Agent Kenneth Rodgers, a big, beefy man, walked in with another man, whom Scott did not recognize. This was David Lagerveld, top criminal investigator of the Prince William County Police—the county in which the Quantico base was located. In the cramped interview room they began a barrage of questions that would continue for several hours.

"Where were you last night?"

"Did you loan your car to anyone?"

"Who were you with last night?"

"Can you prove to us you're not our man?"

Bewildered, Scott didn't know how to respond to their rapid-fire questions. This had to be a bad dream. He tried to remain calm, but he was petrified, angry, deeply hurt that his colleagues should abruptly turn on him for what he now believed was no other reason than his race. He answered their questions as best he could; still they kept at him, hammering away, repeating themselves, trying to catch him in a lie, to wear him down. Time and again Scott denied any knowledge of the attack.

"Cut the shit," Rodgers finally said. "You're our prime suspect."

Scott felt dizzy, felt his heart pounding as he heard them inform him of his rights and offer him a chance to summon a lawyer. No, he said, he didn't need any lawyer and he would answer all their questions. He then told them, in considerable detail, where he had been the previous day and what he had done.

Scott said he'd left work in the afternoon to go to his recently vacated apartment at Spanish Gardens. His former landlady, Maxine Knight, had told him he would have to scrub down the apartment, mop the floors, and scrape the stove clean before she would return his $220 security deposit.

While cleaning, Scott remembered that he had to stop by his bank to get cash because the next day was his wife's birthday and he wanted to buy her a present. He got to the Virginia National Bank just before the seven P.M. closing, returned to the apartment to finish cleaning, and then got his security deposit. From there, Scott said, he went to the nearby town of Dumfries, where he bought Lola a foot massager at a discount drugstore. Her pregnancy made this a special birthday, and though it was around 7:30, he decided to look for a second gift. He drove about twenty miles to a Zayre's department store in Woodbridge. There he browsed for a while, looking at things for his wife and at some men's clothes. He didn't find anything he wanted. At the soda fountain he bought a Coke, then headed back to his new apartment at the Chesapeake Apartments, located off US 1. On the way home he stopped at a place called Quikee's for ice cream, but though staff were inside, it appeared closed, so he continued on to his apartment, arriving about 9:30.

If true, Scott's alibi would have made it impossible for him to have committed the assault on Judy Connors sometime between eight and nine P.M.

During the lengthy questioning, Scott was allowed to make a phone call home. To his astonishment he discovered that Lola already knew what was happening. She told him that Rivers and Martin of NIS had been to the apartment. She said they told her they were cops who were also friends trying to help her husband, so she'd given them permission to take away some of his clothes. For some strange reason, she said, they'd also taken away her aluminum chili cooking pot.

This last item puzzled Scott until he learned later about Judy Connors's statement that she heard the rattling of a metallic bucket on the backseat of the rapist's car. Actually, during the course of his questioning, Scott had mentioned using a green plastic bucket for cleaning the old apartment; he would never have used the cooking pot for cleaning, so why would they take that pot away? He was dumbfounded until a thought occurred to him.

"I'm innocent!" he shouted when he got off the phone. "I didn't do it!" The most bizarre part, to Scott, was that Judy Connors knew him. Surely she would tell NIS that he was not the man. The Connorses and the Scotts had lived in the same apartment complex until just the previous day, when the Scotts had moved. They'd seen each other around. He and Lola had even bumped into Kevin and Judy a few days earlier outside a K Mart. It was grotesque! "We're neighbors!" Scott explained. "Just ask her. She'll tell you the truth. She'll tell you it wasn't me. She'll tell you Kevin carpools with me. We were in training together!"

Scott's words fell on deaf ears. He sensed the interrogation was turning more hostile. Ugly. He had waived his rights to a lawyer; now, however, after another lengthy, exhausting session of questioning, he said that if the harassment continued he would demand an attorney. With that the questioning stopped.

Scott did consent to a search of his work locker and his car. The agents found nothing of value. The Prince William County police crime-scene technicians dusted his car for fingerprints. They found none.

They did, however, discover something they believed was extremely significant. It appeared to the county police that the passenger-side window, the inside surface of the passenger door, and the front seat had been carefully wiped down—to remove all fingerprints, they concluded. Confronted with this, Scott vehe-mently denied it. Nevertheless, to the NIS investigators it was clear evidence of his guilt. They believed that using his back-ground knowledge as a criminal investigator, Scott had removed or erased from his car anything that might incriminate him.

Less than twenty-four hours into the case, the NIS agents were thoroughly convinced they had solved the crime. Their investiga-tion had started with Lindsey Scott and it would end with Lindsey Scott.

3

At Quantico, where the vicious assault on Judy Connors swiftly became known as "the crime of the century," the NIS agents began to tighten the noose around Lindsey Scott. Special Agent James Lindner was well aware that the first forty-eight hours following a crime were the most important for securing hard evidence and cracking a case; after that, memories become increasingly vague and the trail grows cold. Thus, on the day following the crime, while other agents were grilling Scott and checking out his apartment, his car, and his locker, Lindner returned to the hospital at Bethesda to conduct a "photo lineup" with Judy Connors. This would serve as a preliminary to a live lineup.

The victim was still sedated, weakened from loss of blood, when Lindner presented her with six photographs, including one of Scott. According to the agent's subsequent written report, the photographs were "similar in photographic composition" and all the individuals "approximated each other in physical characteristics." Initially, Lindner showed her the photographs one by one. She shook her head at the first three. When she came to the fourth—Scott—she became "visibly upset," according to Lindner, and said, "That looks like the man."

The agent continued, and when they reached photograph number six, again "the victim became visibly upset" and said, "That looks like the man also."

Lindner then showed her all six photographs together, spread out on a manila folder, with Scott again number four (from left) and the other man she'd picked out again number six (from left).

Judy picked out Scott.

"How do you recognize this man?" Lindner asked.

"That's the man that raped me."

"Can you be sure?"

"Well . . . this man here also looks like the man," she said, pointing to the other photograph she'd selected.

"Do you have a preference?"

"Yes, number four [Scott] looks a little more like him because number six's lips are a little too wide."

Agent Lindner's report goes on to state, "Victim added, however, that they both looked like her assailant."

Though the NIS agents didn't have enough on Scott to charge him, they immediately suggested to his battalion commander, Lieutenant Colonel Philip Hemming, that he be removed from the Criminal Investigation Division. Hemming ordered Scott transferred to a supply unit on the base, and immediately rumors began to fly about his guilt. He was shunned, isolated, particularly by white Marines. A few friends told him there was even a rumor that Judy's husband, Kevin, was gunning for him.

Scott had barely unpacked his bags on his new assignment, however, before Lindner decided he was a serious AWOL risk. He recommended Hemming have Scott arrested immediately. Hemming agreed, and now, fewer than forty-eight hours after the crime, Scott was handcuffed and taken into custody. Unlike civilian suspects who must be arraigned within seventy-two hours, Scott could be held indefinitely at the pleasure of his commanding officer.

Scott was allowed a phone call to Lola, and she raced to his side at the infamous Quantico brig, the federal prison facility that had recently housed the would-be assassin who shot President Reagan, John Hinckley. In a secured visitors' room, with guards watching, Lindsey and Lola hugged and cried. He told her he was petrified, NIS was out to get him. He said he'd better get a lawyer right away, but he didn't know any, didn't know anybody he could trust to recommend one, either. In desperation, he asked the guards for the Yellow Pages, and looked through the advertisements under *Lawyers*. Perhaps by chance, perhaps proving the efficacy of an ad in the Yellow Pages—Scott never could provide an explanation—he chose Dumfries Law Offices, at Triangle Plaza South, not far from the base. The firm listed twelve different specifics under its general practice headings; last on the list was criminal.

Scott called the law office and asked for either Ervan Kuhnke or Marilyn Rose, respectively numbers one and two of the three lawyers listed for the firm. Since neither attorney was in, the secretary took the call and left a message on Kuhnke's desk. Later that afternoon, when he returned to his office, Kuhnke discussed the call from Scott with Marilyn Rose. She said she wasn't interested, so Kuhnke—a sixty-two-year-old retired CIA agent, telephoned Scott, listened to a brief summary of the situation, and told him he'd come down to the brig to talk to him. It was the beginning of an ill-fated relationship.

At the brig meeting Scott told Kuhnke he was innocent. He related in detail his version of his movements on the night of the crime. The lawyer, a balding, bespectacled man with a pipe that seemed permanently fixed between his lips, listened as Scott outlined his alibi point by point, naming names or at least giving descriptions of people he had seen on the afternoon and evening of the crime. Kuhnke believed his story and agreed to handle the case for a fee of $1,000, implying that he didn't anticipate spending much time on it. Based on what Scott had told him, the absence of evidence, and the seeming solidity of the alibi, Kuhnke felt the case was so weak that the Marines would never bring it to trial.

As subsequent events would disclose, Kuhnke's memory of that first meeting with Scott differed in both substance and interpretation from his client's—as did the memories of both men differ in testifying of further meetings. However, they would not be alone in their struggles with the shifting sands of memory.

Three days later, on the morning of April 25, Scott called Kuhnke again and told him NIS had scheduled a physical lineup for one o'clock that afternoon. Scott asked him to be there to represent him. Kuhnke said that wouldn't be necessary. Instead, he telephoned the office of the staff judge advocate (an equivalent to the attorney general) and spoke to Major Alan Roach, head defense counsel. He told Major Roach he had a client, suspected of rape and attempted murder, who was to appear in a military lineup at Security Battalion that afternoon. He asked for a military defense counsel to be sent over to represent his client (this was an automatic entitlement for any accused military person).

Realizing the seriousness of the offense, Major Roach assigned himself to the case, called Security Battalion, arranged a meeting with Scott, then called Special Agent Lindner to request that he be present during the lineup. Before the actual lineup, a preliminary was held using the men chosen by NIS; Major Roach objected to two of the men on the grounds that they were too thin compared with Scott. Finally five men were chosen: a corporal, three sergeants, and, interestingly enough, Major Donald Thomson*, a prosecuting attorney with the staff judge advocate's office. Selected because he was stockily built along the lines of Scott, Major Thomson had to shave off his mustache for the lineup; as the most experienced trial counsel at SJA, the major reappears later in this surreal drama as a much more important player.

That afternoon, NIS agents took a frightened Judy Connors from her hospital bed back to Quantico for the live lineup. She was brought there in a wheelchair, her neck and face heavily bandaged, and she was shaky and fearful at the prospect of confronting the man who had raped and stabbed her. By now she had given a full statement about the crime, adding a few chilling details: when the rapist had initially forced her to perform oral sex, he asked whether she did this to her husband, whose name he knew. When she was being choked and losing consciousness, she remembered, her assailant had laughed at her; a weird, high-pitched laugh.

The Quantico base newspaper and the local media carried sensational stories about the case now, though Scott had not been formally charged. Pressure was building on Lindner and the others to wrap things up, and they were more determined than ever. They brought Judy Connors to the base television studio for the lineup, and they marched Scott from the brig to the studio—in handcuffs and shackles, for all to see.

Inside, the six black Marines lined up were dressed alike in white T-shirts, camouflage fatigues, and black boots. They faced a wooden partition while the bruised and haggard victim, with a nurse attending her, viewed them through a peephole.

Two crucial factors could be said to affect the integrity of this lineup: Scott was the only man among the six whose picture had also been in the photo lineup, so his face would seem familiar to Judy. And in any case, Judy already knew Scott from Spanish Gardens and had seen him as recently as four days prior to the assault, when the Scotts and the Connorses bumped into each other at the K mart and the two men had exchanged pleasantries.

With everything ready, the Marines were ordered to turn in unison to the left, then to the front, to the right, to the rear, then again to the front, at which time the victim was asked, "Do you recognize anyone?"

"The two on the right look like him," Judy said. Scott was fifth in the line.

One at a time the two men were asked to step forward and face left. The victim was asked if she could identify either of them.

"Number five looks like him," she said.

"Can you be sure?"

"Number five and number six both look like the man. Number six has longer hair, more like him, but I can't be sure which one looks more like him. I'm sorry. I didn't really get a good enough look at him. But number five scares me the most."

As veteran criminal lawyers know, eyewitness identification makes for dramatic courtroom theatrics on TV shows, but is notoriously unreliable in real-life courtrooms — particularly in the case of cross-racial identifications. Studies have shown that witnesses, regardless of their ethnic background, are much more accurate when identifying people of their own race and consistently less reliable with people of different races. However, this was, arguably, not real life but the military. Judy Connors's qualified identification of her attacker was good enough for NIS; though there were obvious problems with it, thus far it was the best single piece of evidence they had to nail Lindsey Scott.

In a case like this, a kind of collective delusion can take hold; the investigators, once they believe in the victim's identification, tend to see the rest of the case with blinders on. If they accept her identification, then they must believe that the other pieces of evidence fit. If those pieces don't fit, the nuances and outright contradictions tend to be ignored rather than explored.

Indeed, there were contradictions. There was a significant discrepancy, for example, between Scott's car and the car described by the victim. Judy Connors said originally she was attacked in a yellowish or brownish car that she believed was a Chevy Nova. Scott's car was a 1976 Buick Skylark, similar in design to a Nova—but two-tone. It was beige with a white landau roof and it had distinctive mag wheels, details that had never been mentioned in her statements.

Right after the physical lineup, though Judy was still heavily sedated, NIS agent Richard Wardman drove her around the base to see if she could spot the car in which she'd been attacked. Significantly, in the backseat was her angry husband, Kevin; significant because he had carpooled with Scott and knew his car; questionable investigative procedure, certainly. There were many ways Judy's husband, inadvertently or deliberately, might taint any identification she made—a cough, a look, a suggestion to Wardman, for example.

For a time, as they drove around the base, though Judy saw a few cars that she said were similar in size and color, she could not make a positive identification. Then, in the parking lot of the Provost Marshal's Office, she said she saw a car that looked the same in color, size, and general body style. According to the official NIS report, she got out of the NIS car and peered into the interior of the suspect car. "The victim became visibly upset" and said that such things as the location of the ashtray, the gas gauge, and the general interior "appeared similar" to her attacker's car.

This indeed was Lindsey Scott's car. It had been impounded and placed in the PMO parking lot.

Another important question of identification was the knife used in the attack. Scott had admitted borrowing a small, serrated steak knife from his landlady on the day of the crime, to use in cleaning the crud off the stove of his old apartment. The NIS agents wanted him to produce it. Scott didn't have it. He said that as he was gathering up all his cleaning supplies and leaving his old place, he must have thrown it away along with the garbage. The agents didn't buy the story. They believed it was the weapon used in the attack.

The problem with their conclusion was that in her statements Judy had described a knife—even did a sketch for NIS—showing a definite hilt. This was not a feature of a household steak knife, and Scott's landlady definitely said the knife he had borrowed had no hilt.

Meanwhile, NIS agents had not been idle. Agents Claude Rivers and Kenneth Rodgers had been out to the Dumfries Pharmacy to interview the salesclerks. One of the women there stated—according to the agents' report—that she remembered seeing Scott on the night of April 20 and selling him a foot massager sometime between 7:30 and eight. She remembered him saying it was for his wife, who was pregnant. She remembered that he was wearing glasses and seemed to be in a hurry.

The gaps in the evidence against Scott were still huge by normal investigative standards; in particular the lack of forensic evidence usually needed to link a rape victim with an alleged rapist. Scott, behind bars in the Quantico brig, was asked to grant what was called "a permissive search authorization" so NIS could get a sample of his blood. Through his military defense counsel, Major Roach, Scott told them no.

NIS was not to be denied. The following day Lieutenant Colonel Hemming issued a command authorization for a "search and seizure," based on "probable cause." The affidavit supporting this forcible taking of a blood sample, executed by NIS Case Agent Lindner, states, in part: ". . . there is reason to believe that within the blood of Corporal Lindsey Scott, USMC 407–78–9524 . . . there are now identifying constituents matching those found on victim's and suspect's clothing; and also in the sperm mobility slides, pubic hair samples, and vaginal swabs taken from the victim. . . ."

A Navy medic took the blood sample while Lindner watched. Scott, resigned to the entire procedure, mindful of the power now of "command authorization," caved in to Lindner's request for samples of his saliva and pubic hair.

With Scott in confinement, Major General Twomey, as base commanding officer, ordered a magistrate's hearing for April 27, to determine whether or not Scott should remain in the brig or be released while the investigation continued. The military magistrate was Lieutenant Colonel Richard T. Harry, a colorful, much-decorated twenty-year Marine veteran who had been a combat helicopter pilot in Vietnam.

Scott, who had been passing his days in the brig reading and praying, was once again shackled and handcuffed and marched by the MPs to the Quantico courtroom at LeJeune Hall. Named for General John A. LeJeune, a revered former Marine commander, the four-story red-brick building also housed, on the third floor, the offices of the base commander, Major General David Twomey.

Lieutenant Colonel Harry convened the hearing the next day. Scott was there with his wife, Lola; Major Roach and Ervan Kuhnke were there for the defense; Special Agent Lindner was there, Lieutenant Colonel Hemming, and, acting as trial counsel for the prosecution now, Major Thomson, who had been in the six-man physical lineup with Scott.

Lindner presented the evidence gathered thus far against Scott; this included the Identi-Kit, the photo lineup and the physical lineup, and Judy Connors's statement that Scott's car "appeared similar" to her recollection of her assailant's.

Scott told his story all over again. However, he added one detail of possible significance regarding his alibi. He remembered that at Zayre's, when he bought his Coke, he spoke to the clerk at the counter, and he recalled that her name was Pat, or Pam, and that she was white. Scott still counted on that visit to Zayre's because he felt that if he could prove that he was there—more important, that he was there *when* he said he was there—then he could not have committed the crime. During the course of the hearing, Lola showed Lieutenant Colonel Harry a pair of civilian-style glasses with lighter frames and rounder lenses than the standard military-issue glasses both described by Judy Connors and used by Lindner in all three identification procedures. Lola said, and Scott confirmed, that this was the pair of glasses he was wearing on the night of the crime.

For Scott's defense, neither Kuhnke nor Major Roach offered any evidence.

When the hearing was over, Lieutenant Colonel Harry said he wasn't entirely satisfied either with Scott's story or with the prosecution's case. He ordered Scott to be retained in custody, but said he would hold a second hearing on May 5. In the interval, he said, the prosecution would have to bring in more conclusive evidence of Scott's guilt if they wanted to keep him in the brig.

The NIS agents wasted no time. They had eight days to dig up enough hard evidence to keep Scott in jail—and not only keep him in jail, but serve as a base on which they could build their case against him for a general court-martial. That, after all, was always to be the goal of their investigations.

And all concerned in the Quantico command structure—from Major General David M. Twomey, to Battalion Commander Hemming, to prosecutor Thomson on down the line—were well aware that if he was found guilty at a general court-martial of rape and attempted murder, Scott faced the death penalty.

From the hearing Lindner went over to the Provost Marshal's Office to interview Captain Andrew Unsworth, legal officer of the Security Battalion. The captain offered information about Scott's itinerary on the night of the crime that Scott had not provided in his first statement to the NIS agents on April 21. According to Captain Unsworth, as he was about to go off duty at the Provost Marshal's Office at about eight P.M. on the night of the crime, he saw Scott and stopped to talk to him for two or three minutes. He remarked to Scott that his clothing was unusual, to which Scott replied that he was wearing it because he had been cleaning his old apartment. The captain described the clothing as "an old pair of green sateen utilities. The trousers were not bloused and his shirt was hanging out over his waist. He was wearing a light tan, waist-length, leatherlike jacket."

Lindner showed Captain Unsworth a pair of black frame military-issue glasses. The captain said, "These glasses are almost exactly the same as the glasses Scott was wearing in regards to shape and color." Captain Unsworth said he left the building then and could not say when Scott left.

The captain went on to say that two days later, on the twenty-second, about 0845, he was walking through the Security Battalion building when Scott approached him and asked him what time they had seen each other on the night of the twentieth. "I told him it was sometime after 1830. . . . Scott said it was later. I then told him it must have been after 1915 to 1930 because

I was securing for the evening. I did not want to commit myself to him because I felt he was trying to question me, to pin me down to an exact time. Realizing that he was at that time a suspect in the investigation, I did not want to give him an exact time and I only gave him a general time, even though I knew approximately the exact time I had seen and spoken to him that evening."

If true, this account would smash Scott's alibi by overturning the timetable of the itinerary he had given for that night. However, Captain Unsworth's alleged eight P.M. chat with Scott at PMO conflicted with an earlier report of Agents Rodgers and Rivers stating that the clerk at Dumfries Pharmacy remembered selling a foot massager to Scott between 7:30 and eight.

This conflict in times took on particular significance when Rodgers and Lindner began driving around checking distances and times traveled between Scott's apartment, Judy Connors's apartment, PMO, the spot where Judy was found, and the various places Scott said he'd been. With the deadline of the second hearing before Lieutenant Colonel Harry very much on his mind, Lindner checked out the manager and three female employees at Quikee's who were on duty the night of the twentieth. The manager confirmed that all employees punched out at 2050 that night. Lindner showed the three female clerks photos of Scott. None recalled seeing him.

He actually found a Pam, named by Scott, working at Zayre's soda fountain. She said she had been working the night of the twentieth, but when Lindner showed her a photo of Scott and asked if she recognized him, she said she did not. He asked her if she recalled serving him or talking to him that night. She said she didn't.

Lindner then did some more time/distance measurements from PMO to Zayre's to Quikee's. He concluded that there would have been "insufficient time for subject to arrive at Quikee's prior to all personnel having departed." In other words, Lindner was saying that Scott could not have seen staff at Quikee's, as he'd claimed, since by the time he would have arrived, they all would have been gone—thus nailing Scott with another lie about his alibi.

What appears to be missing from all this time/distance study is Scott's purchase at Dumfries, which the report by Rodgers and

Rivers appears to confirm. Lindner also had to use the site where Judy was found, not the actual crime scene (since they never found it) as a focal point. Scott felt, whether rightly or wrongly, that Lindner may have been swayed by preconception and allegation.

However, the pressure was on him, and he had no reason to doubt Unsworth's word that Scott had been at PMO at eight P.M.

Lindner was now reasonably satisfied that he could shoot down Scott's alibi based on his time/distance evidence and his interviews with the employees of Quikee's and Pam at Zayre's. Now he wanted to complete the picture of Scott's guilt with damning forensic evidence.

On the twenty-eighth, Special Agent Wardman sent an urgent letter to the director of the FBI in Washington, D.C., with a formal Request for Laboratory Examination. Wardman outlined briefly the case against Scott and the forensic evidence obtained. Wardman stated that Scott was in pretrial confinement, but, "the magistrate has requested that additional evidence [forensic evidence] be presented. . . . Due to the extreme seriousness of these offenses, it is requested that this evidence be processed as expeditiously as possible. . . . If any pertinent determinations are made prior to all examinations being completed, please notify the case agent whose name and telephone number appear below. . . .

"All evidence will be hand-delivered to, and picked up at, the FBI laboratory. Upon completion of the examination, contact Special Agent James F. Lindner."

On the twenty-ninth Lindner duly delivered to the FBI forensic laboratory all the physical evidence NIS had collected: the victim's clothes and the clothes the agents had taken from Scott's apartment that Lola said she thought he had worn on the night of the crime; blood samples from Scott and the victim, vaginal swabs and sperm motility slides from the victim, pubic hair and saliva samples from Scott, everything vacuumed from his car, and anything else NIS thought pertinent.

On both May 4 and 5 (before the hearing began on the fifth), Lindner got a telephone call from the FBI. The agent gave him an account of the lab results thus far. It was not good news for NIS.

There was no cross transfer of hair or fibers between subject and victim. Hair of victim did not match the hair found in vehicle.

There was no cross transfer of fiber between victim's clothing and the results of the vacuum bag from subject's vehicle.

Examination of cigarette butts revealed they were not victim's brand.

No semen was found on victim's or subject's clothing or hair samples. Examination of sperm motility slides revealed there was insufficient semen present to obtain a blood grouping.

The FBI agent further advised Lindner that the examination of all items for blood and the grouping of any blood found would require about two weeks.

The sole item that excited Lindner's interest was the lab report that they had found, on the inside of the victim's sweater, one head hair of Negro origin, about two inches long.

True, that hair was too long to be Scott's—but could it belong to Lola, Scott's wife? What connection Lola might have had with the crime Lindner did not explain in his written report, but he wasted no time getting Lola's permission to take a sample of her head hair. This he dispatched to the FBI lab for comparison with the head hair of Negro origin found on Judy's sweater.

At the hearing later that day, Scott's civilian attorney, Ervan Kuhnke, made an opening motion for Scott's release from custody on the grounds that holding him in the brig was unconstitutional. Lieutenant Colonel Harry reserved his ruling pending the hearing of evidence. Scott's military defense counsel, Major Roach, did not appear at all for the second hearing. Kuhnke offered no evidence or called any witnesses on Scott's behalf.

Major Thomson for the prosecution once again referred to the identification of Scott in the lineups and to the rest of the evidence introduced at the first hearing. Lieutenant Colonel Harry asked for the forensic evidence. Lindner gave him the FBI lab report, well aware that it was negative, or at best inconclusive. However, NIS had an "ace up its sleeve," a "bombshell" that would make the negative forensic evidence irrelevant: Captain Unsworth's statement that Scott had been at the Provost Marshal's Office at eight P.M. Major Thomson introduced this statement in triumph, since it destroyed Scott's alibi, particularly since he had never even mentioned stopping at the PMO that night.

Lieutenant Colonel Harry questioned Scott about Captain Unsworth's allegation. Visibly embarrassed, fumbling in his words, Scott admitted that he had been at PMO, just for a few moments, to use the toilet, but had forgotten to mention the incident to the NIS agents and at the first hearing. He said, however, that according to his recollection, he'd been at PMO earlier, about 7:20 or so, not at eight as Captain Unsworth claimed. Lieutenant Colonel Harry appeared to listen with some sympathy to this account.

At the close of the hearing, which lasted about forty-five minutes, Major Thomson made a motion to keep Scott in custody on the grounds that he had no ties in the area and, if released, might go AWOL.

Lieutenant Colonel Harry denied the motion and announced his decision: he said that after listening to and receiving evidence over a two-week period, he saw no direct evidence linking Scott to the crime. The forensic evidence proved nothing. The photo and physical lineups left room for honest doubt. And since in his opinion Scott was not an escape risk, he ordered him released from confinement in the brig.

Joy in the Scott camp; fury in the Quantico command.

That was the last ruling Lieutenant Colonel Harry ever made as a military magistrate. The next day Commanding General Twomey relieved him of his duties. Harry believes he was fired. The Marines say Harry had previously put in for retirement and that the timing was coincidental.

4

Lieutenant Colonel Harry, the former Vietnam helicopter combat pilot, a twenty-year Marine veteran, did not walk away from what he considered to be a slap in the face from Major General Twomey. He promptly sent him a scathing letter of protest.

Sir:

You crucified me without representation and have convicted Corporal Scott without a trial. Please allow me the opportunity to give you the "evidence," and I use that term loosely, presented to me in this case.

Report of Confinement . . . the one and only statement with some credibility, cannot be vindicated on its own merits because the victim identified *two,* not just one from that lineup.

Statement of Captain Unsworth, in which he states he saw Corporal Scott between 1955 and 2005 on the night in question; he personally told me it was 1930. Therefore, this evidence is not as condemning as it might have been.

Reports from the FBI lab: as related by the NIS agent there was nothing produced that could indicate Corporal Scott or anyone else was the perpetrator of the crime.

The prosecuting attorney . . . tried to justify the retention of Corporal Scott on the grounds he has no ties to the community. This doesn't even wash, as his wife, who is pregnant, is here, his lawyer, Mr. Kuhnke, is here, and his family and his wife's family are greatly concerned about the case.

If you ask my honest opinion, I feel the case stinks and the prosecution is not doing their job. I felt the retention of Corporal

Scott would be embarrassing to you, to the Marine Corps, and detrimental to any case that may be brought at a later date against Corporal Scott.

I do not argue the merits of whether or not Corporal Scott is guilty; that will be determined if and when he is charged before a general court. What I do say is that we have to perform according to the laws on the books . . . which state, "In those cases where the military magistrate, based on the evidence initially presented, determines that there is a need for further inquiry, additional information may be sought about the case. In no event, however, shall the decision concerning the release of the serving member be delayed significantly after commencement of the initial hearing." I delayed that decision eight days to allow the prosecution to come up with something. They provided nothing.

Also, the same reference states, "In the absence of clear evidence affirmatively establishing a need for pretrial confinement under existing military law, the service member is entitled to release from pretrial confinement."

. . . In summary, I agonized about this case for eight days while awaiting some results from the lab. In the absence of clear evidence pointing to Corporal Scott I felt I was duty bound to release him from pretrial confinement.

Therefore, I respectfully request you to rescind your order of May 6, 1983, in which you appoint Major Dorman as military magistrate/traffic-court officer.

Major General Twomey did not comply with this request. In fact, he totally ignored it. Shortly afterward, Lieutenant Colonel Harry was forced to retire from the Marine Corps.

As expected, the Quantico command denied Lieutenant Colonel Harry's accusations. The staff judge advocate said it was pure coincidence that Major General Twomey replaced Harry the day after his decision to release Scott from confinement for what was considered lack of evidence. Harry, he said, was due to retire shortly in any case, a replacement would be needed as military magistrate, and Major Dorman was available immediately.

However, the Marines had not heard the last of Lieutenant Colonel Harry. And not only the Marines.

Interestingly enough, this was not the first time Major General Twomey had been involved in serious controversy. In 1975, when he was chief of staff, a colonel at the San Diego Marine Recruit Depot, a scandal erupted when a young recruit was killed during a training exercise and a drill instructor court-martialed for manslaughter.

Lynn McClure was a five-six, 115-pound misfit at San Diego. He never got past the tenth grade at school. Rejected by the Army and Air Force, with a police record and time spent in a mental institution, he was nevertheless accepted by the Marine Corps. He went AWOL shortly after reporting to San Diego. When he was captured he was put into a "correctional platoon" and then into a "motivation platoon," designed for difficult recruits. One day the DI sent him out to fight another Marine with pugil sticks, a long, padded pole used for bayonet training. This routine was so grueling, indeed, so punishing, that the rules stated no man should fight consecutive bouts. But McClure was forced to fight one man after another, men usually twice his weight. He was taking a terrible beating until, after a particularly hard blow to the head, he fell to the ground unconscious, in a coma. He never came out of it and died three months later.

The DI sergeant was court-martialed for involuntary manslaughter. The jury found him not guilty.

The fatal beating of McClure touched off a nationwide uproar over Marine recruitment and training. The House Armed Services Committee investigated. Colonel Twomey, unscathed by the scandal, was promoted to brigadier general and assistant commander at San Diego. He promised reform. McClure's death, he said, was "a black mark against the Corps . . . a black mark against me, because I was chief of staff at the time."

Also, at that time the draft had ended, and the Marines were running short of new recruits. To help fill the quotas, they began accepting volunteers rejected by the other services, men often poorly educated, doubtful material for the tough Marine boot-camp regimen. Men like Lynn McClure. They were difficult to train, difficult to discipline. Many of them washed out. The

Marines weren't happy about the high attrition rate. Twomey wasn't happy.

He wanted to make as many Marines as possible out of the raw recruits sent to him. So he tried, as he put it, "one last thing."

He instituted a punishment routine: recruits who broke discipline, disobeyed orders, were tied hand and foot with shackles and forced to stand out in the sun all day, helmets on heads.

"I shouldn't have done it," Twomey admitted later in an interview with *The Washington Post*. "It was illegal. . . . I didn't know it was against the rules."

Nevertheless, Twomey was promoted once again, this time to take charge of the largest Marine base in the United States. He arrived at Quantico as the quintessential "hard-ass" Marine general, square-jawed and clear-eyed, a no-nonsense commandant. He was totally the man in charge and let no one doubt it. Colonels looking for that first brigadier star on their collars, majors looking for promotion to lieutenant colonel, indeed any officer on the base looking to be "upwardly mobile" knew the power of the commanding general to make or break them.

Major General Twomey did not overturn Lieutenant Colonel Harry's decision to release Lindsey Scott from the brig. On the other hand, he didn't free him completely, either. He ordered him confined to barracks. Scott protested to his battalion commander, Lieutenant Colonel Hemming, that his wife was suffering through a difficult pregnancy, aggravated by the stress of the situation, and she needed his help at home. Hemming refused him. Days later Lola Scott fell ill and was rushed to the hospital. Only then did Hemming relent. He placed Scott under house arrest. This restricted Scott to moving only from his apartment to the base and back again.

Soon afterward, however, with Lola back home, Hemming once again ordered Scott confined to barracks. That same night Lola began to hemorrhage and again was rushed to the hospital. Scott brought Hemming letters from the doctors saying Lola needed to rest at home, to stay off her feet as much as possible, and needed his help. Hemming agreed to put him back in house arrest, with frequent telephone calls to check on his movements. Scott was also required to call his superiors frequently day and night to verify his whereabouts. Disgusted, Scott felt this was sheer harassment.

Meantime the NIS investigation continued relentlessly, agents searching anywhere and everywhere for anything that they might be able to use as solid evidence against Scott.

NIS Agent Lindner paid a visit to Hardee's, the fast-food restaurant where Judy Connors had worked until the day of the crime. The agent knew it was important that he keep good investigative records on the victim as well as the accused. The very afternoon of the alleged sexual assault and attempted murder, by coincidence, Judy had quit her job. She was tired of the hours, she'd told Lindner. The NIS agent interviewed a few of her colleagues. What he discovered of interest, if anything, he did not include in his written report.

Vital forensic evidence still eluded the investigators. Lindner decided to send Judy Connors's and Scott's shoes to the FBI lab "to determine the presence of any foreign debris and if the debris found on each is similar in origin."

The results were negative. So was the result of the lab report on the head hair of Negro origin found on Judy's sweater, compared with the head hair of Scott's wife. The significance of this, if any, was never mentioned in the official NIS reports. If not Lola's hair or Scott's, then whose?

While under close house arrest, Scott wrestled with his nightmare. Lola was visibly depressed, subject to bouts of weeping. At work at the base, Scott's colleagues shunned him. The Quantico newspaper was reporting the story and Scott felt the chill—the accusing stares—everywhere. Every day he called his attorney, Kuhnke, asking what was happening, would the court-martial go ahead, was he checking out the potential witnesses he had named. Kuhnke told him not to worry, he didn't think the prosecutors had enough of a case to proceed against him.

The Marines thought differently. On May 26, 1983, five weeks after the crime, the Marine Corps formally charged Corporal Lindsey Scott with kidnapping, rape, sodomy, and attempted murder, and announced that it would convene a general court-martial under the Uniform Code of Military Justice, in which such crimes are punishable by death.

First, however, would come the next stage in the case against Scott: an Article 32 hearing, on June 1. An Article 32 is held to produce a recommendation whether or not to proceed with a court-martial, somewhat akin to a civilian grand jury. Except that where a civilian grand jury is composed of twelve jurists listening to prosecution and defense arguments, an Article 32 is conducted by a one-man jury—in Scott's case appointed by the base commander, Major General Twomey.

Major Richard E. Ouellette was the investigating officer appointed by Twomey—that one-man jury, in effect. Representing the Marines was, again, Major Donald Thomson. Kuhnke and Major Roach represented the defense.

Major Ouellette said he wanted to make some preliminary remarks about his own background regarding the case; he said that he had not, until that morning, known the name of the accused, although three weeks earlier he had been asked to be the Article 32 investigating officer (a significant fact, since it suggested that no matter what the outcome of the military magistrate's hearing, the commanding general intended to proceed with a court-martial). Major Ouellette added that he knew the case had been written about in the base newspaper, but he had not read the story. He did hear, he said, "that this case involved a woman who was allegedly raped . . . that an accused had been identified, that the case may not have been extremely strong, and that the accused was not placed in pretrial confinement and there was some rumor of some disenchantment because of that. My source for that information was the deputy staff judge advocate."

Major Thomson then said he would call just two witnesses, victim Judy Connors and Case Agent James Lindner.

In order to secure a decision by Major Ouellette to proceed with a general court-martial, Major Thomson needed first to examine Judy Connors carefully and extensively, setting out for legal reasons all the intimate details of the assault, to prove the government's case that a sexual attack had taken place as specified in the indictment.

The transcript of the Article 32 hearing, as a prelude to the court-martial proceedings, is important enough for substantial portions to be narrated here, parts reproduced verbatim. In effect, both prosecution and defense produce virtually the same evidence and arguments they would reveal in a trial. And the investigating officer could recommend no court-martial should proceed.

Called to the stand, Judy, still wearing a surgical collar, her scars and deep bruises clearly visible, stated that though still married, she was now living with her parents in Columbus, Ohio, and was working there. (Gossip around Quantico was saying she had separated from her husband, Kevin.)

Recounting the events of the night of the twentieth, she now stated that there were two phone calls starting about 8:15 P.M. in which she picked up the phone but no one answered. At a third call, a man who identified himself as a military policeman, she said, told her that her husband had been in a serious car accident and had been taken to Camp Upshur Hospital. She said the man asked if she was alone. She replied that she was and asked if someone could come and pick her up. She said the man told her someone from CID would come over.

Judy said he asked her to be outside in her parking lot, standing by her car, in two minutes.

Judy said then that she quickly changed her clothes, putting on a sweater and coat, and rushed down the stairs to the parking lot. She noticed a car to her left, with the motor already running. The car backed toward her and stopped, the driver asked if she was Mrs. Connors. She said yes and, before she got in, asked if he was from CID. He said he was.

Responding to Major Thomson's direct questions, she then proceeded to describe her journey—out of the parking lot, onto Fuller Heights Road, and into Route 619. From 619 the driver turned left onto a dark road with woods all around. She said he seemed lost after a while, stopped on a dirt road, and began rummaging through a bucket on the backseat, saying he was looking for his radio.

(The following is verbatim question-and-answer.)

Q. You mentioned a bucket. What did this bucket look like?

A. It was round and it was fairly large in size. It was not plastic, I noticed, because when he was rummaging through it, I heard cans and stuff hitting against it. It was not real deep but round and large.

Q. What color was it?

A. It was dark. From what I could see it was like a metal bucket.

Q. What happened next?

A. He seemed to be angry that he could not find his radio and turned back around and started the car and we kept driving. We drove a little ways further until he came to a point where he backed into a—what looked to me like a little dirt area in the middle of nowhere.

Q. And what happened next?

A. He stopped the car and he turned the lights off, and he said, "Here we are."

Q. And what happened next?

A. At that point I knew that there was something wrong, and the first thing I did was I went for the door to try to get out. Before I even—as soon as I had my hand on it, he grabbed my arm, and said, "Don't try anything. I have this," and I turned around and looked and it was a knife.

Q. To the best of your knowledge, what did the knife look like?

A. I just saw the blade—I saw the blade shining. It wasn't a little pocketknife. It looked longer than that. The blade was pretty long.

Q. And what happened next?

A. I kept asking him to please not hurt me, because I knew that he was going to do something to me, and I just kept asking him not to hurt me and he told me not to panic. He said, "Stop talking. Don't say any more." And he opened his pants and he told me to—

Q. Go ahead.

A. He told me what to do. He told me to pump his penis.

Q. Did you comply with his order?

A. Yes, sir.

Q. What happened next?

A. He said, "Okay," after a minute or two, and then he told me to suck it.

Q. And did you comply with his order?

A. Yes, sir.

Q. What happened next?

A. Then he said, "Okay," after a few minutes, told me to sit up. He still had the knife in his hand all this time, and he told me to take off my pants and turn around in the seat and put my legs up on the seat.

Q. During this time when he forced you to have oral sex with him, was he saying anything at this point?

A. Just that he told me what to do and not say anything.

Q. What happened next?

A. He put his pants down a ways. He had the knife in his hand, and he proceeded to rape me.

Q. Mrs. Connors, tell us—and I know this is difficult for you—tell us exactly what he did.

A. He entered me.

Q. Did he put his penis into your vagina?

A. Yes, sir.

Q. Do you remember what type of seats he had in his car?

A. Bench seats.

Q. When he forced you to have sex, did he still have the knife in his hand?

A. Yes, sir.

Q. And how long did that last?

A. Approximately five-to-eight minutes.

Q. During the course of the conversation that you had with him, did you give him permission to have sex with you?

A. No, sir.

Q. Did he do this forcibly?

A. Yes, sir.

Q. Did he do it against your will?

A. Yes, sir.

Q. When he forced you to have oral sex with him, to put your mouth on his penis, did he force you to do that?

A. Yes, sir.

Q. Did he do it against your will?
A. Yes, sir.

Judy then described how, afterward, the man told her to get out of the car. He walked her down into the woods, told her to lie down, then knelt down and started to strangle her. He choked her harder and harder till she passed out. When she came to, she realized she had been slashed on the neck and the man was standing over her, the knife in his hand. The man laughed then, she said, a kind of low laugh. Then he walked away. She heard the car door shut and the car drive away. She said she believed she passed out again for a few minutes. Finally, she got up and started walking back to the road.

She wanted to flag down a passing car, but afraid the man might be coming back, she let the first two vehicles pass by before successfully waving down the third.

Major Thomson then asked Judy to describe in detail her assailant's car, both exterior and interior, as she remembered it that night. Then:

Q. Have you seen a car similar to that of your assailant since that time?
A. Yes, sir.
Q. And do you remember when that was?
A. Yes, sir.
Q. When was that?
A. That was after I had talked to the Naval investigators, and I believe it was Mr. Wardman who drove me to the car, which was somewhere around PMO, I think in the next parking lot over from PMO.
Q. Are you able to give a description of your assailant?
A. Yes, sir.
Q. Would you please describe him?
A. He was a black man. He had glasses on.
Q. What type of glasses did he have on?
A. The glasses looked to me like they were not tinted. They looked like fairly larger lenses than what the military glasses

looked like to me. And that's about all I remember about the glasses.

Q. Continue, please, with your description.

A. He looked to me to be between the ages of maybe twenty-three or twenty-four to twenty-eight. He was clean-cut. He was approximately five-eight. He was not fat, but he was not skinny. He was medium-built.

Q. Mrs. Connors, do you see that man present in this room?

A. Yes, sir.

Q. Would you please point to him and describe who you are pointing to?

(The witness pointed to the accused.)

Q. Would you please describe who you're pointing to?

A. His name?

Q. What he looks like?

A. Black hair, glasses, the same build, same approximate age, the features on his face look exactly the same.

Major Ouellette: Let the record reflect that the witness has pointed to the accused.

In his cross-examination of Judy Connors, Kuhnke took her through the phone calls, the lighting in the parking lot at Spanish Gardens, and her identification of Scott's car. He obtained, here, a contradiction of Agent Wardman's statement about her identification. As Judy answered questions regarding her drive around the base with Wardman and looking at cars, Kuhnke asked her:

Q. Did you look in the interior of any of those other cars?

A. No, just the one.

Q. So you only looked into the interior of the car at PMO?

A. I don't think we got out of the car. Mr. Wardman took us around the parking lot but I don't remember getting out of the car.

(In his statement, Wardman said she did look into the car she identified as Scott's and became "visibly upset" when she did so, and described items such as gas gauge and ashtray and general interior appearance as similar to those in her assailant's car.)

Kuhnke continued, referring to the lighting inside the car on the night of the crime.

Q. While you were in the car, it was always dark, wasn't it?
A. Yes, sir.
Q. The lights were never on?
A. No, sir.
Q. And so except for that brief period that you were—right after you were picked up, the lighting was—is it a fair statement that the lighting was very bad all the time?
A. No, sir.
Q. Well, it was hard for you to really get a look at your attacker, wasn't it?
A. Yes, sir.
Q. Could that explain, ma'am, the difficulty you had in the photo lineup and also in the physical lineup in identifying the man?
A. Yes, not only that but the fact that all the time I was in the car driving supposedly to where he said he was going, to Camp Upshur, I was looking out the front window. . . .
Q. Um-hmm.
A. Ninety-nine percent of the time.

After getting from Judy the fact that she smoked two or three cigarettes during the drive and put them out in the ashtray, Kuhnke then took Judy through her recollections of what the knife looked like, about what her assailant was wearing, the color of his jacket, the type of glasses he was wearing, and the length of his hair. Once again Kuhnke questioned her identification of Scott.

Q. Now, when you—your attacker, you indicated he had short hair?
A. Yes, sir, he did.
Q. And you picked out two men, did you not, at the lineup?
A. Yes, sir.
Q. And number six had longer hair than number five?
A. Yes, sir.
Q. And for that reason—is that the reason you thought initially number six was your attacker?

A. No, the first person—the first number I picked out was number five, and then I said, "But his hair looks too short." From what I remember his hair was longer than what it was in the lineup.

Q. I ask you to look at this man now (indicating accused). What was he, number five or number six?

A. Number five.

Q. I ask you to look at him. Is his hair longer or shorter than the man that attacked you?

A. Shorter.

Kuhnke continued in this vein through several more questions about hair length and the lineup, then:

Q. The person that attacked you, you think his hair was longer than this? (Again indicating the accused.)

A. A little bit longer.

Q. Did you say words to the effect that you weren't sure, you just didn't get a good enough look at him?

A. I said that I did not get a good enough look at this person to be able to say, without any doubt in my mind, that I was sure at this point that that was him. I said, "It looks just like him." I said, "His hair is too short in this lineup," and that I wanted to be absolutely positive.

Q. Well, it's important that you be absolutely positive, and it's important now because a man's life is at stake. You know that?

A. Yes, sir.

Q. I know you don't want to make a mistake, do you?

A. No, I do not.

Q. You're not really sure this is the man that attacked you, are you?

A. I am pretty sure that this is the man who attacked me.

Q. You're pretty sure, but you're not absolutely sure?

A. It looks just like him.

Q. But you're not absolutely sure?

A. I can't say I got a good enough look at this person to say, "This is definitely, absolutely him." I had a good enough look at him throughout that night to say that this person looks exactly like him.

Q. It looks like him?

A. And I believe that it is him.

Q. You believe that it is him, but you're not sure, you're not absolutely sure it's him?

A. I'm as sure as I can be.

Q. You're not absolutely certain. You weren't absolutely certain in the photo lineup?

A. Yes, sir, I could not be absolutely certain at the photo lineup.

Q. And you're not absolutely certain now?

A. He looks like the man, yes.

Q. But you're not absolutely certain that this is the man who attacked you, are you?

A. No, sir, not without—

Q. So when you responded to Major Thomson's question, "Do you see that man in the courtroom?" and you said, "Yes," and you pointed at him, you were not absolutely certain that that man is the man, are you?

A. I am as certain as I can be that this is the man, but I—when I saw the photo lineup, you know—I wanted to be positive. I said, "I want to be absolutely positive," and I said, "This person looks just exactly like him. That's as good enough look as I got of him that night to say what I believe and what's true."

Q. Twenty or thirty minutes in the dark car?

A. Yes.

Q. You saw him for twenty or thirty minutes at most in a dark car?

A. I was not staring at him constantly, but in the time that I did see him, his face.

Q. You didn't see any distinguishing marks, scars, or a chipped tooth or anything like that?

A. No, sir.

Q. You didn't remember anything about his teeth, did you?

A. No, sir.

Kuhnke had no further questions.

Major Ouellette and then Major Thomson questioned Judy Connors briefly, then, with no further questioning requested by either Thomson or Kuhnke, Major Ouellette excused Judy and told her she need not remain in the area, but could return to her home in Ohio.

The time was 1210. Major Ouellette called a recess until 1400, at which time Special Agent James Lindner would be called to testify.

5

Special Agent Lindner, a key witness for the prosecution, identified himself as the primary case agent in the investigation. Immediately, in beginning his narration of events, he mentioned, more or less in passing, that at the clinic where Judy was taken from the MASH unit, it was felt "she was injured too seriously to do any of the normal rape examinations." Lindner said he contacted the NIS agent at Bethesda and asked for the appropriate rape examination to be done there. What makes this statement important is that thus far nobody—least of all the defense—had introduced or had asked to be introduced as evidence the medical reports on Judy from the Bethesda Naval Hospital. Whatever those reports might have indicated—or not indicated—consistent with a rape assault, is a moot point within the chronological context here of the case against Lindsey Scott. Nevertheless, it is an arguable example of questionable procedure by both sides in a prosecution where a verdict of guilty could mean the death penalty for the accused.

Lindner continued his testimony with a detailed account again of the time/travel studies, which, he claimed, destroyed the itinerary alibi claimed by Scott. Again, however, his presumption placed Scott at PMO at eight P.M., Lindner still quoting Captain Unsworth to that effect. Whether or not Lindner was aware of Lieutenant Colonel Harry's letter to Major General Twomey in that regard is irrelevant. He would be confident, of course, of whose testimony would count before a military court.

Kuhnke objected to Lindner's introduction of "hearsay evidence," that is, repeated what other agents and what Captain Unsworth had told him. Major Ouellette overruled, but said he would note the objection, listen to the testimony, and decide later whether or not he would consider it.

Lindner testified to the photo lineup and the physical lineup, admitting that in both cases Judy had picked out *two* men, and had not been able to say with absolute certainty which had been her assailant.

Major Ouellette asked Lindner if during the physical lineup they had tried switching the men's positions around for a further ID. Lindner replied no, they had not.

Did Lindner know whether or not the victim had come into contact with the accused at any time since the lineup? Lindner said no, not to his knowledge. But Major Thomson, the government counsel, said it was his belief that the victim had come into contact with the accused on the previous day. Kuhnke stated that the defense would so stipulate. (Such contact would be highly irregular, and it could be claimed that this might have had an effect on the victim's subsequent identification of the suspect in court.)

Kuhnke cross-examined.

Replying to Kuhnke's questions, Lindner said he'd known Scott for about a year, and no, he had never before participated in an investigation of anyone he'd known. He denied Kuhnke's accusation that this was not proper and contrary to good investigative practice, or that knowing Scott had affected his judgment.

Kuhnke asked Lindner about the hair sample taken from Judy's sweater. Did it match the hair sample taken from Mrs. Scott?

Lindner: "No, it didn't match."

Did he ever ask the victim about the possible origin of that hair sample from her sweater?

Lindner: "No, I didn't ask her that. I have no idea whose hair that is, no."

Perhaps unfortunately, Kuhnke did not pursue that line of questioning.

Instead, he turned to the results from the FBI lab. Lindner admitted they were all negative. As for fingerprints, they did take the victim's fingerprints because they did find a print on the window of the car. That came back negative. It didn't match the victim's.

Lindner: "If it matched the suspect's, big deal—it was his car."

So there was no physical evidence linking the suspect with the victim?

Lindner admitted there was none, no physical evidence.

Abruptly changing tack, Kuhnke asked Lindner about investigating other suspects.

Lindner: "I'm not aware of any investigations of any other suspects in this case. There are no other prime suspects. . . . We limited our search to Security Battalion because it was obvious that the individual knew military-police procedures."

Did they look for past members of the MPs?

"No, we didn't. I suppose it's possible that a lot of people in the Marine Corps have had some law-enforcement training and know a little bit about military-police procedure. I doubt it, though."

Strangely, then, though he had just said he was not aware of any investigations of any other suspects, he proceeded to contradict himself.

Kuhnke changed the wording of his earlier question. Was it not a fact that NIS was pursuing other leads?

Lindner: "Yes, it's true that NIS is pursuing other leads in this case."

Kuhnke: "Would you care to tell us about those other leads, because I'm sure the major [referring to Ouellette, the investigating officer] would like to know if there is any other evidence, since the evidence you've told us is pretty inconclusive at this point."

Immediately Major Thomson leaped from his chair and objected to any such testimony until the NIS had an opportunity to follow through on those leads. He said he realized that the rules of evidence were relaxed, but he did not think unsubstantiated leads would be helpful in the determination of the matters before the hearing.

Major Ouellette's curiosity seemed to be piqued by the prosecutor's lightning reaction, and he asked Lindner if the leads might involve the accused, and could he release his information to the defense.

Lindner: "As for whether the leads we are following involve the accused or go elsewhere, they could go either way. If someone says, 'Hey, he wasn't the one,' we'll follow up on that. I'm not out to hang anyone. When you ask me about releasing that information now to the defense, my answer is that I am not at liberty to do that now."

Major Ouellette advised Kuhnke that as investigating officer he did not have the power to order the witness to divulge the information. And so the sudden opening of a door possibly leading to new and exciting passageways was just as suddenly slammed shut.

Kuhnke could do little but shrug and go on. "I realize that," he said, "but I wanted the major to know of this aspect of the case."

Major Ouellette: "I am fully aware of the defense's purpose in bringing this out *to show the weaknesses in the government's case in showing a nexus between the accused as the alleged perpetrator of the offenses*" (italics added).

The major said he would take note of the fact that the investigation was still progressing, and advised Major Thomson that anytime he wished to reopen the investigation, he would be amenable to doing so.

Kuhnke continued his cross-examination of Lindner by asking him why NIS had limited its search for suspects to the Security Battalion.

"We felt we had a good suspect in Corporal Scott," Lindner said. "He matched the physical description and the composite. His car matched the description. There were no others within Security Battalion that matched that description. He was an individual who knew something about military-police procedures and may very well have likely known Mrs. Connors and Corporal Connors. *As a matter of fact, the assailant did know Corporal Connors and Mrs. Connors*" (italics added).

It is not a case of trotting out hindsight's famous twenty-twenty vision to speculate on why, if it was known and admitted that Scott and the Connors knew each other, Judy could not positively identify him in a live lineup. Why indeed the need for any lineups?

Or an Identi-Kit? Why would she not say at the outset, "It was that Lindsey Scott guy who did it"? In the course of his first interview by NIS agents the day after the crime Scott protested his innocence with that very fact: "We're neighbors!" Scott had said to NIS Agent Rodgers. "Just ask her. She'll tell you it wasn't me!"

Strange to say, neither before the Article 32 hearing nor at the hearing itself did the defense or anyone else ask the question. When Lindner made this admission, defense attorney Kuhnke did not pick up on it. Lindner just kept on going. "He [the assailant] knew Mrs. Connors by name and Corporal Connors by name. We felt it was enough."

Kuhnke: "But a lot of people would have known Mrs. Connors by name, wouldn't they?"

Lindner: "Yes, I'm sure a lot of people could have known Mrs. Connors by name."

Kuhnke asked him how many black men he thought were on the base with the same general physical structure as Scott.

"I would not venture to say how many black men there are on the base with the same size and structure as the accused. There could be hundreds, even thousands."

And when did NIS first begin thinking of Scott as a suspect?

"I would say we first established Corporal Scott as a suspect after the composite was developed and I reviewed it. I'm sure in some people's minds he was a suspect before that. Our focus in narrowing suspects began in Security Battalion. It was the logical place to begin for the reasons I alluded to earlier. I know defense counsel has raised an objection, but it was the logical place to begin, and in the beginning we found what we felt to be a good suspect and we pursued our investigation toward that end."

Kuhnke had no more questions to ask Lindner, and the government rested its case.

Kuhnke called just one witness for the defense, Captain Unsworth. There was no way the defense counsel could know of the letter sent to Major General Twomey by Lieutenant Colonel Harry, and there was no way he could shake Captain Unsworth's testimony about Scott's visit to PMO on the night of the crime.

The captain stated, "I saw him as I was securing sometime after

1930 or so. I was working late that night. I locked up the S-1 area, and I was in the lobby area in front of the desk sergeant. That's when I saw Corporal Scott. . . . Yes, it was sometime after 1930. I've been thinking all day long and reviewing exactly what time it was that I did see Corporal Scott. I went from there out to the gym. I was at Larson Gym just a little bit after 2000. Larson Gym is about a three- or four-minute car drive away. I was at the gym as late as 2015 or so."

An area of contention regarding the identification of Scott by Judy Connors concerned the type of glasses she said her assailant had worn. She had described them as square, black-framed glasses. At the first hearing before Lieutenant Colonel Harry, Scott's wife, Lola, had brought in as evidence a pair of civilian-type glasses with larger, rounder frames. These, she had claimed, and Scott had confirmed, were the glasses he was wearing on the night of the twentieth.

Kuhnke asked Captain Unsworth if he could recall what kind of glasses Scott had been wearing.

"I did not pay particular attention," Captain Unsworth said. "But it seemed to me he was wearing the glasses he normally wore. Now, whether he normally wore the same glasses he has on now or not, I don't have a specific memory of." The captain stated that to the best of his knowledge, the glasses Scott was wearing that night were very similar to the ones he was now wearing in court.

The defense rested.

Major Ouellette advised both parties that after he had read the transcript of the hearing and thoroughly examined the NIS report he would contact both sides regarding their desire to reopen the proceedings, and if they had no request, he would then make his recommendation in the case.

On August 9, Major Ouellette handed down that recommendation: a general court-martial. Scott's battalion commander, Lieutenant Colonel Hemming, agreed with the decision. Major General Twomey—who as commanding general always had the right at any time to drop the charges—also agreed.

The only break Scott got—if in the circumstances any mitigation could be called a "break"—was the advice on sentencing given by the staff judge advocate, Colonel David Cassady. He pointed out in his summation of the case that although according to "the book" (Table of Maximum Punishments), if found guilty, Scott could get the death penalty, "the Supreme Court has ruled that the death penalty in rape cases is generally forbidden. The legality of the death penalty in the military under the Uniform Code of Military Justice is presently being argued before the U.S. Court of Military Appeals.

"I am of the opinion," Colonel Cassady went on, "that the maximum permissible punishment would be a dishonorable discharge, forfeiture of all pay and allowances, and confinement at hard labor for life."

(Eventually the U.S. Court of Military Appeals ruled that the death penalty for rape was not unconstitutional.)

Two weeks later, Scott was in the delivery room with his wife as she gave birth to a daughter, Latavia. His joy was blunted, however, by the fear that he might never get to know her.

An overwhelming sense of dread and disbelief enveloped Scott as he awaited trial. He knew the military justice system. He knew the methods of the NIS. He asked his lawyer, Kuhnke, about locating and subpoenaing potential witnesses, but Kuhnke only humored him, again reassuring him that the evidence itself was so flimsy the Marines would not even dare proceed to trial.

Scott did not share his lawyer's confidence. All he saw ahead of him was a lifetime spent in a military prison.

The odds were strongly against him, and he knew it, because of the very nature of military justice, a heavy-handed system that historically was designed primarily to maintain discipline rather than assure justice; a system with a conviction rate of approximately ninety-five percent.

In a civilian trial, if even a single juror is not convinced of guilt, the case ends in a hung jury. But a military defendant can't be saved by a lone holdout, or even two. At a court-martial only a two-thirds majority is needed to convict, even for capital crimes. In Scott's case, only five votes of the seven-member jury could send him to prison for life (the death penalty in military trials requires a unanimous vote).

Civilian-trial procedures also guarantee the defendant's rights, a process that is governed by a hallowed old tenet of the judicial system: "Better a hundred guilty escape than one innocent man be punished unjustly." In the military the tradition is far different, however, based on chain of command being a far more important principle than protection of the accused. Court-martials are convened by the base commander, who is the absolute authority with unilateral power to order trials and even overturn verdicts. This power is total, imperial, as described by a World War II–era law review: "It is almost entirely up to the commander to determine not only who shall be tried, for what offense, and by what court, but also what the result shall be in each case." The military reformed the system in the 1950s to guarantee more protection for defendants, but for the accused there still remains the specter of "command influence," in which base commanders sway the outcome of a court-martial.

To understand the powerful role that command influence can play in the outcome, one must appreciate that a court-martial, unlike a civilian trial, is not conducted within an open and free society. It takes place within the rigid world of chain of command on a military base. Commanders put people on trial when they believe they are guilty, and then appoint officers under their command to serve as jurors. These military jurors, known as "members of the court," are men and women strongly indoctrinated by years of training to obey their commander. They also depend on that commander for promotions, for favorable assignments, and for protection in a system where poor behavior could mean a questionable discharge, or perhaps a transfer to some remote, dead-end post, or, as in the case of Lieutenant Colonel Harry, a prompt transfer from an important position to shuffling papers till retirement.

Although military jurors are sworn to higher ideals, it is the rare career officer who is prepared to buck the system, the rare juror who would relish being a holdout when the Marine mission is "loud and clear."

* * *

As the day of his court-martial loomed closer that September, Scott's anxiety deepened into panic. It seemed to Scott that his military lawyer, Major Roach, had been virtually invisible throughout the proceedings; in any case he wasn't sure he could trust a career Marine to fight vigorously for him. And his civilian lawyer, Kuhnke, still voicing his empty reassurances, clearly was not preparing for a trial. He hadn't even bothered to interview the witnesses Scott had named; he hadn't talked to the soda jerk at Zayre's, for example, because the NIS report said that agents had already talked to her and she said she didn't recognize the photo of Scott they showed her.

A desperate Scott sat down and wrote out a long, detailed account of his situation. It was an impassioned letter, a rambling, fourteen-page document, a cri de coeur from a man who felt that nobody believed him, that he was being railroaded to prison by NIS—from a man who declared his innocence. Scott mailed his letter to several public officials, seeking their help. His letters went unanswered. Then, one evening, as he and Lola sat in lonely desolation in their apartment, she showed Scott an article she'd been reading in the Potomac newspaper. It concerned a civil-rights activist who had been pressuring local government into stronger affirmative action for minorities. This woman pursued other causes, such as desegregating a local restaurant that refused to serve blacks.

"This is the kind of person you need to contact," Lola said. "I'll bet you get an answer." Scott got the woman's telephone number from the newspaper, called her, and told her his story. She asked him to send her the letter, too.

Scott sent it, ending his letter with these words: "I would not jeopardize my life, my marriage, or my career to such horrendous actions. I have come this far being very cooperative and patient, by trusting and keeping my faith in the Lord, the help of my wife, family, and friends. I implore you to come to my aid in this time of need."

A religious woman herself, his plea touched her. But she felt she needed to know more, to meet this man and his wife. She called

Scott and made an arrangement to come to their apartment that evening.

Enter Lori Jackson.

Enter a whole new dimension in the case of *United States* v. *Corporal Lindsey Scott*.

6

Lori Jackson was a tall, striking woman of forty-six, with prominent cheekbones and strawberry-blond hair. She was part black, part white, part Cherokee Indian—and all energy. She was also the mother of seven mixed-race children. Civil rights and social justice were more than mere causes to her, they were crusades. She waged these wars with almost reckless intensity sometimes, allowing herself to be overwhelmed, at the expense of her family and friends. Born in Decatur, Alabama, she had vivid memories of the South of the 1940s. She was six years old when she stood with her family on the banks of the Tennessee River, watching the badly beaten bodies of her cousins being fished out of the icy waters. They had cinder blocks chained to their bodies to keep them from surfacing.

She never forgot their deaths, the firebombing of homes and churches by the Ku Klux Klan, the constant fear of beatings and lynchings by night riders. She remembered, too, the secret trapdoor underneath a table in the kitchen, carefully camouflaged, a small escape hatch constructed as a refuge when the hooded horsemen of the Klan attacked the crude shacks of the black neighborhoods. That refuge became more than just an escape hatch from the Klan for Lori (born Minnie Lorene), it became a haven from the real world of hate and bigotry, from a world war she could not comprehend. It was in that shelter that Lori created imaginary friends of all colors who lived happily ever after in a perfect, secret world.

The torment of little Minnie Lorene was not confined to the night riders of the Klan, however. At her all-black elementary school in Decatur she was the target of her classmates, who bullied her unmercifully because of her light skin and beautiful long black hair that fell to her waist. She was not one of them. She was almost white. They would tie her to a tree and abuse her as "Minnie-Ha-Ha," after the Indian heroine of Longfellow's *Hiawatha*. They would steal the lunches she brought from home; in the school hallways they would sneak up behind her with scissors and snip patches off her long hair. When her mother braided it, they cut that, too.

One day several of her classmates approached her, and in what appeared to be a friendly gesture, one held out a paper bag and said to her, "Here, Minnie, have some." So anxious to make a friend, any friend, seven-year-old Minnie Lorene thrust her hand into the bag—and felt the writhing of slimy snakes. Bursting into tears, she ran away, heading blindly toward the Tennessee River, desperate to escape, though she couldn't swim. The gang caught up with her at the riverbank, threw her to the ground, pulled up her blouse, and emptied the bag of snakes over her bare skin. Minnie Lorene carried a morbid fear of snakes with her forever after.

Lonely, shy, friendless, unhappy, unable to cope with the vicious bigotry of whites and the cruelty of her black schoolmates, little Minnie Lorene was soon given a lesson in "affirmative action" long before the modern popular phrase was ever coined. She was walking home from school when, as usual, a group of her classmates followed her, bullying her, knocking her books to the ground. One girl in particular was tormenting her, calling her names, pushing her, hitting her, challenging her, when out from behind a large tree stepped Minnie Lorene's twenty-year-old sister, Vera.

"Minnie," she said, "put the rest of your books down and come on over here." She grabbed Minnie Lorene by the collar then and said to her, "Now you whip that girl's ass or I'm gonna whip your ass when you get home." Minnie Lorene knew the wrath and reputation of Vera, and rather than face a beating later from her sister, she turned around and fought her tormentor—and won.

At home later Vera said to her, "I'm proud of you. You did what you had to do, and you're going to have to keep on doing it till people stop beating on you."

Still, that wasn't enough for Vera—a very tough lady, as an older Lori was later to remark many times. When she learned from Minnie Lorene that not only the kids, but the teachers as well, were treating her badly because of her looks and her mixed blood, she marched to the school with two .38 Special revolvers and a bucket of ammunition. She sat down cross-legged on the grass of the football field, next to the school, and began firing her pistols into the air. The school principal came to the door and looked out to see what the shooting was all about.

Vera shouted at him, "If any motherfucker sticks his head out the door, I'm gonna blow it off! Now I want my little sister to get better treatment around here or I'm gonna have to start killing some people!"

The principal ducked back inside and called the sheriff, who laughed and said, "Don't worry, she'll run out of ammunition eventually."

Later, Minnie Lorene said to her, "Would you really kill anybody, Vera?"

"Well, I don't think so, Minnie, but anyways they wouldn't do anything to me if I did. Nobody around here cares if you kill blacks."

Minnie Lorene had no trouble after that, and in fact became one of the most popular girls in her school. The incidents etched themselves indelibly on her mind. It was a lesson she never forgot.

Within the context of her extended family of aunts and uncles and cousins, Minnie Lorene's physical features—for a person legally black—were not unique. She had relatives who were black, and relatives with blue eyes and blond hair. This, Lori once traced back to a female African ancestor sold into slavery in 1809 to a German plantation owner. She had thirteen children by him. One boy escaped and took refuge with a Cherokee tribe and married a Cherokee girl. One of their daughters, at thirteen, was captured during a raid and sold as a house servant to a white slave owner. This girl, who was called Mary Wahaleha, bore eight children by her white owner, and two by her slave "husband." Set free after the Civil War, some of the various offspring from these white and black and Indian forebears managed to remain in touch as a family of many colors, but one spirit.

This "Rainbow Coalition" (again, long before today's popular phrase was born) caused consternation in various quarters more than once. At a family reunion in Alabama some years ago, the local sheriff turned up after a call about a strange group of people having a picnic. "What's going on here?" he demanded, looking around at the various hues of the score and more people sitting around the picnic tables. "Just a family reunion," said Lori's grandfather.

"Family reunion, hell!" exclaimed the sheriff. "Looks like you got the whole goddamned You-nited Nations here!" he said, walking away, shaking his head in disbelief.

Lori, as a matter of fact, could have had herself and her children legally declared to be Cherokee Indian instead of black.

During the 1980 national census, she ticked three boxes under *Race*—black, white, and Indian. The first call she got was from the local census bureau. "We have a problem with your census form," the woman said. "You have checked three boxes. What race are you?"

"I don't know what race I am," Lori said. "I'm all three. You tell me what I am."

"Well, our computers aren't set up to take this kind of information."

"Then the government will just have to get a new computer to fit people like us," Lori said.

The next day a man from the Federal Census Bureau called her and they went through the same routine. Finally he said, "What mixtures exactly are you?"

"Caucasian, Black, and Cherokee, and probably a bit of French and Blackfoot Indian on my father's side. So how can I designate myself as one particular race? If you can find a way out, then you change it."

"Okay, what was your grandmother, your mother's mother?"

"Cherokee Indian."

"That simplifies the whole thing!" he exclaimed. "That makes you a Cherokee Indian!"

"Oh yeah? And my kids, too?"

"That's right."

"Now, how did you come up with that?" Lori asked.

"Well, Congress has declared that whatever the dominating race of the mother is, that's what the children are."

"You're telling me I'm a Cherokee Indian?" said Lori. "After all these years of the government putting me in segregated housing and segregated schools and telling me I'm black, now you're telling me I'm a Cherokee Indian?"

"Yes, ma'am, that's it," the government man said.

He probably thought that was going to be the end of the story, but he didn't know Lori. When she got hold of something she did not let go. She promptly telephoned the Bureau of Indian Affairs and related the story. The man at the bureau cracked up with laughter. "That's the funniest thing I ever heard!" he said.

"I'm not calling you because it's funny," Lori said. "What I want to know is, if I'm an Indian now, and my kids are Indian, are we entitled to Indian benefits?" (She never had the intention of claiming them, but thought what a wonderful way to tease government bureaucracy!)

"Certainly you are, ma'am."

"What are these benefits?"

"Well, college scholarships, medical, things like that, and if your grandparents were or are on a reservation, then you could be entitled to cash benefits, perhaps a hundred dollars a month or so." But first, he explained, she'd have to get the Council of the Cherokee Nation to accept her as a member.

That didn't faze Lori one bit. She wrote to the council at Cherokee, North Carolina, detailing her background, and some sixty days later got back a letter of welcome to the Cherokee Nation, an identification card, and a title of minister.

Back to the Bureau of Indian Affairs she went, asking when they'd send her, among other benefits, her monthly check. "And you'll make that check retroactive, of course?"

Silence at the other end of the telephone.

"Hello, hello, are you there?" said Lori.

"Yes, ma'am. Did you say retroactive?"

"Sure. If the government says I'm a Cherokee Indian, I didn't just become an Indian yesterday. I was born an Indian. Right? So you have to pay me from the day I was born."

Badly shaken, the man from the bureau said he would look into it.

However, Lori never followed up on this bizarre turn of events. It was shortly overshadowed by a more serious and sinister occurrence: a telephone call from Corporal Lindsey Scott.

Lori could never explain, even to herself, why as ten-year-old Minnie Lorene she began to hang around the county courthouse at Decatur, Alabama. The courtroom fascinated her. Wise beyond her years as the result of her traumatic experiences, she understood and absorbed the injustices dealt out to blacks by white judges and juries. And in the artless fashion of a child, she vowed to herself that when she grew up, somehow, in some way, she would change all that. Never for a moment could she have foreseen then how successfully she would fight to fulfill that vow.

She was just seventeen when she married James Collier, a white, career U.S. Army man. They had seven children, blue-eyed children who could pass for white, children who were dark black, others of various hues in between. By this time Lori had dropped the Minnie from her name, with all its humiliating memories. She became Lorene Collier, but everyone called her Lori. She was also well into her civil-rights battles, on Army bases where her husband was stationed, overseas with him in Germany, where she helped blaze a new image for blacks with the Germans, who had, under Hitler, considered black people to be *untermensch*—subhuman.

Back in the United States, Lori managed to be wife, mother, and civil-rights activist. She did voluntary work for the American Civil Liberties Union, she marched in the 1960s with Martin Luther King, Jr., and she knew what it was like to be pushed and beaten, to be hit with fire hoses, to be attacked by dogs. To be sneered at as "nigger," of course, was not a new experience for her. The taunts merely reopened old wounds.

It did not take long for the military to recognize Lori Collier as a maverick, and regard her as a nuisance. She was not the kind of Army wife they liked: a wife who would cook and clean house, bear and raise children, play bridge with other Army wives, mind her own business and dutifully follow her husband around the world from base to base, dragging her equally docile children behind her. Unofficially, the military frowned on mixed marriages, and as biblical Joseph's "multicolored dreamcoat" offended his brothers, so did Lori's multicolored brood act as a bur under the neatly starched shirts of the Army brass.

It all came to a head in February of 1971, at Fort Campbell, Kentucky, home of the 101st Airborne Division, the famous "Screaming Eagles" of the Second World War. Lori and her family had been living at Campbell since August of 1969, when Collier, now a master sergeant, was shipped out to Korea. When he returned the following summer he was transferred to Fort Knox, Kentucky, about 120 miles from Fort Campbell.

Lori was ordered by the base housing officials to leave the base and join her husband at Fort Knox. The Army said they gave her until December; Lori said she wasn't even notified until February 18 and told to leave by March 8. Lori protested that family accommodations were unsuitable at Fort Knox, and asked that she be permitted to stay at least until June, the end of the school term.

And so the battle was joined, a battle whose smoke and noise reached across the country and into the pages of *The New York Times.* Lori accused senior brass at the base of calling her "a troublemaking black militant" and of trying to evict her because of her involvement in civil-rights activities, because of her repeated requests to introduce the teaching of black history into the curriculum of the base school.

The Army counterclaimed that she had indeed caused disturbances at basketball games, where her son James was a star player for the Fort Campbell school team, and that she had been in trouble for loud parties. Neither of these complaints could be documented; on the contrary, a number of students said Lori often acted as a calming influence when friction developed between blacks and whites at the school, or between black students and white military police.

The Army was adamant. Lori and her family had to go. However, "If she had kept quiet," said one senior officer, articulating the Army's protocol, "she could have stayed here until June and nobody would have cared."

Said a senior personnel officer about the eviction order: "We believe in preventive maintenance. It's like a pimple. You remove it before it gets too sore."

The Army eventually backed down in the face of all the publicity, allowing Lori and her family to remain at the base until the school term ended in June. Unhappily, as an aftermath of the battle, she and Collier divorced. But Lori got two clear messages out of her tangle with the Army: the military was infected with racism; it responded to the pressure of important media publicity.

Thus Lindsey Scott's telephone call and fourteen-page letter came as no great surprise to her. She had moved to Woodbridge, Virginia, near the Quantico marine base following her divorce and immediately had become involved in local political and civil-rights activities. She had been working with Victor Glasberg, an attorney specializing in civil-rights cases, gathering information for him, interviewing potential witnesses, helping in any and every way she could.

Lori was particularly intrigued by Scott's letter because she already knew the atmosphere of racism that pervaded the southern military base, where blacks performed the lowest military and civilian jobs and where incidents such as cross burnings and racist graffiti were seared in memory—but dismissed by the base command as simple foolishness, trivial vandalism.

Yet she needed to know more, and so that momentous evening, as she rang the doorbell of the Scotts' apartment, she felt a tingling of anticipation. What would they be like, Lindsey and Lola Scott?

Lindsey answered the door. "Hello," he said, smiling. "You must be Lori."

For a moment Lori was too startled to answer. She ignored Lindsey's outstretched hand and stared at the gold tooth in his mouth. A light in the hallway seemed to illuminate it. My God, it's like a beacon, she thought. God is pointing things out to me. This man needs me. I must help him.

7

For the first time in her life, Lori now felt overwhelmed by her commitments, caught in a wave of activity that threatened to engulf her. She was the victim of her own success. She had a calling for helping those who could not help themselves—and many were those who called her. Now she worked with the American Civil Liberties Union, with the Equal Opportunity Conference, the National Association for the Advancement of Colored People (NAACP), with civil-rights attorney Victor Glasberg, a day often of twelve or even sixteen hours long, a week of seven unrelenting days. She fought bigoted restaurateurs who refused to serve blacks, she fought against discrimination in housing, in employment, against police brutality. She fought in the trenches of the jails and the courtrooms.

Lori was well-known in northern Virginia as a tenacious seeker of justice, a battler for the underdog, whether black or white. She intimidated her opponents, and she knew it, used it, used without inhibition the unwelcome glare of publicity as an unspoken threat. A favorite tactic during a confrontation was to say, "Well we can settle this right here in your office, or we can settle it in the courtroom."

She considered herself, and indeed was, a woman of action. She deplored the bureaucratic red tape of some self-serving civil-rights groups and their obstructive procedures, which led to her leaving the NAACP just before she met Lindsey Scott. She was chairwoman of the legal committee of her local branch, because all the cases were coming to her, but she was becoming impatient with the formalities. It wasn't a civil-rights organization anymore, she complained, it was a business, a corporation. The situation came to a head when she received a phone call from a mother who said her son had been arrested, beaten so badly at the station house that he was taken to the hospital, beaten on the way there, beaten on the way back, and then thrown into a cell and forced to eat a broken lightbulb.

This required quick action. Lori took the case that night to a NAACP meeting and asked for immediate intervention. The president reminded her of their procedures: they needed a letter from the complainant. Then the executive board would have to meet and vote on it, and thirty days after that the body had to vote on it.

"Hey, look," objected Lori, "I don't have time for votes and all that rhetoric you people like so much because by that time the man could be dead." She resigned, took the case on herself, and, shortly afterward, began to organize her own civil-rights action group, Women for Equal Social Justice.

Somehow, amid all this frenetic activity, Lori found time to get married again. At a fund-raising party one evening, she was introduced to a young engineer named Paul Jackson, white, some twenty years her junior. He was liberal-minded, but indifferent to politics and the civil-rights movement. To Paul, brought to the party by a friend, it was just another pleasant way to spend an evening. He and Lori began to talk—exchanging the usual pleasantries of a first meeting—a talk that lasted more than three hours. He was totally captivated by this warm, yet dynamic woman. He knew immediately that he wanted her for his wife, and he in turn charmed her with his youthful enthusiasm and inquiring, open mind. He could respect her work without becoming an activist himself, and that was good enough for her.

Their marriage was not blessed by Paul's family. They did not believe in mixed marriages. His parents disinherited him; they and his two brothers disowned him. Lori's seven children accepted him without reservation. They might never call him Dad, but he was family now.

On the day that Corporal Lindsey Scott telephoned Lori, she and Paul were beginning to pack for a honeymoon in Hawaii.

They had the plane tickets and the hotel reservations and were looking forward to a much-needed break.

As that oft-quoted Scots poet Robert Burns wrote: "The best laid plans of mice and men oft go astray."

On that Saturday night late in September 1983, with Scott's court-martial barely two weeks away, Lori Jackson sat with Lindsey and Lola and their newborn baby girl and listened to their story, her eyes continually straying to that protruding gold tooth. She listened and she learned, as much from tone of voice, facial expression, and body language as from the words that tumbled from Lindsey Scott's lips. Lori had that rare facility, a blend of instinct and knowledge, that enabled her to make quick and accurate judgments of people.

Within the hour she knew that helping Lindsey Scott was something she had to do, above all other things in which she was involved. She believed Scott was innocent, but she did not reveal that to him—not yet.

Perhaps sensing Lori's reluctance to commit herself to his cause, Scott said to her, "I have a transcript of the Article 32 hearing. Would you mind reading it? I believe it'll show you what I've been telling you is the truth. The NIS is out to get me. They don't have any real evidence. They just want to get me because I'm black and she says a black man did it to her."

"I'll do that," Lori said, rising to leave. "I'll read it over the weekend and call you on Monday."

"Please, please," Scott said. "I'm desperate. I know you help people. Please help me."

All day Sunday Lori read and reread the Article 32 transcript. And that evening she said to Paul, "I'm afraid we're gonna have to postpone that honeymoon a little bit."

"Postpone it? What on earth for? We have the tickets, we have the hotel reservations. Lori, you need a break! We both need this time together, you've been so busy."

Lori held up the Article 32 transcript. "The Marines are out to frame this guy. They aim to railroad him right to Leavenworth for the rest of his life for something he maybe didn't do."

"But maybe he did do it?"

"I don't think he did, not from talking to him and to his wife, and from what I read in here. There are so many discrepancies, like about the description of the attacker, and so little real evidence . . . but all that is beside the point, Paul. I feel this isn't just about Lindsey Scott. It isn't even about whether or not he's guilty or innocent. This reminds me too much of the old lynch mobs when I was a kid in Alabama. They didn't care who, so long as he was black.

"Paul, this is about Women for Equal Social Justice. This is about civil rights. This is about a person's constitutional rights to a fair trial, which this boy is not gonna get, unless maybe I can help him in some way. I've gotta do it, Paul. God is telling me I have to help."

"Well, I'm not about to argue with God," Paul said. "I know when something is that important to you, Lori, then you just have to go ahead and do it. I love you and respect you for that. Hawaii will still be there when this is over."

Monday morning Lori telephoned Scott and agreed to do what she could to help him. "But I can't make a move without talking to your attorney first. He has to agree with my helping and he will have to know what I'm doing out there."

Scott gave her Ervan Kuhnke's telephone number. She called him immediately, introduced herself, and told him Scott had asked for help. "But I told him I'd have to get in touch with you and make sure that was okay with you."

"It certainly is," Kuhnke said. "I've heard about you. I've read a lot about you in the paper. You do a lot of work with Vic Glasberg, don't you?"

"That's right, I do."

"I worked with him once on a case, too," Kuhnke said. "Listen, I welcome your help in any way that you possibly can."

"Well, I can do the footwork," Lori said, "and, you know, try to come up with some information."

In the absence of any specific instructions from Scott's lawyer, Lori decided to read through Article 32 again. Confiding in her husband, she said, "It seems to me the best thing I can try to do is reconstruct Lindsey's alibi. What I'll do is make a note of all the witnesses mentioned in this Article 32 and go out and talk to them."

"Hasn't Scott's lawyer already done that?"

"Scott says no."

Though Lori had some previous experience conducting volunteer civil-rights investigations, this was her first major criminal case. Immediately she began coming up with pieces of information that could be important: she went into Quantico town and asked questions, and discovered that since April there had been two other rapes in the area, committed by black men of similar description—while Scott was under house arrest. She also heard allegations that the victim and her husband had not been getting along, and that she might not have been as innocent as first appeared.

Reading in the Article 32 transcript that there was a conflict of evidence about the length of the assailant's hair as described by Judy Connors and the way Scott normally wore his hair, Lori tracked down his barber. She told the man Scott's lawyer would be in touch with him, and reported this to Kuhnke. "Good work," Kuhnke said, "but don't worry, it's in the bag, this case will never come to trial."

Lori then focused on Scott's alibi, retracing the steps he said he had taken on the night of the crime. She went to Dumfries and spoke to the same clerk NIS Agents Rodgers and Rivers had interviewed. She again confirmed Scott's purchase that evening. Then she checked with the three women at Quikee's interviewed by NIS Case Agent Lindner, and got the same story he did. Lori realized these were not the most important witnesses; the key was at Zayre's, because Scott claimed to have been there at more or less precisely the time Judy Connors claimed she was being raped and knifed.

She called Kuhnke and related what she had done, and told him next on her list was Zayre's. She intended to find the soda jerk named Pam from whom Scott said he'd bought a Coke that night.

Kuhnke told her not to bother. It wasn't necessary to question her because the NIS had already done that, had showed her a photo of Scott, and she couldn't identify him.

That was not good enough for Lori; she did not have that much confidence in the official NIS reports. She went out to Zayre's to find Pam herself. That proved to be difficult; Pam was in the process of moving to another job, the manager told her, and it was against company policy to give out addresses or telephone numbers of employees. However, she said, Pam would probably be at the store in a day or two to finalize her arrangements. Lori could try to telephone her for an appointment.

Stymied for the moment, Lori talked to several other employees at the store and showed them photos of Scott. Nobody recognized him. Two days went by, two precious days with nothing accomplished, except that as word got out around the Quantico base that Lori Jackson was snooping around trying to help Lindsey Scott, a number of black Marines asked to meet with her at Lindsey's apartment. There they related to her an extraordinary tale of harassment and discrimination at the base. They alleged that some officers were racist, that one way or another they were trying to get rid of the black Marines in the battalion.

This she filed away for future reference; it might be useful to Kuhnke, but what was needed now was indisputable evidence to back up Scott's alibi—and that means Pam at Zayre's. Again she telephoned the store. This time she got Pam (her name turned out to be Pam Biller), explained briefly it was about a case involving a rape, and she had some pictures to show her. Pam agreed to see her the next day.

She was a very young, pleasant, polite white girl. They chatted for a few minutes, then Lori showed her a black-and-white mug shot of Scott—the same one Lindner had showed her, the NIS photo.

Pam Biller shook her head. "I'm sorry," she said. "I hate to say this and I don't mean to offend you, but to me he just looks like any other black man."

Lori was well prepared for that reaction. "Well, I have some personal pictures here I'd like to show you." She pulled from her purse a series of color photos given her by Lola, photos of Lindsey and Lola and Lindsey's family on the beach. One of the photos showed Lindsey standing alone by his car, wearing a cap, the same sort of cap he said he had been wearing on the night of the crime. When she saw that picture, something clicked with Pam Biller.

"Oh yes, I recognize him now," she said. "I've seen him in the store before. I sold him a Coke. I remember it because he paid for it with change."

"Could you say that he was in the store on the twentieth of April?"

"Five months ago? I'm sorry, I couldn't say if I saw him on the twentieth, or the twenty-first, or whatever day it was."

"Well, okay," Lori said, "but listen, Scott's lawyer, Ervan Kuhnke, he'll be in touch with you anyway, to talk to you."

Disappointed, Lori telephoned Kuhnke with the news. Pam Biller had identified Scott but couldn't pinpoint the date he'd been in the store.

"If she can't place him there on the twentieth, then her testimony would be insignificant," Kuhnke told her. "But don't worry about it. It's in the bag. The case will never go to trial."

Lori felt as though she had run into a brick wall. With a week to go before Scott's court-martial, she had turned up nothing really tangible to support his alibi, and all Kuhnke kept telling her was that it was "in the bag," the case would never go to trial.

Lori went home that night a disturbed woman. Scott was calling her regularly asking about progress and she had nothing encouraging to tell him. Kuhnke was advising her not to worry, "but," she said to Paul that night, "it's fine for him not to worry, he's not the one going to Leavenworth for the rest of his life."

"Maybe he's right, Lori," Paul said. "Maybe they won't go to trial."

"Oh, they'll go to trial, all right. Mr. Kuhnke doesn't know the military like I do. They've gone down the road this far and there's no way they're gonna stop now and back off. No way."

"Well, what can you do now?"

"I've been sitting here thinking, Paul, there's got to be somebody at Zayre's who saw him that night and remembers him, and I've got an idea. If he was in Zayre's for maybe fifteen minutes or so, like he says, then maybe security picked him up."

"Why would security pick him up?"

"Hey, if there's some black guy wandering around Zayre's for fifteen minutes and not buying anything except maybe a Coke, there's a good chance somebody at security would have taken notice of him and kept an eye on him. Anyway, I'm gonna call Kuhnke and try it out on him."

The lawyer agreed it was a good idea, certainly worth a try. So the next day Lori went out to Zayre's again, to try to discover who in security was on duty the night of April 20. The security manager, who knew of Lori's reputation, went back through five months of schedules to find the answer.

"It was Ruby Hills*. She was on duty the night of the twentieth."

"Great! Can you put me in touch with her?"

"We don't give out address or telephone numbers of any of our employees. Certainly not security people. But if you come back tomorrow, she might be here."

Ruby Hills was not there the next day. But on the following day Lori caught her at Zayre's, and she agreed to talk. They sat outside at a table near the concession stand. The first thing Lori showed her was the black-and-white mug shot of Scott.

"Don't show me those things. I see those things every day. I couldn't identify him from that."

Lori then followed the same routine she'd used with Pam Biller. She showed Ruby Hills the set of personal color photos—and got the same reaction.

"Oh yeah, I remember him all right. I can even tell you what he was wearing when I saw him."

"Would that have been on the night of April the twentieth?"

"Five months ago? I'm not even sure I was working that night."

"Your security manager says you were."

"Maybe I was, then. But I'd want to check my own records to be sure."

"Can you do that now?"

"No, it will take too much time. Come back tomorrow and I'll tell you."

"I'll be back. Meantime I'll be telling Lindsey Scott's lawyer, Ervan Kuhnke, about you, and he'll be getting in touch."

Excited now, Lori called Kuhnke and told him about the meeting. "I'm going back there tomorrow, and I'll call you again," she said.

At their meeting the next day Ruby Hills was able to verify that she had been on duty the night of April twentieth.

"And you remember seeing Lindsey Scott that night?"

"I didn't say that. All I can say is I worked that night, and that I remember seeing that guy in the store. But I can't put those two things together. I don't know what night I might have seen him."

"Can't you find out?"

"Maybe. It is possible. I'll have to check my records again to see if I made any notes about busts, suspicious characters, things like that."

"It's very important, Ruby. Will you do that for me?"

"Okay, but it might take a day or two."

"Good. I'll report this to Mr. Kuhnke again and he'll be in touch."

Lori called the lawyer and told him how excited she was, that Ruby Hills definitely was working security that night, and she recognized Scott, even described the clothes he was wearing. The only thing was, she couldn't tie the things together, Scott being there on the night of the twentieth. But she was going to check her records further.

"I think she's a very potential witness," Lori told him.

"Lori, if she can't put him in the store on the twentieth, then her testimony would be just as insignificant as Pam Biller's," said Kuhnke.

Lori became very upset at this remark. "Well, aren't you gonna subpoena her, and those other people I've been getting for you? Aren't you going to talk to them, interview them, or something?"

"Lori, I keep telling you it's nothing to worry about. You worry too much. It's in the bag."

Exasperated, Lori asked Kuhnke if it would be all right if she set up a personal meeting between Ruby Hills and Lindsey Scott. "Maybe if she could see him in person it would help jog her memory and she could put him in the store on the twentieth."

"Sure, go ahead if you want to," said Kuhnke.

On September 29, five days before the scheduled trial, Lori set up a meeting in the Zayre's parking lot for two P.M. At the meeting were Lindsey and his wife, Lori, Ruby Hills, and another security guard named Philip Quarrels.

At once Ruby pointed to Scott and said, "Yes, he's the one I saw in the store."

"On the night of the twentieth?"

Ruby shook her head. "I don't know. I haven't had a chance to go through all my records yet."

Lori sighed. "All right. There's not much more we can do now. Thanks for your help. I'll have Mr. Kuhnke get in touch with you about your records. It's really vital, you know, if you could put Lindsey there on the night of the twentieth."

"I know. But I can't perjure myself. I'll have to be absolutely sure."

Once again Lori had hit a brick wall. All she could do was telephone Kuhnke about the results of the meeting and listen to him repeat his advice "not to worry."

Lori decided to back off then. She said to her husband, "Maybe there's something going on behind my back Kuhnke doesn't want to tell me. Maybe there's a plea-bargain deal working out."

The Saturday before the trial was scheduled to open she called Victor Glasberg and explained the situation. "It's driving me bananas," she said. "My nerves are jumping. I keep calling Kuhnke and asking him if he intends to interview any of the witnesses I sent him or subpoena any of them and all he keeps telling me is I worry too much. 'It's in the bag,' he keeps telling me. 'The case will never go to trial,' he keeps telling me. Well, I'm telling you, Vic, I'm getting hives all over my body from this guy!"

Glasberg couldn't do anything for her but lend her a sympathetic ear.

Lori couldn't do anything more for herself or for Lindsey Scott but wait and hope for the best.

And all Lindsey Scott could do on that pretrial weekend was sit mutely in his apartment with his wife and new baby daughter and wonder what would become of him. And them.

On Monday morning of October 3, 1983, Military Judge Lieutenant Colonel H. S. Atkins, U.S. Marine Corps, called the court to order. The trial of *United States* v. *Corporal Lindsey Scott* began.

8

The military prefers to operate in a world of its own design, creating well-defined perimeters, its commanders, in their illusion of benevolent despotism, rewarding their own, punishing their own, away from public gaze, within the soundless seclusion of their moated fortresses. Lori Jackson, however, was determined that in the case of *United States* v. *Corporal Lindsey Scott*, the Marines and NIS would not enjoy a quiet court-martial.

"If they think they can get away with a paragraph buried somewhere in the Quantico newspaper," she said to her husband the weekend before the trial, "they better start thinking again. And they will not fill that little courtroom with their people. I will get some of ours in there, the press, civil-rights people. We need souls to bear witness to this trial, because I've got a bad feeling about it."

Her power to generate publicity was swiftly in evidence even before Military Judge Harry S. Atkins banged his gavel to open the pretrial proceedings. A collection of local news media and civil-rights activists descended upon the Quantico base, a rare event in the traditionally closed world of military justice. But the first bright spotlight of any major coverage of this case came when *The Washington Post* responded to Lori's call suggesting that this was a dramatic story of racial bias and injustice.

"It's an outrage that the military even chose to take this case to court," Lori proclaimed to the few reporters who assembled on the steps of LeJeune Hall for the first of what would be several impromptu press conferences. "I feel they were under pressure to get a suspect, and Lindsey was available."

Kuhnke, standing next to Lori, chimed in with an announcement that he would seek a change of venue. "I am convinced my client cannot get a fair trial," he said. "I am confident about this case, but there is always a chance for something to go wrong when it is an emotional issue like this one, where the woman almost died."

True to his announcement, at the pretrial formalities on the overcast morning of October 3, and before Judge Atkins asked Scott, "How do you plead?," Kuhnke submitted a motion for a change of venue, "on two grounds, the ground that Corporal Scott cannot, in our opinion, receive a fair and impartial trial because of command influence—undue command influence—and also because of pretrial publicity."

To substantiate his charge of command influence, Kuhnke asked to call as witnesses (among others) Lieutenant Colonel Harry (Retired), Major General Twomey, and Colonel Bruce Truesdale, Twomey's chief of staff.

Kuhnke didn't stand a chance, but to be fair to him, he probably had little or no knowledge of how the military worked in these circumstances. Unlike a civilian trial, Kuhnke could not demand the appearance of military witnesses. The trial judge and the military command themselves had almost unlimited decision-making power over which military personnel could be called. Thus the government, i.e., the prosecution, simply denied his request for the appearance of Harry and Truesdale on the grounds that their testimony would not be material. Major General Twomey, conveniently, was vacationing overseas.

Kuhnke argued that Harry would testify that because he released Scott from confinement, he was dismissed as military magistrate by Twomey's order, carried out by Truesdale, and that when he seemed ready to confront Twomey and make an issue of it, Truesdale warned him to keep his mouth shut. Since Twomey was, in any case, unavailable, Kuhnke argued, he should be granted a continuance of his motion for change of venue until Harry and Truesdale could be produced and testify.

Judge Atkins: "Is it your contention, Mr. Kuhnke, that the relief of Colonel Harry in some way influenced the referral of this case to a general court-martial?"

Kuhnke: "It is my contention that because of his release and the signals that were sent to the command that Corporal Scott cannot get a fair trial with members appointed by this command. I have . . . indicated that we would have no objection to holding the trial here provided that the members be made up of either headquarters Marine Corps personnel or Navy personnel. This, Your Honor, would be a clear indication to all concerned that Corporal Scott could get a fair trial. There is doubt now . . . and that is why I would like to call both of these gentlemen."

Judge Atkins: "Now, these gentlemen would be able to testify as to how the prospective court members would be unable to impartially and fairly sit?"

Kuhnke: "No, I submit if their testimony is that he was relieved because of that decision, which I submit the evidence indicates now . . . it's telling everybody in the command that the command is unhappy about that decision, and that this man must be guilty. The command believes he's guilty and I submit that to erase that possibility, I should at least be given the opportunity to call them and you should be able to hear from their own mouths and make that determination of whether there is undue command influence."

Judge Atkins: "Can you show that the members are aware of this action by General Twomey?"

Kuhnke: "No, I can't. I can't at this point. But I can show that the chief of staff, acting in the name of the general, relieved the military magistrate and that that action could well signal that that decision was a bad one and that the command wanted Corporal Scott incarcerated and, therefore, believed he was guilty of this offense."

Major Jim Messer, who was assistant trial counsel to trial counsel Major Thomson, objected to Kuhnke's statements; as he put it: "The defense counsel is starting to mix apples and oranges. Now we have all of a sudden switched in midstream from trying to show what had appeared from the pleadings to be a classic case of command influence to now talking about whether the court members have been afforded by this decision to relieve Lieutenant Colonel Harry to such an extent that they cannot render a fair and impartial verdict in this case." Although he was assistant trial counsel, it will be seen that Major Messer from the very beginning was to act as chief prosecutor throughout the trial, with Major Thomson in a supporting role only.

Messer, famous in the military as a "killer prosecutor," effectively trashed Kuhnke's pleadings. "If the defense counsel would like, the government would certainly stipulate that Lieutenant Colonel Harry was the military magistrate on the fifth of May, that he released Corporal Scott from pretrial confinement, and that he was subsequently relieved on the sixth of May. The government has contended all along, so what? There's no nexus between that and command influence, which is what the basis of these pleadings was apparently all about."

Judge Atkins: "The defense request for a continuance is denied."

Kuhnke's frustration was evident as he mopped sweat from his forehead and from around his lips. In his attempt to prove command influence, he was allowed to call as witnesses Lieutenant Colonel (promoted from Major) Ouellette, Lieutenant Colonel Hemming, Lieutenant Colonel Richard Walls, who was deputy staff judge advocate under Staff Judge Advocate Colonel Cassady. It was Walls, who, upon reading the transcripts of the Article 32, recommended to Colonel Cassady that the command proceed to a general court-martial.

It was a brave but futile gesture by Kuhnke. None of the three high-ranking officers could offer any testimony indicating pressure from Major General Twomey. Neither would any of them agree that Harry was relieved because he released Scott from confinement.

Kuhnke (to Walls): "Was there disenchantment within the JAG [sic] office when Corporal Scott was released?"

Walls: "Well, disenchantment is not a very technical term. I personally thought that the decision was inappropriate, based on the evidence of which I was aware."

In his final argument for a change in venue, Kuhnke reiterated his accusation of command influence by Major General Twomey. "I submit that other evidence of command influence in this matter is apparent," he said to Judge Atkins, "with my denial of calling witnesses that I believe will establish command influence in this case. Especially with respect to Colonel Harry, there is the

matter . . . that he would have testified about subsequent conversations with Colonel Truesdale—conversations in which he
was told not to open his mouth. I have been precluded from
putting the colonel on the stand. I have been precluded from
putting a man on the stand who gave him these instructions,
presumably in the name of Major General Twomey.

"I submit that the refusal of the government to let me take the
testimony of these two men that I believe in all due respect would
show command influence is in and of itself evidence of command
influence, denying me and raising a serious question about the
ability of Corporal Scott to get a fair trial before this court. I again
renew my motion for a change of venue and urge the court to grant
it."

For the government Major Messer countered that "after being
allowed to call a string of witnesses in its behalf the defense
counsel even in his closing argument failed to aver a scintilla of
evidence that there was in fact command influence connected with
the disposition of this case."

Judge Atkins: "The defense request for a change of venue is
denied. Does the defense have any more motions?"

"None, Your Honor."

"Very well. I'll receive the pleas of the accused, then."

"Your Honor, the accused pleads not guilty to all charges and
specifications."

That ended the first day of the proceedings. Pretrial continued
the following morning, first with the calling by the prosecution of
Special Agent James Lindner in special session to give evidence
on the Indenti-Kit identification by Judy Connors. After that, jury
would be empaneled and the trial begin.

Trial counsel Major Thomson, who was black, could feel the
stony stares of Lori and other civil-rights activists fixed upon him
as he took Lindner through all the stages of the Identi-Kit. The
NIS agent showed the judge, and defense counsel, exactly how it
worked, testifying to Judy's reaction to each stage. This, said
Thomson, lays the foundation to authenticate the photographs that
would be given the members, saving trial time; otherwise the

entire procedure, stage by stage, would have to be done and another photograph given the members at each stage.

Kuhnke cross-examined Lindner at length about the Identi-Kit process in an attempt to show that he might have influenced Judy by the way he worded his questions. The result was questionable, since as yet there were no members present or even empaneled. In any case, he knew he would have the opportunity again, when, during the course of the trial, the prosecution called Lindner as a witness.

Finally that morning came the selection of the members who would sit in judgment of Corporal Lindsey Scott. Nine prospective officers had been selected by the Quantico command, of which seven would be selected in a voir dire session. The phrase is a legal one, meaning a preliminary examination concerning the competence of a prospective juror or witness. The origin is Old French, meaning "to speak the truth."

In questioning each prospective member, Major Messer concentrated on two principal points: reasonable doubt and circumstantial evidence.

To the first prospective member, Colonel J. O. Marsh, Messer read out the following, taken from the Military Judges' Bench Book: "By reasonable doubt is intended not a fanciful or ingenious doubt or conjecture but an honest, conscientious doubt suggested by the material evidence or lack of it in this case. It is an honest misgiving caused by insufficiency of proof of guilt. Proof beyond reasonable doubt means proof to a moral certainty, although not necessarily an absolute certainly. . . . The rule as to reasonable doubt extends to every element of the offense, although each particular fact advanced by the prosecution which does not amount to an element need not be established beyond a reasonable doubt. However, if you are satisfied beyond a reasonable doubt of the truth of each and every element, then you should find the accused guilty.

"Sir, do you feel that you understand the difference between doubt and reasonable doubt?"

"Yes, I do."

"And would you agree with government counsel that the

government does not have to prove its case to a mathematical certainty against the accused?"

"Yes, I do."

Messer then summarized the circumstantial evidence instruction from the same book: "Colonel Marsh, there are two types of evidence you can use in deciding the facts of this case, direct evidence and circumstantial evidence. Direct evidence is based on actual knowledge or observation; circumstantial evidence, on the other hand, is indirect evidence or circumstances which convince you that some fact may or may not exist. For example, if you wake up in the morning and look out the window and see a wet street, that circumstance may cause you to conclude that it rained during the night. Sir, do you believe that you can take into consideration the fact that circumstantial evidence has the same weight as direct evidence?"

"Yes, I can."

"And if the government were to present the case based entirely on circumstantial evidence, could you vote to convict the accused of the offenses of which he's charged—based on circumstantial evidence?"

"Yes, I can."

In questioning Colonel Marsh, Kuhnke raised—and lost—an interesting point regarding direct evidence as opposed to circumstantial: "Would you agree with the position that circumstantial evidence should be held to a greater scrutiny?"

Major Messer: "Objection. That's not a premise based on law."

Kuhnke: "Not in military law, perhaps—and if that's the case, I withdraw it."

That brief exchange in effect established the basis of the government's entire case: the prosecution was relying on its circumstantial evidence, but in military law that carried just as much weight as direct evidence—of which they had none.

The questioning by both Major Messer and Kuhnke was moving along smoothly until the prosecutor stumbled over Lieutenant Colonel Rafael Negron, an operations officer. This officer agreed with Major Messer that the government did not have to prove its case "to a mathematical certainty." However, when Major Messer asked, "If the government were to construct a case based solely on circumstantial evidence, could you convict the accused of the offenses alleged?"

Lieutenant Colonel Negron replied. "No, I could not."

The colonel elaborated, in that he would need direct evidence to convict, such as a witness. "Circumstantial evidence is not enough to convict somebody," he said.

Perhaps needless to say, after all the other prospective members had been called and questioned, Major Messer "challenged for cause" Lieutenant Colonel Negron and got him dismissed as a member. One other officer was dismissed, Captain Brian Murry, on a "peremptory challenge" by Major Messer. The captain was hesitant about whether or not he could find Scott guilty on circumstantial evidence alone. On a "peremptory challenge," which he was allowed, Major Messer did not have to explain to the court why he didn't want the captain to sit as a member. The reason, however, was obvious.

Thus the final seven-member panel consisted of three majors, two lieutenants colonels, and two colonels; four of the members were white, two Hispanic, one black.

Judge Atkins seated the members, spoke to them briefly about their duties and responsibilities, and recessed the court for a brief break.

At three minutes past two o'clock, on October 4, the first salvos in the trial of Corporal Lindsey Scott were fired, with opening statements by trial counsel Major Thomson and defense counsel Ervan Kuhnke.

9

The afternoon was unseasonably warm and humid, and the small military courtroom at LeJeune Hall was stifling. The seven members of the court, sitting on a raised platform at the head of the wood-paneled room, were visibly uncomfortable in the oppressive heat. To their left stood the judge's bench, occupied now by Lieutenant Colonel Atkins. Below and perpendicular to the bench, not more than perhaps ten feet away, stood the cluttered table and straight-backed chairs of the defense. Here sat Kuhnke, unlit pipe as always clenched in his teeth, Major Roach, and Corporal Lindsey Scott, in full dress uniform as decreed by court-martial protocol. On the opposite side of the small room, facing the members and the judge, were the chairs and the table of the prosecution, occupied by trial counsel Major Donald Thomson and assistant trial counsel Major Jim Messer. The witness chair, a floor microphone at its side, was placed with its back against the wall between the members' dais and the prosecution table. A clock on the wall overhead ticked off the minutes.

Behind a low wooden barrier four rows of modest seats held just twenty-seven spectators. On that afternoon, except for several members of the press, this gallery was largely filled with friends, supporters, and relatives of Lindsey Scott. His parents had come up from their home in Louisville. Lori, carrying her many handwritten notes, was there along with two of her five daughters and representatives of her activist group, Women for Equal Social Justice; also on hand were observers from the Southern Christian Leadership Conference, and, from the Prince William County branch of the NAACP, two former high-ranking black military officers, retired Vice Admiral S. L. Gravely, Jr., and retired Army Major General R. C. Gaskill. Lori had her "souls to bear witness."

As opposing counsel shuffled their papers and the sweltering spectators squirmed restlessly in their hard wooden seats, Judge Atkins with one bang of his gavel called for order and asked for the opening statements.

Trial counsel Major Donald Thomson rose and, standing at military attention, spoke first, addressing, of course, the jury.

"Mr. President and members of the court, we've come just a little ways down the road through the process that this particular proceedings will take us. Generally, as the United States, we carry the burden of proof in proving that Corporal Scott is guilty beyond a reasonable doubt of what he's been charged with. The defense has a duty and a function to represent their client zealously and to the best of their ability. It is these functions that should determine perceptions of what we say and what we do, for what we say as counsel is not to be taken as evidence and what we say as counsel is not to be taken as the law. There is one individual in this courtroom who is qualified, according to law, to instruct you on what the law is, and that is the military judge.

"In this particular case, *United States* v. *Scott*—although the evidence may take a long time and the exhibits may be numerous—we are talking about conduct that transpired over less than an hour's period of time. The United States will present testimony as to that event by evidence both direct and circumstantial.

"Mrs. Judy Connors, the victim in this case, obviously will be intimately involved with the facts, the representations, and the circumstances on the twentieth of April, 1983, because in an hour's time, between 2000 and 2100, memorable events happened to Mrs. Connors which she will testify to. She will testify, we expect, that she was lured from her apartment by a telephone call . . . taken to a dark area onboard Marine Corps Development and Education Command, forced to commit sodomy upon her assailant. She was raped . . . she was choked, she was stabbed, slashed, and left in a remote area.

"There will be others who will testify as to the consequences and subsequent events. . . .

"We would suggest at this point that it is the quality and not the quantity of evidence that you will have before you . . . but the indicators point to Corporal Lindsey Scott as the individual who perpetrated this offense against the United States and against Judy Connors. We are at this time confident that when it comes time to deliberate on that evidence, you will find that a verdict of guilty of all charges and specifications will be mandated."

Solemnly removing his pipe and placing it carefully on the table before him, Kuhnke then addressed the court with his opening statement: "Mr. President and members of the court, I join with my colleague, trial counsel, in urging you to listen very carefully to the evidence—all of the evidence. Neither what I tell you or he tells you is evidence. The evidence will come in the form of testimony from the stand and documents that are produced. What I would ask you and where I disagree with the major is that you look—and where we have a disagreement as to the nature of that evidence—I ask you to look at the quality—the quality, gentlemen, of the evidence. We insist—we believe that after you have examined that quality of evidence that you will return a verdict of not guilty on all charges and specifications.

"You gentlemen—each and every one of you, collectively— are the judges of the facts—are the judges of the credibility of the evidence that you will hear as the trial unfolds. Again, I urge you to pay careful attention not only to what is said, but to the demeanor of all the witnesses.

"Now, in this case the defense has no burden whatsoever of putting on any evidence. We will. If the case were to stop, the government has the responsibility of proving to you beyond a reasonable doubt each and every element of the crimes that are charged. We have no burden of producing any evidence, but we will, and let me briefly tell you—give you the rest of that road map of the type of evidence that we will put on. We will call a witness who saw Corporal Scott that afternoon and who will describe the witness's [sic] clothing and put him in a given area at a given time. We ask you to listen very carefully for the discrepancies in testimony as to clothing, as to appearance, because one of the keys to this case is identification, whether there was in fact a good identification. We will then call a barber who has cut—who is the sole barber, if you will, of the corporal, and he will testify because the length of the hair is very relevant, as you will see in this case.

"We will call two witnesses who will place the corporal at a time which, we submit, makes it impossible for him to have committed these offenses. One of the men is a sergeant who was working on his car near the residence of Mrs. Connors, and it's expected that he will testify that he was working on his car until 2030 hours that evening and did not see the corporal or the corporal's car during that time. In fact, I believe he will testify that he did not see Mrs. Connors during that time. Again, I ask you to listen to the times and the testimony.

"You will then hear . . . a witness who saw and will identify Corporal Scott some thirteen, fifteen miles from where the crime was supposed to have been committed, putting him in a position where he could not have committed the crime. This person is a security guard in a store in Woodbridge who saw the corporal that night, has identified him, and will testify.

"Then the corporal will take the stand and he will testify as to those events that evening, as to his previous acquaintance of the victim. He will be available to answer any and all questions that you gentlemen or the opposing counsel may have.

"I'm convinced, as I indicated before, that after you hear all of the evidence that you will return a verdict of not guilty."

As Major Thomson called the first prosecution witness, NIS Special Agent James Lindner (conservatively dressed in a dark suit), Judge Atkins interrupted and asked the bailiff to open the outer door "and see if we can't get a little cross breeze in here." The packed courtroom was airless, stifling.

After swearing him in, Major Thomson walked Lindner through the investigation of the crime from the beginning, setting out for the members of the court his experience as a NIS investigator, the use of the Identi-Kit (the members each had been given the complete set of overlays), and the results of the photo and physical lineups. Lindner admitted that in both situations Judy Connors picked out two men as possible assailants.

Major Thomson: "What if anything did you say to her during the physical lineup?"

Lindner: "I asked her did she recognize any of the individuals."

"And what was the result?"

"She stated that the two on the right end, which were number five and number six looked like the man that attacked her."

"What happened next?"

"I had each man—number five and number six—individually step forward, do some facing movements, and then step back into line. I again asked Mrs. Connors could she pick out the man that attacked her, and she said that number five looked like him. I asked her, 'Can you be sure?' and she said, 'Number six also looks like him.'"

"What, if anything, happened next?"

"I asked her one more time could she be sure whether it was number five or number six and Mrs. Connors said, 'Number five scares me the most, but I'm still not quite sure.'"

"Were there any comments made by Mrs. Connors as to hair?"

"Yes. She said the hair on number six was longer and more like that of her assailant."

"And would you please tell the court who number five was?"

"Number five is the accused, Corporal Lindsey Scott."

Major Thomson continued his questioning with a summary of where Judy Connors lived, where she was found, and where the crime allegedly took place. Lindner identified these on an area map introduced by Major Thomson and marked the map with these and the location of the PMO office. This was the prosecution's maneuver to establish the Marines' jurisdiction over the crime, which was of course basic to the entire court-martial, had always been in question, and in fact never proven.

Having set it up, Major Thomson proceeded with Lindner: "Special Agent Lindner, the markings that you've put on the map, are they accurate as to the facts of this case, to the best of your knowledge?"

"Yes, they are."

"Due to where the victim was picked up in this case, where does jurisdiction lie?"

"Aboard the military reservation."

Kuhnke rose. "Your Honor, I object to the offer of this exhibit into evidence unless the crime scene, which was identified—

unless there is more testimony—unless it's clarified—may I voir dire the—"

Judge Atkins: "Your objection is to the identification of the . . . ?"

"Identification of the crime scene, which has been described as the crime scene."

Judge Atkins: "I will then sustain your objection."

Major Thomson tried again: "Special Agent Lindner, you've marked on the map 'location where victim found.'"

"Yes."

"As case agent in this case, as the agent in charge, do you have an opinion as to where the offense took place in regard to where the victim was found?"

"Yes, I believe the offense took place aboard the MCDEC and the victim was found aboard MCDEC."

"Objection to the opinion!"

"Sustained.

Major Thomson tried a third time, entering from a different direction. He asked Lindner, "What, if any, efforts did you take to locate the crime scene?"

"We got tracker dogs out that night from Prince William County to try to pick up a scent, see if we could trace it back to the crime scene. We were unsuccessful. They brought out military police and investigators from CID and our office—out to the crime scene and canvassed the area to try to locate it, and they also brought Mrs. Connors back to the general area to see if she could pick out where the crime scene was, but she was unable to do so."

On the basis of that testimony, Major Thomson again asked that the map and Lindner's opinion be introduced as evidence to establish jurisdiction.

Again Kuhnke objected. "That document should not be admitted. Special Agent Lindner has admitted that they were unable after exhaustive efforts to locate the crime scene. The proximity of the boundaries and everything makes it purely speculative at this point whether it was in Prince William County or in MCDEC. We don't know where the crime was committed, and I submit that it would be misleading to the jury to submit this into evidence. You have sustained my objection as to the agent's opinion where the crime was committed. I submit now that you should sustain my objection to admission of this document."

"I will sustain the defense objection. There is nothing before the court as to the time or location where the victim was found."

Important point scored by Kuhnke. Major Thomson withdrew the map as possible evidence.

Following further brief questioning of Lindner by the prosecution, Kuhnke cross-examined.

He took Lindner at some length through the Identi-Kit process, referring to Lindner's testimony at the Article 32 hearing in June, challenging the agent's procedures and once again Judy Connors's identification of Scott as her assailant.

Kuhnke: "Now, when you prepared this Identi-Kit likeness, was Corporal Scott a suspect?"

Lindner: "No, he was not, sir."

Kuhnke: "Would you read from the cross-examination on page 40, this paragraph?" Kuhnke handed the witness the transcript of the Article 32 investigation.

Lindner (reading): "I've known Corporal Scott about a year, give or take. I have never participated in an investigation on anyone I've known for this length of time or even known. When you suggest it's not proper and contrary to good investigative practice, I would say no. Yes, I prepared the composite picture. It's true I regarded him as a suspect and I was the case agent. . . ."

Kuhnke: "Those first few lines. Do you find anything inconsistent with that statement?"

"Yes, I do."

"Would you tell the court what's inconsistent and what's the truth?"

"The 32 says he was a suspect, but the truth is he was not a suspect. His name had been mentioned that night when they rolled Mrs. Connors into the hospital. Somebody said, 'That sounds like Scotty' "—it was his partner of that evening, NIS agent Rivers—"and we both laughed it off. And then the next morning his name came up again."

"So this testimony was inaccurate?"

"Yes, sir."

Kuhnke continued with questions about the photo lineup and the physical lineup, as Messer and Thomson exchanged uncomfortable glances and whispered to each other. Lindner had to admit, of course, that Judy Connors had not been able to make a positive identification of Scott and had picked two men out of both lineups, saying "I just can't be sure."

Still hammering away at the jurisdiction controversy and the victim's identification of Scott, he said to Lindner: "You still don't know where the crime scene was, do you?"

"No, sir."

"When did that search stop—an attempt to locate it stop?"

"I'm going to say on the twenty-sixth of April, after Mrs. Connors was released from the hospital and we were able to take her out through the area and she finally just said, 'I can't remember for sure.'"

"And no attempt was made after the twenty-sixth to locate where a crime of this magnitude was committed?"

"Not to my knowledge, no, sir."

"The description of the car. How did she describe the perpetrator's car?"

"Two-door sedan, yellow, gold exterior, a similar interior, light color."

"What does Corporal Scott's car look like?"

"I believe it's a gold two-door Buick Regal."

"Would it surprise you that it's actually beige and has a white landau roof?"

"No, I guess you could call it beige."

"But did you notice the white landau top?"

"Yes, sir."

"Did the victim say anything about a white landau top?"

"No, sir."

Kuhnke turned to forensic evidence. "Did you conduct any laboratory or cause to be conducted any laboratory tests?"

"I didn't conduct them personally, sir. I sent them off to the FBI lab."

"What type of tests did you send off?"

"Serology examinations."

"Explain to the court what that is."

Lindner went through the list of tests: blood, semen, hair, soil from the shoes of both victim and suspect. All tests, he said, came back negative or inconclusive.

"Fingerprints? Were there any fingerprints?"

"No, sir."

"His car was vacuumed, and the results of that vacuuming—the material that was picked up from his car—that was tested. Was there any identification of the victim?"

"No, sir."

"Were there any other tests that were taken, any other forensic tests caused to be taken by you?"

"Blood, hair, semen, fingerprints. No, I can't think of any. Soil, debris."

"All negative?"

"Or inconclusive."

"Did the victim tell you what kind of cigarettes she smoked?"

"Marlboro Lights."

"Did you find any of that type?"

"No, sir, we did not."

"So there was absolutely no physical evidence that you took—was there anything that you missed—any possible physical test?"

"No, sir, I believe we covered them all, all the standard tests, in the investigation."

"With negative or inconclusive results?"

"Yes, sir."

At that point, the time being 4:20 P.M., Judge Atkins nodded to the bailiff, who bellowed, "All rise!" and the judge dismissed the members of the jury first, as the protocol dictates. The court was now adjourned until the following morning, when Kuhnke would continue his cross-examination of Special Agent Lindner.

Lori was not happy with the results of that first day in court. Her concern was that Kuhnke still had not subpoenaed any of the possible alibi witnesses, or any other witnesses she had suggested to him, or even contacted them. She was particularly disturbed by the fact that in his opening statement Kuhnke had alluded to a witness he intended calling who was a security guard in a store and who would give Scott a perfect alibi. This, of course, was Ruby Hills of Zayre's. Lori knew very well that Kuhnke had not even telephoned her, much less issued a subpoena for her appearance in court. Furthermore, the denial by Judge Atkins of Kuhnke's motion for a change of venue, the lawyer's defeat in trying to prove command influence, reconfirmed her certainty that Scott had no chance of a fair trial.

Scott, too, was mournfully pessimistic. He left the building with Lola and five-week-old Latavia realizing that some critical elements of Kuhnke's defense had already been wiped away. "I can only hope for a miracle," he said to the few reporters who asked him for a statement.

The continued cross-examination of Lindner the next morning elicited nothing startling—but it might have, when Kuhnke questioned Lindner about the possibility of suspects other than Scott.

"During the Article 32 you were reluctant—in fact, you refused—to tell me of any other suspects in the case. Can you tell me and the court now if there were any other suspects in the case?"

"No, sir."

" 'No, sir'? You can't tell me?"

"No, sir, I mean there were no other suspects in the case."

"Are you aware of the fact—let me restate that. Did someone bring to your attention a possible suspect that resembled Corporal Scott and had a car similar in color to Corporal Scott's?"

"Not to my knowledge, sir, no."

"And is it a correct summarization of your testimony that your investigation was limited to Security Battalion?"

"Yes, sir."

That ended Kuhnke's cross-examination of Lindner.

The probing of other suspect possibilities might have gone deeper, however. There was the unsettled matter of the hair discovered on the inside of the sweater Judy Connors had worn on the night of the crime. Lori had reported to Kuhnke of other rapes around Quantico in which the suspects were black, and related to him that there was some gossip at Hardee's about Judy. Allegedly black colleagues of hers were involved. Lindner had certainly implied during the Article 32 hearing that the investigation was still ongoing, though refusing to elaborate, and being supported by Major Thomson in that respect.

What, if anything, Kuhnke might have gained for the defense by pushing Lindner harder in this direction is a moot point. Nevertheless, it might well have caused a bit of a stir in the courtroom.

After a bit of redirect by the prosecution and re-cross-examination of Lindner, primarily about Judy Connors's description of what she called a metal pot or bucket on the backseat of her assailant's car, the prosecution called Judy herself to the stand.

10

Despite the saturating heat, Judy Connors wore a turtleneck sweater to hide the scars from her neck wounds. As she settled into the witness chair a conspicuous quantity of tissues in her hand, Major Jim Messer rose to his feet to take over the questioning. Messer was a Marine's Marine, a recruiting-poster Marine, an imposing six-foot-plus, muscular, with clean-cut, unsmiling features that could have been carved from stone.

Quietly he led Judy through the events of April twentieth, from the time she returned home from her last day's work at Hardee's—though this fact was bypassed—to the time she said she received the phone call about her husband and raced down to the parking lot of the Spanish Gardens complex where she lived.

She remarked that it was dusk but getting dark. A clear night, with stars and a moon. There was a light on top of a pole, she said, some twenty-five to thirty feet away from where she stood, waiting for the car she said was already in the lot and backing up toward her. She said, in reply to a question from Major Messer, that there had been a brief exchange of conversation with the man in the car before she entered it.

Judy: "The person in the vehicle said, 'Mrs. Connors?' And I said yes. And he said, 'Come on, we've got to get going.' I naturally presumed this was the man from CID. I walked over to the car, to the passenger-side door. I opened the door and I bent down and I looked at him and I said, 'Are you the man from CID?' And he said yes."

As she continued her narrative she said that as they drove off and she was asking him about what had happened to her husband,

95

she was smoking a cigarette and he said to her, "Can I have one?" She gave him a cigarette, and lit it for him with her lighter.

For the benefit of the court, Judy described in detail all the things she said had happened to her—the sodomy, the rape, and the knife attack by her assailant. She described how as her attacker knelt over her, choking her, she tried to push his arms away. She blacked out briefly, she said, and when she awoke, "He was standing over me and he had the knife in his hand and he was laughing—in a weird way."

Major Messer: "Judy, if you ever saw this person again, would you recognize him?"

"Yes, sir."

"Now, Judy Connors, I want you to look at this courtroom and tell me, do you see the man that forced you to orally sodomize him, who raped you, who choked you, stabbed you, slashed your throat, and left you in the woods?"

"Yes, sir."

"Is he in this courtroom?"

"Yes, sir."

"Would you please point him out to the members of this jury?"

For six months leading up to this moment she had been uncertain. She had seemed frail and vulnerable, unsure of her own judgment. Now, having enjoyed many opportunities to review the case with the prosecutors, and being obviously well-prepared, Judy rose from the witness chair, approached the defense table, and pointed dramatically at Lindsey Scott, declaring, "This man right here."

With Judy's identification of Scott as her assailant a principal target of the defense, Major Messer framed four rapid questions aimed at justifying her accusing finger.

"Judy . . . when you first bent over to talk to the accused in his car, how far away were you at this point?"

"Approximately two to three arms' lengths."

"When you sat in the car with the accused, how far away were you from him?"

"Approximately two arms' lengths."

"When the accused was raping you, how far away were you from him?"

"Very close. Inches."

"When the accused was choking you, how far away were you from him?"

"Probably about—oh, an arm's length at most."

When Major Messer asked, "Judy, can you estimate how long you were in the accused's car on the evening in question?" Kuhnke objected to the phrase "in the accused's car" and the other, similar phrases used by the prosecutor. Kuhnke was objecting to the use of the word "accused" within that context because it implied that there was no doubt whatsoever that Judy was in Scott's car, that it was he who was choking her, and so forth, and that therefore he was the assailant.

Kuhnke: "There have been several leading questions of this nature, but I've let them by. I submit that the form of the question is improper."

Judge Atkins: "What is the nature of your objection, Mr. Kuhnke, that it's leading?"

"The implication is that—"

Major Messer interrupted: "There is no implication here, sir. She identified him."

Judge Atkins: "She has identified him."

Kuhnke: "I submit that's misleading and prejudicial, Your Honor."

Fuming, Major Messer abruptly banged the prosecution table with his hand, startling the entire courtroom. "There is only one person that was prejudiced in this courtroom, sir! That's the victim in this case!"

Judge Atkins attempted to restore order as the spectators buzzed at the prosecutor's outburst. "Now, just a minute, counsel," he said. "I will permit you to use that phraseology. She has identified him. But there is no need to get any more upset about it. Carry on."

And to Kuhnke: "Overruled."

Major Messer continued, and brought Judy to the point of the photo and physical lineups, in order to introduce them formally as prosecution evidence. He handed her first the photo lineup pictures.

"Did you pick anyone out of those series of pictures as the person who did this to you?"

"Yes, sir."

"Who did you choose?"

"Number four."

Then photographs of the physical lineup.

"Did you identify anyone in that lineup as the person who did this to you?"

"Yes, sir."

"And who did you identify?"

"I identified number five."

(No equivocation by Judy Connors this time. No mention of the fact that at the original lineups and in all subsequent sworn statements she had admitted to picking out two possible assailants.)

Major Messer, ever the clever trial dramatist, then had Judy face the jury members, pull her hair back, and show them her neck.

In sepulchral tones, almost as though what he was about to say was too terrible to pronounce in open court, the "killer prosecutor" turned to the members: "The record should reflect that exposed on the neck of the witness appear to be several horizontal slash marks around the throat area . . . and they appear to be between three and five inches long."

Turning quickly back to Judy: "And would you tell the members what they are?"

"They're scars from when Corporal Scott stabbed me."

Murmurs from the spectators in the courtroom. Judge Atkins banged for quiet.

Major Messer: "The government has no further questions from this witness, Your Honor."

Kuhnke, dabbing his brow with a handkerchief: "The defense would request a ten-minute recess."

Lori immediately approached the attorney and led him out into the hallway, where she huddled with him about something she had only recently discovered about Judy's former employment at Hardee's.

(It will be remembered that Special Agent Lindner had also been told at Hardee's that Judy had been "very friendly" with a couple of the black employees there; anything more than that he might have learned had not been included in his official report.)

When the trial resumed, Lori changed her seat so that while taking her copious notes she could get a better view of Judy's face during the cross-examination to come.

Kuhnke, ever the mild-mannered Virginia gentleman, approached Judy Connors to cross-examine as though walking on eggshells.

"Mrs. Connors . . . I don't intend to embarrass you. I don't intend to upset you. If I do it is only to get at the truth. . . . Now, when you were asked if you saw the man who did this to you, you stood up and pointed to the corporal. I want to know, Mrs. Connors, why you weren't so certain before . . . you just testified that you picked his picture out of the photo lineup and the physical lineup. But you also picked out of each lineup another man, didn't you, ma'am?"

"Yes, sir."

"And you also said that you couldn't be sure which one it was, didn't you?"

"There was a reason why I picked out another person in the pictures."

"Please tell me and the court."

"Because the picture of the person that I originally picked out and said that this person looked exactly like him, which was the picture of Corporal Scott, his hair was a little bit shorter than what I remembered it to be. And I looked at another picture, and I said that this person also looks like him, but that—because his hair was more the length of what I remembered it to be."

"You remembered your attacker to have longer hair than Corporal's Scott's?"

"A little bit longer, yes."

"And at the physical lineup you also picked out two people, didn't you? And you said you were sorry, you couldn't be sure?"

"I was 99.9 percent sure."

"But didn't you say you were sorry, you couldn't be sure?"

"Yes."

This was a softly delivered but well-aimed cross to Judy's unequivocal identification of Scott under Major Messer's direct. Kuhnke followed quickly with questions prompted by the fasci-

nating information Lori had given him during the recess—
questions that raised a few eyebrows around the courtroom.

"Ma'am, there was a Negroid hair, two inches long, found on
your sweater. Do you remember that? Are you familiar with that?"

"I guess they told me, yes."

"Do you know where that hair came from, that two-inch hair?"

"No."

"You don't know what the source of it is?"

"No. I assume it came from him, but it could have been a hair
that was on his clothing from someone else."

"You don't know whether that hair sample was checked, do
you? Was examined?"

"I don't know if they told me about that or not."

"Do you have any male Negro friends?"

"I used to when I was working at Hardee's. I knew a couple
guys that worked there, friends of mine."

"It wouldn't surprise you if I told you that we talked to your
supervisor at Hardee's?" The witness shook her head in the
negative. "And it wouldn't further surprise you if I told you that
the supervisor told my investigator Mrs. Jackson that you were
very friendly with the black employees there? Would that surprise
you?"

Defensively, appearing angry and just a bit shaken by the
direction of the questioning, Judy replied, "I was no more friendly
with them than I was with anyone else."

"But you were friendly with them," Kuhnke pressed her.

"As far as saying hello and talking with them, like I'd talk with
anyone else, yes."

Having made his point—which was that there could well have
been other suspects in the case, other men with other motives—
Kuhnke had no place to go. The best he could have hoped for, in
any case, was sowing a few seeds of doubt in the minds of the
members of the court.

The lawyer moved to what appeared to be firmer ground. He
pursued Judy with the facts that she had lived for many months in
the same Spanish Gardens complex as Scott, her husband had
worked with him and carpooled with him, and she herself had met
him, according to Lindsey.

"Do you remember four days before the incident Corporal Scott—do you remember another military policeman right outside the apartment, four days before the incident, stopping you and saying hello to your husband?"

"A lot of people that he knows live in that apartment building, have said hello to him. But I don't remember anybody in particular."

"You don't remember a black—you don't remember seeing Corporal Scott four days before the incident?"

"If I did, I didn't take any notice to him, or recognition."

"Did you ever see him—did you ever see Corporal Scott while you were shopping at K Mart?"

"If I ever laid eyes on him I wouldn't have known who he was and I wouldn't have taken any recognition to him, no. I don't remember ever seeing him before."

"But you admit that since he lived there and you lived there that there is a possibility that you saw him? Do you admit that?"

"I could have seen him sometime. But I wouldn't have—I, just like anybody else, just glance over at people. I wouldn't—"

"And you have lived there for eight months?"

"Yes, since September of last year."

Fumbling with his words, seemingly unsure of where he was going, Kuhnke dropped this line of questioning (though it was patently obvious to the prosecution, to Scott, and to a chagrined Lori, sitting in the front row of the gallery, where he had intended to go) and questioned Judy at some length on her routine of the early evening, beginning at five o'clock. He then took her through her identification of her assailant's car—and got back on course.

Before he could continue, however, there was an interruption by the court reporter, a gunnery sergeant (always called "Gunney" in the Marines). He sat at a table on a small platform just below the judge and just above the prosecution and defense tables. "Your Honor, I've run out of the paper roll on my Stenotype," he announced.

A scattering of titters ran around the gallery. Judge Atkins banged his gavel for silence, but he was smiling. "Okay, let's take five minutes for Gunney to get his paper roll back in business."

Standing at the defense table, Kuhnke went over with Judy her experiences of the evening, including her brief conversations with her assailant, as she had recounted them earlier under questioning by Major Messer. However, whereas the prosecutor successfully elicited testimony from Judy that on a number of occasions she had been close enough to her assailant to identify him in the lineups, Kuhnke turned the same information on its head for the defense. He established with Judy that the parking lot was partially lighted when she was picked up by the waiting car.

"Did you get a pretty good look at the man at this time?"

"No, not at the time. All I knew was, you know, that he was a man, that he had glasses on, that he was black. That's about all I noticed at that time."

"And you didn't recognize him or his car?"

"No, sir."

"When you got to Route 1 was there a red light?"

"I believe so, yes."

"And so the car was stopped?"

"Yes, sir. Not very long."

"Was there much light from that inside the car?"

"Yes, as much as there would be from the lights. Not a lot."

"You kept asking this man about your husband?"

"Yes, sir."

"And you were looking at him all the time?"

Judy hesitated for a moment, appeared puzzled, as though not sure where Kuhnke was taking her and wary of falling into a trap, a damaging admission. "No, not all the time. I glanced at him once in a while . . . and I didn't look at him all the time, no."

"But you looked at him—you looked at him in the parking lot and . . . you looked at him when you lit the cigarette for him?"

"I think so."

"And you certainly looked at him when he was sexually attacking you?"

"I tried not to look at him as much as I—you know, I didn't want to look at him, but I—"

"But you did look at him?"

"I glanced at him a few times, yes."

"And you looked at him later in the woods? You were looking up at him?"

"I couldn't—yes."

"You remember in the Article 32 I asked you if there were any distinguishing characteristics about this man's face?"

Judy nodded affirmatively.

"I asked you if he had any chipped teeth or anything like that, and what was your response?"

"I—I didn't know."

"Did you notice anything about his teeth?"

"No."

"Have you subsequently learned that Corporal Scott has a very prominent gold tooth in his mouth?"

"Yes."

"And you didn't see it that night?"

"No."

"The cigarette that you lit for the man that attacked you, was that your cigarette or his?"

"Mine."

"And you lit it. And did you light it and put it in his mouth or was it in his mouth when you lit it?"

"I don't remember. I think I held the lighter up and lit the cigarette for him while he had it in his mouth. That's what I remember."

"During that time you obviously were watching him, so you didn't burn him?"

"I was watching the end of the cigarette and my lighter."

"And you didn't see that gold tooth at that time?"

"No, sir."

"You didn't see it at any other time?"

"No, sir."

There it was—the conundrum; a puzzle for anyone in the courtroom who cared to recognize it: if, as Judy implied, and was meant to imply by the direction of the prosecutor's questions, that she was a number of times close enough to her assailant to easily pick him out of two lineups, then how could she possibly have missed that prominent gold tooth and hairlip scar?

Kuhnke didn't press her. Although he continued to question her at length about other events of that night, he extracted just one item of possible useful information for the defense. In describing the assailant's knife, Judy said that it had hilts, and remembered having drawn a sketch of a hilted knife. The importance of this would be highlighted by the evidence that would be given by the prosecution's next witness.

It is a peculiarity of military trials that the members could ask questions of a witness after the judge and all the attorneys had approved of them. This was not done directly; members could write down the questions (signing their names but remaining anonymous to the courtroom). The questions would be handed down to the bailiff, who would then hand them to the judge for first viewing. If he felt they were relevant, he would then have the questions asked by whichever counsel had called that witness.

The members had many questions for Judy, largely concerned with the layout and lighting of the parking lot at Spanish Gardens. While they were writing them down Judge Atkins ordered the bailiff to close the courtroom windows and turn on the air-conditioning. For October, it was absolutely suffocatingly hot and humid.

Judy answered the members' questions, read out by Major Messer (since Judy was his witness) and one from Judge Atkins about the location of the light pole in the parking lot. Excused finally after her long session in the witness chair, she hurried from the courtroom with quick little steps, biting her lip, dabbing at her eyes with a tissue, looking neither right nor left, ignoring the pointed stares from some of the gallery spectators.

The government called Mrs. Maxine Knight, the office manager at Spanish Gardens. As Mrs. Knight took the witness chair, Major Messer, who had effectively taken over the chief prosecutor's role from Major Thomson, remarked to Judge Atkins that since the dinner hour was approaching, "her direct and cross shouldn't take more than ten or fifteen minutes."

The judge smilingly obliged. "Ten or fifteen minutes. That will be fine. Go ahead."

The prosecutor introduced via Mrs. Knight the knife allegedly used in the attack. She testified that since Scott was leaving Spanish Gardens he had to clean the apartment he was vacating, and had neglected the stove. "He didn't have anything with him to expedite the cleaning of it. And in my desk I had a knife which I had used myself when I cleaned stove parts, and I loaned it to him."

"Did the accused in this case ever bring that knife back to you?"

"No."

"Do you have any idea where that knife is today?"

"No, I certainly don't."

"I have no further questions of this witness, Your Honor."

Kuhnke was equally brief, simply developing with the witness an important, detailed description of that knife. "It was a very ordinary steak knife, not an expensive one. It was an old one. It was about eight inches long and had a serrated edge."

"Did the knife have any—right between the handle and the blade did the knife have any objects sticking out?"

"No."

"What military people call 'hilts'?"

"No."

"You're absolutely sure of that?"

"I'm absolutely sure of that."

Mrs. Knight was not a lady to waste words. Succinct but telling. In direct contrast to the hilted knife described by Judy Connors.

Mrs. Knight was excused. With a "hmmph" of what was no doubt meant to be her opinion of the entire proceedings, the landlady strutted from the courtroom, head held high.

Major Messer reminded the judge of the time. "Your Honor, the government has other witnesses, but due to the nature of the hour we would anticipate—"

In a genial mood, Judge Atkins nodded his agreement. "You're commended for your accuracy of prognostication." He beamed at the prosecutor. "Okay, shall we, gentlemen, then be in recess until 1300?" he said, as though addressing his cronies at some business meeting.

Deadly serious a trial it might be, a man's life and that of his family be at stake, but the "normalities" of life had to continue; the lunch break was decreed.

Next on the witness chair was Master Sergeant David Martin, who was an active-duty Marine currently detailed as an NIS special agent. It was Martin, who with his partner, NIS Agent

Rivers, had gone to Scott's new apartment on the day after the crime while Scott was being interrogated at the Quantico base. The object, said Martin, was "to speak to Corporal Scott's wife and seize any evidence that was deemed appropriate at the time."

What he seized, he testified under examination by Major Messer, were articles of clothing Lola Scott had said her husband had worn that night, when he'd gone out to clean their old apartment at Spanish Gardens, and a silver metal pot that he said contained cleaning materials.

The question of the length of Scott's hair also came up again. Martin said Scott usually wore it short, Marine style, but on the day of the physical lineup it seemed to him to be "shorter than it was normally."

Under Kuhnke's cross-examination, Martin admitted that he'd known Scott for about a year, had for a time been his superior, and that Scott had been "above average. When he worked for me I had no problems with Corporal Scott. He did good work."

Martin said he knew the Scotts socially, and Mrs. Scott had invited him and Rivers into the apartment and had cooperated fully in their "search and seizure" mission. Among the clothes Lola gave them was a brown-colored cap and a light scarf (neither of which had been mentioned by Judy Connors in the description of her assailant's clothing).

According to Martin, later that day, upon their return to the base, Scott asked to talk to them and, though adamantly denying his guilt, did admit that the silver-colored bucket had been in his car that night when he went to clean the apartment.

Obliquely, Kuhnke brought in the racist issue during his questioning of Martin: "In April of this year, how many black CID officers were there?"

"Two."

"Two. And the other man's name?"

"Sergeant Raymond Collier."

"Do you know anything about Sergeant Collier's duty status on April twentieth?"

"I believe it was the day after he went on leave."

"So, that would have made Corporal Scott the only black CID officer at Quantico?"

"On duty."

There were nods of approval from Lori and the civil-rights activists in the gallery. This was precisely what they had been agitating about for many months: the Marines' policy at Quantico, and not only at Quantico, of discriminating against black Marines, holding them back from promotion, keeping them out of the more elite battalions like CID.

However—and Lori only questioned this afterward—the singling out of Scott as one of the only two blacks in CID seemed an illogical point to highlight here for the defense; at the outset of the trial Kuhnke had publicly declared that he didn't think the prosecution was "racially motivated." More important, exposing Scott's exclusive status particularly on that fateful night could very well strengthen the prosecution's contention that since he was the only black in CID on duty and since the assailant had identified himself as a CID man (according to Judy), then Scott was not only the likely suspect—he must be the guilty man.

Kuhnke did not take the racial issue any further, however, and other than several routine questions about the search of Scott's car and the timing of his itinerary as he had related it to Martin, he had no more questions for the witness.

Major Messer had a few questions for Martin on redirect examination, principally: "Do you know what kind of vehicle the accused drives?"

"A light-tan-colored—I'm just guessing now—a '73 or '74 Chevy."

On that note Kuhnke came back with a recross: "When did you last see the corporal's car?"

"That's a good question. I—"

"Because he doesn't have a Chevy, Sergeant."

"I didn't—I don't know the brand name. It could have been a GM-type vehicle."

"And the color?"

"Light brown. I don't—I can't remember."

"Could the car have been a Buick and could it have been beige with a white landau roof?"

"It could have, yes."

That was all for Martin. The prosecution next called Richard

Leonard of the Prince William County Police Department to testify about his examination of Scott's car on the day after the crime. The first thing Lenoard testified to was the identification of Scott's car—which was correct, while NIS Agent Martin's was completely wrong.

"It was a 1976 Buick Skylark. It was white over yellow in color and a Virginia tag."

Leonard continued with his description of the car, in which he reiterated his opinions stated in early NIS reports that to him it appeared as though the inside passenger door, the window, the seat, and dashboard had been wiped down. The floorboard around the passenger seat was damp, he said, as though water or some kind of liquid had been spilled there. The ashtray was empty.

Cross-examination by Kuhnke: "Did you dust this car for fingerprints?"

"Yes, sir, it was dusted."

"Did you find any?"

"Only smeared, nothing identifiable."

"The car had a white landau roof?"

"It's a white vinyl roof. I would call it a half roof."

"But it was white?"

"Yes, sir."

"What was on the rear seats, if anything?"

"I believe there was a scarf."

"What color scarf?"

"I don't recall, sir."

Before the prosecution's penultimate witness was to be called—NIS Special Agent Richard Wardman, who had driven Judy Connors around the base trying to spot her assailant's car—the defense asked for a special session, called an Article 39(a) session. In such an instance, the jury members leave the courtroom while opposing counsel argue aloud in the open courtroom before the judge. The defense here was objecting to seven photographs of the victim that the prosecution was planning to introduce with the calling of its final witness, the Navy doctor who treated Judy at the emergency clinic. Because of certain technicalities peculiar to evidence allowable at military trials, Kuhnke asked Major Roach to make the argument for the defense.

The major referred to a rule stating that "even if evidence is relevant, it may be excluded if the probative value is substantially outweighed by—one—the danger of unfair prejudice or—two—the fact that there's going to be needless presentation of cumulative evidence." He argued that the photos, which were of the victim's neck wounds, had no value as proof of guilt or innocence of the accused. The defense did not deny that there was a crime and that there were wounds; furthermore, the victim had already exhibited her scars.

"The danger is great," said Major Roach, "that these photos will unduly prejudice the members . . . with all of the blood and the scars and the little bits of stitching and the number of those photographs, the real danger is that the members might base their decision on emotion rather than reason."

Major Thomson, for the prosecution, claimed that the photos were necessary because the "United States in this case is alleging attempted murder."

After listening to much legal wrangling back and forth, Judge Atkins sustained the defense objection to five of the photos, and overruled on two.

Major Messer made short work of NIS Special Agent Richard Wardman. Did he conduct an investigation on the twenty-fifth of April with Judy Connors? He did. What type of investigation? To observe the corporal's car and see if she could identify it as the one that she had been transported in on the evening that she was raped. And did she make any identification of a car? Yes, she did. And whose car did she identify? Corporal Scott's car.

No further questions by the prosecution.

On the other hand, Kuhnke conducted a lengthy cross-examination, starting from the ride around the base. Wardman obliged by painting a very detailed picture of every parking lot they had entered, and included the trenchant comment that Judy's husband (who, as we said, had carpooled with Scott and knew his car) had accompanied them on the drive, sitting in the backseat.

During the search, Wardman claimed that before identifying Scott's car, "she pointed out two other vehicles as possibly being similar to the one she was transported in."

"And those two other vehicles, were they similar in color?"

"They were—one was whitish, and the other was an off-white."

"Did she examine the interior of these two vehicles?"

"She examined the interior of one of the others." Without further prompting, Wardman gave Kuhnke and the court a travelogue of the journey, ending with Judy's identification of a car, which turned out to be Scott's. According to Wardman's testimony, Judy spotted a car she said looked similar to her assailant's, got out and studied the interior for about a minute, and said, "This has a similar appearance to the vehicle I was in."

Wardman said she pointed out four things: the car had bench seats, a pull-down ashtray in the center, and the same round gas gauge on the far left of the dashboard. That was only three things, but Wardman, perhaps engaging in mental arithmetic, added as a fourth: "She said, 'Well, on the mirror there was something hanging. It was squarish, and it was like on a dark string. But it's not there now.'"

Kuhnke: "Similar in appearance to the vehicle. She didn't say, 'That was the vehicle'?"

"Not at that time. After she had restudied it and I'd ask her, you know, 'What specifically do you recall?' and then she'd explain it to me and continued to look into it, she became emotional over it, and she said, 'Yes, this is the vehicle.'"

"After your discussion?"

"Yes."

"Would it surprise you to learn, Special Agent Wardman, that Mrs. Connors does not remember this matter in any way near the detail that you just related?"

"No, it would not surprise me."

"And she, in fact, makes no reference to a whitish car."

With little else to be gleaned from Wardman, he was excused, and the prosecution called as its final witness Lieutenant Commander Ronald Schubert, of the Naval Reserve Medical Corps. Major Thomson took over the questioning.

The doctor explained that on the night of April 20 he was the staff emergency-room physician when Judy Connors was wheeled in. He described her condition when she was admitted: ". . . the injuries seemed to be centered about her neck . . . multiple stab wounds and slash wounds. She also had a bite mark, a contusion, bruise on her tongue. There didn't seem to be any imminent or immediate threat to her life."

Major Thomson: "Are you the doctor who treated Judy Connors?"

"Correct. I did the initial treatment and evaluation. And subsequently when I felt like the injuries could be life threatening I referred her to Bethesda Navy Regional Medical Hospital after consulting with her surgeons."

Initially, Lieutenant Commander Schubert said, he had controlled the bleeding and Judy did not seem to be in distress; however, further examination showed the wounds to be deeper than originally thought, and though he didn't see any immediate risk to her life, he felt that she should have exploratory surgery.

Major Thomson produced the two photos that had been allowed in as evidence by Judge Atkins, and the doctor pointed out the various stab wounds.

Major Thomson: "Have you formed an opinion as to whether those wounds are consistent with an object, a sharp object, with a serrated edge?"

"Yes. In my opinion—"

Kuhnke rose quickly. "Objection, Your Honor."

The doctor continued to speak. "In my opinion—"

Judge Atkins, visibly annoyed, stopped him. "Excuse me. Excuse me!"

Witness: "I'm sorry."

Judge Atkins, to Kuhnke: "On what grounds?"

Kuhnke: "I think we should have a 39 session, Your Honor."

The judge agreed. The members of the jury left the courtroom.

Kuhnke's basic contention was that while the doctor was an expert in his own field, he had no training in forensic evidence, and therefore the conclusion the prosecution was asking him to make "would be purely speculative and prejudicial."

The judge allowed a voir dire by both prosecution and defense to question the doctor about his expertise in knife wounds.

Major Thomson: "Doctor, have you received any training as to being able to assess wounds of this nature?"

Lieutenant Commander Schubert: "With the exception of forensic pathologists who study in detail such wounds, most physicians do not receive specific training."

"Do you feel that qualification as a forensic pathologist for training in forensics is necessary to render an opinion as to whether or not the wounds in this case were inflicted by a sharp object with a serrated edge?"

"I feel I could say these wounds are consistent with a serrated object. However, I don't feel I have the qualifications to state in fact it was."

The doctor replied more or less the same way in response to Kuhnke's questions. His opinion was that the wounds could be consistent with a serrated knife, but "like I said before, I can't say for sure that's what it was."

Kuhnke renewed his objection.

Judge Atkins: "My ruling is such that trial counsel or defense counsel can elicit from the doctor the extent of his experience as treating such wounds and lacerations . . . but as to his opinion as to whether or not those puncture wounds were made by a serrated edge, I will not allow those."

A rare victory for Kuhnke's defense. Scott, who up till now had sat expressionless and had hardly exchanged two words with his attorney, nodded in approval.

When the members returned, Major Thomson resumed his questioning of Schubert: "Doctor, while you were present at the hospital when Judy Connors was admitted, was a rape examination done?"

"No. A rape examination was not done."

For the moment the prosecutor appeared stunned—and he was not the only one in the courtroom to register surprise. There was a stir from Lori's front row on back to the fourth and last row, where members of the press were busily scribbling their notes.

"Well, do you think that would have been a good idea?"

"Ideally, that would have been what we would have done." The doctor went on to explain that he felt the risk of keeping Judy at the emergency clinic outweighed any other considerations. "We had no other options but to ship her via ambulance to a larger hospital where the neck could be better evaluated."

Perhaps hoping the doctor's startling revelation could be muted by further discussions of the wounds, the prosecutor returned to that subject before releasing the witness to the defense.

Kuhnke, however, did not miss the implication of the doctor's admission. "Doctor, did you testify that no rape examination was conducted at your facility?"

"Correct."

"So, there's no independent corroboration that she was, in fact, raped? You have no way of knowing whether she was or was not raped?"

"I know what the patient told me and—"

"But you didn't corroborate that by any medical examination?"

"No, sir, I did not."

Pausing for a moment to allow the members to digest the astonishing fact that the rape for which Corporal Lindsey Scott had been charged had never even been medically verified, Kuhnke went on briefly to reestablish with the doctor that he could not say with any degree of certainty what kind of instrument had caused Judy's neck wounds.

Kuhnke had no more questions.

Major Thomas stood up stiffly at the prosecution table. "Your Honor, United States has nothing further. United States rests."

Immediately Kuhnke called for another Article 39 (a), "for the purpose of several motions."

With the members absent from the room, Kuhnke moved for a dismissal of all charges, "based on the government's lack of subject-matter jurisdiction over the offense. The government has not established where this offense was committed."

There ensued a protracted battle by opposing counsel, with Major Roach entering the fray for the defense and Kuhnke retreating due to his lack of expertise in military law. Realizing that this was not going to be a short session, and the time being 3:26 P.M. Judge Atkins recalled the members and excused them, and recessed the court until the following morning. The 39(a) session continued.

An hour later, all the arguments pro and con exhausted, Judge Atkins denied the defense motion to dismiss.

"Any other motions?" testily he asked Kuhnke.

"Your Honor, we have—we *had* another motion. We had

intended, Your Honor, to move the court to strike—which is, I believe, a motion for not guilty, a finding of not guilty. Based on the advice and review of applicable military procedure, we now withdraw that motion.

"Unfortunately," Kuhnke said, with a weary shake of his head, "the government has an easier burden in that area than it would have if we were trying this case in the Commonwealth of Virginia."

11

At just about midnight of the day the prosecution rested its case against Corporal Lindsey Scott, the telephone rang in Lori Jackson's bedroom. Startled out of a restless sleep, she fumbled for the phone in the dark. "Yes, hello, who is it?" she mumbled, still not fully awake.

"Lori, it's me, Ervan Kuhnke."

Instantly alert with foreboding, she switched on the bed lamp and sat up. "What's wrong, Mr. Kuhnke?" she said, glancing at the bedside clock.

"I apologize for calling you at this hour," the lawyer said, "but I'm getting worried about the case."

Lori bit back the words that sprang angrily to her lips—"it's too late now, you should have started worrying four months ago." Instead she said, tactfully, "Well, I'm not surprised. It doesn't look too good, does it? But . . . well, what can I do? Why are you calling me now?" she said, eyebrows raised at her husband, Paul, who was looking at her questioningly. She covered the mouthpiece for a second. "Kuhnke," she said.

"Honey," he said—Lori once moaned to her husband that Kuhnke called her honey so many times she was getting hives—"honey, I need you to go out and find Ruby Hills, Scott's neighbor, Tammy Martin, his haircutter, John Worsley, and an MP named Sergeant Gaither and make sure you get them to the courtroom tomorrow no later than 8:30."

Lori's mouth fell open. "You what? Mr. Kuhnke, do you know what time it is? You want me to go out *now* and find these people? In the middle of the night? How am I supposed to do that?"

Kuhnke sighed. "I don't know, honey. But I'm counting on you. It's vital we get them on the witness stand. For Lindsey, for his alibi, for the identification business. Everything."

Lori shook her head. "This is crazy, Mr. Kuhnke. But all right, I'll see what I can do. But I can't guarantee anything. Not this time of the night. The only good thing I can tell you is that I already got in touch with Worsley and he promised to be there."

"Good, good," said Kuhnke. "Well, I'll hang up now and let you get to work."

Lori cradled the phone and stared at her husband. "Can you believe this? You understand what's coming down here?"

"Yeah, from your end of the conversation."

Lori shook her head and sighed deeply. "He is not going to have a picnic in that courtroom tomorrow—worse luck for Lindsey Scott." She got out of bed and began dressing.

"You're going out there, then?" Paul asked.

"*We* are going out there," Lori said. "Better get dressed, Paul. We got a lot of work to do, and frankly, I don't know where to start."

"Let's start in the kitchen with a cup of coffee at least," Paul said.

"Smart idea. And meanwhile I can start doing some thinking."

As they sat in the kitchen over their coffee, with Lori thinking out loud about how to get started, two of their younger daughters walked in from their bedrooms, rubbing their eyes, yawning, having been disturbed by the ringing of the telephone and the voices from the kitchen.

"What's going on?" asked one. "Why are you dressed?"

Lori explained.

"Is it worth it, Mom?" she asked. "I mean, all this work you've been doing, knocking yourself out for this Lindsey Scott. You're not even getting paid for it!"

"Of course it's worth it," Lori said quietly. "This is something I got to do. And not for him, not just for Lindsey Scott. I got to do it because it could be anybody out there in his place being railroaded into prison because he is black and the powers that be at Quantico are in a hurry to pin that crime on some black Marine.

I told you all that before. Now get back into bed. Paul and I are going out and I don't know when we'll get back."

She turned to her husband. "The most important witness is that black store detective, Ruby Hills. She's the one who can give Scott his alibi. But I don't know her home phone number and Zayre's is closed now, of course. Sergeant Gaither? He's an MP on the gates. Maybe I can find him. Worsley I've already taken care of. Tammy Martin? I don't know what good she'll do but if Kuhnke wants her . . ."

Unable to find Tammy Martin's telephone number either in the book or via the operator, Lori and Paul set out for the Bayview Apartments in Woodbridge, where Tammy lived with her Marine husband (after moving several months earlier from Spanish Gardens). There, Lori knocked on the apartment door. No reply. Worried about disturbing the neighbors, she left a note on the Martins' door asking Tammy to telephone her or Lola Scott as soon as possible.

"I don't know where they are, if he's on base working a night shift or if they went to the movies or something," Lori said. "Leave a note is all I can do. So let's go to Zayre's."

"But it's closed."

"I know, but maybe there's a security guard around who can help us. Maybe he can call Ruby for us. I don't know, Paul, but we just got to try anything."

Off they went to Zayre's, but found nobody. Back they went to the Bayview Apartments on the chance that Tammy or her husband might have found the note. No, it was still on the door. Lori scribbled another one and taped it to the door, with an URGENT in big capital letters on it.

"Now what?" said Paul. "This Sergeant Gaither?"

"Why not? Let's see if we can find him." They drove to the main gate at the Quantico Marine base. Gaither wasn't there. The MPs on the gate said they could not give her any information about him: against the rules. Lori asked if they could at least get a message to him or if he turned up at the gate to please tell him that Lori Jackson was looking for him—he would know why.

"That's that," Lori said to Paul. "Let's just hope he turns up tomorrow."

"What's he got to do with the case?" Paul asked.

Lori shrugged. "Don't know. No idea. Kuhnke said he wants him, that's all I know." She looked at her watch. "It's after two already with all this running around. I sure wish there was some way we could get in touch with Tammy Martin."

"I don't think there's any more we can do, Lori."

"No, I guess you're right. We'll go home and wait up awhile to see if Tammy calls us. And then first thing in the morning, before Zayre's opens, I'll start calling. The workers must get in early, especially security."

Back home they went—Paul to bed, Lori, unable to sleep, to the kitchen, to write down her thoughts and add to her already voluminous notes about the case. After a time she went to her bed and lay down, fully clothed, her mind racing in circles, wondering how she could help, if she could help, despairing of any hope for Lindsey Scott.

She dozed, in and out of a light sleep, until at just after six A.M. the telephone rang. She jumped up on the first ring and grabbed the phone. "Lori Jackson here." It was Tammy Martin. Lori explained the situation and Mrs. Martin agreed to be in the courtroom on time.

Wide-awake now, Lori returned to the kitchen and prepared coffee. Then she called Zayre's. Nobody answered. She continued to telephone until she got a reply from a security guard who had just checked in. Ruby Hills wasn't there and wasn't expected that morning. Under normal circumstances there was no way the store would give out any employee's telephone number, much less that of anyone in security; fortunately Lori got someone who knew who she was and knew of the case, and gave her Ruby Hills's telephone number. At 6:30 Lori called.

Ruby was astonished to hear from her. She said she knew nothing about the case, wasn't really interested, hadn't been subpoenaed, and nobody had been in touch with her since that last meeting in the parking lot with Lori and Scott. Lori was persuasive as only Lori knew how to be, reminding Ruby that working security for Zayre's, she had been in courts many times and so knew how important a witness could be. Ruby was badly needed in court. Could she be there no later than 8:30?

"Oh, I don't know about that," she told Lori. "I just got up. I got to wash my hair and everything. I really don't know if I can make it."

"Try," Lori said. "Please try. I'll call you again later."

Lori called again at seven and spoke to Ruby. She called at 7:30, this time from a public phone at LeJeune Hall, where the day's court proceedings were due to begin at 8:30 with another Article 39(a) session. Just before the 39(a) began, Lori called one more time, trying to extract a promise from a wavering Ruby Hills that she would be coming right down to the courtroom. Then she rushed to find Kuhnke and fill him in.

The lawyer nodded his approval, then gently took her by the elbow, steered her out to the hallway, and pointed to a bench outside the courtroom door. "Please wait here," he said, "because I'll be calling you as a witness today."

The Article 39(a), preceding the calling of defense witnesses, covered several important items. First Judge Atkins had to get on the record that on the previous afternoon he had denied the defense motion to dismiss on the basis of jurisdiction, having decided arbitrarily that the offense took place on the Quantico base. Then the judge officially announced to Scott his rights as a defendant, which included the fact that he was not obliged to present any evidence at all. "The burden is on the government to prove your guilt beyond a reasonable doubt," he said. "You have the right to remain silent and the fact that you do not take the witness stand cannot be held against you in any way."

Kuhnke stood up to complain that despite his request to have Lieutenant Colonel Harry subpoenaed (which was the government's responsibility) this had not been done. Further, he had asked the prosecution to produce certain documentary evidence, consisting of MP logs and other reports, and had not received them.

Once again the power of command influence displayed itself. To Kuhnke's first complaint Major Thomson simply replied, "Your Honor, Lieutenant Colonel Harry has not been subpoenaed and has not been made available by the convening authority"—meaning

Commanding General Twomey—"due to the grounds of relevancy." As for the records Kuhnke wanted, the prosecution could
produce just one of the three; the other two, in particular a military
police alert, were not in existence. The major added (significantly)
that "all other matter either was not kept in accordance with
routine or has been destroyed during the normal course of military
police procedure."

Judge Atkins looked at the major with some surprise. "You are
saying that the MP alert and dispatch logs do not exist?"

"Yes, Your Honor."

Judge Atkins: "What is an MP alert?"

"From what I understand, Your Honor, when the Provost
Marshal's Office is notified that an incident takes place, it alerts
the MPs at certain gates that an offense has been committed. And
a note of that is made at different gates. But after the time period
passes for which they are alerted, the alerts are routinely destroyed. And there is no record of any of them being kept at this
time, and indeed Security Battalion suspects that they were
destroyed days after the incident happened."

"Was one made?"

"There is no record of one made, Your Honor. A record of MP
alerts is not kept."

Kuhnke stood quickly and vehemently contradicted Major
Thomson. "Your Honor, one of the witnesses we intend to call,
Sergeant Keith Gaither, is expected to testify that the MP alerts *are*
kept and are available. They're kept in a folder behind the MP
sergeant's desk, and we would like to see them for the date in
question and the date after."

For the best part of an hour the mystery of the missing
documents was debated back and forth. Should Sergeant Gaither
run over to PMO and try to find them—if they existed—or should
someone else go. Strangely, Kuhnke allowed Judge Atkins to
accept the prosecution's suggestion that Major Thomson himself
try to locate the documents. There followed a short recess while
the major left the courtroom.

When he returned, it was with the statement that he had called
the military police desk, he had also called operations, and he had

talked to the battalion commander (Scott's battalion commander, Hemming).

"There is no military police alert for this incident on the night of twenty April, 1983, present there now. The information we have is that there was a check about a month ago by a defense witness and it wasn't there at the time. The battalion commander says that from his memory there was not a military police alert because they did not receive a description of the vehicle on that date in order to put the MPs on alert. And his statement was, 'All we have was a description of the accused and putting out an MP alert for a description of a black male, or whatever the description might be, would be untenable.' So from his recall a military police alert was not released."

The argument was finally resolved by Kuhnke's admission that maybe there wasn't a document after all, maybe it was just a telephone call, but his witness would testify that he definitely received an MP alert.

To the spectators in the gallery—now filled not only with several journalists, Lori's people, and other supporters of Scott, but with those few curious Marines of all ranks who had managed to squeeze into the twenty-seven-seat section—all this argument about an MP alert seemed petty; but its significance would shortly be revealed.

To use a baseball metaphor—Kuhnke began his defense of Corporal Lindsey Scott with two strikes against him and the umpire on the payroll of the other team. Unlike his opposite numbers at the prosecution table, Kuhnke had not prepared his witnesses, as was customary—indeed necessary before putting them on the stand. This pretrial rehearsal, perfectly legal and proper, clues the witness in to the questions to be asked on direct examination, how best to answer them, and what is likely to be asked on cross-examination—lessening the danger of surprise.

Kuhnke had not even prepared Scott, the defendant, whom he had decided to call, and his prize alibi witness—Ruby Hills—had just emerged from the shower to take Lori Jackson's second persuasive telephone call just about the time Judge Atkins was convening the Article 39(a).

Kuhnke's first defense witness was Worsley, the barber. The brief questioning by Kuhnke and the equally brief cross-examination had to do with the length of Scott's hair as he sat in the courtroom compared with how he was wearing it in April, about the time of the crime. Since it transpired that Worsley couldn't remember whether or not he had cut Scott's hair in late April, his appearance was negative.

Next was Sergeant Stephen Chaplin, a witness found by Lori. The sergeant lived at Spanish Gardens, and on the night of the crime, almost exactly at the time Judy Connors said she was picked up in her assailant's car in the parking lot, he was right there inserting a radio in his car. His testimony appeared promising at first, since he said that although between the hours of 2000 and 2030 two cars owned by residents pulled into the lot and one left the lot, if there had been a car parked with its motor running near his car, it was likely he would have heard or seen it.

However, when Kuhnke tried to pin him down more precisely to times and what he actually saw or didn't see, the sergeant confessed he had no sense of time, wasn't wearing a watch, and couldn't really remember.

Kuhnke: "You're positive that there were no cars back there between 2000 and 2030 hours?"

"I'm not positive of that, sir."

"But you didn't hear or see any?"

"I can't remember, sir."

Kuhnke showed him a drawing of the parking lot. "Do you remember seeing any cars about 2015 hours or thereabouts stop in the vicinity of what's marked B in the chart?" (Where Judy said she was picked up).

"I cannot remember again, sir."

Kuhnke shook his head in apparent exasperation at his own unhelpful witness. "Do you remember anyone walking around the area about 2015 hours?"

"No, sir."

Perhaps in wonder or suspicion about his witness's lapse of memory, Kuhnke asked him, "Has anyone talked to you about Corporal Scott recently?"

"Mrs. Jackson, the investigator for you, sir."

"Who else?"

"No one else, sir."

"You don't recall a conversation with Special Agent Lindner?"

"That wasn't recently, sir."

"That wasn't recently," Kuhnke repeated, the touch of sarcasm apparent in his voice. "When was it?"

"The first time I spoke to Mr. Lindner was one week exactly after it happened."

"Yes? And . . ."

"I spoke with him also by phone approximately two days after that. I spoke with him again several weeks later. And that's all, sir."

"Did he indicate that he may call you as a witness in this matter?"

"Not as a witness, no, sir."

With nothing more to be gained from Sergeant Chaplin, Kuhnke deferred to the prosecution.

Major Messer rose from his chair and started his cross-examination. "Sergeant Chaplin, I just want you to relax. These are not going to be hard questions. You testified that you were installing your car radio the evening in question?"

"Yes, sir."

"Okay. And would you tell the members how you installed your car radio?"

"Okay, sir. I had to put it into the dash, sir. A lot of time was spent reading the directions, getting tools from the trunk of the car, and also being under the dash."

"When you said you were underneath the dash, what exactly do you mean?"

"I mean that I was on the floorboard, sir, on my back facing up underneath the dash."

"Now, Sergeant Chaplin, in answer to Mr. Kuhnke's question as to whether or not anyone else had talked to you about Corporal Scott or this case, do you remember talking to me very briefly before you came in here to testify?"

"Yes, sir."

"And do you recall what I told you?"

"You ensured me that—not to be nervous, take a deep breath, and tell the truth."

"Do you recall me telling you to tell the truth?"

"Yes, sir."

"Okay. Now, is the truth of your testimony simply that you don't remember anything about the events concerned with this case?"

"Yes, sir."

"No further questions, Your Honor." The major sat down, well satisfied with rendering Sergeant Chaplin's testimony useless to the defense. The sergeant simply didn't remember anything to do with the case.

Kuhnke was more successful with Sergeant Keith Gaither, who did get the message that Lori Jackson had been looking for him—and understood why.

The sergeant was able to testify that, as Kuhnke had insisted during the Article 39(a) session, there had been an MP alert.

Kuhnke: "Sergeant, did you receive a report of any kind concerning an alleged rape near Camp Upshur?"

"Yes, sir. I was the gate sentry at Gate 4. I was out in the lane directing traffic and—my other gate sentry was Lance Corporal Hardy. He was out there, too, in the gatehouse . . . and he received a call from the desk saying that a vehicle—it was alleged—it was a rape that occurred on base. And it had an MP out on the vehicle. They called an MPA, military police alert, on the vehicle. It was supposed to have been either a tan or a brown Maverick or a tan or brown Duster. It was supposed to be a two-door and gave a description of a black male, about anywhere from five-eight to five-eleven. He was supposed to be wearing a mustache, long hair, and black-rimmed glasses."

"Who called this report to you?"

"The first time, I'm not sure, sir. The other gate sentry took the call, but it either was the desk sergeant or the dispatcher. They are the only two people who really call us out on that. The second time, Sergeant Kanthak called and asked us—"

"Sergeant, who?"

"Kanthak. He was the desk sergeant that night."

"What did you call this type of report, this type of alert?"

"It's an MPA, sir. Military police alert."

The sergeant continued with his testimony that it was Standard Operating Procedure that a written MPA was supposed to be filled out after a verbal alert is sent to the gates and "that's usually kept on the desk in the military-police-alert folder. And then they are supposed to send a copy of the MPA out to all of the gates."

"Did you ever see a copy of this?"

"No, sir."

"But you have seen other copies of MPAs?"

"Yes, sir, as a desk sergeant I have filled out a few myself."

"Have you ever looked for this MPA?"

"A month ago, sir, I was going through the book, but I didn't see an MPA on that night for this case."

"And there is a book where these MPAs are kept?"

"Yes, sir. There is a book. It's a black binder . . . it's a book that's kept on our desk with all the MPAs in there, sir."

"And you looked at that book, and there was no report of this incident in that book?"

"No, sir."

Kuhnke had no more questions; the significance of the "missing" written MPA report was the description of the alleged assailant as given in the oral MPA alert—of a black man with long hair and a mustache, and driving a car that did not match the description of Scott's car. Without a written backup to the testimony, what Sergeant Gaither said was pure hearsay; it could not be proven one way or the other that there ever was an MPA report; the sergeant's testimony of the description he got was worthless as evidence, in particular since Kuhnke had no other MP to call upon to testify that he, too, had received such a telephoned MPA.

It was easy therefore for prosecutor Major Thomson, with a brief cross-examination to dismiss the testimony of another defense witness as irrelevant.

"To your knowledge was there any recording of an MPA? Was there a written MPA?"

"To my knowledge I couldn't be sure, sir, because I never did see—never did look for it."

"You checked the book, right?"

"Yes, sir, a month ago. But I couldn't be sure they wrote one out that night because I never did see the one. The only thing I got was the verbal one from the gate."

"So, to your knowledge there never has been any written recordation of an MPA?"

"Not to my knowledge, no, sir, but Sergeant Kanthak, he was the one that broke me in on the desk and I just couldn't see something of that magnitude not going without an MPA."

"Isn't it a fact that there was no MPA because there was no description of the vehicle?"

"It was a description of the vehicle that was delivered to us, sir, due to what they say that the witness, the person that was allegedly—"

The prosecutor cut him short. "You testified that there was no MPA. Isn't that correct?"

The sergeant valiantly tried to retain the integrity of his testimony, of his recollection of events on the night of the crime. "No MPA being written out on the desk, I can't testify to that, sir, but the MPA that was given to us on the gate."

"You checked the book, right?"

"Yes, sir, a month ago."

"Was there one in there?"

"Not a month ago, sir."

"No further questions."

Kuhnke was not out of ammunition yet on the point of the MPA, however. He called to the stand next Sergeant William Bryant, a military-police patrolman who came on duty at 5:30 A.M. on the morning after the crime.

Major Thomson stood immediately and voiced an objection: "Your Honor, United States at this time believes that the defense is going to call witnesses that have been sitting in the courtroom throughout the trial." Sergeant Bryant, the major said, had been sitting in the courtroom on the previous afternoon. That was improper and the prosecution believed he should be excluded from testifying. "We move to suppress his testimony," Major Thomson said.

Kuhnke argued that he hadn't known either that Sergeant Bryant would be a witness, but information had come to his attention that the sergeant had relevant testimony about the MPAs.

Judge Atkins questioned him closely about this: "Was the existence of this witness known to you prior to today?"

"He was not, Your Honor. And I do not know whether he was in the courtroom or not. In any event, there was no request by the government for a rule on witnesses."

Judge Atkins: "The government objection is overruled. You may proceed."

A deep breath of relief from Kuhnke as he called the sergeant to the stand.

Bryant related how as he walked into the Provost Marshal's Office early that morning he asked a Sergeant Stone, who had been on duty the night before, "Was there any action last night?" And Stone replied, "Yes. Read this."

Stone showed him a CID report of the rape and attempted murder. "And anytime we have an incident like that," Sergeant Bryant testified, "there's always a military police alert. So I picked up the Military Police Journal and the Military Police Word Book and I picked up a military police alert. And on that alert it stated that the suspect was driving a tan or brown Duster, the person was black, heavyset, and had military glasses."

Kuhnke nodded at the sergeant to continue; he could sense that Bryant, sitting squarely in the witness chair, was confident within himself and with his story.

"Now, as far as the military police alert being on the gates," the sergeant said, "all three gates, I do not know. But I know for a fact that at six o'clock that same morning we started our brief. I personally took the military police alert in there myself and I passed the information to the oncoming shift, which would have been six gate sentries and approximately five, six patrolmen."

Kuhnke: "Sergeant, when did you first learn that Corporal Scott was a suspect in this case?"

"I'd have to say a day, two or three days after that. The description that they gave wasn't exactly that good. The one that they gave could have fit Corporal Scott. But then at the same time it could have fit about a hundred Marines aboard this base."

Major Thomson announced with a slight shrug of the shoulders that there would be no cross-examination—to the surprise of Kuhnke, Judge Atkins, and even one or two of the members, who of course always sat properly stony-faced and ostensibly, at least, disinterested. The fact was that Sergeant Bryant was too sure of himself to be shifted, and no matter what he testified to, there was no MPA to be found of the kind described by Sergeant Gaither. The prosecution could afford to let Kuhnke win a small point.

When the defense attorney next called Lori to the stand, Major Thomson objected to her appearance on the same grounds as he had for the previous witness: Lori had been sitting in the courtroom since the beginning of the trial. The judge, however, made the same ruling and allowed Kuhnke to proceed with Lori's testimony.

While that little argument was taking place a small drama was being enacted in the hallway: Ruby Hills had just arrived in an agitated rush, almost three hours later than Lori had hoped, but still in time for her turn as a defense witness.

"Thank God you got here!" Lori said. "I just got called and I think Kuhnke wants you next."

"What am I doing here?" Ruby cried. "I don't even know what's going on! And look at me, I'm a mess!" she said. A woman who always prided herself on her looks and dress, she complained to Lori, "My hair isn't even dry yet, I didn't even have time to put my panty hose on!" She pointed to her bare legs.

"Don't fuss, you look just fine," Lori said, patting her on the arm. "The main thing is, you're here. I'm grateful to you for that. I got to go in now, they're calling me again. You just sit here and catch your breath, relax for a couple minutes."

As Lori had feared, and as she would relate to her husband later that day, her appearance on the witness stand was another waste of time. She had in fact little to contribute of importance to Scott's defense, and what little she had was blocked by a successful objection by Major Thomson.

Lori began her testimony with an account of how she had

investigated other rape attempts in the area by a Marine who fit the general description of Scott.

Major Thomson objected on the grounds of relevancy; the trial was about one particular rape, and any other similar crimes had no bearing on this case.

Kuhnke retorted by claiming that the testimony could point to the fact that there might be other suspects, besides Scott, who had not been investigated.

Another of the many Article 39(a) sessions was called for during which the prosecutor argued that Kuhnke could be damaging his own defense; Lori's potential testimony, Major Thomson said, was not only irrelevant but in fact prejudiced Scott's position. If the members were allowed to hear testimony about other rapes where the assailant generally fit the description of Scott, "we come dangerously close to exposing the defendant in this case to misconduct not charged."

Kuhnke wanted to introduce that testimony nevertheless. "I submit it's relevant," he said to Judge Atkins.

Judge Atkins: "You're not concerned that there is a possibility of inference by the court members adverse to your client?"

Kuhnke: "I have weighed and considered that, Your Honor, and I believe in the interest of justice that this testimony should come before the court."

The judge would not allow it, however. He sustained the prosecution objection, "because of the danger of evidence of misconduct not alleged and the possible adverse influence to your client."

Thus, in a trial filled with contradictions and surprises, there was now added the strange incident of the prosecution appearing to come to the aid of the accused, over the objections of the defense attorney. The end result, however, was that Kuhnke had nothing to get out of the remainder of Lori's testimony but the subject of jurisdiction, which he covered with her at some length. Not a word that Lori said about blocked roads and construction around Route 619 and Belfair Corner was of any use to Scott's defense, because no matter what she might claim that clouded Special Agent Lindner's or Judy Connors's testimony, Judge Atkins had already ruled that the government had proved jurisdiction; it was a dead issue as far as the prosecution and the judge were concerned, but with little else to offer, Kuhnke was still not quite ready to sever that tenuous thread to a dismissal verdict.

To the witness chair came a feisty Ruby Hills*, unhappily conscious that she was not looking her best, resentful at being hustled into testifying when she was unsure of what she would be asked and how to respond. Her job with security for Zayre's had given her ample experience in courtroom procedures, and in the normal course of such events she would have testified with complete confidence. Now, as she waited for the questions by Kuhnke, whom she had never met or spoken to, she was bemused and irritated—but ever the professional.

Ruby immediately threw Kuhnke off stride when he asked her to state her name, for the record.

"Ruby Wilson."

Obviously surprised (though he should not have been) Kuhnke examined the paper in front of him. "I have it down as Hills."

"That's my erroneous name at work. No one is supposed to know my real name."

Kuhnke's opening questions filled in her general employment credentials at Zayre's before getting down to the crucial specifics: "I invite your attention to the afternoon and evening of twentieth April, 1983. Where were you employed on that day?"

"At Zayre's in Woodbridge."

"What time did you come on duty, ma'am?"

"About 4:30."

"And you worked how long?"

"About ten or eleven that night. I'm not sure what time I left. The store closes at ten. Sometimes we leave at 10:30. It depends on when the staff finished cleaning up."

"Now I ask you to look at this man here"—pointing to Scott. "Have you ever seen that man before?"

"I'm trying to figure out how many times."

"Well, when was the first time you saw him?"

"I only seen him once."

"Yes. When?"

"It was back in the spring."

"Did you see him on twenty April—on the evening of twenty April, 1983?"

"That's kind of hard for me to pinpoint whether I saw him on April twentieth."

This statement, too, should have come as no surprise to Kuhnke; it was precisely what Lori had told him some two weeks earlier. In fact, Kuhnke had said to Lori then that Ruby's testimony would be insignificant if she couldn't place Scott in the store on the twentieth. And when Lori had asked him if he was going to interview and subpoena Ruby, the lawyer, still confident that the case would never come to trial, advised her not to worry about it. Now Kuhnke was stuck with Ruby's limited recognition of his client.

He probed again, hopefully: "You don't know whether you saw him on April twentieth?"

"I remember the last time I saw him was in the spring," Ruby said adamantly.

"About what time?"

"It was during the time I was doing the pickup. I do a pickup between eight and 8:30."

"Would you please explain the circumstances?"

"Well . . . I had just cleared the service desk when I saw him walk in. And I saw him go to the first rack, which is in the men's department, and start looking at some clothes. And I saw what he was wearing, and I was checking him out to see if he could be a potential shoplifter. After I didn't get a feeling, I stopped watching him."

"How long did you watch him?"

"I watched him go from the first rack to the third rack. From there he went to the back of the wall, and I stopped observing. He looked like he was clean-cut, so I didn't bother watching him."

"What was he wearing?"

"He was wearing a dark cap. He had on a leather jacket. He had it zipped all the way up. And he had on like—looked like green fatigue pants. I remember looking at him because the jacket did not go with those fatigues. The jacket is a jacket that should be worn with dress slacks. And because the jacket was zipped up—a lot of shoplifters would come in with their jackets zipped up, enough to conceal, you know, they can always stash inside."

"Did he wear glasses?"

"Yes, he did."

"What kind of glasses? The same kind he's wearing now?"

"I don't know. I'm not sure. I didn't really notice. My thing is looking at clothes."

"Did anyone show you a picture of this man?"

"Yes, someone did. A lady. I don't remember her last name."

"Describe that picture."

"To be quite honest with you, the pictures were lousy. It looked like him, but the pictures did not look like what he looked like that night."

"Were you told how he was dressed that night?"

"No, I told *her* what he was wearing. She asked me if I had ever seen him before. I told her yes and what he had on and where I saw him at."

"Have you seen him since?"

"I see him now."

"No further questions," said Kuhnke, retreating with much less than he might have hoped for from Ruby Hills (or Wilson). At which point Major Messer rose to object on the basis of relevancy. "We move to strike the testimony," he said. "It's apparent from this witness's testimony that she cannot talk about the events on the twentieth of April, 1983, which are really the only events in issue."

Judge Atkins overruled the prosecution and allowed the testimony. Major Messer sat down and said there would be no cross-examination.

The members had several questions of significance, however, which Kuhnke read out to Ruby.

"At the time you were contacted by Mrs. Jackson, could you remember the date you saw Corporal Scott?"

"I could not remember the date. But I remembered during the time he was in the store was during the time that my mother was dying. And I remember seeing him. It was in relation to what was happening at that time because of the hours I was working."

"Mrs. Wilson, how many people entered Zayre's the night you saw the accused?"

"You really want me to answer that question? I think it's rather dumb."

"To the best you can, answer the question."

"Why don't you ask me how many black people entered the store? I can answer that."

Major Thomson stood up to address the judge. "Your Honor, the United States is going to ask if the witness is going to be asked a question by a member that she be instructed to answer the question."

Kuhnke: "Please answer the question as best you can, ma'am."

"I cannot answer how many people enter a store at night. I can only tell you how many black people I notice enter in a night because the Woodbridge store doesn't have that many black clientele."

"Why do you remember the accused so well after only seeing him once several months ago?"

"I don't forget faces. When I was showed his picture I remember seeing him. I remember what he had on. That's my job. I'm an ex–police officer. I know my job."

"In trying to pinpoint this date, you indicated that you made a bust?"

"I made two busts that day."

"Is there any way of associating those busts, those arrests, with your seeing this gentleman?"

"No."

"There isn't? When was your mother ill?"

"From March until June, when she died."

"At that time you were working late all that time?"

"Mostly ten to six, two to ten. Because I had a nurse at home with my mom, I would go in staggered. That day I was working from 4:30."

"And how did you verify that?"

"No sooner had I walked in the store than I got a bust at 4:30."

"But have you checked records? And you were working on the twentieth of April?"

"I had a bust at 4:30 and I had one between seven and 7:30."

"And that was on the twentieth of April, 1983?"

"That's correct."

"Do you think that's the day you saw him?"

"I only seen this man twice in my life. Am I allowed to just speak freely?"

"Please speak your mind, ma'am."

"I noticed this man because, like I said, we don't get that many black clientele in the store and the ones we do are regular customers. I know they're not going to do anything, so I don't notice them. Whenever I get someone new in the store and he's black, I check them out to see if they are potential, and that's why I noticed this man. After I didn't get any feeling that he was going to do anything, I stopped watching him."

Then came an exceedingly penetrating series of questions by a member (as usual, recited by Kuhnke).

"Mrs. Wilson, isn't there a record kept of each bust made at your store? If so, wouldn't you have access to it?"

"That's correct."

"There is a record?"

"Yes."

"And you have access to it?"

"Yes."

"And you have verified that there were two busts on the twentieth of April 1983?"

"That's right."

The questioning by members died right there, but the facts that emerged from that series of questions would develop an afterlife in the years to come.

The delicate balance of Ruby's testimony was such that Major Thomson felt it necessary to cross-examine on the one crucial point—the point that could swing a perfect alibi for Corporal Lindsey Scott one way or the other.

"Mrs. Hills—is it okay if I call you Mrs. Hills?"

"You can call me whatever."

"Mrs. Hills, on direct examination you said it would be hard to pinpoint when you saw Corporal Scott in the store."

"The date."

"The date. It is now your testimony that you saw him on April the twentieth?"

"My testimony still stands that I saw him in the spring."

"And you don't know what date it was?"

"No, I will not commit myself to a date."

"No more questions."

And no more answers from Ruby Hills.

12

Following the lunch recess, Kuhnke called Lola Scott to the stand. With the Scotts' five-week-old daughter looked after in the hallway by a family friend, Frances, Lola walked to the witness chair nervously, twisting a handkerchief in her hands. Clearly terrified, Lola exemplified the undercurrent of tension and pressure existing within the courtroom. She sat down and looked around her, at the symbols of power that towered over her as she sat stiffly there in the witness chair as though on trial herself: the mighty judge, the forbidding prosecutors, the somber, shadowy members, all of them in their beribboned uniforms with their oak-leafed and eagled badges of rank. She looked at her husband for help and Lindsey gave her a little smile of encouragement.

Kuhnke proceeded carefully. "Mrs. Scott, I know you're nervous. Just be as calm as possible . . . now, you were interviewed by two CID agents on the twenty-first of April, 1983"—actually, Kuhnke should have identified the two as NIS agents, not CID. "Please tell the court about that interview."

"I arrived home from work about four. Dave Martin, who I know, came to my house between 4:30 and a quarter to five. When I had come home from work, I opened my birthday present, which was a foot massager, that I was sitting in my chair using when he arrived. I asked him who he was and he said, 'It's me, Lola, Dave Martin.' I opened the door and let him in and he told me who the man with him was. They just started talking socially, about my furniture, how nice it was, and Rivers—he was the other man—Rivers said that he liked my foot massager, that he was

136

trying to get one, and where did I get it, and I said, 'Well, today is my birthday. Lindsey got it for me.'

"After that Dave asked me, 'Did you talk to Lindsey anytime today?' and I said, 'Yes, he called me this morning.' And then Dave said, 'Did he tell you anything?' I said he just told me he was working on a big case down there and he would go into more detail about it that afternoon. After that there was just normal conversation, then Dave said, 'Well, that's what it was, then,' and he explained to me that the night before Mrs. Connors had, you know—whatever—and they were questioning everybody down there and they had to ask me some questions.

"I said okay and he said they were questioning Lindsey, too, and I said, 'Well, you know Lindsey—' I laughed a little bit and I said, 'You know Lindsey couldn't possibly do nothing like that,' and he said, 'Yeah, we know, we know,' and Rivers said, 'We know he's a good guy. There ain't no way he could do anything like that.' He said, 'We just have to do it because we have to question everybody. She said the guy was black and we have to question all the black guys down there.' And I said, 'Well, I know Lindsey's upset, you know, his pride. Just asking him something like that would hurt him.' And he says, 'Yeah, he's pretty upset.'

"So they asked me what time did he come home that Wednesday and I said he came home between five and 5:15. Well, first I just hesitated to think about it because he said, 'Well, just give me the time like between such and such, like that,' so I said, 'Okay, just put down between five and 5:15 when he came home to get me.' That was to go back to the apartment that we had cleaned the night before that he had to go back to that day to clean the stove and floors and something like that because they didn't pass inspection. And he came back to get me to see if I wanted to go, but I was too tired, you know. I told him, 'No, I don't think I want to go today. I'm too tired and I'm going to lay down.' He said, 'Well, I just want you to go with me. You can sit down.' Because, you know, usually I go just about everywhere with him except to work. We do everything together because we're not just husband and wife, we're best friends."

With that, all the emotional tension Lola had been suppressing broke. She began to cry. "Just leave him alone! Leave my husband alone!" she shouted.

Kuhnke tried to calm her. "Please . . ."

Lola became hysterical, weeping and screaming loudly and uncontrollably. "He didn't do it! He did not do it!"

Kuhnke asked for a recess.

Judge Atkins nervously called the recess, but as he and everyone else in the courtroom looked on in shocked silence, Lola continued to weep and cry out.

"Why are they messing with us? I'm sick and I'm tired. They tried to kill my baby and everything! Leave him alone. Leave him alone, leave my husband alone! He hasn't done nothing to nobody. He's good. He's nothing but good. Why do they want to do something to good people? Why?" Looking at the prosecution table, the judge, the members: "Why? Why do you want to make us suffer? Why do you want to make the good suffer?"

The entire courtroom seemed frozen, unable to stop her, with several spectators in the gallery adding their sobs, moaning loudly, until Scott himself broke the tension by rushing to his wife's side and with the help of one of Lori's activist women, escorted the still-weeping Lola outside (two men in dark suits, presumably NIS agents, left the gallery and followed on Scott's heels).

Kuhnke, as dumbfounded as everybody else by the outburst, began to apologize to the court, but was cut off by Major Messer.

With a cold sneer on his face, the prosecutor said to him, "You might not have planned it, but it looked pretty good, didn't it?"

Kuhnke stared at the major openmouthed, his face turning purple with rage, fists clenched at his side. But it was Judge Atkins who intervened. Leaning over the bench, he pointed his finger at the prosecutor and said, his anger evident, "That was uncalled for, Major. You will apologize directly to Mr. Kuhnke. Now. And loudly enough for everyone to hear."

Lola returned to the witness stand after a fifteen-minute recess, composed but still palpably nervous, with Frances, her companion, at her side, holding her right hand throughout the rest of her testimony. (Out in the hallway Lola's mother, Jewel, took over the baby-sitting chores for the moment.) Judge Atkins had no objections to the presence of Frances, but he made it clear to the members that Lola's outburst must not affect their deliberations. "All you need to be aware of," he said, addressing them directly, "and what you take into the deliberation room is the admissible evidence you have received here in court from the witness stand."

Kuhnke: "Now, Mrs. Scott, I know this is hard for you. I just want to ask you a few more questions. Were you asked what Lindsey was wearing that night?"

"Yes, sir."

"And did you tell the investigators?"

"Yes, sir."

"And did you give them everything Lindsey was wearing?"

"Yes, sir."

"You're sure you gave them everything?"

"Everything but his jacket."

"Why didn't you give them the jacket?"

"They did not want the jacket. It was with his clothes, and they said something about that the jacket was brown that was described."

"Did they see the jacket? Let me show you a jacket. Ma'am"—showing her a red jacket—"is this the jacket Lindsey was wearing that night?"

"Yes, sir."

"And that afternoon when you saw him?"

"Yes, sir."

"And did you show this jacket to the investigators?"

"Well, they were all laying together and they picked up what they wanted themselves."

"But did you tell them that he was wearing this jacket?"

"Yes, sir."

"What did they say?"

"That they didn't need that jacket, that the jacket was brown that had been described or something."

"But you made it clear to them that he was wearing this jacket?"

"I made it very clear."

Kuhnke offered the jacket as evidence and continued. "Mrs. Scott, was Lindsey wearing glasses that night?"

"Yes, sir."

"What kind of glasses?"

"They're brown, not exactly round—I don't know what you would call them. But they're brown-tinted—"

Lola's companion interjected: "Schoolboy."

"Yes. Schoolboy is the word that they use for style or fashion or whatever-you-want-to-call-it glasses."

"Did you give the investigators anything else that night?"

"As they were taking his clothes, Rivers—"

"What clothes did they take?"

"Green fatigue pants, Army fatigue pants, a green Army fatigue jacket, a brown hat, and shoes."

"What else? Did they ask about anything else?"

"Everything was in a room. We had just been moving and there were a lot of boxes in that room, and Rivers came inside the room with me while Dave stood out in the hallway—in the doorway. And Rivers asked me was that his cleaning gear that was laying on the floor in a plastic bag, and I told him yes it was. And he said, 'Well, can we take this pot?' I said to him, 'Why do you want this pot? He doesn't use this pot. This is what he used,' and I pointed to a green mop bucket that had two mops and a broom in it. And he said, 'Well, we have to show it to Lindsey.' I said that was okay, but I told him that was my cooking pot and that they had to excuse the house, that we had been moving and that I had emptied that box out the night before—pots and dishes and stuff like that. And he said, 'Well, that's okay, we just need it to show Lindsey.'"

"Now reflect, ma'am. You told him that he had not used that pot that night?"

"Yes. I said, 'Why do you want this? He didn't use this.'"

"What did he use?"

"A green mop bucket. Olive green."

"Did you point out the olive-green mop bucket?"

"Yes, sir, I plainly pointed it out."

Kuhnke picked up a green bucket and showed it to Lola. "Is this the green bucket that you referred to in your testimony?"

"Yes, sir, that's the bucket."

"And the investigators didn't pick it up?"

"No, they didn't take that and the jacket."

Kuhnke introduced the green bucket into the formal evidence, then turned back to Lola. "You're absolutely certain that there were no other articles of clothing you gave the investigators?"

"I didn't give them nothing. They picked the clothing up themselves. I never did hand them anything."

"Which NIS agent told you that they didn't want the red jacket?"

"Rivers was the only one doing the talking. He was in the room with me."

"And which NIS agent told you they didn't want the green bucket?"

"Rivers."

Kuhnke had no more questions to ask of Lola, and perhaps prudently, considering her previous outburst, neither Major Messer nor Major Thomson asked to cross-examine her. However, members had questions, which were asked by Kuhnke.

"Mrs. Scott, does your husband own more than one pair of glasses?"

"The glasses that he's wearing and he has about two or three pair, I guess, of those military glasses—black, square-framed."

"Do you know where the other ones were on the night of twenty April, 1983?"

"At home. The black ones? They were at home. He keeps them on the dresser."

"Do you recognize the silver bucket introduced as evidence? It's this silver bucket here"—indicating the prosecution's exhibit.

"Yes, sir. It's my bucket—but it's a pot, my pot. It's a cooking pot, it's not a bucket."

"It's your cooking pot?"

"Yes, sir."

"If so, where was it the night of twenty April, 1983?"

"In my home in the bedroom in some boxes we had been moving."

Lola's responses about the silver pot prompted Major Thomson now to cross-examine. He had just one question. "Mrs. Scott, are you aware that your husband told Master Sergeant Martin he had that bucket the night of the twentieth of April?"

"No, I'm not."

Lola was excused and left the courtroom, her troubled eyes meeting Lindsey's as she passed by the defense table.

Kuhnke was ready to call Tammy Martin, but since she was not expected to arrive for another fifteen minutes or so, an Article 39(a) was called to discuss how Judge Atkins intended to instruct the jury on the charges. The judge thought it was premature to start talking about the prosecution and defense agreeing on the charges to be presented to the members—but since they had fifteen minutes to kill anyway, he said they might as well make a start.

"Certainly the court is going to instruct the members on the elements of the offense, on expert witness, on credibility—"

Kuhnke interrupted and said the defense would like to see the credibility instruction, then changed his mind, said he had no problem with credibility. "I'm sure that's not the one I was thinking about," he said. "It's circumstantial evidence."

Judge Atkins concurred, and here Major Roach, the court-appointed military defense attorney who had been quiet thus far, took over from Kuhnke, since he was more familiar with court-martial procedures. "The defense is going to propose two instructions, one on alibi and one on prior inconsistent statements. The defense agrees with the government that at this point discussion on the alibi proposal is premature."

Kuhnke did point out to the judge, however, that after the defense rested, he intended to renew his motion on lack of subject jurisdiction, "in light of additional evidence as to the location today." He was referring to Lori's testimony about blocked roads and his unrelenting questioning of whether or not the crime was committed within the boundaries of the Quantico base.

Tammy Martin arrived and took the witness stand. Considering the trouble Lori had gone through to get her there, Mrs. Martin had little to contribute. True, she did say that while she was still living at Spanish Gardens, on April 20 she did bump into Lindsey Scott and they held a brief conversation. He told her he was moving out and since the apartment didn't pass inspection he had to go back and reclean it. She identified the clothes he was wearing as green pants, a burgundy jacket, and a tan cap. He was also wearing brown plastic-frame glasses and carrying "cleaning stuff." In a box or a bucket, she wasn't sure and she couldn't remember. However, since all this had occurred at about noontime or shortly afterward, as Mrs. Martin testified, it in essence proved nothing about what Scott might have worn later that night.

It came down then to the last witness for the defense: Corporal Lindsey Scott.

The packed courtroom stirred in expectancy as Kuhnke called him, expecting some new, perhaps sensational disclosures. What would he say, what could he say in the face of Judy Connors's "99.9 percent sure" identification of him as her assailant? How could the defense attorney counter all the evidence against his client—circumstantial though it might be?

Settling into the witness chair, Scott looked out into the nearby gallery, searching for friendly faces that might hearten him. He saw his father, thin, erect, dignified, trying to mask the concern on his face, and next to him his mother, wearing yet another of the large flamboyant hats for which she had become famous during the trial, sobbing softly into a handkerchief. Scott braced himself; he would not show weakness before this courtroom.

Under questioning by his defense lawyer, Kuhnke, Scott began a long, rambling account of his movements on the day and evening of April 20. He stressed that everybody at the Provost Marshal's Office knew that he would be cleaning his old apartment early that evening because he discussed it openly with his superior, Gunnery Sergeant Martin, telling him that Mr. and Mrs. Knight were not satisfied with the job he'd done before moving and insisted he return and do it again or he would lose his deposit. Scott said that Sergeant Martin told him, "Go and clean it again tonight. If you have any trouble I'll go back with you tomorrow and we'll talk to the lady and we'll go over to the apartment together at the same time."

Scott said he left the PMO and returned home to change his clothes, putting on a brown hat, red leather jacket, green sateen pants, brown shoes, and a red scarf for his hair to keep the dirt off it as he cleaned. That was about 1:45 or two P.M., he said, and when he ran into Tammy Martin and spoke to her about where he was going. He said he was carrying a green plastic bucket at the time, two mops and a broom, and plastic bags filled with cleaning materials. When he got to Mrs. Knight's office, Scott related, she asked him if he had a knife with him, because he would need one to clean the stove properly.

"At that time," Scott testified, "she went in a drawer and pulled out a little bitty steak knife. It was old, and she had some stove parts sitting on her desk. She picked it up and she started showing me the particular parts of the stove where I had to get the dried grease out of them, which she said couldn't be done with a scouring pad, that I was really going to need a knife. So I took the knife and the scouring pads."

Scott continued his account of how he cleaned the stove, scrubbed the floors on his hands and knees, and thoroughly cleaned the apartment for the Knights' inspection so he could get his deposit back. That took till about 1700 or so, Scott said, and he decided to go home for a break before he returned to the apartment once more for a final once-over before showing it to the Knights.

"I knew my wife usually gets home from work about 1630— she's a clerk stenographer at Fort Belvoir—and she expects me to be home to greet her because usually we get off work at about the same time. So I went home to see how she was. I asked her if she wanted to come back to the apartment with me to clean it or whatever and she said she was tired . . . she would wait for me at home."

When Scott finally finished cleaning his old apartment, he got Mr. Knight to come up and inspect it—that was about 1840 or so, Scott said. Mr. Knight was satisfied and returned his deposit check, but then "going through the apartment he found some discrepancies. He found the mattress was stained. He said I would have to pay a twenty-five-dollar fine for that. Then a lightbulb was burned out in the icebox. I had to pay him a dollar for that."

He didn't have that much cash with him, Scott said, so he offered to go to his bank, which was open late, and get the money. Mr. Knight agreed, and began switching off the lights in the apartment at the fuse box while Scott began to gather together his cleaning materials.

"I had four or five sponges and all types of scouring pads and paper, and I had the knife that I borrowed. It was sitting there, but it was in the middle of all the trash. It was on the counter and I just scooped everything into the empty plastic bag that I had. I really didn't think too much of it then. We left. He locked the apartment door and I went down to my car. As I was leaving the parking lot there's a Dumpster. It's on the far side of the back parking lot. I rolled up to it and I threw the bag in the Dumpster."

He returned to Spanish Gardens, Scott said, paid Mr. Knight, and went to the Provost Marshal's Office, where he used the rest room, thought he might weigh himself (he was self-conscious about a slight weight problem), and was going to call his wife to tell her he'd finished at the apartment, but changed his mind because she would then expect him to return home, and he wanted to "use this time and opportunity to go out and buy her some birthday gifts. I'd say it was approximately 1730 [sic] when I was at PMO, when I arrived." (He meant to say, of course, 1930, not 1730.)

"Who did you see at PMO?"

"When I first—first, I want to explain. When I went into PMO I took off the scarf that I was wearing. I was wearing a pink scarf on my head. I can't go into my place of work with a scarf on my head. I had on my brown hat, maroon jacket, my green sateens, suede shoes. As soon as I walked through the door, I saw Captain Unsworth . . . and he stopped and he said, 'Good evening, Corporal Scott, you're dressed unusual tonight,' because I imagine I did look unusual. He said, 'Are you undercover tonight? Are you working undercover?' and I said, 'No, sir, I just got through cleaning my apartment,' and that was all that was said."

Scott said he left PMO shortly afterward and went to Dumfries Pharmacy, where he bought his wife the foot massager, arriving there about 1950. He put the gift-wrapped package on the backseat of the car, where he'd previously placed the green bucket and his cleaning materials. He then went to Zayre's.

"About how far would you estimate that to be, Corporal?"

"I would say eleven or twelve miles."

"And about what time was this?"

"Well, I'm pretty sure when I left Dumfries Pharmacy it was approximately 2000, 2005 . . . no later. I was in a hurry to get home for the simple fact that we had just moved . . . it was a new apartment and my wife wasn't too comfortable about it. And I didn't want her to be alone too long. Without me she gets uncomfortable."

"How long were you at Zayre's?"

"First, when I walked in the door, I looked around in the men's section. That's a habit with me. I just looked. I would say approximately fifteen or twenty minutes."

"Where did you go from the men's section?"

"I walked over to the clocks, the TVs, stereos, kitchen appliances, and a lot of things like that."

"Did you buy anything at all at Zayre's?"

"I stopped at the concession stand on the way out and I asked the lady who was working behind the stand for a Coke. I bought a Coke, and in the process of her getting the Coke for me, somebody came up . . . and spoke to her and called her by her name."

"What did they call her?"

"They called her Pam. I left Zayre's. It was approximately 2030, 2035."

"What time?"

"Twenty-thirty or 2035, somewhere around there. I wasn't really looking at my watch or paying any attention to the time. I knew that I was in a hurry, but I didn't really look. I drove back down to my apartment, which sits right off US 1. On the way home I stopped at the Chesapeake—no, it's the Quikee drive-in restaurant. I was going to get us both a chocolate sundae to take up to her. I went up to the girl and I asked her for the sundaes. She told me they already turned the ice-cream machines off and the grill was closed. She said I was welcome to buy anything that was on the front of the windows like potato chips, but I said, 'No, thank you.'"

"What time was that?"

"It was approximately 2050, around there."

"How do you know?"

"Judging from the time approximately I left Zayre's, it didn't take me more than ten or fifteen minutes to get down there. My apartment's right across the street almost. I left there and went straight to my apartment. I took the present out of the backseat and I moved some things around in my trunk because I wasn't going to take it up. Tomorrow being her birthday, there was no sense in her seeing her present then. I put it in the trunk of my vehicle. I had a lot of junk back there.

"I took the green bucket, my two mops, my broom, and my two plastic bags and I went to the apartment. I went to a side bedroom . . . there were several boxes not unpacked. There was stuff laying everywhere. I set the green bucket in there, the two mops, the broom, and the two bags with the cleaning gear. I went back into the bedroom . . . undressed. I took my clothes back into the other bedroom. I just laid them over the boxes. . . . I looked at my clock. I knew I had to get up the next morning. I looked at my clock and I set it, and my clock at that time, it said 2105. That's all I did that night. I laid down and I went to sleep."

Kuhnke continued by showing Scott a jacket and glasses and asking him to identify them as the jacket and glasses he wore that night. Then he asked about his hair: "Lindsey, when's the last time you cut your hair on top?"

"I would say . . . the sixteenth of April."

"You haven't cut it since?"

"No, sir."

"Have you had it trimmed since?"

"Yes, sir, but only on the sides and in the back."

"When was that?"

"I'd say the last time was two or three weeks ago."

After ascertaining that only John Worsley ever cut Scott's hair, and he'd had it trimmed just before the physical lineup back in April, Kuhnke asked: "After the lineup—why didn't you cut your hair after that?"

"I was ordered not to."

"Who ordered you not to?"

"My battalion commander, Lieutenant Colonel Hemming."

Kuhnke turned to the investigator's examination of Scott's car on the day after the crime. "Were you present when your car was searched?"

"Yes, partially, but not all the time."

"Did you see them empty your front ashtray?"

"Yes, I did."

"Yesterday there was testimony that there was water—it was wet near the front seat. Can you account for that?"

"I don't see any way anyone can account for that. There was no water in the front seat of my car. My car had not been wiped down. I arrived at PMO that morning at approximately 0700. That car sat in the parking lot until 1930 that evening. The windows were rolled up. It was a hot day. So how could something like that even be damp from being wiped? I don't understand it. Then again, the Prince William County officer testified that my door was dirtier than the other door . . . either my wife would use that car—we both work—or I would use it to go somewhere, but most of the time it was just one person driving the car. The door got more use. Yes, it would be more dirty."

"Corporal, where were you at 2015 hours on twenty April?"

"I was either at Zayre's Department Store or was on the way."

"Did you see Mrs. Connors on twenty April, 1983?"

"No, sir, I did not."

"You're charged with four offenses against Mrs. Connors. You didn't see her?"

"No, sir, I did not."

"Prior to that time—did you see her?"

"I saw her on the sixteenth of April. When I say 'her' I mean her and her husband. Me and my wife, we were out to K Mart department store. We were doing some shopping, and her husband, Lance Corporal Connors—I went up to him. I spoke to him. I asked him how he was doing, how he was coming along on the job, just things of that nature. And at that time she was standing there. She turned around. She looked at me. I didn't say anything to her. He didn't introduce me to her or anything like that. But I had seen her."

"How long had you known Mr. Connors?"

"We went to MP school together down at Fort McClellan, Alabama. That was in January of '81. We were there together for eight or nine weeks."

Kuhnke showed Scott a plastic bag filled with cleaning materials and Scott identified it as his, the one he was using to clean the apartment. He identified the cleaning materials inside as his, but with several items missing that he had thrown away in the other plastic bag.

"Again, Corporal, what did you do with the knife?"

"I threw it in the Dumpster in the plastic bag with the paper, old sponges. Scouring pads, and stuff of that nature."

Kuhnke had no more questions. Major Thomson asked for a ten-minute recess, then began his cross-examination.

The standing-room-only crowd in the gallery stirred as Major Thompson rose to his feet, paused, and looked squarely at Scott. Some in their seats strained forward expectantly. A distinct heightening of tension enveloped the courtroom.

"Corporal Scott, since this happened, you've had quite a few opportunities to tell different individuals your time and location that night, haven't you?"

"Sir, I don't quite understand what you mean. A lot of opportunities? Do you mean to speak to my defense counsel or during the interrogation?"

"The question is exactly as I stated it, Corporal Scott. You've had several opportunities to tell people where you were that night, haven't you?"

"I spoke to my defense counsels, yes."

"You testified that you were in a hurry to get home that night, is that correct?"

"Yes, I was."

"You were in a hurry to get home when you were at the pharmacy—the Dumfries Pharmacy?"

"I was in a hurry to get to Woodbridge."

"You stated on direct that you were in a hurry to get home."

"Well, you've got to get to Woodbridge before I get home, sir."

"Woodbridge is on the way home from Dumfries Pharmacy?"

"No, but what I was looking for was there."

"What did you get in Zayre's in Woodbridge?"

"I looked at a lot of things, but I—"

"I asked you what did you get in Woodbridge at Zayre's?"

"I bought a Coke."

"When you left the pharmacy, you stated it was 2005, is that correct?"

"Approximately around there, sir."

"Yet when you arrived home it was over an hour later, isn't that true?"

"When I got in the bed the clock said 2105."

"But you were in a hurry to get home?"

"I was concerned about my wife, sir."

"You were so concerned that you went all the way to Woodbridge to Zayre's to buy a soda?"

"To look at presents, sir. Gifts. Something to buy."

"Corporal Scott, let's discuss some of these other opportunities that you had to tell people where you were on that night. Isn't it a fact that you were interviewed by Special Agent Rodgers on the twenty-first of April?"

"Yes, sir, along with another agent."

"Isn't it true that you told him that you went to Zayre's that night?"

"Yes, sir, I did."

"Isn't it true that you told him that you did not see or speak to anyone at Zayre's that night?"

"No, sir, it's not."

"Isn't it a fact that you spoke to Master Sergeant Martin on the same day, Corporal?"

"Yes, sir, it is."

"Isn't it a fact that you told him also that you hadn't seen or spoken to anyone at Zayre's?"

"I don't believe I mentioned the part that I spoke to anyone."

"You had a magistrate's hearing on the twenty-seventh of April, 1983, is that correct?"

"Yes, sir."

"Isn't it a fact that's the first time you've mentioned that you had stopped at the soda fountain and gotten a soda?"

"No, sir, it's not."

"Corporal Scott, this pot which has been marked as Prosecution

Exhibit 23—isn't it a fact that when it was brought into NIS, you denied having that in your car on the twentieth of April?"

"I still deny it."

"Isn't it a fact that you told Master Sergeant Martin that same night that it was in fact in your car on the twentieth of April?"

"No, sir, I did not tell him that."

"You deny that?"

"Yes, sir."

"When you were interviewed by Master Sergeant Martin and by Special Agent Rodgers, you told both of them the time schedule that you had on the twentieth of April, isn't that correct?"

"That's an error, sir—"

"Isn't it a fact that you told them of the times and the places you went on the twentieth of April?"

"No, sir. I told—do you want me to tell you what I told them, sir?"

"No, Corporal. I want you to answer my questions."

"They—"

"I want you to answer my questions, Corporal."

"Yes, sir."

Rapidly, persistently, the prosecutor fired questions at Scott, cleverly switching his subjects back and forth, keeping his witness off balance.

"Between the night of the twentieth of April and the afternoon of the twenty-first of April, you wiped down the passenger side of your car, didn't you?"

"No, sir, I did not."

"Isn't it a fact that you wiped down the windows?"

"No, sir, it's not."

"Isn't it a fact that you washed down the seats?"

"No, sir, that's not true."

"Isn't it a fact that you washed down the panels?"

"No, sir, that's not true."

"Isn't it a fact that you washed down the upholstery?"

"No, sir, that's not true."

"You did a good job on your car between the twentieth and the twenty-first of April, didn't you, Corporal Scott?"

Kuhnke leaped to his feet. "Objection, Your Honor. He's badgering the witness. That's not a question."

Judge Atkins: "It's argumentative."

"Your testimony was that you saw the crime-scene technician empty your ashtray?"

"I looked right at him, sir. He even showed to me what he got out of the ashtray. He held it up in a little plastic bag."

"What was that, Corporal Scott?"

"It looked like cigarette butts to me, sir."

"You heard Officer Leonard testify here today?"

"I don't know which officer it was. It could have been Officer Leonard or it could have been the other Prince William County crime-scene technician."

"Did you hear him testify, Corporal Scott?"

"Yes, I did."

"Did you hear him testify that the ashtray was empty?"

"Yes, sir, I did."

"Is he lying, Corporal Scott?"

"I know I'm not lying, sir."

Major Thomson questioned him about his movements and the timing of them on the night of the twentieth, from the time he said he arrived at PMO till he arrived home.

"What time did you leave Zayre's?"

"I'd say approximately 2030, 2035."

"What time did you arrive home, Corporal Scott?"

"Well, I probably pulled up in the parking lot about 2055—about there."

"You've heard the testimony of Master Sergeant Martin, is that correct?"

"Yes, I have, sir."

"You've heard the testimony of Officer Leonard, is that correct?"

"Yes, I have, sir."

"Are they lying?"

"I'm telling the truth, sir."

"That's not my question, Corporal Scott."

"Yes, sir, they are lying."

The prosecutor asked Scott about the circumstances during

which his landlady gave him the knife. "And you threw it away?" he asked.

"Yes, sir, I did."

"Why didn't you give it back to her, Corporal Scott?"

"I forgot about it, sir. I was in a hurry."

Finally, Major Thomson asked Scott about his familiarity with the area where Judy Connors was picked up after the assault. Scott said he knew the area, but not very well. "I believe I wouldn't get lost. I know how to get around. I don't know it as well as others."

"No further questions," Major Thomson said, and sat down. The gallery spectators stirred again; murmurs and sighs.

On redirect by the defense Kuhnke brought out from Scott his allegation that Special Agent Rivers had offered him a deal during questioning at the NIS office on the day after the crime.

Kuhnke: "What kind of deal?"

"I don't know, sir. When I got over to the office they sat me down in a little chair and they—all of them gathered together and they were talking. They sat me there for almost half an hour or forty-five minutes or something like that."

"Did they read you your rights?"

"Special Agent Rodgers—and there was an investigator from Prince William County—Legerfield or Legavera or something like that—they read me my rights. And I said I would talk to them. They immediately started on me, badgering me from both sides. I was trying my best to cooperate with these men. One would ask me a question, and the other one, before I could answer him—the other one would ask me a question. Special Agent Rodgers—he told me that before he became an NIS agent he used to work somewhere investigating dirty cops. I tried my best. I was very confused. I was very upset. I just couldn't function, get my head together the way they were after me."

When the investigator from Prince William County called him a liar, Scott said, he refused to continue with the interview without a lawyer present.

Kuhnke closed out the defense questions and gave way to Major Thomson, who went back to Scott for a recross that covered no new territory. The members had quite a few questions for Kuhnke to read out, but so many of them in areas already asked by both prosecution and defense and answered by Scott, that at one point Judge Atkins, apparently becoming impatient with it all, gave Kuhnke permission to skip some of them.

Late that October afternoon, as dusk began to settle over the Marine base and the lights came on in LeJeune Hall, Scott was excused from the witness stand and resumed his seat at the defense counsel table. And Kuhnke said: "The defense rests, Your Honor."

13

In the gathering gloom of that late afternoon of October 6, 1983, a small knot of concerned, unhappy people stood around the back steps of LeJeune Hall, chattering among themselves and to the few journalists covering the trial. Lori Jackson was prominent among the group, lashing into the prosecution, into the Marine command. "Lindsey Scott is a victim," she said to the journalists, "a victim of the Quantico hierarchy looking for a quick solution to the rape of a white woman by a black man. And the prosecutors are under pressure to get a conviction."

James Scott, Lindsey's father, tall and sad-eyed, nervously smoking one of his endless chain of cigarettes, shook his head in disbelief at his son's ordeal. "We're a close and proud family," he told the questioning reporters. "Nothing like this has ever happened to us before. If he murdered someone defending himself, I could understand it, but he'd never do anything like this."

One of the journalists, looking for an angle for his story, said to Mr. Scott, "Do you think your son was singled out for some reason?"

"Well, maybe they thought he was moving up too fast," Mr. Scott said. "That's the only explanation I can think of. But I'll say this, if I was to be hung today if he did this, then I'd say go ahead and hang me, because I know my son is not guilty."

As Lori and two of her daughters, Scott's parents, the reporters, and the various other onlookers dispersed into the autumn twilight, an Article 39(a) session was being held in the courtroom, in an attempt to schedule the remainder of the trial and conclude it as expeditiously as possible; the coming Monday was a national holiday,

Columbus Day, and Judge Atkins hoped to close out the trial before that, on Friday or Saturday. However, while Kuhnke was ready, the prosecution said it would probably ask for a continuance to call a number of rebuttal witnesses, including NIS Agent Claude Rivers, who would have to be brought back from his current posting in Okinawa. Major Thomson said the prosecution needed him back to rebut Scott's claim that Rivers had offered him some kind of deal.

Kuhnke had no objection to the continuance, but at the same time took the opportunity to renew his motion for a dismissal on jurisdiction, repeating his claim that the government had not been able to prove that the crime had been committed on the Quantico military reservation.

Once again and with finality Judge Atkins denied the motion and adjourned the court; it convened again briefly the following afternoon to confirm the extension of the trial until Tuesday morning. At that time, Major Thomson said, the prosecution might have as many as seven rebuttal witnesses; in addition, the major said, it would be cooperating with the defense to try to get Colonel Harry to Quantico to testify in what was called surrebuttal. This was Kuhnke's condition to agreeing to the prosecution request for a continuance until Tuesday.

Both defense and prosecution assured Judge Atkins that they would be able to finish the case on Tuesday.

Over the weekend and the holiday Monday, while others associated with the trial might have been enjoying a well-deserved respite from the pressure and tension, and still others, such as Lindsey, Lola, and his parents spent the best part of those seventy-two hours in troubled speculation and fervent prayer, Lori Jackson was busily preparing herself for a worst-case scenario.

On Tuesday morning, October 11, just before Judge Atkins arrived to signal the opening of court at 8:30, Lori marched into the courtroom with two of her five daughters and collared Kuhnke at the back of the gallery. Scowling, her face so tight with anger the veins fairly popped out, she pointed to the two armed MPs standing either side of the main entry door (everyone but the members had to enter by this door, which opened into the gallery; members had their own private door at their end of the courtroom).

"Look at *that*, Mr. Kuhnke," she said to him. "Sidearms and all, ready to take Lindsey away to prison, else why would they need armed MPs in the courtroom? If that doesn't prove they're already sure they'll get a guilty verdict, I don't know what would!"

"Don't worry about it, honey," Kuhnke said. "It doesn't mean anything."

"Well, I think you should complain to the judge about it. It's—it's intimidating. It might even affect the jury."

Kuhnke patted her on the arm. "Don't worry about it. Take your seat, honey, you and your fine daughters—I see your friends have saved your seats for you, and we'll see how the day goes. Okay?"

Grumbling, angry, upset, reconciled to a bleak day in that courtroom, Lori sat down, daughters at her side, as the court came to order at 0839.

Officer Richard Leonard, the Prince William County investigator, was the first witness to be recalled by the prosecution. His rebuttal to Scott's testimony was that as senior technician processing Scott's car, he noticed that the front pull-down ashtray was empty, and, said Leonard, "the passenger side of the inside of the vehicle had been wiped clean."

Kuhnke couldn't penetrate that testimony with any of his questions; Leonard remained adamant that he'd been on top of the investigation and none of the other officers working on the car could have emptied the ashtray when he wasn't looking.

"I observed everything they were doing."

NIS Special Agent Kenneth Rodgers, testifying next, denied that in his interview of Scott the day after the crime he threatened him, promised him anything, or offered him inducements of any kind. Rodgers also denied that Special Agent Claude Rivers had made any promises to Scott (the prosecution never did get Rivers back from Okinawa to testify).

Since this account, of course, conflicted with Scott's testimony, Kuhnke in his cross-examination asked Rodgers, "Did you reduce the results of this interview to writing?"

"Yes, sir, I did."

"Do you have that?"

"No, sir, I don't."

"Did you record it in any way? Was there a tape recorder going?"

"No, sir."

Kuhnke did not press Leonard on the absence of his written record, and the agent was excused shortly afterward.

The rebuttal of Master Sergeant David Martin was particularly contradictory of the testimony of both Lindsey and Lola Scott. First, he claimed that contrary to Scott's account that during the crime-scene search he was deliberately made conspicuous by wearing his dress blues when everyone else was wearing "cammies," other Marines were also in dress blues. Next, he said that when he took the silver pot from Scott's apartment, Lola Scott never mentioned anything to him about a green bucket.

Major Thomson: "Was there any discussion about a maroon jacket?"

"Not a maroon jacket. We asked if Mrs. Scott knew what kind of jacket her husband had been wearing on the previous night and she said she had no idea what he was wearing as far as the jacket was concerned."

Predictably, Kuhnke couldn't shake Martin's testimony.

"You asked for a tan jacket?"

"No, sir."

"Did you ask for any jacket?"

"We asked if she knew what Corporal Scott was wearing the previous night and she did not have any idea what sort of jacket her husband was wearing. She brought the utilities and other garments from the rear bedroom. Apparently he must have changed back there. That's the only thing I can assume."

"And you deny saying that the maroon jacket was the wrong color?"

"She never showed me any jacket, sir."

Later in the cross-examination, Kuhnke asked Martin, too, if he had made any recordings of his interview with Scott.

Martin: "It's reported in the NIS report of investigation."

Kuhnke: "No, I know it's reported. Somebody else wrote it in the NIS report."

"Yes, sir."

"But did you write it, Sergeant?"

"I didn't write it."

"Did you write any notes down?"

"I'm sure I did, yes, sir. That's why Mr. Lindner was able to tell—"

"Do you still have them?"

"No, I don't, sir."

"Because there are a lot of inconsistencies, Sergeant, and it's important that your recollection be correct."

"I realize that, sir."

"Did you record these conversations with Corporal Scott?"

"I don't know what you mean recorded—"

"I mean did you record them with a tape recorder?"

"No, sir, I did not."

"And you didn't take notes?"

"Yes, sir, I did take some notes."

"Where are the notes, Sergeant?"

"I don't know, sir. They've probably been destroyed by now."

Kuhnke didn't press Martin either, on why an investigator's notes, so pertinent to an important criminal case, should have been destroyed before the case came to court.

And so the litany of rebuttal testimony continued in this vein, as well-prepared witness after witness for the prosecution marched to the stand and contradicted vital parts of the story told by Corporal Lindsey Scott and his wife.

There was little Kuhnke could do about it. He could challenge and cross-examine at will, but inconsistencies and contradictions flew about like confetti at a wedding. They hung in the stale air of the courtroom like some malignant virus, waiting to infect the weak, or the unwary, or those indifferent to truth. It would have been an unwarranted benefit of doubt to forgive every twisted piece of dangerous evidence as lapses or blurrings of memory.

No, the more logical explanation was that fabrications were being employed here, as they always are at a trial. Either Corporal Lindsey Scott and wife were lying, or one or more witnesses for the prosecution were lying. Who was doing so was a matter for the seven members of the court to decide.

When the parade of prosecution rebuttal witnesses ended,

Kuhnke brought Harry to the stand—his surrebuttal witness who could challenge Captain Unsworth's testimony about the time Scott had appeared at PMO on the night of the crime. A few moments earlier, the captain had appeared in rebuttal and repeated all his statements made when first called as a witness.

Kuhnke: "Please state your full name for the record."

"Richard Thomas Harry."

"Your occupation, sir?"

"I'm retired—thank God."

Kuhnke immediately slipped into quicksand when he tried to question Harry about the circumstances of his release as military magistrate by General Twomey. Major Thomson objected that it was irrelevant, and Judge Atkins sustained the objection.

"Mr. Kuhnke, I will allow you to examine this witness, obviously, to rebut anything that's contained—or statements made by a government witness—but I will have to agree with trial counsel that the reasons for his relief, I see at the present time, are not relevant."

Kuhnke also had a problem with the letter that Harry had sent to Twomey. The prosecution was successful in getting it suppressed as evidence; Kuhnke was restricted to using it solely to refresh Harry's memory.

"Does that letter refresh your memory concerning your conversation with Captain Unsworth?"

"Yes, it does."

"And can you tell the members now when Captain Unsworth indicated that he saw Corporal Scott at the PMO on the evening of twenty April?"

"Okay. At the second hearing there was a statement in there from Captain Unsworth stating he saw Corporal Scott at PMO between 1955 and 2005. When I had talked with Captain Unsworth, he assured me it was 1930, so when I looked at that, there's a thirty-minute variance there between what he put on paper and what he assured me—he said he was positive at that time."

"What other investigation did you conduct?"

"I talked with NIS. I talked with Corporal Scott's CO. I waited eight days on the results from the lab, which came up totally negative."

"What action did you take at that second hearing?"

"My orders stated that if there's clear evidence, then Corporal Scott should be retained in custody. Because I saw no clear evidence, I saw no reason to retain Corporal Scott."

"So you ordered his release?"

"I ordered his release."

And once again Kuhnke announced, "The defense rests, Your Honor."

The sudden rise in tension throughout the courtroom crackled like electricity in the air. That was it. No more witnesses, no more testimony. All that could be said—perhaps—had been said in the case of *United States* v. *Corporal Lindsey Scott.* There remained now only the final arguments of prosecution and defense, in which each would try to convince the members of the jury with irrefutable logic that his case was the stronger. But of course this was more than just a contest in rhetoric; a man's life might hinge on the skill or lack of it by prosecutor or defense attorney—unless, which was eminently possible, the members had already decided on the guilt or innocence of the accused.

At 1:30 on the afternoon of October 11, Major Messer rose to present the final arguments for the government. The major opened his speech with a reminder to the members that "whatever either counsel says is not evidence. You should remember that you are the sole triers of fact in this case." For whatever it was worth, for whatever impression it might have made on the members, it was a true statement of law, however breached in the course of final argument, when testimony is presented as "fact" and the integrity of some evidence is open to question.

"The first point the government counsel will discuss with you," said Major Messer, "is what can best be described as absolutely unrebutted facts in this case, that is, facts which anyone with common sense would certainly not disagree about. The second point we're going to discuss is jurisdiction. The third point we're going to discuss is identification. The fourth point the automobile used in this crime; the fifth point, the knife, and last, but not least, the alibi defense of the accused in this case."

For the next hour and five minutes, during which he alluded to Scott as "evil incarnate personified in the uniform of a corporal of Marines," the major talked about his six points, each one of them ostentatiously represented by a three-by-five file card that he flourished in his hands, and each torn up ceremoniously as he concluded a point. The prosecutor skillfully mixed bombast with sarcasm (e.g., Scott's gold tooth: "That tooth appears most prominently when the accused smiles, and he didn't take Judy Connors out into the woods the night of the twentieth of April to smile at her").

Jurisdiction? Major Messer brushed aside Lori Jackson and her testimony about blocked roads. "The government would contend that Miss [sic] Jackson is a goodhearted woman, who's trying her best to figure out what the defense counsel wanted her to do."

Trashing Ruby Hills's testimony was easy: "The defense counsel simply couldn't deliver on that witness. She testified that she saw the accused once in the spring. Close isn't good enough. . . . Gentlemen, no matter how hard he tried, the defense counsel could not establish that the accused was at Zayre's the evening of the night in question. Why? The logical answer: he wasn't. . . ."

The testimony of Lola Scott, about Scott's glasses and the bucket? "Why did the defense counsel call Mrs. Scott? The government has no idea. Now, gentlemen, let's not shred Mrs. Scott like the rest of the witnesses. Let's just fold her gently and place her aside, because there's enough tragedy in her life."

Major Messer did his job, protecting well his reputation as the "killer prosecutor."

Sarcasm and bombast were not Ervan Kuhnke's style. He rose slowly to his feet and addressed the court quietly. "Gentlemen and members, I have no cards to tear up. I have no theories to talk about. I want to talk about the evidence, the evidence that you and I heard from that stand, the evidence that you will take back into the jury room with you. No theories. No speculation."

Kuhnke pointed out that the government's case depended on

circumstantial evidence, and that the evidence was weak, with poor identification and absence of any laboratory evidence. The government had not proved its case beyond a reasonable doubt.

He made what was probably his most important point in disputing the evidence of identification. "Notwithstanding what the major just told you, Corporal Scott was not positively identified until the identification was made in this courtroom, several months later after he was charged and is on trial. You'll remember in the photo lineup she picked out two men, men that she said both looked like her attacker. You'll remember four days later in the physical lineup she picked out two men. Both men that she said scared her.

"I submit that in light of these poor identifications Mrs. Connors's dramatic identification of Corporal Scott is suspect."

Kuhnke reminded the members that all laboratory tests were either negative or inconclusive. He said that Judy Connors had never described Scott's car correctly, had called her attacker's car at various times tan, yellow, gold, a Nova or a Duster, none of which fit Scott's beige Buick with a white top.

He raised questions about the entire conduct of the investigation: pinpointing of Scott by NIS agents from the very beginning, before they had even begun an investigation. He mentioned the MP alerts, and the strange disappearance of official documents.

Kuhnke committed a serious error, however, on alibi, saying, "I admit the defense did not prove an ironclad alibi case."

Valiantly he continued, though at times appearing to lose his train of thought: the crime scene was never found, there was no medical evidence of rape. Mrs. Scott and Tammy Martin had testified Scott was wearing a maroon jacket, but since that didn't fit the description given NIS agents, they didn't take it from Scott's apartment. They said Lola Scott never showed them a jacket; Judy Connors had described hilts on her assailant's knife, which the steak knife used by Scott to clean the stove did not have.

In the front row of the defense side of the gallery, Lori despaired; her heart sank with every sentence. This was not good enough, she thought. Kuhnke was not powerful enough, convincing enough to overcome the more dramatic, more persuasive arguments of Major Messer.

*　*　*

Just before four o'clock on a gray, drizzly afternoon, Judge Atkins began to instruct the members on the law to be applied before they retired privately to begin their deliberations. He told them that an agreement by at least two thirds of the members was necessary for a guilty verdict; since there were seven members, at least five would have to agree on guilty. If fewer than five voted guilty, then the verdict would have to be not guilty.

The jury needed just three hours to come to a verdict. Judge Atkins asked Scott and Kuhnke to rise, to hear the findings of the members, which were read out by the president of the court.

Guilty on all four charges. The sentence: to be dishonorably discharged and to be confined at hard labor for thirty years (the prosecution had asked for life imprisonment).

Scott, standing at attention, slumped and lowered his head in disbelief. Shouts and cries came from his supporters. "No! No! Not guilty! Not guilty!" Lola burst into tears then screamed frantically as the MPs came forward, handcuffed Scott, placed him in leg irons, and began to lead him from the courtroom. Weeping and shouting, Lola rushed to his side, grabbed at his arm, desperately trying to hold him back. "Let him go! Let him go!" she cried. Gently, Frances and other friends pulled her away, holding her as she fell back into a seat, inconsolable.

Lori had not waited to hear and see all this turmoil, which continued in the courtroom for some time before the room was cleared. While the shouting and crying was going on around Lola, she, her two daughters, and several of her followers strode purposefully from the courtroom and headed for the parking lot. There, at her station wagon, she issued instructions and placards. Then, just before sliding into the driver's seat, she turned and stared angrily at the red-brick walls of LeJeune Hall.

"This is not the end of it," she said aloud, to no one in particular (but perhaps to the world in general). "This is just the beginning."

She got into the wagon, slammed the door shut, and with her two daughters in the rear seat and a small contingent of cars following, drove out the main gate of the Quantico Marine Base to the Iwo Jima Memorial some one hundred yards distant.

There they parked their cars, and in the cool mist and the rain, Lori and her daughters and some dozen civil-rights activists began to march slowly and silently back and forth in front of the memorial, carrying the signs that Lori—in her apprehension—had prepared over the weekend; signs that read:

JUSTICE FOR LINDSEY SCOTT

LINDSEY SCOTT WILL NOT BE FORGOTTEN

PART TWO

Justice in the military is at the whim of the commanding officer. . . . It's time to stop this circus, this persecution, this racial attack on Lindsey Scott.

—Lieutenant Colonel R. T. Harry, USMC ("fired" trial magistrate)

14

Lori Jackson was a fighter. Ever since as a little girl she was compelled by her older sister Vera into facing down a bullying schoolmate who had been tormenting her, Lori had been a fighter. Toughened through her adult years in the crucible of civil-rights marches, protest movements, and affirmative-action groups, Lori developed into an independent champion of civil rights and justice. Scornful of what she felt was the time-wasting bureaucracy of the formal civil-rights organizations, she waged single-handed warfare against bigotry and injustice; essentially a caring, warmhearted, generous woman, Lori Jackson was in her own way the proverbial iron fist in a velvet glove.

Now, with her heart and soul, she immersed herself in the cause of Lindsey Scott.

The night Scott was dragged off in chains to the Quantico brig, a perturbed, angry Lori paced the kitchen of her house, bouncing her fury off the patience of her husband Paul.

"We've lost the battle," she said to him, "but the war goes on. This case will not die until we see justice done for Lindsey."

"Well, what can you do now, Lori? How can you fight the whole Marine Corps?"

"By doing what I do best. Making a nuisance of myself. I'll keep up the publicity campaign, keep this story in the newspapers, on television if I can, I'll organize marches and rallies, I'll write to Congress, to the Pentagon, to the president, to anyone who'll listen. And maybe most important, Paul, because there's an appeal coming up, I'm getting together with Scott's wife and his parents and persuade them to fire Kuhnke and get some real lawyers in there to fight for Lindsey."

"That could cost a lot of money, Lori."

"We'll raise it. Somehow we'll raise it. And maybe we can find a lawyer who'll want to fight with us on Lindsey's side and not charge too much."

As was her custom, Lori wasted no time converting plans into action. The next day she visited Scott at the brig, bringing him a Bible and two cartons of cigarettes. (Marine Corps procedure specified that a prisoner would be held in the brig until the "convening authority," i.e., the base commander, reviewed and acted on the case. Major General Twomey's options as base commander included reversing the jury's decision, ordering a new trial, or changing the sentence.)

In the austere, green-walled interview room at the brig, Lori sat across the metal table from Scott and told him of her plans, promised him that she would continue the fight. And she arranged with Scott a meeting with his parents and Lola to discuss the firing of Kuhnke and the hiring of new lawyers to handle the appeal before the Navy–Marine Corps Court of Military Review.

"You have to keep up your spirits, never lose hope and your faith in the Lord," Lori told him. "It could take months before your appeal is heard. Twomey is in no hurry to get his review done. I don't have much use for that general. Anyway, it gives us time to find new lawyers for you."

Lori's critical judgment of Major General Twomey further crystallized three days later. After leaving Scott that day, she wandered into the base PX, intent on overhearing some "scuttle-butt" about the Scott case. She knew it was still the hottest topic of conversation around Quantico and thought perhaps she might catch something that could be useful to Scott, or at least get some general idea of what the base Marines were thinking about the case.

As soon as she entered the PX, however, what caught her eye—not her ear—was the front page of the weekly base newspaper *The Quantico Sentry*. She bought a copy and quickly scanned the lead three-column story on Scott to get to the group photo—also three columns wide—of Scott's former unit, Security Battalion. The picture showed the Marines in a semicircle around the commanding officer, Lieutenant Colonel Hemming, as he presented a check for $1,686.76 to Colonel J. M. Romero, the Quantico coordinator for the annual combined Federal Campaign (for the United Way and other charities for the needy).

What astounded and infuriated Lori was the photo caption, which said: *The (forty) Marines and (one) sailor (of Security Battalion) earned the money while on leave during August by acting as extras in the filming of a television miniseries entitled* George Washington. (Note: the eight-hour miniseries aired in April 1984 on CBS-TV.)

Lori stared at that photo, and the more she stared the angrier she got. She dashed out of the PX and headed for the parking lot and her car. She could hardly wait to get home and show the photo to Paul and share her anger and her idea with him. As she drove home, the front page of the newspaper beside her on the seat, she stole an occasional glance at that photo, at that smug face of Lieutenant Colonel Hemming that was driving her to distraction, that face evoking a bitter memory in her mind: she remembered Scott telling her when she first met him that during his "house arrest" through the summer months, and in particular during August, he had wanted his attorney, Kuhnke, to get in touch with Hemming and verify certain details with him, but the battalion commander was always "unavailable."

Sure, Lori thought, now I know why he was unavailable. He was too busy with Scott's battalion fighting the Revolutionary War.

What aroused Lori's indignation was the very noticeable absence of any black faces in the photo. There were plenty of black extras in the series, playing slaves or servants, of course, she thought. Why didn't they any black Quantico Marines?

This was it, she thought. This was the time and this was the trigger she would use to fire off all those letters she'd been meaning to send to powerful people in government about the complaints she'd been getting in recent weeks from black Marines about race discrimination on the base, all pointing the accusing finger at a senior officer.

That evening, after showing the newspaper story and photo to

Paul, Lori began looking through her contact files and researching names to whom she could write. While letters flew off in all directions Lori organized activities closer to home. Day after day she led vigils and demonstrations outside the front gate of the base, held rallies at local churches and gave interviews—all of which generated columns of publicity in both the local press and the prestigious *Washington Post*.

On the day after Lori led a contingent of more than 250 Scott supporters in an hourlong prayer vigil at the Iwo Jima Memorial outside the front gate, the *Post* ran a lead article (by Molly Moore) in its Metro section about the vigil and about Scott, headlined CONVICTED MARINE LOVED THE CORPS. The lengthy, well-documented article discussed Scott's background, the case itself, and noted that while he could be eligible for parole in one year, he would receive a dishonorable discharge if his appeal was unsuccessful, while remaining of course in Marine custody.

The reporter quoted Lori saying that "demonstrations would continue until we can get a new trial for Corporal Scott and away from Quantico. This case should never even have been brought to court." (Scott was no longer a corporal, of course. He had been busted to private.)

Kuhnke was quoted: "No civilian court would have found Scott guilty."

Replying to accusations alleging Scott was a victim of blatant racial prejudice among some base officers eager to arrest a black man for an attack on a white woman, Captain William Hayes, a Quantico legal officer, admitted, "There are some racists [on the base] just as there are in almost all communities. We get what society gives us. But I don't think that played a role in this case."

The wheels continued to turn, spurred on by Lori's tenacious efforts. The local NAACP offered a thousand-dollar reward for information leading to the arrest of "the real criminal." Several churches began collecting money to help out Lola, because as part of Scott's sentence, for thirty-six months he would be docked $500 a month from his $927 a month pay and allowances.

Several days later, as Lori marched outside the entrance to the Quantico base with Lola Scott—infant daughter in her arms— and some dozen or so other supporters, inside the base Reverend

Curtis Harris, president of the Virginia chapter of the Southern Christian Leadership Conference, was meeting with Marine officers to charge that racial discrimination was "flagrantly practiced" in both the military and civilian sectors.

Harris requested a new trial for Scott. He told the Marine officers, who included Chief of Staff Colonel Paul Lessard and Staff Judge Advocate Colonel Cassady, that he was concerned about "the process used in the investigation and prosecution of the case. I am concerned about the circumstantial evidence," Harris said, "whether this particular black man was actually the assailant or whether they were concerned that this one was as good as any."

Harris said that the SCLC was contacting Senator John Warner (R., VA), who was then a member of the Senate Armed Services Committee, to urge him to call for a congressional investigation into employment practices at the base.

A Marine Corps spokesman, Major Rick Stepien, said, "there is no basis to that in our opinion." As for a new trial, that decision would be up to the base commanding general. Unfortunately, Major General Twomey was away from the base that day and did not take part in the meeting. Neither could he be reached for comment.

Outside the base, holding a sign saying JUSTICE FOR LINDSEY SCOTT, Lori told a local reporter, "A new trial is what we want for Scott. We know somebody did this to this lady and we want that person caught. A black man did this, but it wasn't Lindsey Scott. I'm a mother of five daughters, and if I thought he did it I'd be out here picketing for a longer sentence for him."

Suddenly the Scott case and Lori's action groups around Quantico were overshadowed by a tragic event many thousands of miles away from the base, but very close to the heart of it; on October 23, the Associated Press flashed a bulletin: "A terrorist explosion kills 237 Marines in Beirut."

Immediately the newspapers and the Washington, D.C., television stations dispatched reporters to Quantico to get the Marines' reaction. For several days the tragedy took over the lead stories in the nation's media. Along with millions of other Americans, Lori expressed her outrage at the terrorist attack, and her sympathy for the grieving families of the dead and wounded Marines. Quietly, however, she pursued her own goal and continued to focus her attention on the plight of Lindsey Scott, shut in his Quantico cell with little going for him but hope and prayer, and the unremitting exertions of Lori Jackson on his behalf.

Lori's flurry of impassioned letter writing to various public officials had thus far gone unanswered, but now, on November 1, she sent a long detailed letter to Representative Ron Dellums (D., CA), head of the powerful Congressional Black Caucus (now Chairman of the House Armed Services Committee). Lori requested a Congressional investigation, asserting that Scott had been singled out for arrest based solely upon the fact that he was the only black CID Investigator in his unit and asserting that Scott was the latest victim of a pattern of race discrimination in his unit. She pointed out that nearly half the blacks in Scott's unit had been discharged since the fall of 1982 and that the promotion of blacks had decreased considerably. She informed Dellums that in the course of her investigation she had received what she termed "documented complaints" of race discrimination within the unit, all pointing to a senior officer. She described a cross burning incident KKK style that had been dismissed as a joke.

The response from Dellums's office was immediate. Special Counsel Robert Brauer telephoned Lori the next day to ask her if she had any further or detailed information she could send. Lori promptly sent along details of three specific cases, two involving criminal allegations against white MPs and one a minor, noncriminal alleged infraction by a black MP, indicating by the disposition of these three cases "a double standard of treatment within Corporal Scott's unit, under command of Colonel Hemming."

In response to Lori's letters, Congressman Dellums next day sent a letter to the Honorable John F. Lehman, Jr., Secretary of the Navy, with copies of Lori's letters attached, asking the secretary to give "prompt personal attention to a possible miscarriage of justice."

Referring to Lori's allegations in her letters, Dellums wrote, "Given these allegations of possible racism and possible defects in the process, I urge your prompt personal investigation. I urge your review of the attached and respectfully suggest you contact Ms. Jackson."

(In the final analysis none of the petitions to the secretary of the Navy or any other public authority had any tangible effect on Scott's situation or the allegations of racial discrimination at Quantico, in particular within Hemming's Security Battalion. In January of 1984, two months after receiving the letter from Congressman Dellums, the then assistant secretary of the Navy, Chapman B. Cox, dismissed Lori's allegations as more or less irrelevant, and referred to the cross burning at Quantico as a "tasteless prank." Of course, since the litigation in the Scott case was still ongoing, in effect sub judice, Mr. Cox was necessarily constrained in his comments.)

Clearsighted woman that she was, Lori knew that all her letter writing, all the vigils and the picketing and the media publicity, were but sideshows to the main event. All would be in vain should they succeed in obtaining a new trial for Scott—but fail in finding a new defense lawyer or team of lawyers powerful enough to take on the command influence backing up the government's prosecutors.

Together with Scott's parents, his wife, and supporters from his hometown of Louisville (where his parents still lived), Lori searched for such men. Time and again, among recommended legal firms, the name of Howard & Howard turned up.

Lori had heard of Howard & Howard of Alexandria, Virginia. Few people who read newspapers diligently or had anything at all to do with the courts in the Washington, D.C., area—either as clients or counsel—had not heard of Howard & Howard. T. Brooke Howard, the senior partner with his son Blair, was a legend in his own time. Now semi-retired, acting in an advisory capacity while Blair carried the major burden of trial work, T. Brooke Howard had a record of defending more than three hundred first-degree murder cases without a single one of his clients ever being convicted of murder in the first degree. He always managed to get the charges reduced for a client who either pleaded or was found guilty by a jury. T. Brooke was also famous in the area—indeed, perhaps nationally—as "the judge maker," because down through the years so many of his partners went on to become senior judges in the Virginia judiciary system.

On November 4, in the midst of all the letter writing and the picketing outside the Quantico main gate and the daily visiting of Scott in the brig, Lori made the crucial phone call to the offices of Howard & Howard. The receptionist put the call through to the only person available at that moment, John Leino, an associate counsel in the firm.

For the better part of an hour Leino listened patiently to Lori's story. Yes, he told her, he had heard of the Scott case, or read about it, and he thought perhaps his wife, Patty, had mentioned something to him about it. However, he and Blair Howard were terribly busy at the moment and he wasn't sure they could handle it. Lori persisted. And Leino really liked what he heard: the sound of her voice, the sincerity, the honesty. He, too, was a religious person, and he felt something inside him stir to her pleadings.

"Okay," he said to her finally. "I don't promise anything. But come up to the office on the eighth. Tuesday. That's it, local elections that day. The phone won't be ringing off the hook and we can talk about it some more."

At their meeting on November 8 Lori and Leino talked about many things, some personal, some legal, much to do with the Scott case, but a fair amount, too, about each other. It was in a sense like two boxers sparring, searching for strong points and weak points, for feints and bluffs and where the truth lay; except that these were not opponents, but potential allies, and it was vital that if they were to work together, they knew and understood each other. It was, as John Leino would interpret later, a searching for each other's souls.

When Lori left the office, Leino went to the office library, where Blair Howard was researching for case law among the floor-to-ceiling volumes. Blair looked up from a thick tome. "What'd you think of her?" he asked Leino.

Leino laughed briefly. "That," he said, "is one tough cookie."

"And?"

"And I think this is something we should take on. I like what I heard. I like what I saw in her eyes. But I made no promises. I told her before we made a decision we would have to study the trial transcript and everything else connected with the case, and meet and talk to Scott himself. But before we made a move, I told her, Scott would have to fire Kuhnke. Officially."

Blair smiled at him. "That's fine, John. Except for the 'we.' It's you. I'm up to my ears in cases. I couldn't get involved in another thing, not for months. So this is the one you'll finally have to take on yourself. We won't be able to help you."

Leino agreed, gladly, albeit a bit apprehensively. Up to that point, as an associate, all his cases had been handled in conjunction with Blair. Now he had the opportunity to prove he could succeed as a defense attorney on his own. And this "test case" looked like a very difficult one indeed.

However, working in the library at that moment was Gary Myers, an attorney who from time to time worked with Howard & Howard on specific cases. He spoke up now: "Listen, John," he said to Leino, "for what it might be worth to you, when I was in the Army I spent my time in the judge advocate general's office, so I know something of how the military mind works. If I can be of any help to you . . ."

"You're on," Leino said at once. "We can act as cocounsel. If we take the case on, of course. Meantime we can't do anything till we're informed that Ervan Kuhnke has been taken off the case."

That did not happen as quickly as Lori would have wanted, due to the procrastination of Scott, his family, and his supporters from Louisville.

Thus, during this delay, Kuhnke sent a letter to Major General Twomey via Chief of Staff Colonel Lessard, requesting that Scott be released from confinement pending a new trial or pending appellate review. Twomey refused the request, stating that he didn't see any basis for Scott's release, and in any case, he hadn't yet received Colonel Cassady's record of the trial (Twomey was away at the time, it will be recalled) and therefore he had not, of course, decided on any action, nor would he until he reviewed the staff judge advocate's report.

Several days later, Scott fired Kuhnke, opening the door to a meeting with John Leino. That took place in the interview room of the Quantico brig. Over a four-hour period, with Scott's nervous chain-smoking clouding the room in a blue haze, Leino grilled him as thoroughly as he would a hostile witness. At the end of it, as Leino rose to leave, Scott said to him, "You never asked me if I did it. I didn't do it. I would never do anything like that."

Leino nodded and shook Scott's hand. "I know that. I'll be in touch with you again, soon."

When he returned to his office in Alexandria, Leino marched into the library, where, as usual, Blair Howard and Gary Myers were bent over law books, scribbling notes. "We're in business," he announced. "I got a gut feeling during the first hour talking to the guy. Scott didn't do it. The man is not guilty."

15

As alike as they were in their love and respect for the law, so were John Leino and Gary Myers unlike physically. Leino was thirty-four, a big cuddly bear of a man, with a bristly brown mustache, who dressed casually and was built like the inside linebacker he had been briefly with Notre Dame before the load of his premed studies made football an impossible luxury. Myers, a slim, dapper thirty-nine-year-old who favored well-tailored three-piece suits, earned a degree in chemical engineering from the University of Delaware before switching to law at the highly regarded Dickinson School of Law in Pennsylvania. Leino, during his senior year at Notre Dame, decided medicine was not for him, and eventually got his LL.B. degree from what was then the newly opened International School of Law, later to be renamed and become renowned as the George Mason School of Law in Arlington, Virginia.

Significantly, both men had distinguished military careers. After being graduated from Notre Dame, Leino was unsure of his career direction and enlisted in the Marines. He had always wanted to be a Marine, always felt the time would come when he should do what he could to serve his country, a country that had welcomed his Finnish parents escaping from Soviet domination following the Russo-Finnish War (during which his mother had been a combat nurse, decorated for valor). Following Officer Candidate School at Quantico, Leino was assigned to Camp LeJeune, North Carolina, the largest amphibious training base in the world, where he commanded a weapons platoon, a platoon rated at the time, "the best platoon in the 2nd Marine Regiment." He served more than three years, reaching the rank of captain before leaving to attend law school, a decision largely inspired, he always said, by reading F. Lee Bailey's autobiography, *The Defense Never Rests*.

Myers served four years in the U.S. Army, rising to captain in the judge advocate general's office. In 1971, he was the detailed military defense counsel in the *U.S.* v. *Medina* case that arose out of the infamous My Lai massacre during the war in Vietnam. He remained fascinated with military law, taught it at Georgetown University, and still practices it.

Thus it would have been surprising if a certain frisson—not of pleasure but of concern—did not pass through the entrails of Quantico's command structure at the news of Howard & Howard's takeover of Lindsey Scott's case. These were heavyweights in the criminal-defense league, compared with Kuhnke, a man with good intentions, but neither with the training nor the experience of Leino and Myers—nor, indeed, their drive and energy.

It was reported in the media that Leino and Myers took on Scott's appeal pro bono; that is, free of charge for a good cause. That was not true. Leino and Myers asked a fee of $10,000 to cover the appeal and subsequent proceedings; however, considering the unforeseen duration and legal complications that were to follow and the attorneys' forbearance regarding how, when, or even if the money might eventually be paid, the asking fee did develop into a virtual pro bono.

Immediately following the Thanksgiving holiday Leino and Myers huddled with Lori Jackson to plan the strategy for an appeal. They sensed that there was little or no hope that Scott's conviction could be reversed; the appeal would be for a new trial. What they needed was a solid reason why Scott should get one. Lori gave it to them.

It was at this meeting that the lawyers heard for the first time Lori's detailed account of how she felt—and Scott felt—that Ervan Kuhnke had botched the defense. In particular, Lori stressed the part Ruby Hills could have played in providing Scott with an alibi, had she been told to check her records further before the trial and been able to place Scott definitely at Zayre's on the night of the crime. Lori told them how Kuhnke had called her in the middle of the night to get Ruby into court the following morning and how

Ruby had arrived unprepared, flustered, and too vague to be a credible witness. But Lori said she was convinced that Ruby now could be more precise, could and would say that she remembered Scott was in Zayre's, and could back it up by her records.

At the conclusion of the session, which lasted for more than three hours, Leino and Myers decided that their appeal for a new trial would be based on the claim of a totally inadequate preparation and conduct of Scott's defense, denying him his right to a fair trial as guaranteed by the Sixth Amendment to the Constitution. They would use the Ruby Hills alibi as a prime example—providing, of course, that she would cooperate.

On December 13, Leino went to see Ruby at Zayre's, accompanied by Major Roach, technically still the detailed military defense counsel. Leino thought that regardless of what happened at Zayre's, having Roach along was a kind of insurance; he could verify if necessary the propriety and proper legal process of the interview with Ruby. Leino carefully explained to her the situation regarding an appeal and handed her an affidavit to sign. "I'm not pressuring you on this," he said to her. "It's your decision whether or not you want to do this, and you may well have to testify again if there is another trial. The major and I will leave you now, wait outside the store for half an hour, then return. Think it over carefully. Take your time."

When Leino and Roach went back to see her, she handed Leino the signed affidavit, which said in effect that she could state "unequivocally" that she saw Scott in Zayre's between 8:15 and 8:30 on April 20.

With that weapon in hand, added to all the information Lori had given them, and the evidence of the trial transcripts, Leino and Myers thought they had a strong case for the granting of a new trial. Further, they knew that they did not have to wait for their appeal to be heard by the Navy–Marine Corps Court of Military Review—the first step in the formal appeal process. They could go directly to Major General Twomey. As "convening authority," it was within his province to order a new trial.

By now Twomey had on his desk the record and review of the trial sent to him by the staff judge advocate, Colonel Cassady. The defense team also received a copy from Cassady. Immediately

Leino and Myers sent the general a letter that was both a rebuttal of Cassady's review and a formal request that Twomey order a new trial based on the "ineffective assistance" given Scott, appending Ruby Hills's affidavit.

Cassady countered by sending to Twomey an "addendum" to his review. He dismissed Ruby's affidavit as posttrial "improved memory" that had no credibility, and therefore the defense of alibi "is not applicable in this case based upon the competent evidence of record."

He pointed out to Twomey that contrary to the criminal trial itself, where the burden of proof is on the prosecution, when there is an allegation of inadequate representation by defense counsel the burden of proof is on the accused to prove "serious incompetency . . . and that such incompetency affected the trial result."

As far as he was concerned, Cassady said, "I am of the opinion that Corporal Scott was represented by a competent attorney who provided him effective assistance from the time he was retained until he was relieved of his duties. . . . Furthermore . . . even if the allegations of Corporal Scott are true, he was afforded a fair trial and the alleged instances of ineffectiveness did not affect the outcome of the trial."

An affidavit from Kuhnke was attached, in which the attorney stated that "all defense witnesses were interviewed by me or cocounsel before they were put on the stand."

However, Cassady added, Twomey could, if he wanted to, determine that Scott was not adequately represented, and order a new trial. But, he wrote, "I do not recommend that action."

It came as a disappointment—but no great surprise—to Scott, to Lori, and to Leino and Myers—that Twomey did not want to order a new trial. His reply to the defense attorneys was that the trial judgment would stand. In which case, an appeal to the U.S. Navy–Marine Corps Court of Military Appeals was mandatory.

Pending the process of that appeal, Leino and Myers wanted at least to get Scott out of the brig. They had little hope about their chances with Major General Twomey, but they thought it was at least worth a try. However, where Kuhnke had made the same attempt with a brief, three-paragraph letter to Twomey, Leino and Myers sent Lori out into the civilian community with a petition for freeing Scott pending his appeal. Within a week Lori collected dozens of signatures and affidavits from people who believed in Scott's innocence and/or believed that if he was released pending an appeal, "he would not be a danger to anyone . . . and not run away."

The lawyers sent a ten-point letter to Twomey along with the petition and affidavits, detailing Scott's clean record as a Marine, submitting that there was no possibility that he would become a fugitive. What Scott wanted, the request said, was that "he might have ready access to assist his current counsel in the preparation of his appeal, and, certainly, that he be allowed to be with his wife and child in order to fulfill his responsibilities as husband and father to them."

Twomey's response came four days later, stating, in part: "I specifically find that Corporal Scott has not met the burden of demonstrating the improbability of flight or the lack of likelihood of further criminal acts should the request be granted. . . . Accordingly, Corporal Scott's request for deferment of confinement is denied."

The lawyers were not surprised by this denial either, though they were shocked by the specific language of it, as though Scott had a record of violent crime. "Incredible," said Leino to Myers and Lori, "but that's the way they want it. As far as they're concerned, they got their man behind bars and he's gonna stay there."

With Christmas just a few days away, Scott was crushed by Twomey's refusal to let him out of the brig to join his family. His hope, buoyed for a few golden days by the rapid, professional legal moves of his new lawyers, were now dashed by the intransigence of the Quantico command.

"It's a shame, a disgrace," Lori said to her family as they gathered over the holiday. "Here it is, just twenty years since I marched in Washington with Martin Luther King, twenty years since that wonderful speech of his saying 'I have a dream.' Well, that dream hasn't come true yet." She sighed. "Not for poor Lindsey, anyway."

*   *   *

Nineteen eighty-four opened with renewed resolutions by Lori and by Scott's legal defense team of Leino and Myers to press their attack for a new trial. While the lawyers drafted the brief that they would present to the Navy–Marine Court of Military Review, Lori planned her approaches to the media to attract continuing publicity about Scott's plight.

One evening, sitting in her living room paying little attention to the program on her television screen, her mind occupied elsewhere, Lori suddenly began to focus on that program: *60 Minutes,* the CBS-TV news show that has been consistently among the highest rated in the country.

She grabbed the telephone and rang John Leino at home. "John, you know that TV program *60 Minutes*? That's just the kind of show to get Lindsey on! It's seen all over the country. Won't that help keep the pressure on the Marines to give Lindsey a new trial!"

"It'll certainly be a great publicity coup if you can pull it off, Lori," Leino said. "It won't be easy to get on it, but it's worth a try."

That same night Lori wrote a letter to CBS, outlining her story, and mailed it early the following morning, uttering a silent prayer as she dropped the letter in the mailbox: "Dear Lord, let them say yes."

Warned by John Leino that the coming fight for a new trial could be long and difficult, Lori decided it would be prudent to advise her family of her place in that impending struggle. After dinner one evening, she called together her five daughters and two sons and her husband, Paul, and painted the picture for them. She reiterated that this was something she just had to do, that in a very real sense to her, she had been called upon by the Lord to fight for Lindsey Scott's civil rights, not only for Lindsey himself, but because he represented a principle that was being violated by the Quantico military.

"This is 1984 and people are still not being treated as equals," she said. "If we don't win this battle, how many more military personnel will fall between the cracks? Next time it may not be a black person. Some general might want to get rid of an Hispanic, or maybe someone who's Jewish, or even a woman.

"What I'm saying is I need your help and cooperation. I will have to be spending so much of my time with this, what with the appeal coming up and everything, that I just don't know how I'll cope without your help around the house, without your moral support and understanding. My poor head's spinning already with all the things I got to do."

Lori's eyes misted as one by one her children and her husband pledged their loyalty and support. She was moved all the more because she knew in her heart that though they didn't say so, not all of her children believed Scott was innocent. Yet they would back her fight for him all the way.

On January 20, 1984, Leino and Myers filed their defense brief with the Navy–Marine Corps Court of Military Review. This was the necessary prelude to oral hearings that would be held before the court after it had read and digested both the defense brief and the government's subsequent counterclaim. The Quantico command felt no pressure to hurry its reply; it could afford to ignore the interest surrounding the Lindsey Scott case as a minor distraction, when the Marines' situation in Lebanon still occupied the minds of many in the nation, including President Reagan, the Pentagon admirals and generals, and the media. Besides, orders were already being cut to take care of Lindsey Scott.

In the waning days of the month, a routine settled in among Scott's family of allies. In his hometown of Louisville, his parents were literally knocking on doors trying to raise money for a defense fund, organizing cookie sales in the church, seeking help from any possible source. Howard & Howard started receiving checks in the mail: odd amounts, $20, $6.78, $100, $9.54 . . . and a few checks with more significant amounts raised by Louisville supporters.

Lori made regular visits to the brig, bringing Scott the latest, if any, news about the appeal, chatting to him cheerfully, keeping up his flagging morale. Each day his wife, Lola, came to see him, always bringing the daily newspaper and photos of their five-month-old daughter, Latavia. Their nerves stretched to near breaking, Lola and Scott puffed on cigarettes incessantly. The stress began to tell on Lola's eating habits, too; she rarely bothered to cook meals for herself, indulging in bouts of junk food. She gained weight. Scott noticed, but said nothing.

Every day Scott called John Leino (he hadn't met Gary Myers as yet) to ask about the appeal, and every day Leino explained that it was "in the works," but it had to go through the plodding process of the legal system.

Just before the end of the month Lori got the call she had prayed for—from CBS. A senior producer with *60 Minutes* told her that her letter had impressed him, and he was seriously considering her story. However, he needed more information. Did she have anything else she could send him?

"You bet I have!" Lori said. "It'll be in the mail to you tomorrow special delivery!"

Lori put down the phone, her head buzzing with excitement. She phoned Leino with the news, she phoned Lola Scott, and together they drove to the brig to tell Lindsey. She went to see Leino the next day to discuss with him how they should approach the program if it indeed came off. "I know it will!" Lori exclaimed. "I feel it! It will! And it'll light a fire under some of these people in the Congress who don't seem to care what's going on in this country!"

While Leino readily agreed that prime-time TV coverage would spotlight the Scott case, he knew it would have no effect on the appellate judges, if indeed they ever even saw the program. Nevertheless, the prospect of national television coverage was heartening news. Lori's excitement was infectious. Everyone caught it. Things were looking up for Scott.

And the blow fell.

Just after midnight on February 2, John Leino and his wife, Patty, were preparing for bed when their phone rang. They looked at each other in apprehension: good news did not come by telephone at this hour. The lawyer picked it up. "John Leino," he said softly.

"John! John! It's me, Lori! They're taking Lindsey away to Leavenworth!"

"What? When?"

"Now! In about two hours! Lola just called me. She's in a panic. I'm going down to the brig!"

"I'll meet you there," Leino said grimly. He turned to his wife. "Patty, they're shipping Lindsey out to the prison at Fort Leavenworth. Now, right now. Throw some clothes on, we're driving right down to Quantico to see what the hell's going on there."

An angry Lori, a weeping Lola, and a frightened Lindsey Scott greeted Leino and his wife. Confinement in the Quantico brig was bad enough—but the U.S. (Army) Disciplinary Barracks at Ft. Leavenworth, Kansas, was notorious throughout the military services as a major prison that held serious military felons.

There was nothing Leino could do about the transfer. It was Marine Corps policy that "long-term" prisoners were sent to Leavenworth—"long-term" meaning a male prisoner who had received a punitive discharge and would have at least five years to serve.

While Lola cried and Lori told Scott that his friends would keep on fighting to free him, Leino, the former Marine captain, felt that sympathy at this point was not enough, that a dose of strong military medicine was needed.

"Lindsey, you can't afford the luxury of feeling sorry for yourself right now," Leino said. "I'll give you the advice old T. Brooke Howard always gave the young men and women who came to work for him: 'You have to make time work for *you*.' Lindsey, you can't become the slave of time while you're in there. You have to utilize the time you've got. You have to go at this just like it's a job. As though you're doing a tour of duty in Vietnam or wherever. Just consider this part of being a Marine. You've got a real shitty tour of duty coming up. The worst in the Corps. But you keep it together and one day it'll be over."

At 4:01 that afternoon, flanked by two security escorts, Lindsey Scott flew off on a commercial flight from Washington National Airport to Ft. Leavenworth, Kansas, to begin serving his thirty-year prison sentence.

Many months later, Lieutenant Colonel Fred C. Peck of the Marine Corps Public Affairs Office, replying to a query from author Ellis A. Cohen, stated that he was informed by trial counsel Lieutenant Colonel Messer that "Scott, his family, and his military and civilian counsels were given ample, advance notice before

Scott's transfers were effected. In general, notice of an impending transfer was given one or two weeks before the event."

John Leino's comment on this: "Bullshit! I was never notified of Scott's transfer to Leavenworth."

16

In the aftermath of his transfer to Ft. Leavenworth, a numbing cloud of gloom settled over Scott's family of supporters. While he had been just a touch away in the Quantico brig, a routine of daily visits and telephone calls somehow lessened the gravity of his incarceration, inviting a delusion that this nightmare would vanish with morning's first light and life return to normal.

Now that gossamer thread was cut; reality was Lindsey Scott far away in the military's grimmest prison.

Lori and the defense team, however, could no more allow themselves the luxury of despondency than could Scott, and they knew it. Quickly they steered themselves back on course. While Leino and Myers continued to prepare for the upcoming appeal, Lori kept the publicity pot boiling, competing with the announcement by President Ronald Reagan (on February 7) that he had ordered all the Marines out of Beirut immediately. The reassignment of many of those Marines to Quantico had the base and the local press buzzing, but Lori prevailed. She called the newspapers and expressed her outrage at the way the Quantico command "tried to sneak Scott out of here. But if they think moving Scott to Leavenworth is going to stop the actions of this community, they're in for one big surprise."

Rockets from Lori flew off in all directions, landing on the desks of newspaper columnists, television-news-assignment editors, members of Congress, and prominent members of various civil-rights action groups (some of which Lori continued to refer to as "no-action" groups).

As the weeks hurried by, a certain amount of noise was created by several of the well-placed persons Lori contacted: comments in the press, letters to the Navy, murmurings of indignation and concern—all, however, met with the usual polite platitudes by the military or ignored completely. In truth—and Lori realized this but felt it was useful to maintain the publicity campaign—while the legal wheels were in motion for an appeal, there was nothing to be done about Scott unless Major General Twomey so willed it. And certainly he would see no reason to take any action other than keeping his commanding general's eye on the progress of the legal maneuvers.

In April, Leino and Myers received their copy of the government's reply to their "Assignment of Errors"—their brief to the Navy–Marine Corps Court of Military Review requesting a new trial. The reply was filed with the court by Lieutenant Commander (U.S. Navy) John B. Holt, who was appellate government counsel in the Office of the Judge Advocate General of the Navy. Holt's argument echoed the government's case against a new trial established earlier by Staff Judge Advocate Colonel Cassady: that is, in sum, "the government submits that the appellant"—meaning Scott—"has not met his burden to demonstrate either serious incompetency by Mr. Kuhnke or that any incompetence affected the results of the trial. . . ."

This raised not a flutter in the offices of Howard & Howard. Nothing else had been expected. The motions by both defense and the government were all part of the rules in a kind of legal chess game, but with the grim irony that the real winner—or loser—was neither of the two players. Next would come oral arguments before the court, which were scheduled for sometime in May.

The good news in April was that CBS News in New York called Lori to tell her it was official: *60 Minutes* would do a story on the Scott case. Joe Wershba, a senior producer, would fly down to Washington then drive to Virginia to meet with her. He would prepare a script for the correspondent assigned to the story, Morley Safer. Could she give him some of her time?

Could she? Lori almost jumped out of her shoes. "Are you serious? Of course! I'll be more than glad to help," she said. "I'll give Mr. Wershba all the time he wants to find out whatever it is he needs. He can count on me."

Lori was so excited she ran out to her car and drove the forty miles to the offices of Howard & Howard in Alexandria to tell John Leino and Gary Myers the news in person. "I didn't want to call," she said, breathless with emotion. "I just had to come here and tell you. Isn't it fantastic!"

Leino and Myers were equally ecstatic. "Brilliant!" Leino exclaimed. "Who do they intend talking to? When is this happening?"

"I don't know, I don't know any of that. I was too excited to ask questions. All I know is producer Joe Wershba is coming down here soon to start working on a script and they want me to help. They said they'd call me to tell me exactly when he's coming down. When they call me I'll call you." And with that she was out the door and down the steps in a whirlwind, galvanized into action.

This is the best thing that's happened since I got that first phone call from Lindsey, Lori reflected as she drove back home. Lord, could it really have been . . . what, eight months ago!

Wershba and the crew of *60 Minutes* arrived in early May and began filming at various locations in the Quantico area. At the same time, on location at the Washington Navy Yard, a different but related drama was unfolding: Leino and Myers faced their opposite number, Lieutenant Commander Holt, before the three judges of the Navy–Marine Corps Court of Military Review: J. S. May, Edward K. Sanders, and C. J. Cassel.

At Lori's suggestion, Wershba and Safer, along with Lori, traced for the CBS camera the route Scott said he had driven that fateful night in April of 1983. In Lori's kitchen the next day they interviewed her, Lola Scott, and Ruby Hills. In Alexandria, in the library of the Howard & Howard offices, they interviewed John Leino. Again at Lori's suggestion, Wershba and Safer and camera crew drove down to Palmyra, Virginia, to interview the former Quantico magistrate, Richard Harry, now a civilian running a two-pump gas station and general store and coaching high-school football. Harry was as forthright as ever; Wershba and Safer did not regret making that trip.

Wershba asked the Marine Corps to designate a spokesperson who could be interviewed on camera to give the Quantico side of the story, but the offer was declined. However, the base public-affairs officer, Major Rick Stepien, got permission to allow the CBS camera crew to film inside an empty LeJeune Hall courtroom.

The filming completed, Wershba told Lori that after editing in New York, the story would be given an air date by executive producer Don Hewitt for later that fall or early winter.

The other drama was also played out, and now the players had to wait for two events: the airing of the *60 Minutes* story and the decision of the Court of Military Review.

On Monday, June 18, the court handed down a unanimous decision.

The court, properly, did not concern itself with the verdict in the case but with the appeal of "ineffective assistance" versus the government's refusal to concede that there was defense-counsel deficiency, and its contention that "the weight of government evidence at trial eliminates any reasonable probability of a different outcome."

In an important opinion, the court said,

The government's argument, however, fails to recognize that the impact of inadequate trial preparation may not be discernible in any degree from examination of the trial record or from the view of the in-courtroom observer. The presentation of a defense case, particularly an affirmative defense, obviously is dependent upon the quality and associated weight of the defense evidence. Inadequate case preparation by the defense counsel may enervate the accused's response to the government's trial evidence. . . .

We cannot, therefore, unconditionally accept the premise of the government's argument of "no prejudice. . . ." Our reservations regarding the government's contention . . . is not based on any lack of prosecutorial vigor. . . . The government's case was ably presented. It is the uncertain nature of the defense effort, when considered in the light of the posttrial affidavits submitted on behalf of the appellant which presently concerns this court. . . .

Both the oral and written presentations by appellate government counsel and the civilian counsel . . . present a battle of affidavits and unsworn arguments. . . .

We agree with all parties that on the face of the record this was a hard-fought criminal trial. At obvious issue in this case, however, is whether the appellant was, *beyond all reasonable doubt* [italics added] regardless of any defense-attorney deficiencies, the perpetrator of the offenses as the government contends, or was he some twelve to fifteen miles from the scene of the crime at the time these apparently premeditated offenses were in progress, as appellate counsel contends via an asserted alibi defense?

What we specifically find at this stage of appellate review, however, is a lack of sufficiency in the trial record, the appellate briefs, affidavits, and the oral assertions of appellate government and defense counsel related to the performance of trial defense attorney in this case.

We emphasize that we are not now ruling on the sufficiency of the evidence related to the *findings* in this case. That in our view is presently subordinate to the issue of whether or not in the pretrial preparation and courtroom response to the charges brought against him, appellant was afforded the level of defense-counsel effort and performance mandatory in any court-martial of a member of the naval service.

We are not unmindful of the impact of our interim decision here. A brutal and premeditated attack was obviously perpetrated upon the person of a terrorized young wife. . . . The tragic impact . . . upon the victim would be compounded, however, if the legal standards applicable to the trial of a member of the naval service who is accused of the attack have not been met.

Accordingly, the record of trial and all related appellate documents are returned to the judge advocate general of the Navy for transmittal to the appropriate convening authority. The convening authority [meaning of course Major General Twomey] may take one or more of the following courses of action:

A. Order the conduct of an evidentiary hearing. [Authors' note: this hearing was called a DuBay hearing, based on an appeal in a 1967 court-martial case, *United States* v. *Private Robert L. DuBay.*] That hearing will be conducted solely on the issue of the level of defense counsel assistance rendered on behalf of appellant in this case. The appellant as well as the government will be afforded the opportunity to call witnesses and present documentary evidence in compliance with the Military Rules of Evidence, on this issue. Specifically, at a minimum, the following areas of inquiry shall be addressed:

1. Date civilian defense counsel's services formally retained by appellant.
2. Number/length of conferences between appellant and civilian defense attorney from date of retention until date attorney discharged by appellant.
3. Names and relevance of defense witnesses who were interviewed by defense counsel, detailed military defense counsel, or other defense agents prior to trial.
4. Dates of interviews, approximate length of interviews, and specific identity of the interviewers of all defense witnesses prior to trial.
5. Specific circumstances related to appellant's retention of the services of Mrs. Lori Jackson and the extent of control and instructions issued by civilian defense counsel to Mrs. Jackson, prior to, and during trial.
6. Extent of pretrial preparation including visits, if any, by defense counsel or their agents, to scene of the victim's abduction and sites of asserted alibi contacts.
7. The instructions transmitted by civilian defense counsel to detailed military defense counsel relative to that associate counsel's pretrial and trial responsibilities.

B. Order Rehearing. The convening authority may, subsequent to the above hearing or if the evidentiary hearing described above is not deemed practical, order a rehearing of the case.

The court decision added a footnote stating that there was nothing in their opinion "intended to divest the convening authority of his authority under the code to dismiss the charges in the event he believes that an evidentiary hearing or rehearing is impractical."

Thus Major General Twomey was formally given a choice by the Court of Military Review: he could take this opportunity to dismiss the charges against Scott, order a new trial, or call for a DuBay hearing to be held on the subject of Kuhnke's conduct of Scott's defense.

The court's decision was greeted with cautious optimism by Scott and his defense attorneys. It was not the complete success they had hoped for: an order for a new trial; but, as John Leino remarked to the press, the decision "opens new doors." There was no doubt in his mind or that of his cocounsel, Gary Myers, that Major General Twomey would not dismiss the charges or order a new trial but would choose the option of a DuBay hearing (Twomey was given three weeks to decide). Ervan Kuhnke made the same presumption and said he "would welcome a hearing" to determine his competency.

In Leavenworth, where he had been assigned to the kitchen, peeling potatoes and scrubbing pots and pans, Scott was informed by Leino of the decision and the probability of a DuBay hearing. He was "pleased," Scott told a reporter from the *Potomac News* who telephoned him for an interview. At least the decision offered "a bit of hope," he said.

(It was at this juncture in the Lindsey Scott case that author Ellis A. Cohen became involved, alerted by CBS News producer Joe Wershba that he was working on something important that could interest CBS Entertainment, Cohen's employer. Cohen, supervising the post-production of a CBS-TV movie he'd recently produced, flew to New York from his Los Angeles base for a meeting with Wershba to learn some general facts in his piece. Wershba told him he could not be specific with any details at that point, but would call and leave him a "signal" days before the story would be aired. This policy prevented any advanced leaks to upcoming stories on *60 Minutes*.)

Though John Leino cautioned him about impatience, Scott now began to telephone him and Lori—collect—every few days, asking the same question of both: "Have they decided to hold a hearing?" The answer of course was that Major General Twomey would announce his decision when he was good and ready, no doubt at the last minute of the three weeks he was allowed for reflection.

Leino and Myers, meantime, quietly and continuously working behind the scenes on Scott's behalf, suddenly won a major concession from the Marine command at Quantico. For months they had been fighting to get Scott back to the brig at Quantico, where he could have accessibility to his attorneys and to his family. While waiting for Twomey to make up his mind, they got a phone call on July 3 from Quantico with the word that Scott would be returned to Quantico the next day—July 4 (an incidental irony).

Leino immediately called Lori with the news. Seeing this surely as a sign of even better news to come, Lori told her husband she would have to cancel her family plans for the holiday. She must go to the brig to welcome Scott when he arrived. (Neither for the first time nor the last time, Lori's children were unhappy with her order of priorities.)

With Scott back at Quantico, Lori called Joe Wershba at CBS News and suggested he come down with his crew and interview Scott—a logical element in the show, but an impossible one while he was in Leavenworth. Wershba loved the idea and flew down to Virginia to meet again with Lori. However, there was the delicate legal position to consider, and when Wershba met with Leino, the attorney said he would speak to Myers about the idea, but in any case, he said, they should not go ahead with a Scott interview until Twomey made the expected announcement about a DuBay hearing.

That came finally in mid-July with an order from Twomey to Lieutenant Colonel Atkins, the military judge who had presided over Scott's court-martial. Against the background delirium of the Democratic National Convention in San Francisco, which nominated Walter Mondale as its presidential candidate, Twomey broke the story that he had "directed" Lieutenant Colonel Atkins to conduct "an evidentiary hearing." Lori claimed Twomey had hoped to muffle press coverage of his decision by timing it to coincide with the convention, particularly since Mondale made history by choosing Geraldine A. Ferraro as the first woman vice-presidential candidate. This selection sent a chill of recollection through Lori as she reflected that sixteen years earlier she'd led the failed campaign for the Democratic presidential nomination of Shirley Chisholm—a pioneering campaign since Ms. Chisholm was not only a woman, she was black.

The local media, at least, jumped on the Scott story. It quoted Quantico spokesman Major Stepien's cautionary statement about the DuBay hearing: "The conviction still stands and the government stands firm in its case," he said. He added that "information gathered will be forwarded to the appeals court, which could then order a retrial or uphold Scott's conviction. A date for the hearing has not been set . . . it will probably be held within sixty days."

Gary Myers told *The Free Lance-Star*, "This is the first step in getting the Scott case reheard."

A DuBay hearing to challenge the efficiency of a defense attorney in a major criminal case would be every bit as complicated as the criminal trial itself; the preparation, the legal paperwork was enormous. Before the actual hearing could take place, Lieutenant Colonel Atkins called a conference on August 6 to discuss areas both defense and government might agree on to argue about. Leino, Myers, and Major Roach, still on the team, lined up against assistant trial counsel Lieutenant Colonel Messer (promoted from major after the Scott trial). Major Thomson, still nominally the government's trial counsel, did not attend, indicating again that it was Messer to whom the government looked to lead its case.

It was agreed that the defense might call all the witnesses who appeared at the trial. The government said it would call Ervan Kuhnke. The DuBay was scheduled for September 24, but before that, the defense was required to give the government a list of requested witnesses, and to give Judge Atkins a list of suggested "findings of fact" in addition to the seven mandated by the Court of Military Review.

On a somewhat lighter note, Leino told CBS News producer Wershba that he could interview Scott for *60 Minutes,* but before the filming he and Myers would insist on briefing Scott (based on the court-martial transcript and Lori's opinion, they were concerned about Scott's ability to handle vigorous questioning). Wershba agreed to this, and immediately before Morley Safer and the film crew were to begin the interview at the Quantico brig, the attorneys met there with Scott privately.

Leino explained to him that since they had no idea what kind of questions Safer might throw at him, it was important that he "hang tough." Myers cautioned: "This is strictly a publicity exercise. We don't want you to start sounding off with any bitterness toward the Marines."

"That's right," said Leino. "More than fifty million people will be watching the program, and that's a lot of folks who can be convinced of the government's rush to judgment."

Scott nodded his understanding. "That's easy. I don't really feel bitter toward the Marines anyway."

"Good," said Myers. Then, abruptly: "What the hell, Scott, you're just another nigger who raped a white woman."

Scott stiffened in anger; then, understanding that this was Myers testing his reaction to a possible attempt by Morley Safer to provoke his anger, of course, not with these words, he relaxed and smiled.

Myers chuckled briefly and turned to Leino. "He's ready. Send him out!"

Leino grinned. "Yeah. He's ready." He called in Safer and the television crew then, and the interview for *60 Minutes* went ahead.

During the rest of August and into early September, Leino and Myers and the government counsel argued over procedures and motions relating to the coming DuBay hearing. The defense sent in a list of some twenty-five possible witnesses. The government prosecutors (Lieutenant Colonel Messer and Major Thomson) countered with a motion requiring the defense to file, relative to that list, "a synopsis of the expected testimony sufficient to show its relevancy and necessity."

This Leino and Myers did; additionally, they filed a motion asking the court to command Kuhnke to produce every record he possessed that referred to his experience as a criminal trial attorney, his activities as Scott's defense attorney, and all records pertaining to the activities of the detailed military defense counsel, Major Roach. This, said the defense attorneys, was necessary since Kuhnke had filed an affidavit saying he had interviewed all defense witnesses before their appearance in court.

This bout of legal jousting turned the opening of the DuBay hearing, held on September 5, into another procedural argument. The government was objecting to the defense plans to call so many witnesses, claiming that the defense was in fact planning to retry the case, which was far outside the scope of the DuBay hearing set by the Court of Military Review.

Gary Myers, arguing for the defense, with Scott sitting by his side, disagreed. It was not a question of retrying the case, but, he said, "the reason"—for the witness request—"is because we feel that effective assistance of counsel must be measured against the test of omission as well as commission. The failure, for example, to investigate in depth the background of the complaining witness in this matter, the defense views as relevant to the question of preparation. It is an act of omission, a failure to do that which reasonable counsel would do. There were many acts of omission, many failures to investigate. I merely point out a few: the failure to deal with the alibi witness, Mrs. Hills, in a meaningful way; the failure to interview at all Miss Pamela Biller in a timely fashion. We cannot limit these proceedings to negligent commissions; we must instead deal with all the elements of the impropriety of Mr. Kuhnke's representations.

"As Colonel May, Judge May [of the Court of Military Review] said," Myers continued, " 'Get the warm bodies on the witness stand; test them in the caldron of the witness box, find out what really went on here at this trial, at this place, and find out also what didn't go on here.' Only in that way," insisted Myers, "can we get at the fundamental question of whether this young man sitting here on my left received a fair trial; and that is what this DuBay hearing is all about."

In rebuttal, Lieutenant Colonel Messer argued that for purposes of a DuBay hearing, "The witnesses could be limited to Mr. Ervan Kuhnke and at most Mrs. Lori Jackson, Major Roach, and Private

Scott. What the defense would try to do over and above that is contend that this hearing can be used as a springboard to in essence rehear the case by calling an entire panoply of witnesses. The government would say the defense position would be a speculation on a better way to do it, a speculation as to how could the case have been tried, what could have been developed, who could have been interviewed, and the government position is that within the confines of relevance, those sorts of answers are not relevant to a DuBay hearing."

Myers retorted that the judges of the Court of Military Review were very expansive with respect to questions that could be raised, that the seven questions specifically mentioned were "the minimal range of inquiry."

Judge Atkins then asked Myers, "Should I rule today that using the Court of Military Review's criteria as the minimum and the criteria for this DuBay hearing, what would be your position?"

Myers said he would appeal that ruling. "I think the Court of Military Review would certainly be disappointed in defense counsel," he said, "if all it got back were the answers to those seven questions."

Atkins did rule that day as he suggested he might, including his decision that the defense could call just the four witnesses named by the government: Kuhnke, Roach, Scott, and Lori. Leino and Myers did appeal to the Navy–Marine Corps Court of Military Review, which in effect kicked it back to Judge Atkins and the DuBay proceedings to decide.

And so the legal conflict of motions and rebuttals, affidavits and sworn statements, continued. A new hearing, set for later that month, was postponed, according to Major Rick Stepien, "for procedural reasons." Leino and Myers, meanwhile, produced six new affidavits from witnesses in the first trial who swore that Kuhnke never interviewed them before putting them on the stand.

One of these was Ruby Hills, who in her affidavit said she was now able to place Scott in Zayre's about 8:15 on April 20, the night of the crime. Ruby said that the date now stood out in her memory because she had made two shoplifting arrests that night, and she and a coworker reviewed arrest records from the spring of

1983. Ruby said that she wasn't interviewed by either Kuhnke or Major Roach, but was interviewed by Lori Jackson.

Lori told the *Courier-Journal,* "If Kuhnke had gone out to the store early on, we could have had a good witness."

Kuhnke again maintained that "all defense witnesses were interviewed by me or cocounsel before they were put on the stand."

Major Roach, his cocounsel, filed an affidavit saying he interviewed three defense witnesses; however, none of those three was among the six Leino and Myers wanted to put on the stand for the DuBay hearing, who said they had not been interviewed.

John Leino, talking to the *Courier-Journal,* said, "When half a dozen people with no interests in the case say the same thing, you know something is wrong."

Scott, interviewed in the brig, was asked if he had applied for parole, to which he was now entitled. "I'm not interested in parole," he said. "I want to be exonerated. I want to be proven innocent in a court of law."

Following another flurry of defense motions and government replies, Judge Atkins set December 5 for a hearing, at which time he would make a final decision on which witnesses the defense could call for the DuBay. Most of this activity was ignored by the press, diverted as it was by the presidential election of November 7, which returned Ronald Reagan and George Bush by a landslide.

Half-forgotten in the intensity of the complex legal maneuvers leading up to the DuBay hearing was *60 Minutes,* when the announcement came that the Scott story was to be aired on Sunday night, December 2.

(Two days earlier author Ellis A. Cohen got the cryptic phone message from producer Wershba that *60 Minutes* would be doing a story about "a U.S. Marine corporal who is serving a thirty-year sentence for a crime he said he didn't commit." With that vague information, Cohen phoned around various Navy and Marine bases to find out who the Marine was. The public-affairs department at Quantico admitted knowledge of the case, but refused any information except to give author Cohen the telephone number of Lori Jackson, described as "the official contact for the case.")

The following evening author Cohen reached Lori and expressed his interest as a CBS-TV movie producer in getting her support as well as the corporal's that very night "before my competition saw the telecast."

"Give me an hour," Lori said, "then call me back."

Cohen did, and Lori said, "You're okay. When do you want to meet?"

Caught off guard, Cohen asked, "Who did you speak with?"

"With Joe Wershba and Lola," Lori said.

(That began the relationship of author Cohen with Lori Jackson and the Lindsey Scott case.)

Sunday evening at 7 o'clock Lori Jackson and her seven children, husband, and other relatives sat around the TV in her living room to watch the *60 Minutes* story, entitled, "Corporal Scott, USMC." For some of those gathered, the national spotlight that would be put on the Scott case by the program was secondary to the excitement of seeing "Mom" on the television screen.

Scott appeared, dressed in fatigue uniform. "Did you rape her?" Morley Safer asked him. "No, I didn't," Scott replied calmly. "I'm innocent of this." He went on to say he was not embittered, that he still believed in the Marines and in the system, and that eventually he would be exonerated.

The show moved on to Lieutenant Colonel Harry (Ret.) at his gas station and general store. "Do you still say this case stinks?" Safer asked.

"I still say that," Harry replied.

Ruby Hills appeared, dressed smartly and demurely in a white suit. Safer asked her: "Had you been able to look at your records, you could say that it was Lindsey Scott you saw at some point between 8:15 and 8:30 that night?"

Ruby: "There was never any question on the time I saw him."

Safer: "On the twentieth of April?"

Ruby: "On that date, yes."

Lori's family was very impressed with Ruby Hills's statement on camera before the entire United States. She would be a vital witness in the upcoming DuBay hearing thanks to "Mom."

But as Morley Safer wrapped up the show they all sat there in stunned silence. For some reason, never explained, the interview with Lori was cut (as was John Leino's). There was not even a mention of Lori in the narration. All looked at Lori for some explanation. She did not utter a word, simply walked out of the room and into the kitchen.

After a moment one of her daughters broke the silence. "She didn't do it for herself," her daughter said, a touch of bitter sarcasm in her voice. "She did it for him. For Scott."

17

There was no better measure of the impact of the *60 Minutes* story than the blast of fury it sparked off immediately at the Quantico Marine Base. It drew blood. On the morning after, December 3, Colonel David Cassady, the staff judge advocate, authored a stinging press release that totally denied the *60 Minutes* charge that Lieutenant Colonel Harry had been "fired" as a result of his releasing Scott from pretrial confinement. Cassady stated that "the charge was denied by the command to the producers of *60 Minutes.*" (*60 Minutes,* of course, said they stood by their story.)

As the holiday season of 1984 approached, there was little time for the protagonists on both sides of the Scott case to prepare for the traditional festivities. For the December 5 preliminary DuBay hearing called by Judge Atkins, the government prosecutors had the easier task. They had only to hold successfully their hard-won ground that for the ultimate DuBay hearing the defense could call just the four witnesses approved by the judge: Scott, Kuhnke, Lori, and Major Roach. Since the Court of Military Review had refused to rule on the defense appeal, by deciding not to decide, the formidable challenge facing Leino and Myers was changing Judge Atkins's mind.

This was a key issue, and once again the small courtroom at LeJeune Hall was packed with supporters and observers, including Scott's wife, his parents, Lori, and several members of the local press.

Judge Atkins expressed surprise, as the hearing opened, to find that the defense had proffered once again its entire list of possible witnesses. Gary Myers explained that since the Court of Military Review had neither recommended nor rejected the list, "we feel that it is wholly appropriate to move to reopen the question of the witness list, since as we argued previously, the ruling of the court we felt was severe and restrictive."

Government prosecutor Major Thomson, of course, immediately objected, arguing that by its abstaining from a decision, the Court of Military Review "saw fit not to disturb anything the judge had done to that point. And we feel it's a waste of judicial time and economy to relitigate an issue that has already been decided."

Myers replied: "It is time now to examine this in a little broader perspective. We have come to this court in an attempt to demonstrate that an American citizen was deprived of his right to counsel because the counsel he retained was simply ineffective in the defense of a very serious matter which has resulted in a very serious sentence. We believe that the witnesses we submitted to you are relevant to the question of effective assistance of counsel. If we limit the scope of this hearing to the four or five witnesses that are before this court at the moment we simply do not do justice to this inquiry.

"What we have here is a darkened room into which we are trying to let light. And the foreclosure of the ancillary witnesses in this matter from this hearing will not shed light on the entirety of counsel's ineffectiveness in this case. It is fundamentally wrong to call this an evidentiary hearing with the four or five witnesses that have been described by this court as acceptable. It does not reflect the reality of what went on at the prior trial . . . it will not come to a just result, because this court will not have the opportunity to hear the testimony of the entirety of the case.

"And I suggest to the court that any solution short of the broadest-based appraisal of what happened in this matter of defective assistance of counsel is a denial of ultimate justice for this young man . . . who is incarcerated, it is our position, as a result of a lawyer who shouldn't have been there in the first place.

"Now, how do we get at this question of why he shouldn't have been there in the first place? We get it by finding out whether he met certain minimal standards that we expect from law students.

And we get at it to determine whether what he didn't do or did do prejudiced the outcome of that trial."

John Leino then rose and said, "I just have a couple of things to add. The United States Supreme Court talks about a criminal trial as being a crucible that tests the truth. It talks about a criminal defendant being entitled to be armed by his defense counsel in the form of a gladiator. It's our submission that the crucible the first time around was an ashtray, and our client was armed with a manure fork.

"Guilt or innocence here isn't the issue. It's a higher standard, the constitutionality of the case. The fairness of the case. If it wasn't fair, if representation was ineffective, I submit to the court, that first trial never happened. And that's why this examination is crucial, because this is the springboard that we use."

Judge Atkins, nodding his head several times as Leino sat down, remarked to defense counsel, "Gentlemen, I have had a very good argument. But could you please state a motion for me?"

Myers: "We would move that the witness list submitted on the record be approved by the court as the relevant and material witnesses for purposes of the evidentiary DuBay hearing."

Both Major Thomson and Lieutenant Colonel Messer objected. Messer complained that "we have been down this road before. And when the military judge [Atkins] ruled at the last session, the ruling encompassed Scott, Roach, Kuhnke, and Jackson as relevant witnesses. That was a clear ruling . . . and they would be asked questions, examined within the framework of the seven certified questions by the Court of Military Review."

Myers rose again and, carefully buttoning the jacket of his three-piece suit, said solemnly to Judge Atkins, "If I may impose upon the court for one more moment, the difficulty with the government's argument with respect to Mr. Kuhnke is that one of the best ways to test the credibility of a witness is to bring in people around him who he says did this or didn't do that. Now, if Mr. Kuhnke says no to a question, whatever question it might be, that's where we're left, if that's all I've got up there. I've got cross-examination. But if I have another witness who comes in here and says yes, then—then I have a search for truth, which is what this is all about. You close this hearing down and you lose credibility and you lose parts of the truth. I need these people if I am to discharge the duties that I took upon myself when I became a member of the bar and a member of the Court of Military Appeals and when I took the oath before this court. I can't do it without them."

Judge Atkins: "I'm sorry, Mr. Myers, I don't quite follow your 'no' — 'yes.'"

Myers: "Well, Your Honor, it's very simple. I need to test the credibility of Mr. Kuhnke in an arena other than cross-examination. I need to bring in other witnesses."

Judge Atkins: "For instance, you said if he says no."

Myers: "Well, for example . . . Mr. Kuhnke says he interviewed Ms. Hills, personally. Now, if I didn't have Ms. Hills come in, what would I have? What would I say to him? 'Are you sure you interviewed her?'"

Judge Atkins: "Okay, I understand. . . . Mr. Myers, is your client willing to take the stand for the purposes of this DuBay hearing?"

"Yes, Your Honor, he will testify."

"And I understand it would be limited for the purposes of this hearing."

"Absolutely. Having nothing to do with the substance of the matter, it would merely be limited to his relationship to counsel."

"Right. I am prepared to rule. After rereading the initial opinion of the Navy–Marine Corps Court of Military Review—opinion and subsequent opinion—I am of the opinion that this hearing should take the following format:

"That the purpose of this hearing is for investigation of the defense preparation and presentation of an alibi defense. To that end I would ask that the following witnesses be called, and that I will question initially within the framework of the seven questions ordered by the Court of Military Review. And I would ask that they be called in the following order: PFC [sic] Scott, then Mr. Kuhnke, Major Roach, Lori Jackson, Ruby Hills, Pam Biller."

The judge said that he himself would call the witnesses as court witnesses, with the defense cross-examining each one. He would allow no other witnesses to be called, but six affidavits from witnesses stating Kuhnke had never interviewed them, which had been in the record, would remain in the record.

Thus the stage was set for the final DuBay hearing. Due to the holiday period, this was scheduled for January 28, 1985.

Unquestionably, Judge Atkins's decision to allow Ruby Hills and Pam Biller to be called as additional witnesses was a victory for Scott and the defense team, and indeed, as the hearing ended, Scott, ushered out of the courtroom by two armed guards, turned and flashed a gold-toothed smile at the front row of the gallery, where his family and Lori were seated.

"This is the best I've seen him in months," Lola Scott said. "We're all real hopeful."

Scott's father, James, said he was sure that the judge's decision had lifted his son's spirits. His eyes filling with tears as he spoke to the newspaper reporters, he told them, "It's going to take some time before this is resolved, but he knows he's got a lot of people working for him, working to see that justice is done."

(A week later, on December 11, author Ellis A. Cohen arranged with Lori to have her introduce him to Scott. They met at the Quantico brig, where Cohen signed in, was searched, surrendered keys, wallet, and coins, and was asked to explain why he was there. During the ensuing one-hour chat, Scott said to Cohen, "I just want you to know I'm innocent of this. I didn't do anything to the victim!" Lori told Scott he could trust Cohen; at the end of the meeting, Scott agreed to work "exclusively" with Cohen on his literary and/or TV-movie projects about this case.)

Just when all the legal potholes seemed to have been filled in by the preliminary hearings and the final DuBay ready to proceed in late January, yet another obstacle suddenly appeared. Leino and Myers had earlier issued a subpoena for Kuhnke's records pertaining to his work for Scott, including his preparation for trial. Now Kuhnke made a motion to quash the subpoena on the grounds that Scott owned him $1,500, and therefore he had the right to hold back some of his "work-product" under what was called, legally, "an attorney's lien."

So another preliminary was called by Judge Atkins, for January 17, to clear up this problem.

Following arguments by John Leino and Kuhnke's attorney for this hearing, Admiral Charles McDowell (Ret.), Leino called Kuhnke to the stand.

Leino: "Mr. Kuhnke, how much money does Lindsey Scott owe you for this entire proceeding?"

Kuhnke: "Fifteen hundred dollars."

"And if Lindsey Scott pays that money to you or you receive that money on behalf of Lindsey Scott, you will then turn over your entire file with regard to the preparation of the defense of Lindsey Scott?"

"I'll turn it over for you for—for copying. I expect it back."

"Yes, sir, we understand that. But the file that will be turned over will be your entire file. Is that correct?"

"It will be the entire file."

"No further questions."

Following this exchange came a surprise motion from the government prosecutor, Lieutenant Colonel Messer, urging Judge Atkins to decide in favor of Leino and enforce the subpoena.

No one was more surprised than Leino, who rose and said, "I suppose hell has frozen over because we stand shoulder to shoulder with the United States in this matter. I kind of feel like I'm playing a bit part in *The Merchant of Venice,* here. I thought that because of the importance of this matter—literally the life of a human being and the lives of his family—when trial counsel [Kuhnke] alludes to certain records without qualification and makes the broad statement that these records are, in effect, going to demonstrate clearly that he has done what is necessary, and that all of us can rest peacefully that the Constitution has been served, and then for him to come in here and sit there on the witness stand and smile and say, 'Well, there is such a thing as a lien,' and the principles of lien, in his opinion, far outweigh the principles of constitutionality . . . We're asking for those documents. We understand money is owed. If it's necessary, we'll get the money, and the pound of flesh will be here in time for us to prepare this case, and then we'll have an opportunity, hopefully, to ask Mr. Kuhnke about his preparation and about his file."

Judge Atkins: "The motion by Ervan Kuhnke to quash the subpoena for the materials described is denied. I direct that he allow the inspection by the defense. My ruling on this motion does not extend specifically to the reproduction. . . . The defense is allowed inspection. Is that understood?"

Leino: "Will defense counsel be allowed to make notes?"

Judge Atkins (smiling): "I anticipate that in inspection of it, your hands will not be behind your back."

And so another victory for Leino and Myers. They could call as witnesses Ruby Hills and Pam Biller, and they would have access to all of Kuhnke's files. They felt now that they were as reasonably well armed as could be expected to prove "ineffective assistance" on the part of Kuhnke and thus convince the Court of Military Review to order a new trial. A clear high of optimism was felt in the defense camp as they awaited the climactic DuBay hearing, now set for January 29.

To a large extent the result of the national publicity given the Scott case by the twenty-minute segment on *60 Minutes,* scores of journalists were now in contact with the Quantico public-affairs office asking for credentials to cover the DuBay hearing. On January 25, *The Free Lance-Star* of Fredericksburg, Virginia, ran a page-one profile of Lori by staff reporter Nancy Cook, entitled, RIGHTS: FIGHT IS FULL-TIME FOR LORI JACKSON. Along with a large close-up photo of Lori, Ms. Cook explored the roots of Lori's childhood and her involvement with the civil-rights movement, up to the current status of the Scott case. Lori told the reporter that after eighteen months of work with Scott, she was more convinced than ever that he was innocent, and believed that he didn't have long to wait.

According to the reporter, Scott's attorneys said that "Mrs. Jackson has found two witnesses who saw Scott shopping the night the crime occurred." Ms. Cook quoted John Leino: "She developed the case before we even got involved in it. She is the heart and soul of this case. First comes Lindsey Scott, then comes Lori Jackson."

The day before the hearing the same newspaper ran an interview with Scott, in which he admitted that his confinement was tearing at him, his wife, and his parents. He said that his wife, Lola, had come close to a nervous breakdown, and his little girl, Latavia, born just five weeks before his court-martial, was growing up without him. He said that since his transfer back to Quantico on July 4 he had at least been able to see his wife and daughter on weekends, but in some ways this only added to his anguish. "It's hard," he said. "My little girl grabs my leg when she comes to visit and wants me to go with her. It's hard to say good-bye."

18

When Judge Atkins called the DuBay court to order at 9:40 A.M. on January 29, 1985, it was apparent that the national media were well and truly alerted to the Scott case. So many overflowed the LeJeune Hall courtroom, Judge Atkins allowed nine of them to sit in the jury box (since no jury was needed for the hearing). Among the nine were two sketch artists working for both the printed media and the electronic media. In the second row of the gallery, sitting behind Scott's family and Lori, were, among others, Quantico public-affairs officer Major Rick Stepien, Lieutenant Colonel Richard Harry (Ret.), *60 Minutes* producer Joe Wershba, and author Ellis A. Cohen. Friends, civil-rights activists, and supporters in the gallery included some from Scott's hometown of Louisville and an ex-Marine friend named Josh* who had driven up from Jacksonville, Florida.

At the prosecutor's table were seated the same two from the court-martial, Major Donald Thomson and Lieutenant Colonel Jim Messer. Both wore the winter Marine dress: green wool sweater over the regulation khaki shirt with green wool pants. For the defense: John Leino, clad in light blue blazer, navy-blue trousers, blue shirt, and red rep tie. His partner, Gary Myers, wore a gray striped suit, white broadcloth shirt, and a red striped tie—looking very Ivy League. Between them sat Lindsey Scott, in Marine winter green. Also at the defense table was Major Alan Roach, still the assigned military defense counsel. (At one point during the hearings he had approached John Leino, worried that he would "look bad" for the small part he had played in the original defense team; but Leino had told him he needn't worry, that as far as he

214

and Myers were concerned, he had done his job. He had never been in a position to criticize Kuhnke or take over the defense, even had he been so inclined.)

At the back of the courtroom, two MPs stood stolidly at attention, their eyes fixed on Scott (less conspicuous, two men in dark business suits, doubtless NIS agents, had taken up positions at the back door). Outside in the hallway, waiting to be called, sat conservatively pinstripe-suited attorney Ervan Kuhnke.

As Judge Atkins had ruled, he would conduct the direct examination of the witnesses, then the witnesses would be available to the defense for cross-examination. The defense would also be allowed to call witnesses after they had been examined by the judge. The government would be given the same privileges.

Scott was the first witness called. For more than three hours he was in the witness chair as first Judge Atkins, then John Leino, and finally Lieutenant Colonel Messer questioned him at length about his meetings and his telephone conversations with Kuhnke from the time he hired the attorney through the court-martial. Time and again, in response to questions by Judge Atkins, Scott stressed lack of communication with Kuhnke during the six months between his arrest and the trial. Judge Atkins asked him about the first magistrate's hearing before Lieutenant Colonel Harry.

Judge Atkins: "Did you see Mr. Kuhnke prior to the hearing?"

Scott: "No, sir, I did not."

"During the hearing did you have an opportunity to communicate with Mr. Kuhnke?"

"Opportunity, yes, sir."

"Did you?"

"Not while the hearing was going on."

"Did he try to communicate with you during the hearing?"

"He didn't say anything to me during the hearing."

"Did Mr. Kuhnke participate in the hearing?"

"Beyond stating his qualifications as a lawyer, Mr. Kuhnke had no input into the hearing, sir."

"After the hearing, did you have an opportunity to meet with him?"

"He was in the conference room before he left, sir. We went

nowhere, spoke about nothing, sir. He just relayed that he would be back for the next magistrate hearing and that was it, sir."

"Are you saying, then, that you did not discuss your case in any substance with Mr. Kuhnke on the twenty-seventh of April, 1983, during the magistrate's hearing?"

"That's exactly what I am saying."

Scott testified that at his first meeting with Kuhnke on April 22, he gave the attorney a substantial amount of information he felt could be useful in his defense, including the names of a number of possible witnesses who could confirm his alibi for the night of the crime.

Judge Atkins: "When, after the twenty-second of April, did you next have a meeting of substance with Mr. Kuhnke where presentation of evidence or exploration of defenses was discussed?"

Scott: "I didn't, sir."

"Never again?"

"Never again, sir."

Scott maintained that he asked Kuhnke on several occasions to have the witnesses he had named subpoenaed, but Kuhnke repeatedly told him not to worry about it, that he didn't believe the case would go to trial, the prosecution didn't have a case. At one point Scott called Kuhnke's attitude "lackadaisical."

Speaking in a quiet, measured tone of voice, Scott told Judge Atkins he had also asked Kuhnke to bring in expert witnesses to help in his defense, particularly an expert in forensics. He asked Kuhnke to subpoena Quantico's investigation reports that might have showed that the victim's original description of her assailant didn't match him, and Scott mentioned the fact that Kuhnke failed to protest when NIS investigators searched his home and car without a warrant.

Judge Atkins: "When the trial commenced, what conversation did you have with Mr. Kuhnke about the presence or absence of witnesses?"

"At that time, sir . . . I didn't know that my witnesses and these things hadn't been subpoenaed. I thought they were coming, sir."

"During the nine days of trial, how much opportunity did you have to meet with Mr. Kuhnke and discuss the progress of the trial and the presentation of evidence?"

"I didn't meet with him, sir."

"Not at any time?"

"No, sir."

John Leino, in his cross-examination, delved into Scott's contacts with Kuhnke in much greater detail than had Judge Atkins, to the point where Lieutenant Colonel Messer began to raise questions of relevancy. When Scott reiterated that Kuhnke kept telling him not to worry, that the government would never bring the case to trial, Leino asked him: "Did there come a time, Private Scott, when your liberty was restricted in any way, and if so, when?"

Lieutenant Colonel Messer objected. "The government would simply submit that's totally irrelevant to why we are here today. It has nothing to do with the alibi defense."

Leino: "With regard to the restriction of his liberty, I think that's a significant point here, and if he told his attorney, 'I've been restricted,' or, in effect, 'have been arrested,' I think that would tend to cause an attorney to think that this is a serious situation and a serious prosecution. I mean I doubt if NIS or the powers that be do this just for fun. They weren't running him up the flagpole to see if somebody would salute."

Judge Atkins: "I'll allow it for purpose of foundation for continued contact between the accused and his attorney."

Encouraged, Leino went deeper into the investigation of the crime itself. "I notice that in your notes on the Article 32 hearing, you say that, 'My phone in my own apartment has been disconnected for over a week.' Why do you think that was important?" he asked.

Scott: "Because the assailant obviously called her from somewhere close."

"How do you know that the assailant called her from somewhere close?"

"Because of what the victim stated."

"And what did the victim state?"

"The victim stated that the assailant was there waiting in two minutes."

"Why was the fact that your phone was disconnected important?"

"I couldn't have called her from Spanish Gardens Apartments."

"There are no pay phones at Spanish Gardens Apartments?"

"No, there's not."

"Now, when did your attorney get these notes from you?"

"Mid-September."

"And at that time did he tell you that he was going to have telephone records subpoenaed? Did he say anything like that?"

"No, he didn't."

"Did he tell you whether or not he had checked the telephone records at the telephone company?"

"No, he didn't."

"Did he drive around the area of Spanish Gardens within two minutes to find out whether or not there were any phones that he might have used?"

"No, he didn't."

"Do you know why he didn't?"

"No, I don't."

Step-by-step Leino took Scott through the crime investigation, always asking whether or not he and Kuhnke had discussed any of the evidence uncovered—or not uncovered.

Leino: "Did there come a time when you became aware of the fact that there had been a trail of blood found in the vicinity of the alleged crime?"

"Yes."

"And did you tell this to your attorney?"

"Yes, I did."

"Did there ever come a time when your attorney received blood analysis, or forensic medical tests, as a result of the discovery, with regard to that trail of blood?"

"No."

"So we don't know if it was blood, from a scientific standpoint. Is that correct?"

"That's correct."

"Did you see the trail?"

"I saw something."

"You were out there and you actually saw what they were calling a blood trail?"

"That's correct."

"And you told that to your attorney?"

"That's correct."

"And what did this blood trail appear to be, to you?"

"It was burnt-orange drippings. A lot of mashed bugs—some of them were bugs. We couldn't really distinguish."

"Do you know whether or not a sample of this supposed blood trail was taken by the investigators?"

"I didn't see them do that. I don't believe it was. No, it wasn't."

"Now, we are going to have to be very specific here. Where was the blood located?"

"On a paved road."

"And it started on a paved road and it ended on the same paved road. Is that correct?"

"That's correct."

"Did your attorney ever talk to you about clotting factors?"

"No, he didn't."

"Did your attorney ever tell you that he had talked to a medical expert—not necessarily hired one, but just talked over the phone with someone considered to be a medical expert with regard to clotting factors?"

"No, he didn't."

"And then it's safe to assume that he didn't tell you that the trail of blood, based on the facts of the case, would have been a continuous trail of blood, and, in fact, most of the bleeding would have occurred at the crime scene and continued until the clotting factor took effect?"

"He never told me that."

"Now, they had dogs out there, didn't they?"

"That's correct."

"Are you aware of the fact that the Virginia Search and Rescue Dog Association will provide you with a search—a private search—and expert testimony for nothing?"

"No, I'm not."

"Are you aware of the fact that the dog Bambi found a dead body in ninety feet of water six days after a death took place?"

"No, I wasn't."

"Did your attorney ever talk to you about tracking dogs and how reliable they are?"

"No, he didn't."

"Did he ever say, 'Well, they couldn't find a crime scene out there, so let's do one of two things. Try and find it ourselves, or build a defense on that'?"

"No, he didn't."

"Was there something in your mind that made you think about the fact that it's kind of peculiar that a blood trail starts here and ends there, and dogs can't find it anywhere else?"

"I just never thought about it."

"Did you think she might have been cut in a car and dumped on the road?"

"Objection, Your Honor!" cried Lieutenant Colonel Messer.

Leino: "I'll withdraw the question."

Lieutenant Colonel Messer: "The government realizes that objections to cumulativeness and relevancy have taken a Roman holiday today, but nonetheless, Your Honor, the government would, at the risk of being tedious, lodge an objection based on relevancy, on the fact that we appear to be hearing more of Mr. Leino than we are of the witness."

Leino: "Well, Your Honor, in response, when you're in Rome you do as the Romans do. This is some information that should have come out a long time ago, and the reason it didn't come out is because that attorney didn't make a couple of phone calls. I found out this information by making two phone calls, one to the state police and to a Mrs. Dianne Stanly."

Judge Atkins: "The purpose of this hearing is for me to gather facts on the preparation by Mr. Kuhnke, that is the benchmark of relevance here."

Leino: "Yes, sir."

Judge Atkins: "The argument of the impact is just that. Continue on."

This was without a doubt a major concession by Judge Atkins, who appeared to be as fascinated by all of Leino's revelations as were the spectators. And so the attorney continued along the same path.

"Now, you also reviewed the NIS report . . . and you point out certain things like the wounds the doctor describes on the victim."

"That's correct."

"And it was alleged that this was a rape. Is that correct?"

"That's correct."

"Do you know what a vulva is—ever hear that term?"

"Yes, I have."

"What is it?"

"It's female sex—part of the female sex organ."

"Do you know what the vaginal introitus is? Ever heard that?"

"No, I haven't."

"It's the entry to the vagina. I didn't know that until last night. I researched it in a book. Now, did your attorney point out to you that in the medical report, which he has a copy of, or should have a copy of, the first examining doctor reports that 'the vulva is within normal limits, there are no lacerations, and no contusions'? And did he point out to you that the vaginal introitus was also within normal limits?"

"No, he didn't."

"Did your attorney ever talk to you with regard to hiring an expert on rape tests?"

"No, he didn't."

Leino went on to develop Scott's desperate call to Lori Jackson for help, and how she was able to find witnesses for him who might sustain his alibi. Leino asked him about Kuhnke's affidavit, which stated that Scott had made "scores of visits" to his office. Scott denied it.

Leino: "Did you have twenty visits to his office?"

Scott: "No."

"Did you have ten visits to his office?"

"No."

"How many visits to his office did you have where you maintained your innocence and you discussed the case?"

"One."

"That's your testimony under oath?"

"Yes, it is."

"Well, what do you have to say about the affidavit that says you visited lawyer Kuhnke on scores of occasions?"

"It's not true."

"He goes on in this same affidavit to state that, quote, 'All defense witnesses were interviewed by me or cocounsel before they were put on the stand,' end quote. Is that statement true?"

"No, it's not."

"I quote further: 'Ruby Hills was located as a result of my efforts to find and develop an alibi defense for Corporal Scott.' Is that true?"

"No, it's not."

Following a brief cross-examination by Lieutenant Colonel Messer, which attempted to establish that between Kuhnke and Major Roach a reasonable defense had been offered at Scott's trial, Leino returned with more questions.

"What did Mr. Kuhnke say to you with regard to cross-examination of the victim?"

"He told me he didn't want to ask her about the attack."

"Why didn't he want to ask her about the attack—that's what you were being charged with?"

"He said he knew it would disturb her and also disturb him."

Finally, Leino asked Scott, "Did Mr. Kuhnke tell you what he hadn't done?"

"Yes, he did."

"What hadn't he done?"

"He hadn't interviewed any witnesses, hadn't subpoenaed any witnesses, he hadn't subpoenaed any of the items that I asked him to subpoena, he hadn't subpoenaed any of the expert witnesses that I asked him to subpoena."

Mr. Kuhnke, called next to the stand and interrogated by Judge Atkins, told a radically different story. Obviously under stress, often stumbling over his words, sweating profusely in the stuffy courtroom, and wiping his brow and around his lips with a white handkerchief, the lawyer denied that at their first meeting Scott had named possible witnesses to support his alibi. Often, too, when Judge Atkins asked him difficult questions, Kuhnke retreated into forgetfulness. Early in the questioning, the judge asked him about the first magistrate's hearing.

Judge Atkins: "What preparation did you do prior to this first hearing?"

Kuhnke: "I tried to find out as much as possible about the case through the conversation that—the evidence that they had on him through Major Roach and others."

"You used Major Roach to find out what evidence there was against Private Scott?"

"I knew that he was over here. He had contact with his counterpart, and it was a valid—yes, I used him for that purpose—initially, I called up—"

"What was Major Roach able to find out for you?"

"I can't recall at this time because I talked to a lot of other people. . . ."

"What other avenues did you explore other than using Major Roach to find out what evidence there might be?"

"I don't recall at the moment, Your Honor, but I made a number of other inquiries, as many as I could."

Judge Atkins asked about the forensic tests sent to the FBI laboratory between the first and second magistrate's hearings. "What were those tests of . . . do you remember specifically of what?"

"I don't remember specifically, but—all the tests that—a good law-enforcement organization would take."

"The results of those tests were delivered to whom?"

"I don't know the answer to that, but I was told they were negative or inconclusive, and that was borne out at the hearing."

"Who told you this?"

"I don't know—perhaps Major Roach."

Kuhnke testified that contrary to Scott's claim, he had between 150 and 175 contacts with him between his being retained and the trial, about a quarter of them face-to-face.

Judge Atkins probed Kuhnke's use of Lori Jackson, and Kuhnke admitted that he had asked her to develop contacts with all alibi witnesses. And the judge asked him, "Why did you not interview Ruby Hills?"

Kuhnke: "Lori was doing a good job. She had apparently established a good rapport with her."

Judge Atkins: "Did you ever visit the Spanish Gardens Apartments, or Zayre's department store, or the potential site of the offense?"

"I know where they—many times. I know where they all are. I have lived in this area for ten years."

"In preparation for your presentation of the defense of Corporal Scott, did you visit these places?"

"No, it was unnecessary. . . ."

"Did you ever go out to the part of the Marine Corps base where there was some evidence of—that the victim was found by a passing motorist, or—"

"I have been by there several times. I knew approximately where it was."

"In preparation for this case?"

"No, I asked—that was one of the things I asked Mrs. Jackson to do. . . ."

"Now, I would like to ask you what method did you use in preparing the witnesses for their actual testimony?"

"I didn't prep any of the witnesses. I expected them to tell the truth and to respond truthfully to any questions on cross-examination."

After questioning Kuhnke about his experience as a lawyer, Judge Atkins called a recess till the following morning.

(All that day, during the extensive questioning conducted in the courtroom, Lori periodically left her front-row seat and wandered the hallway just to check the mood of the Marines walking through the area. In general she sensed that most of the leathernecks just breezed in and out of the area on their business and seemed uninterested in the courtroom drama. However, she did notice the presence of several more men in the dark business suits, whom she assumed were NIS agents, loitering around the benches where witnesses waited to be called. Not that she saw anything out of the ordinary, but as a precaution, because their presence did have a "scary, intimidating effect," she explained later, she got some of her civil-rights activists from inside the courtroom to sit on the witness benches to preclude any possible pressure tactics the NIS agents might be tempted to try.)

The Washington Post next morning, headlining its story CON-VICTED MARINE SEEKS NEW TRIAL IN RAPE CASE, mentioned that Kuhnke admitted to Judge Atkins, "I was convinced that the government didn't have a case." The hearing was expected to continue for two more days, the story said, and after that it would be up to the Court of Military Review "to let stand the original guilty verdict, order a new trial or dismiss the charges against Scott." It quoted Judge Atkins saying that a ruling was not expected for several months.

On that second day, Major Thomson took over the questioning of Kuhnke. In theory it was in the government's interest to give the attorney the benefit of the doubt regarding his handling of Scott's defense, protecting the court-martial verdict. Thus it came as a surprise when the prosecutor subjected Kuhnke to a vigorous and penetrating interrogation.

He got Kuhnke to admit to him, too, that he didn't think the government had a good case against Scott, that it would never get to trial, and therefore he didn't think it necessary to review in any detail with him his defense strategy or what witnesses he, Kuhnke, might call. Major Thomson asked him whether or not he had pursued the question of the rape—had it been proven that the rape ever actually had been committed? Kuhnke admitted he never did because "I was convinced the rape had occurred."

Major Thomson: "What convinced you?"

Kuhnke: "The NIS investigation."

"Did you and Scott ever discuss expert witnesses?"

"He suggested expert witnesses. They cost money, a lot of money."

"Did it ever occur to you that expert witnesses should be called?"

"Yes, I considered."

"And what did you decide?"

"I decided against it."

"Why?"

"I was convinced they weren't needed."

"Did you have the wherewithal to have expert witnesses testify?"

"I said, Major, it costs money, a lot of money, for expert witnesses."

"That's fine, Mr. Kuhnke, but that's not answering my question. Did you in defending Corporal Scott have the wherewithal to have expert witnesses testify?"

"I suppose I could have gotten the money if I thought they were needed."

"If you would have had the money, would the expert witnesses have testified?"

"They were not needed."

"Mr. Kuhnke, in going to trial, you stated that you didn't prep any of the witnesses."

"That's right. I had talked—I had—"

"Wait. Wait. What was Corporal Scott charged with?"

"Attempted murder, rape, sodomy, forceful abduction. We had talked about the case for at least—at least 175 times."

"And you didn't prep the witnesses?"

"I didn't prep them, no."

"Did you prepare Corporal Scott?"

"I didn't have to."

"Why not?"

"Because—because he professed his innocence . . . I told him to tell the truth. . . ."

"Mr. Kuhnke . . . have you testified at a trial?"

"I haven't testified at a trial before. Strike—I take that back. In a civil case years and years ago . . ."

"Considering what Corporal Scott was charged with, knowing that you were a lawyer and haven't testified a whole lot, assuming that Corporal Scott hasn't testified a whole lot, you didn't find it necessary to prepare him for his testimony?"

"No."

After a recess, John Leino began his cross-examination. He hammered at the fact, admitted by Kuhnke, that for a substantial part of his information about the crime evidence, he relied on NIS reports and did not verify those reports himself. Therefore, concluded Leino, Kuhnke was never in a position to dispute those NIS reports; he merely accepted them as accurate.

In a discussion with Kuhnke over his pretrial motion questioning the Marines' jurisdiction, because the crime scene was never found, Kuhnke said he sent Lori Jackson out to the area, and then put her on the stand, "on rather the spur of the moment."

Leino: "On the spur of the moment, you put a witness on with regard to where the victim was found, which was part of your defense?"

Kuhnke: "No. That was evident from the report. I would have gotten that through—I would have gotten that information through Lindner—"

"So you relied on the chief investigator, this time, his report, to assist you in establishing a defense. Is that correct?"

"Yes, establish a defense that the crime scene wasn't found. And they readily admitted it."

"But they found a blood trail?"

"I'm not sure it was her blood trail."

"How are you sure they found a blood trail?"

"There was a report that a blood trail was found."

"And who wrote that report?"

"I do not know."

"Might it have been an NIS report?"

"It probably was."

"So again you relied on the prosecution to establish possible defense information. Is that correct?"

"It was in my interest to do so at that time, counsel."

Under Leino's cross examination, Kuhnke said repeatedly that he didn't subpoena or call a number of the witnesses Scott had suggested because he felt their testimony was unimportant or might even be damaging. He said he didn't go out to places such as Zayre's or Dumfries Pharmacy to check out Scott's story or talk to the personnel, "because I had other people doing it for me."

Before closing out his cross-examination, Leino referred once again to the laywer's negative attitude toward the use of expert witnesses on Scott's behalf. He asked him, "Didn't you think that it might have been important to call in a forensic expert and an expert opinion with regard to the possibility that a man can rape a woman wearing a sweater in a car and not one fiber that is discovered, not one hair, matches? And in fact the only hair that is found is dissimilar. Didn't you think that that might be important to bring out to a panel of officers? That this is close to an impossibility?"

Kuhnke: "All of the tests were either negative or inconclusive."

"Did you think it might be important?"

"It wasn't necessary."

"It wasn't necessary to have a forensic expert come in and establish in the minds of the court the significance of the results of these tests, not just the fact that they were negative, but based on the allegations of the government that there was a rape, and not one fiber matched? And the one piece of forensic evidence that was found, a Negroid hair, two inches long, didn't match Lindsey Scott?"

"I think it would have been unnecessary. It would have been expensive and unnecessary to have a forensic-evidence expert there."

Finally, Leino asked him: "Do you have confidence that the verdict was correct?"

Kuhnke: "I think there was a miscarriage of justice in this case."

Gary Myers took over the questioning of Kuhnke then, assuring the judge that he intended to be brief. Myers said that an area that interested him particularly was Kuhnke's role as an investigator. And quietly, gently, he set a snare for the lawyer, and Kuhnke stepped in it.

Myers: "When you were with the CIA, investigating background checks and sensitive matters, I think you put it, how did you do that? How did you physically effect investigations? I'm not looking for any national security secrets here."

Kuhnke: "You're not going to get any."

"I just need to know how you did it."

"How you conduct an investigation?"

"Well, did you send people out in the field, Mr. Kuhnke?"

"Yes. I did it myself—"

"You went out in the field yourself?"

"For a short time, for a couple of years."

"Now, why did you go out in the field, Mr. Kuhnke? Why did you visit people and talk to them?"

"It's usually the most reliable way to get information."

"Thank you, Mr. Kuhnke. With respect to your role as a

criminal lawyer, is it your view that those of us who practice in the criminal bar have a duty to go out in the field and investigate, or do you think it's our place to sit behind a desk and make phone calls?"

"It depends. It depends on the situation."

"Is there ever a criminal case, Mr. Kuhnke, where witnesses are involved or documents are involved where it's appropriate to do nothing but sit in your office and make phone calls?"

"Lead counsel—do you expect the lead counsel to do that in all cases?"

"Thank you for your answer, Mr. Kuhnke. Now, isn't the truth of the matter, Mr. Kuhnke, that you know as well as I do that the best way to conduct an investigation in any matter is in the field? And that the real reason you didn't do what you and I both know you should have done is because the dollars weren't there to do it? Isn't that accurate, Mr. Kuhnke?"

"That's not accurate."

"It was just a matter of dollars and cents, wasn't it?"

"No, it wasn't."

"It was easier to send Lori Jackson—"

"It was not a matter of dollars and cents."

"I have no further questions, Your Honor. Thank you for your indulgence."

Lieutenant Colonel Messer, who then took over cross-examination for the government, asked Kuhnke why he thought there was a miscarriage of justice.

Kuhnke went on at some length, saying that he felt the investigation was improper. "I am convinced," he said, "that given the circumstances in this case, it would be difficult, not impossible, for a black man to have a fair trial, the only black man, the only CID officer on duty at that time."

The prosecutor sneered back at Kuhnke, saying that this was "sour grapes, because you couldn't deliver what you promised, and that was an acquittal in this case."

"It's not sour grapes," Kuhnke insisted.

Before the third day of the hearing, Lori conferred with John Leino. She told him that she had talked to Ruby Hills, and the

Zayre's security guard assured her that she was ready to take the stand that day and reaffirm the statement she had made on *60 Minutes* that she had checked her security records and placed Scott in the store on the evening of the crime.

Ruby Hills, however, was not the only person on Lori's mind that morning, or even the most important. "John," she said, "last night, after court recessed, I tried to talk to Major Thomson, and he seemed very uncomfortable about a lot of things. In my heart, John, I know something about this case is bothering Thomson."

As to what, if anything, might be disturbing the government prosecutor, neither of them could hazard a guess. They let the subject pass (and it was not to surface until much, much later in this drama).

As Lori walked down the hallway leading to the courtroom that morning, aware that she was destined to be the second witness called (after Major Roach), she carried under her arm all of the daily papers that contained major stories about the hearing. This thrilled her. She knew that her persistence in getting the *60 Minutes* story televised had helped stimulate the media turnout. She counted fifteen major print and TV reporters in the courtroom: Associated Press, United Press International, *The Washington Post,* which had assigned Lee Hockstader, one of their brightest reporters, to do a daily, detailed story. She saw old friends from her civil-rights-demonstrations days in Washington—Jim Clark, the Emmy Award-winning reporter for WJLA-TV, the ABC affiliate in Washington, and Joe Johns of WRC-TV, the NBC-TV affiliate.

This time, thought Lori, unlike the limited court-martial coverage, the truth would be reported on a daily basis, throughout the United States, and particularly to the lawmakers in Washington. And the publicity, combined with a public outcry, would surely result in a reversal of the court-martial decision and at least a new trial for Lindsey Scott.

The testimony of Major Roach, and following him the testimony of Lori, was not notably significant; both confirmed that much of Ervan Kuhnke's work on Scott's defense, when it was conducted at all, had been by telephone. Lori stated that on her own, though with Kuhnke's encouragement, she had tracked down

possible alibi witnesses, including the most important of them—
indeed, the key alibi witness—Ruby Hills.

At seventeen minutes past one that afternoon, Ruby Hills took
the stand and gave the assembled media people their "hot" story of
the day. No longer at Zayre's, she had become a licensed private
investigator for Maryland and Virginia and was working for the
government full-time.

Under tough questioning by Judge Atkins, the prosecution, and
Gary Myers, Ruby Hills stuck to her unequivocal statement that
she could place Lindsey Scott at Zayre's between 8:15 and 8:45 on
the night of April 20, precisely the time when the attack on Judy
Connors was taking place. Major Thomson tried to shake her
testimony, but failed.

The crucial part of her testimony, challenged by the government
as "improved memory" because during the court-martial she could
not pin down the exact date, was why she could now be so certain
it was the night of April 20. Ruby explained that at the time she
was first contacted by Lori Jackson, she was distracted by the
recent death of her mother, she knew nothing about the Scott case,
nobody had ever asked her to recheck all her records, and she was
rushed into court in utter confusion without preparation.

It wasn't until after the court-martial that she had been given the
opportunity to double-check her records, additional records, and
by looking at photos of the men she had arrested that night for
shoplifting, she was able to "marry up" Scott to those two men and
place him in Zayre's that same night. And the photos of persons
arrested for shoplifting were not kept with arrest records, but
separately, "in boxes all the way back in a little cubbyhole in the
back of the store."

Myers: "And until you saw those pictures, Mrs. Hills, the best
you could say was, 'I checked my records and I saw that there
were two busts on April the twentieth, and I can tell you from my
police experience that this was the person in the store, Corporal
Scott, at the time, but I can't yet tell you whether he was there the
same date because I have to see the pictures of these two men. But
once I saw them I knew."

Hills: "That is correct."

"Now, Mrs. Hills, I want you to tell this court when you finally got about the business of looking at the pictures of those shop-lifters."

"After I was called into court and testified, no one contacted me again, so I never researched anything. I did not look at those pictures and confirm anything until I was contacted by Mr. Scott's new attorney, Mr. John Leino."

"And when was that?"

"After the man was tried and convicted."

"And it is now your testimony, under oath, that on the night of April twentieth, 1983, between the hours of 8:15 and 8:30, one Corporal Lindsey Scott was present in Zayre's department store?"

"That is correct."

Following cross-examination by Major Thomson and further questioning by Myers, the judge excused Ruby Hills and was about to call the final witness, Pam Biller, when Myers spoke up and, referring to Ruby's testimony, moved for the "dismissal of all charges and specifications against Corporal Lindsey Scott" and asked the court "to grant that motion now" on the grounds that "under cross-examination a witness provided an absolute defense to the crime alleged."

Judge Atkins said he would defer the ruling until after the final witness was called.

Whatever Pam Biller had to say was at this point anticlimactic; the entire courtroom was holding its collective breath waiting for the judge's decision on Myers's motion. Reporters were scribbling madly, ready to rush out to telephone in their stories should the judge agree to a dismissal of charges; it would be a sensation.

As expected, Pam Biller could add little of importance to the proceedings—not after Ruby Hills's testimony. Biller testified that she remembered Scott coming in to Zayre's and buying a Coke from her, but she could not be precise about the date.

Judge Atkins then said, addressing counsel for both sides, "Well, where do we go from here?"

Where they went was into protracted legal arguments on what options the judge had in his decision. The defense argued that despite the limitations of the DuBay hearing as solely an eviden-tiary hearing, he had the right to make a decision to dismiss. Major

Thomson argued, to the contrary, that the judge could only act in one capacity, that of a fact finder, and only the convening authority, that is, Major General Twomey, could dismiss the charges.

Judge Atkins called a short recess to deliberate. Seven minutes later, at 3:42 P.M., he decreed that "the defense motion for a dismissal of the charges and specifications against Private Scott is denied. I have no power beyond that which is given me in the order."

Myers then said that based on that decision, he would move for a deferral of Scott's sentence until the Court of Military Review ruled on the question of a new trial. Myers pointed out that there was no prospect of Scott leaving the community, since his wife and child were there. "We feel that freeing him to his family, with appropriate restrictions as required by the court, is in the interests of justice."

Again Judge Atkins refused, saying he did not have the power to do this; it was up to Twomey. Myers asked if it was at least possible for Scott to remain at the Quantico brig, instead of being returned to Leavenworth, and once again Judge Atkins said that this decision would be up to the general. "Court dismissed."

As Myers was making these emotional appeals Leino asked Scott, sitting there immobile, his face betraying nothing, "Are you all right?" Scott only nodded. In the visitors' gallery, however, friends and family openly showed their anger; Scott's mother and father were visibly shaken by the judge's decision. Scott's friend Josh, who had driven up from Jacksonville, Florida, began swearing at the prosecutors who were trying to make their way out of the courtroom.

"What kind of Uncle Tom are you!" Josh screamed at Major Thomson, who was black, lunging at him. Two male civil-rights activists restrained him as Thomson turned his head and forced a path out to the hallway.

As Leino left the courtroom with Myers and Lori, a reporter shouted, "What's next, John?"

Emotionally and physically exhausted, he responded that they would be pushing Twomey for a dismissal of charges rather than a retrial, because the people who could have given Scott an alibi in April 1983 were never interviewed and their memories have faded.

Said Leino: "How can Lindsey Scott ever have a trial with due justice when we know there are people out there who are lost forever."

19

The ball now was firmly back in Lieutenant General Twomey's court. No one who knew the general would venture to say that he might dismiss the charges against Scott—one of his options. Leino and Myers's request to do so was no more than a gesture. Nor did the defense lawyers expect Twomey to release Scott from the brig pending a decision from the Court of Military Review.

Scott's lawyers read Twomey accurately, as it turned out. The general wrote to them saying he considered their request for dismissal "premature," but he would review the complete range of options once he received the transcript of the DuBay hearing, the findings of Judge Atkins, and conferred with the staff judge advocate, Colonel Cassady. Meanwhile, said the general, he would not release Scott from the brig.

Grateful for any small mercies from the Quantico commandant, Leino told a reporter from the *Potomac News* that he was cheered by the fact that Twomey had at least agreed to review the case quickly. "He's a general," Leino said. "He can make decisions.

"We're glad he's taken it on himself to review our request, and have faith that he'll make a well-considered decision—whatever it is," said Leino.

Lori, too, was encouraged. "It's really a positive step," she told *The Free Lance-Star*. "To get a response from the general so quickly is very positive."

Prosecutor Lieutenant Colonel Jim Messer, however, immediately dashed this hope with a statement that he believed the general would turn down the requests. "Obviously," he said, "the general can do whatever he wants. But I don't think he would substitute his judgment for the jury's or the Court of Military Review. He's like a rung in the ladder.

"That's why I don't think he'll dismiss the conviction in some gigantic burst of mercy. The general is a functionary in many ways."

To a number of seasoned observers of the military, this was rather a curious statement for a lieutenant colonel to make about the limits of his commanding general's power. Certainly it contrasted sharply with John Leino's assessment of Twomey's authority. A blatant case of lèse-majesté by the powerful prosecutor? A planted "leak" on which way Twomey was leaning? Or perhaps a preemptive strike by Messer to circumscribe the general's options.

Several days later Lee Hockstader of *The Washington Post* wrote a page-one story (for the Metro section) titled QUANTICO QUESTIONS LINGER — NEW TESTIMONY BOOSTS CHANCE OF MARINE'S RETRIAL. While reviewing the Scott case in his lengthy article, Hockstader brought out several new items of information: military prosecutors acknowledged that the testimony of Ruby Hills weakened their case and gave Scott a better chance to obtain a retrial. But if there was a retrial, Ruby's credibility was likely to be attacked. Hockstader quoted an unnamed Marine officer: " 'What she said now is going to be bounced off what she said before.' "

According to the article, if a retrial was ordered, it wasn't certain Judy Connors would return to testify. " 'She wants to put it behind her, she wants to forget it,' " reported Hockstader, quoting "one Marine source who is close to the case but insisted on anonymity."

(Lori told author Ellis A. Cohen that Judy was now divorced and living with her parents in Columbus, Ohio.)

Hockstader went on to say that critics of the military had charged that "top brass at Quantico signaled the all-military jury to convict Scott." The "firing" of Lieutenant Colonel Harry for releasing Scott from confinement was proof of this, the critics said, though the Marines always claimed there was no connection, that Harry was due to retire shortly anyway. However, Hockstader quoted Harry saying that the jury "knew exactly what happened to me. And they didn't want it to happen to them. That's the problem with military justice. It leaves a lot to be desired."

In an editorial headlined PRIVATE SCOTT DESERVES A SECOND TRIAL, the local *Potomac News* asked for justice for Scott: "We do not presume to know whether Private Scott is innocent or guilty," the editorial stated. "However, it is clear that he was not thoroughly defended against charges so serious that he was convicted to thirty years at hard labor. . . . Justice for the young Marine is the only essential aspect of this case. At this juncture there is only one way to determine whether Private Scott was properly convicted—the General [Twomey] should order a new trial."

The general, however, was not then prepared to make the swift decision Lori and Scott's defense attorneys hoped for—because the prosecutors on March 1 requested the reopening of the DuBay hearings. Major Thomson and Lieutenant Colonel Messer did not want to wait for the possibility of a retrial in order to attack the credibility of Ruby Hills. They wanted to do it now, and so they introduced in court affidavits from two Prince William County police officers who claimed that Ruby Hills once lied in court and could not be trusted to tell the truth.

The two officers alleged that while applying for a job as a police officer in September 1981, Ruby told them she had lied while testifying in court about a shoplifter she'd arrested while a security officer at Zayre's.

Ruby denied it. "My life's an open book," she said. "I have nothing to hide."

John Leino objected to the entire exercise as irrelevant. "It is patently unfair and prejudiced to allow a display like this to go on," he said to Judge Atkins. The allegations, he said, were based on meetings four years earlier that took perhaps fifteen minutes. "It still boils down to one thing," said Leino. "Where is the evidence attacking her testimony? It's the old thing . . . if you don't have the evidence, you attack the people. The government is talking about 'bad acts.' Does the government have convictions of bad acts? Does the government have documentation of bad acts? No. They have innuendo. Insinuation. Opinion. Now I understand why people don't want to get involved in the system, because their very character, their very life, is put under the microscope.

"This had nothing to do with whether or not the defendant was afforded due process."

Judge Atkins agreed: the information was irrelevant, and except for allowing the affidavits to be entered into the permanent record of the DuBay hearings, the government's request to reopen the hearings was denied.

Leino and Lori left the courtroom with relief at a victory in one small battle, and Scott, as he was marched back to the brig, flashed them a smile.

Three weeks later—still with no word from Lieutenant General Twomey—Scott was found unconscious in his cell. He was rushed to a local hospital and then transferred to the Bethesda Naval Hospital, where he was kept overnight for observation. The following morning he was returned to the Quantico brig. Apparently, according to a Quantico spokesperson, Scott's problem was an adverse reaction to medication he was given in the early evening for a crick in the neck. "The next thing he knew," said Lori, who had rushed to Bethesda as soon as she got the news, "he had tubes down his throat and IVs in his arm." According to her, doctors initially were unable to say what was wrong with Scott, but at one point sent in a psychiatrist to see him. One doctor did tell Scott he thought the illness was psychogenic, brought on by mental distress.

Quantico officials said that because of confidentiality laws they were precluded from releasing information about the medication he had taken. However, Major Rick Stepien, the public-affairs officer, told Lori and the press, "I do not know how he got sick. The cause of his distress has not been determined." He described Scott's condition as "drowsiness and nonresponsiveness," and said doctors told him Scott had fully recovered by the time he had reached the hospital at Bethesda.

According to Lori, this was not the first time Scott had been rushed to the hospital; two months earlier he had been taken in for stomach pains and vomiting. "This is crazy," she told *The Free Lance-Star*. "Someone ought to have some answers." She said that since the onset of these attacks, rumors had been flying around Louisville that Scott had died in the hospital, but the Marines would not admit it or let anyone see the body.

Lori kept pressing Major Stepien about Scott's condition.

Annoyed by and suspicious of what she considered to be stalling and prevarication regarding the true state of Scott's recurring illness, she eventually got into a fierce argument with the major. Finally she told him that either the Marines allowed Scott to hold his own press conference or she would organize one for herself.

Events overtook Lori's demand and her threat. The following day Lieutenant General Twomey issued a terse statement saying that after reviewing all the evidence and the DuBay transcript, he was making no decision about a new trial but sending Scott's appeal back to the Navy–Marine Corps Court of Military Review. Worse yet, Twomey said he was transferring Scott back to Leavenworth "as soon as possible" to await the court's verdict.

That night Lori told her husband, Paul, that a dramatic step was needed to attract attention to the "inhumane treatment of Scott," who had again, after being found sick in his cell, been taken to the Bethesda hospital. She would go on a hunger strike to protest and try to persuade Twomey to allow Scott to stay at Quantico. Both her family and John Leino tried to dissuade her, concerned about her health.

She began taking only water, no food, though admitting that it might all be in vain, that the Marines "might not do anything. I might die, but it's just something I feel I have to do. As mean as they've been, they won't care about the state of my mind, but it will prove something to the people. There is nothing else I can do."

On the seventh day of her hunger strike, Lori was interviewed by Deborah Bowers, editorial-page editor of the *Potomac News*. Lori told the editor that she didn't *think* Scott was innocent, she knew it. She said she had gotten to know Scott's moods and the way he thought, that on her last visit to him, at the hospital in Bethesda, he told her that even if his lawyers could get the charges against him dismissed, he didn't want it. He wanted to be proven innocent. "Those aren't the words of a guilty man," Lori said to the editor.

Ms. Bowers wrote: "The most important thing to Lori Jackson is to do what she thinks is right. Her goal, she says, is not to prove Private Lindsey Scott's innocence, but to protect the right— everyone's right—to due process." (She had to mention this over and over again to some of her daughters, who didn't believe in Scott's innocence, Lori confided to author Ellis A. Cohen. Two of them in fact were convinced Scott was a rapist.) "She sees the Scott case," the editor continued, "as something that goes beyond the bounds of the Quantico Marine Base. To Lori Jackson what has happened to Private Lindsey Scott is a threat to what America is supposed to be."

Lori's family and friends were worried about her health; she appeared to be weakening at the end of her first week of fasting, but Lori assured them she was fine. Meanwhile, under direct orders from Lieutenant General Twomey, Lindsey Scott was taken in the middle of the night from the Bethesda Naval Hospital and flown by military transport to Ft. Leavenworth prison in Kansas. He was not given a chance to say good-bye to anyone; neither was his wife or any of his family or his lawyers notified of the transfer until it was completed.

This was precisely what Lori had feared and expected. Exasperated, she realized that her hunger strike was useless. It was another round in the battle lost, she said to her family and to Scott's lawyers, but she would go on. She would build back her strength for the march in Washington she had already planned for a week later, on Saturday, April 20. Scott's parents, James and Mildred Scott, were preparing to journey fourteen hours from Louisville to take part in the march, accompanied by ministers and social-justice activists.

The march, which passed by the White House, was a huge success from the point of view of media coverage. Hundreds followed Lori down Pennsylvania Avenue carrying signs and chanting for the immediate release of Scott. Demonstrators handed out a two-page fact sheet about the Lindsey Scott case that had been prepared and paid for by the Kentucky Alliance Against Racist and Political Repression.

After a long, hot summer of waiting impatiently for something hopeful to happen, word finally came down to Leino and Myers that a hearing before the Navy–Marine Corps Court of Military Review was scheduled for October 2. When the media broke that news, *60 Minutes,* coincidentally, aired the first of what were to be three reruns of the Scott story. After the original story was shown, Morley Safer reported that Scott's attorneys would soon be appearing before the Court of Military Review. Safer stated that this time their argument would include the testimony of a credible witness who could give Scott an alibi.

Lori was one of the some forty people who crowded into the small, stuffy room at the Washington Navy yard to witness the proceedings. About half were Navy–Marine brass, the other half supporters of Scott—who did not attend. John Leino said Scott didn't want to come: "It would be too emotional for him to be transported all the way from Kansas to D.C. and then sent immediately back. I think we've had enough of that—and just this past year."

Fundamentally, both government and defense could do little more before the three court judges than reiterate the arguments they had employed at the DuBay hearing, which the judges had already examined in the transcript. Eloquence in oral presentation could strengthen those arguments, however.

The new face at the prosecutor's table, Lieutenant Commander John Holt, told the judges that Kuhnke's defense of Scott "was within the wide range of respectable counsel." Kuhnke made "reasonable attempts" to locate, interview, and prepare witnesses.

Gary Myers, arguing for Scott, countered with a scathing description of Kuhnke's defense as "sloppy lawyering, plain and simple. In this case, the prejudice is not only real, it cannot be repaired."

Said John Leino: "Did the lawyer screw up, and if he did screw up, did it affect the outcome of the trial?"

Myers pointed out, as one example, Pam Biller, the soda jerk at Zayre's who remembered selling Scott a Coke at the precise time of the crime, but couldn't recall the date because she wasn't shown recognizable photos of him until five months later. The day after the crime she had been unable to identify him from indistinct NIS mug shots. "We will never know what she could have told us on that spring day in April 1983 . . . a new trial will never make her know. She is lost forever to the defense."

Lieutenant Commander Holt countered with, "It is mere speculation in this case to say Pam Biller ever could be certain. It is pure speculation that Pam Biller's evidence is lost."

Then Myers brought up the testimony of Ruby Hills at the DuBay hearing. At Scott's court-martial, Myers said, she was "improperly prepared to testify," because she was not interviewed by a trained investigator or Kuhnke prior to the trial. Had she been asked the right questions and pressed to search her records, said Myers, she could have testified unequivocally at Scott's trial that he was at the store at the time of the attack. Instead, it was only after the conviction that John Leino's questioning helped her to recall photographs that jogged her memory and enabled her to state under oath that she had seen Scott at Zayre's on the night and at the time Judy Connors claimed he had raped her and tried to kill her.

Prosecutor Holt challenged Ruby's DuBay testimony, however. "Her recantation is bizarre," he said. "The government asks the court to scrutinize the credibility of Ruby Hills. She is not a credible witness. The real question is, what, if anything, refreshed the recollection of Ruby Hills?

"The United States wants justice," Holt said. "The United States does not want an innocent man going to jail. The defendant did receive a fair trial . . . not a perfect trial, but a fair trial."

The one-day hearing came to an end, and now there was nothing anyone could do but wait anxiously for the court's decision. As before, it could order a new trial, dismiss the charges, or uphold the conviction—but the court this time could not refer the appeal back to Lieutenant General Twomey.

As the weeks passed with no word from the court, everyone began to get fidgety. "This is not a situation of no news is good news," said Lori. "You've got an innocent Marine sitting behind bars waiting for those idiots to make a decision." She was sure a retrial was inevitable, she said, but "they're doing everything they can possibly do to delay it."

Just before Christmas, with still no decision, Lee Hockstader of *The Washington Post*, who had continued to monitor the case closely, wrote a major updated article headlined DECISION STILL AWAITED IN MARINE'S APPEAL, with a subheading *Judges Delay Decision in Case of Rape, Attempted Murder*. According to

Hockstader, there were signs that "the judges may be sharply divided." There had been several indications that the court was having a difficult time deciding.

On Friday, December 20, according to the reporter, the senior member of the panel, Navy Captain John W. Kercheval II, said that two or three rough drafts of the final decision had been circulated among the judges and it was once again with the typist. Kercheval said he expected a decision to be handed down by January 15, then reconsidered, and said it would come at the end of January.

"I honestly don't know if the three judges are going to stay in their current positions" on the case, Kercheval said in an interview (wrote Hockstader). "This is one of the most difficult cases I've been involved in."

(On December 28, Lori Jackson wrote a long letter to author Ellis A. Cohen expressing her frustration at the long delay in the court's decision and her fear of the military, its judicial system, and its political power. "The military is used to fighting with weapons," she wrote. "And, since there are no weapons involved, those that we are using"—the courts—"are out of the norm for them. We"—the supporters of an individual's rights—"shall remain victorious if we continue to use the news media . . . then, add the loyal image of a trusting Marine who still believes in the military and our system and we get the most powerful ingredient of all: a sympathetic public ear.")

On January 22, 1986, the Navy–Marine Corps Court of Military Review announced its decision: the divided court, by a two-to-one majority, upheld Lindsey Scott's conviction for rape, sodomy, abduction, and attempted murder.

20

The court's decision struck a stunning blow to Scott and his family, Lori, and his defense attorneys. The roller-coaster ride of the preceding months, those alternating bouts of elation and discouragement, had taken their emotional toll. Now, once again, all of them, shaken, bitterly dismayed, were being forced to reach deep down to find the physical and spiritual resources to continue the fight.

To Leino and Myers, the reasoning behind the decisions of the two judges in the majority was particularly galling. In refusing to set aside the guilty verdict on the grounds of ineffective assistance by defense counsel, Judge Michael D. Rapp, a Navy captain, wrote, regarding Kuhnke, that "we are astonished . . . by his failure to effectively interview *any* alibi witness under the circumstance of this case. All this is especially troubling to us. . . . Such performance is hardly indicative of a 'diligent and conscientious advocate.'"

Yet, having expressed this negative opinion of Kuhnke's defense work, the judge said the prosecution case was so strong that Scott would have been found guilty anyway. "Despite our misgivings about the quality of Mr. K's representation," wrote Judge Rapp, "we need not make a determination that he was actually ineffective but instead may proceed directly to the issue of prejudice." The judge went on to review the entire case, including the court-martial record and the DuBay hearing, casting doubt upon the credibility of Ruby Hills and concluding that "the appellant's pretrial statements to criminal investigators and his in-court testimony, rather than exculpating him, actually reveal

244

direct evidence of a criminal state of mind and circumstantial evidence of guilt when viewed in relation to all the evidence of record. . . . Furthermore, the evidence of record could reasonably lead the triers of fact to conclude, as we do, that the appellant perjured himself at the trial. . . . We believe the appellant's perjured testimony reflects a guilty mind in regard to matters of significance bearing directly upon his guilt or innocence and we cannot reconcile such testimony, given the evidence in this case, with any explanation other than the appellant's desperate attempt to avoid conviction and punishment for the heinous crimes he perpetrated."

Judge Rapp was joined in his decision by Judge John E. Grant, Jr., a Marine colonel.

Dissenting, the senior judge, Navy Captain John W. Kercheval II, wrote, "I find that Mr. K's failure to adequately investigate his client's alibi, upon which rested appellant's exclusive and entire defense, and his failure to provide even a modicum of preparation for the trial appearance of appellant's alibi witnesses, fall far below reasonable standards of conduct for a defense attorney. I find Mr. K's failure nothing short of astounding.

"My confidence in the outcome of the appellant's court-martial has been so sufficiently undermined by the evidence presented at the DuBay hearing that I would set aside the findings of guilty and sentence and return the record of trial to the convening authority authorizing a rehearing if practicable."

(Judge Kercheval's strong dissent coupled with his earlier statement in Lee Hockstader's *Washington Post* article that he didn't know if the judges were "going to stay in their current positions" led to a flock of rumors that the first, unofficial vote had been two-to-one in favor of Scott, but one of the two in favor had been encouraged to change his vote.)

Immediately following the court's announcement of its decision, Scott's lawyers issued a brief written statement:

> The decision of the Court of Military Review denying a new trial does not well serve the Constitution. Instead of protecting the rights of the individual, this decision serves to protect lawyers who require, not protection, but rather closer scrutiny.

The decision fails entirely to determine whether or not defense counsel provided an effective defense and concludes that, whatever defense counsel did or did not do, there was no prejudice to Private Scott because of substantial circumstantial evidence against Private Scott.

This conclusion is intellectually insupportable. When defense counsel fails to do his job, obviously the government is able to overpower a jury with the prosecution's side of the story. Ineffective counsel inherently causes prejudice.

The statement concluded that an appeal was being filed with the Court of Military Appeals.

This court, the military equivalent of the United States Supreme Court, is a three-judge panel of civilians, appointed for life by the sitting president of the United States. As with the U.S. Supreme Court, the Court of Military Appeals is not bound to consider all appeals sent to it; in fact, according to Thomas Granahan, the court clerk, the court traditionally takes only eight-to-ten percent of the some three thousand appeals filed annually.

Should the court refuse to hear Scott's appeal, his lawyers' only recourse would be to raise constitutional objections in a U.S. District Court to the procedures of the system of military justice. If the Court of Military Appeals hears his case and decides against him, then a final appeal could be made directly to the U.S. Supreme Court.

Scott's wife, Lola, interviewed by the *Potomac News,* said she was outraged by the court's decision. "I thought Lindsey would at least get a new trial." She said that Lindsey had been on a hunger strike and lost sixty pounds. He was tired and despondent. He had been so sure the court would order a new trial that he'd packed to go home. "I don't know how much more he can take," she said.

John Leino confirmed that Scott had been on a hunger strike during the long delay awaiting the court's decision, but that he had ended it "when he was able to readjust to the circumstances he found himself in. It must feel like being in hell," Leino said. "He's maintained all along that he's innocent."

Now, said Leino, there was nothing more they could do but wait to hear whether or not the Court of Military Appeals would consider the case. "I hate to say it," Leino commented, "but realistically it could be another year before this court makes a decision."

Typically, Lori Jackson met adversity head-on and considered this latest misfortune a challenge. She telephoned Lola Scott and lifted the distraught woman's spirits with encouraging words: "You can't quit," Lori said. "Not when you've come this far. We'll win in the end."

Next Lori contacted the staff of the Reverend Jesse Jackson, seeking his support. The prominent black civil-rights leader, head of the National Rainbow Coalition, who had sought the Democratic nomination for president in 1984, was now a political rising star. Though Jackson was away from Washington at the time, Lori spent more than four hours with his staff, presenting all the facts of the Scott case. She even called Joe Wershba from Jackson's office and got him to agree to send tapes of the *60 Minutes* show.

"What I wanted Jesse to do," Lori wrote author Ellis A. Cohen, "is meet with Lola to give her moral support, call Lindsey's parents, visit Lindsey in Kansas, and last but not least, organize a huge march at the White House and at the Marine Corps headquarters in Washington."

Lori said Jackson's staff was outraged at her account and would begin immediately to plan strategy to help Scott's case. Again her hopes rose; surely the intervention of a powerful advocate such as Jesse Jackson would get Scott free.

Scott himself was not infected with Lori's enthusiasm. He called author Ellis A. Cohen (collect) and moaned that he was going to "rot" in prison and "the truth would never be told." He said he was having difficulties with other inmates because they had been reading articles about him in the Kansas newspapers that disclosed that he had been in Quantico's elite Security Battalion.

"When I walk down certain corridors," Scott said to Cohen, "I get yelled at: 'Here comes the poooleese.'" He also said he now felt he had to be careful when he was in a recreational area for fear one of the prisoners would try to get at him. To occupy his time when he wasn't working in the kitchen, Scott said, he was reading law books in the prison library, and once a week or so he would call John Leino and throw ideas at him.

Early in February Jesse Jackson announced that he had committed himself to the campaign supporting Scott and would begin to mobilize local and national groups to publicize Scott's case. Craig Kirby, a Jackson aide, said the purpose was to give Scott "the opportunity for a fair hearing.

"We see the case as a clear example of injustice in the military system," Kirby said.

Jackson's aides set about contacting members of the Congressional Black Caucus and Bishop L. E. Willis, a Norfolk businessman and coordinator for the Virginia Rainbow Coalition, an arm of the organization through which Jackson ran his failed campaign for the Democratic presidential nomination.

Lori greeted the moves with her usual enthusiasm and optimism and, never missing an opportunity for press coverage, spoke to the *Potomac News* about it. "It's unfortunate that we as American citizens must resort to outside forces to ensure the implementation of our Constitution," she said. "But there comes a time when our system breaks down, and when this happens, it is our moral responsibility to make every peaceable effort possible to see that our Constitution stands. When it fails for one of us, we all suffer."

(Lori's relationship with Jesse Jackson and his staff deteriorated rapidly—another case of a disappointing experience with civil-rights groups blemishing her innate optimism. She had so much faith in the inherent goodness of people that though let down time and again by promises of help in the Scott case, she refused to become cynical. Following the announcement of Jesse Jackson's interest in Scott, she spent a great deal of her time traveling from her Dale City home to the Washington, D.C., headquarters of the Rainbow Coalition. There, according to Lori, she found herself being sent around on various Coalition projects that had nothing to do with Scott; the group's grand promises came to nothing—and she walked out.)

Thus, once more Lori was on the emotional roller coaster. On June 19, 1986, *The Washington Post,* under a small headline reading QUANTICO UNIT COMMAND CHANGE, broke the story that Lieutenant General David Twomey was retiring as commander at

Quantico and would be replaced at 9:30 A.M. the following morning by Lieutenant General Frank E. Petersen.

Petersen, fifty-four, a much-decorated Marine pilot with more than 350 combat missions through two wars—Korea and Vietnam—had the distinction of being the first black to become a Marine Corps pilot and the first black to become a Marine Corps three-star general. Quoted in *The Free Lance-Star*, Lieutenant General Petersen said, "As far as black is concerned, if you don't stub your toe, everything you do is a first. It could lead one on an ego trip, but it's meaningless. If you take away 'black,' hell, I'm like any other Marine."

Lori Jackson, perhaps needless to say, was ecstatic. She telephoned author Ellis A. Cohen with the news, shouting, "And he's black!" Lori said she planned to hold a two-day prayer vigil that this new, black general may be "the sign we've been waiting for."

Lori became even more hopeful when she learned that Gary Myers knew Petersen personally, had in fact represented him in a court case a number of years back, and remembered him as "an honest guy, a straight shooter." Surely, this, too, was an auspicious sign, Lori related to her family: the dreaded Twomey gone, and a black commanding general known personally by one of Scott's defense attorneys!

A week or so later (as he related to author Ellis A. Cohen and coauthor Milton J. Shapiro) John Leino received a telephone call at home. The caller, who had a Latino accent, would not give his name, but said he was a marine sergeant. He said he had a friend who was a messman (a waiter with a proper starched white coat and white cloth napkin over the arm) for senior Marine officers. The night previously, according to the caller's friend, he had been serving dinner at the home of the Marine Corps commandant, General P. X. Kelley. Lieutenant General Petersen was there. The commandant asked Petersen, according to the messman, what he intended to do about the Scott case.

Allegedly Petersen replied, "Don't worry, we're gonna get this guy."

Leino listened to all this and said to the anonymous caller, "I want to talk to this messman personally. Tell him to call me and use the name 'Axel Anderson' so I'll know who it is."

That telephone call never came, said Leino. "But it disturbed me. It could have been anything, a nut, someone with a grudge. Or it could have been true. Who could know? Everything about this case had become so bizarre, such a call didn't surprise me, it was just part of the crazy pattern. For some time I had been receiving death threats over the phone, calling me 'nigger lover' among the politer epithets. Lori had received threatening phone calls, too. We never went public with it, there was no point. I didn't take them seriously—well, maybe one or two. I remember finally getting so mad at one guy I yelled back at him, 'Fuck you! Come and get me!'"

Leino felt he had to tell Lori about the phone call, though he knew that nebulous as it was, the story would hurt her, cast a dark shadow over her high hopes about Lieutenant General Petersen. "But we—my wife, Patty, and I both—we were very close to Lori. We always told her everything," Leino said. "It made no sense to be a Pollyanna in this case. We knew we would get no favors from the Marines."

The subsequent experience of the former lieutenant colonel of Marines, Dick Harry, did nothing to raise anyone's hopes about Petersen. Some four weeks after the latter took command at Quantico, Harry sent him an impassioned, handwritten letter on behalf of Scott:

General Petersen, this letter is a plea for justice for a fine young Marine. You are the one who can make that happen. May God be your guide in this matter and all your decisions.

Your predecessor orchestrated a grave injustice to a fine young Marine and hence our Marine Corps. I ask you to look into the Lindsey Scott case and see what you find.

I witnessed lies, deceit, manufactured evidence, threats against me, and other nefarious actions perpetrated against Scott and myself. Ask anyone who knows me—I would be the first to shoot a guilty bastard, but I certainly would not bow to pressure to go against my convictions.

You have the opportunity to change the course of many lives. Please do something.

Harry's letter did no better with Petersen than his earlier one had with Twomey. It was simply ignored.

Over the long, hot summer of 1986 and into early fall, the Lindsey Scott case stagnated in limbo. The Court of Military Appeals presumably was contemplating the briefs filed by Scott's defense attorneys and by the government, Scott fretted and fumed in his cell at Leavenworth prison, Leino and Myers went about their business of earning a living while a few checks continued to trickle in against their $10,000 fee for representing Scott. Three years had now passed since his conviction; three years of battling with no end in sight. Three years of emotional highs and lows, of frustrations, of disappointments, of incarceration for Scott, of sleepless nights and sixteen-hour working days had left their mark on everyone.

For Lori Jackson, the ordeal had taken on even greater dimensions: her single-minded devotion to the Scott case had exerted tremendous stress on her marriage and family life. Her teenage daughters, in particular, were openly resentful of all the time she had been spending working to defend "some stranger." Her preoccupation with the Scott case was also creating a financial strain on the family. Lori was repeatedly rejected for jobs for which she was clearly qualified, a situation she and her husband ascribed to the high profile—indeed, in some quarters to the notoriety—she had won because of her work on the case. Paul, therefore, was being saddled with all the family's bills, which had been escalating alarmingly ever since Scott had been sent to Leavenworth, because he telephoned Lori regularly, collect, and the phone bills often reached $300 a month. Paul was reaching the limits of his tolerance; there were times he was sorely tempted to leave (none of Lori's seven children were his and he never adopted any of them), to tell Lori she would have to choose between her crusades and her family.

During a passionate family discussion of the situation, one of Lori's daughters angrily said she thought Scott was guilty, while another said she had an "eerie feeling" about him. "Why are you defending this man, Mom?" she asked. "What if he is really guilty?"

Many nights were spent in long debates about Scott, about the case in general, about Lori's obsession with it, and its effect on the family. As she had found it necessary to do from the very beginning, Lori explained to her children that the issue was not just the fate of Lindsey Scott; it was the pursuit of justice, it was for the sake of justice for all that she devoted her time and her energies to Scott's defense.

On November 11, 1986, a day of remembrance for the fallen in America's wars, *The Washington Post* (among others) ran a small inside-page story saying that Lindsey Scott had filed a $1.5-million malpractice suit against Ervan Kuhnke. The suit, in Prince William County Circuit Court, sought compensatory and punitive damages from Kuhnke, charging that the attorney failed to investigate the case or interview before the trial a key witness who might have been able to provide an alibi.

Kuhnke responded: "The case has no merit, it'll be defended. I may file a countersuit."

Lori was rather bemused by this civil suit of Scott's. She discovered that it had nothing to do with Leino and Myers. They were not handling the case; Scott had found some other attorney to represent him. She wondered (as she mentioned to her family) how Scott expected to win it when thus far all the military courts had judged that while Kuhnke's efforts in defense of Scott left much to be desired, whatever he might have done would have had no effect on the outcome of the court-martial: Scott would have been found guilty.

This was in any case a minor distraction to Lori; late fall in the Virginia/Maryland area was a time when the pleasant aroma of burning leaves and wood smoke from suburban chimneys perfumed the evening air. The days were cool and pleasant and the rosy cheeks of children in the playgrounds heralded the coming winter. Like many a mother of a large brood, Lori was planning a sumptuous Thanksgiving dinner. Christmas was just weeks away, a time for rejoicing, for the giving of gifts, and for hope and prayer that the year 1987 would bring peace on earth and goodwill toward all men—and maybe, with the good Lord's help, as Lori expressed it, "tidings of comfort and joy" for Lindsey Scott.

A week before Thanksgiving Lori called author Ellis A. Cohen and, swearing him to secrecy, told him something that she said she was telling absolutely no one else.

She hadn't been feeling too well lately and had visited the family doctor, who had put her through a series of tests. The tests revealed that she had developed a small tumor in her stomach area. "I thought it was just high blood pressure," she said to Cohen, "because of all the waiting and the tension and the pressure of the case. But I don't want anyone to know about this. Not my family—they'll worry me too much. Not John—he has enough to worry about with Lindsey. And definitely not Lindsey—he'll panic, he'll think I'm deserting him. Also, since I'm in the press a lot with this case, the last thing in the world I want to become is a sideshow. So promise me you'll not tell *anybody*."

Cohen promised (with a great deal of unspoken reservations) but quietly asked Lori if she was going to put herself into a hospital.

"Ellis, heavens no," Lori said. "You forget a third of me is Cherokee. Before there were all the fancy doctors and hospitals, their methods were the only ways the medicine men could save the sick. I'll be seeing some of my people, very quietly, who will know how to heal me."

On Thanksgiving Day, as she was preparing the huge dinner, Lori suddenly felt sick—sick enough for Paul to rush her to the local hospital. The wonderful dinner disrupted, the family deeply worried now, they all agreed to postpone the festivities, so they wrapped up the turkey and stored it in the freezer, hoping Lori would return home the next day.

Lori did not return home the next day. She was kept in the hospital for several days. For the record, to her family and to everybody else, she said she had a "digestive" problem, caused by the strain of the Scott case. True enough, those close to her, such as John and Patty Leino, knew the case had created problems with her children.

Despite her protestations that she was actually fine, some of

Lori's children did begin to express their concern. Together one evening before Christmas of 1986, they questioned her: "Mom, are you really sick?"

In typical Lori fashion she laughed and replied, "Are you serious?"

21

The year of 1987 opened on an upbeat note. For the first time in many weeks Lori, John Leino, Gary Myers, Lindsey Scott, and his family could afford the luxury of a smile. The Court of Military Appeals announced early in January that it had agreed to hear the Scott case. John and Gary were ordered to present oral arguments before the court on February 23, in Washington, D.C., at its courtroom at 450 E Street Northwest.

For Lori, January brought a special present, one that sent her spirits soaring and that, once again, appeared to her to be an omen of better things. All of her adult life she had harbored a secret wish that one day she would find her "dream house," and had made a promise to herself that if ever she found it, nothing would stop her from getting it. So much of her life had been spent in cramped conditions, on military bases both in the United States and abroad, surrounded for the most part by her extended family.

She longed for privacy, a large, old house in a wooded glade where she could find peace, the early-morning quiet broken only by birdsong. In the middle of the night she would hear the hooting of the owls and the barking of the foxes in the deep woods. This was her dream.

One day, out driving with her husband, she stumbled on her dream house in Woodbridge, Virginia. It was exactly as she had pictured it, set far back off the road on a large plot of ground at the end of a long drive that led to the steps of the front porch. The house nestled in a veritable forest of ancient oak, mature birch, maple, jackpine, and dogwood that spread all the way up from the road.

She fell in love with it at first sight. The house was empty and for sale ("It was as though it was standing there waiting for me to find it," Lori confided to author Ellis A. Cohen), and true to her promise to herself, she got it. Within weeks she moved in, happier than she had been in recent memory. Her dream house acted like a balm that soothed the stings of her many disappointments with the Scott case and the friction within her family. And the pleasure of it helped her bear the pain of her illness.

(After she had settled in, author Cohen telephoned and asked her about her illness. She said that through her Native American connections she was meeting with "healers" trained in holistic medicine. "They have me on natural healing and natural living," Lori said. Cohen asked about her tumor. She replied, vaguely, referring to the holistic "experts," "They feel it's okay. . . .")

On February 23, the date scheduled for oral arguments before the Court of Military Appeals, a blizzard covered Washington, D.C., with some twenty inches of snow, postponing the hearings until March 3.

The Scott case was now a national cause célèbre. Thus on the day of the hearing the small courtroom was packed with military personnel (who had been bussed in from Quantico) and journalists from both newspapers and television. Lori attended, as did Scott's parents, Dick Harry (the former Lieutenant Colonel Richard Harry), and Joe Wershba of *60 Minutes*.

At two P.M., the maroon velvet curtains located directly behind the judges' long desk snapped open, revealing each of the three judges standing in his place. The court clerk called the room to order. After introductions, Gary Myers rose and began a brilliant, eloquent defense argument that lasted forty-five minutes, quoting from memory extracts from previous trial records and court decisions. Occasionally one of the judges would interrupt to ask questions. Myers was ready with answers that (as Lori later remarked) seemed to impress both judges and onlookers, who nodded their heads as though in agreement.

Just as it had been at the DuBay hearing, the focus of Myers's argument was Kuhnke's performance as Scott's defense attorney. "The linkage between Mr. Kuhnke's conduct and the conclusion of the case was palpable and clear," Myers told the court. "We end up with no preparation whatsoever and we end up with a conviction.

"The practice of criminal law involves getting your shoes dirty. All Mr. Kuhnke did was sit at his desk."

John Leino presented an equally compelling argument. He talked about the lack of physical evidence offered by the prosecution during the court-martial that had gone unchallenged by Kuhnke. The government's black prosecutor for the hearing, Marine Captain H. C. Lassiter, argued that the defense had been adequate, that Lori Jackson had been operating in a "team effort" with Kuhnke.

Leino countered in rebuttal: "The government is talking about a team effort. I submit, Your Honor, that the defense team showed up at the stadium five months late," he said, referring to the fact that he and Gary Myers only came into the picture after Scott was convicted and Kuhnke fired.

According to Lori, the atmosphere in the courtroom was completely different from that encountered at the DuBay. She felt that the military observers seemed to be listening with sympathy and astonishment to Leino and Myers's arguments.

A fascinating detail of the hearing was the fact that Captain Lassiter bore an uncanny resemblance to Lindsey Scott. The government prosecutor, whose performance compared poorly with those of Myers and Leino (he rambled and stammered and appeared disorganized, Lori wrote author Cohen), was about the same height and of the same general build as Scott, had the same hair texture and cut, same complexion, same walk, and even wore the same type of large-rimmed glasses. During the hearing many in the visitors' gallery, including some of the press, were whispering to each other about the resemblance.

Lassiter looked so much like Scott that after the hearing a number of people felt compelled to tell him so. Scott's mother went up to him and in a shaken, angry voice said, "You look just like my son Lindsey!"

Patty Leino, John's wife, said that when she first saw Lassiter, before the hearing began, she was under the impression that the Marines secretly had flown Scott in for the hearing. And John himself, when he first saw the prosecutor, said to Gary Myers,

"Who does that guy remind you of?" Gary looked at Lassiter and gasped, "I can't believe it!"

Lori couldn't resist; she, too, had to say something to the prosecutor. She went up to him after the hearing, extended her hand, and introduced herself. She told him that he could pass for Lindsey Scott, and then, barely controlling a grin, said, "Come to think of it, where were you and what were you doing on April twentieth, 1983?" (the night of the crime). Lassiter did not appear amused. He looked away nervously.

Once again an anxious waiting period began; it would take weeks, perhaps even months, before the judges of the Court of Military Appeals announced a decision.

As the days passed the Scott case took another bizarre turn. On the defense desk with Leino and Myers during the court hearing had been Navy Captain David Larson, assigned to them as military appeals counsel. The three lawyers got on very well together, became quite friendly, in fact. Shortly after the March 3 hearing, Leino heard from Larson that the Marines had already begun to prepare for the prosecution of Scott in a second trial. The implication was stunning: the government expected the Court of Appeals to find for the defense, or at least was hedging its bets.

Then, to everyone's surprise, Myers called Scott at Leavenworth. He had never done so before, neither at Leavenworth nor at the Quantico brig. The lawyer told Scott that everything was looking very positive, that he had good feelings about the Court of Appeals' decision. The worst thing he could expect, Myers said, was a new trial (Lieutenant General Petersen, as Quantico commanding general, always retained the power to dismiss the charges).

Never before had Myers sounded so confident. Thus Lori and John Leino figured he must really know something, because he was so friendly with Captain Larson and, due to his years as a captain in the judge advocate general's office, was a member in good standing in the "good old boys" network of the military.

However, the information could not be confirmed at this point; it was still within the realm of hearsay, albeit from a reliable source.

(The authors deem it useful to jump ahead of the story here. Captain Larson's information was accurate. On August 17, 1988, some fifteen months after Larson passed on his tip to John Leino, author Ellis A. Cohen learned from a conversation with Marine Major Ron McNeil that some four months before the Court of Military Appeals handed down its decision, Marine headquarters had "quietly" brought him in from the Norfolk, Virginia, Navy Yard, where he had just finished prosecuting a case for the government. The conclusion was that Quantico's new staff judge advocate, Colonel James P. McHenry, after studying every aspect of the Scott case, had come to his own decision that the appeals court would reverse the lower court's decision. According to McNeil, the SJA told him he wanted him to take over the Scott case.

At that time, in the spring of 1987, McNeil had a reputation as the best government prosecutor in the Navy–Marine Corps ranks. And indeed, he became the chief government prosecutor for the second court-martial of Lindsey Scott. To use a baseball metaphor, ordering McNeil to "warm up in the bullpen" four months before the Court of Appeals even handed down a decision convinced the authors and a majority of military and legal scholars consulted that the Marines had been determined to keep Scott at Leavenworth to serve out his thirty-year sentence.)

In April of 1987, while McNeil's appointment by Colonel McHenry and the government's preparation for a second court-martial were unknown to Leino and Myers (though they fully expected a second trial), the Marines suffered humiliating media exposure in two of the nation's most important news magazines.

The front cover of the April 20 edition of *Time* magazine displayed a Marine officer with a black eye next to a headline: SPY SCANDALS — MARINE CORPS WOES — HIGH-TECH SURVEILLANCE — ASSESSING THE DAMAGE.

This high-profile cover story was about the Moscow-embassy spy scandal that had started with a lonely U.S.-embassy Marine guard confessing that he had succumbed to the charms of a beautiful Soviet receptionist in Moscow and then had "escalated into what appeared to be one of the most serious sex-for-secrets exchanges in U.S. history. Not only had the Marine's partner been charged with helping him let Soviet agents prowl the embassy's most sensitive areas but last week a third Marine sentinel stationed at the Brasilia embassy was taken to Quantico, Va., for grilling about espionage. Several others were recalled from Vienna. More accusations of spying were expected to be filed this week in the still unfolding saga."

(This cover story served as ammunition for Lori as she traveled around the Virginia–Washington, D.C., area campaigning for Scott's freedom. She would pull a copy of *Time* out of her battered briefcase and say, "See, these are the same Marines that railroaded Lindsey Scott and refuse to give him a new fair trial where his innocence can now be proven . . . and beyond a shadow of a doubt!")

That same day *Newsweek* magazine ran a feature article in its National Affairs section headed TARNISHED HONOR with a subhead: *For the Marines, "a dagger in our heart."* The article discussed a series of Marine embarrassments: the embassy sex-and-spy scandal; the Iran-Contra affair, and Marine Lieutenant Colonel Oliver North's part in it through his dealings with Iran—a sworn enemy of the United States; Robert McFarlane, a former Marine who once served as President Ronald Reagan's national security adviser, became so dispirited by the Iran-Contra mess, in which he was deeply involved, that he tried to take his own life.

"'No group is more embarrassed by these events,'" said the article, "'and more concerned than the Marines,' the Marine Corps Commandant, General P. X. Kelley, glumly confessed to a Congressional committee. Brigadier General Walter Boomer, the Corps' chief spokesman, described the scandal as nothing less than 'a dagger in the heart.'"

As spring turned to early summer and nothing was heard from the Court of Military Appeals, Scott became fidgety and once again began calling Lori, John Leino, and author Cohen asking if they had heard anything or knew anything. "How soon do you think the court might decide?" was his constant theme.

Lori, too, was despondent. One day late in April she called author Cohen, wondering: "What if the Court of Military Appeals turns Scott down? What can we do next?"

Cohen told her she was the one person who would say, "We've

got to keep the faith," so he asked her why she sounded so low. She was silent for a moment—an eloquent silence that perhaps spoke of too much. Finally she said that her tumor had grown. The faith healers she had quietly been seeing had noted the difference. But, perking up, she said she had been eating a lot of health foods that she had been buying at specialty stores. She spoke about her leaving the Rainbow Coalition. "I'm better off staying away from their office," she said. "I only have enough strength to keep pushing for Scott." An ominous admission from a woman who had always possessed boundless energy.

On July 1, a former division commander at Camp LeJeune, Lieutenant General Alfred M. Gray, Jr., was named to succeed General P. X. Kelley as commandant of the Marine Corps. In light of the alleged dinner conversation between General Kelley and Lieutenant General Petersen, the Quantico base commander, those who were privy to that allegation wondered whether the change in command would have any effect on Scott's position.

Five days later, the Court of Military Appeals announced that in a unanimous decision, it had overturned Lindsey Scott's conviction.

The official Marine Corps press release sent to journalists worldwide said: "The U.S. Court of Military Appeals on July 6, 1987, set aside the findings and sentences in the case of Corporal Lindsey Scott, USMC. . . . The United States Court of Military Appeals made the following decision: 'The findings and sentences are set aside. The record of trial is returned to the judge advocate general of the Navy. A rehearing may be ordered.'

"The decision whether to retry Corporal Scott could be made by the judge advocate general of the Navy or the convening authority that will be appointed."

Surprisingly, the official release went on to say: "The Scott case received national attention in a *60 Minutes* segment on December 2, 1984." (Surprising in view of the fact that the Marines never officially recognized the story and refused in any way to cooperate with the original showing or any of the reruns.)

In anticipation of journalists' questions, the press release offered a list of six questions and answers of its own:

Q. Will he be released from confinement?

A. If the Court of Military Appeals does not reconsider the decision, a decision to release him or place him in pretrial confinement will be made on July 17, 1987.

Q. Who will handle the retrial?

A. The judge advocate general of the Navy will assign a convening authority to proceed with the case.

Q. Where will the trial be held?

A. That will depend on who is named as the convening authority.

Q. What are the options of the convening authority?

A. To dismiss the case or refer the case to court-martial.

Q. What is the maximum sentence he could get?

A. The sentence is limited to that of the original trial, which was thirty years confinement, total forfeiture of pay, and reduction to private (E-1).

Q. What was the basis of the Court of Military Appeals decision?

A. The court found that Scott's civilian defense attorney provided ineffective assistance during the trial.

This was a turnabout of momentous legal significance, since it upset not only the outcome of Scott's court-martial, but the majority opinion of the lower court—the Navy–Marine Corps Court of Military Review, which had ruled that despite its reservations about the performance of Scott's lawyer, Ervan Kuhnke, the prosecution's evidence was so strong that any lapses on Kuhnke's part made no difference to the guilty verdict.

In setting aside Scott's conviction, the court disagreed with that decision. Judge Walter T. Cox III called Kuhnke's trial work "incredible." His failure to prepare a competent alibi defense, wrote Judge Cox, "casts doubt" on the conviction.

"Viewing Kuhnke's performance in light of prevailing professional norms," Judge Cox wrote, "we can only conclude that it falls far short of reasonable competence. Kuhnke's failure to promptly investigate an alibi defense was not the result of strategy or a reasonable decision not to investigate. Rather, it was simply the result of lack of preparation . . . the inexplicable hope that the case would not go to trial."

Judge Eugene R. Sullivan agreed with Judge Cox, but said, "I only dissent on the remedy to be taken. In my view, justice requires that the truth be determined at a new court-martial. In this case I would order a rehearing. If the convening authority does not want to retry this case, the convening authority can dismiss the charges."

Reaction to the court's decision was immediate and spread across the country's news media. Scott, when informed of the decision, ran up and down the Leavenworth halls shouting to fellow inmates, "I'm going home! I'm going home!"

Lori called author Cohen, exhilarated, almost breathless with joy. "Ellis, praise the Lord!" she cried. "I don't know what to do first! I'm just going out for the day and I'm going to drive up to see John Leino and then I'm going to pray for *this* decision to be the final word from the government!"

Scott's family was equally ecstatic. "We hollered and screamed and jumped up and down and cried," said Scott's wife, Lola, who was now living in Louisville. "It's a big relief, but the biggest relief will be when he walks out that prison door."

John Leino, quietly elated at victory, took a more sober line. "It's not over yet," he said. "By not ordering a new trial, the appeals court could be sending military prosecutors a message that 'you've kicked a dead horse long enough.' There are a lot of variables, depending on who wants the buck to stop where. But we're taking the attitude that we'll have a second court-martial."

The reaction from the military appeared to be one of petty peevishness. Author Cohen, and Scott supporters Lori, Leino and Myers, and Lola Scott were busy day after day telephoning around trying to find out from Quantico, from the Pentagon, from newspaper reporters, and even from *60 Minutes*—from anyone who might have a clue—when Scott would be released from Leavenworth, and where he would be going. The Marines were not volunteering any information, neither were they giving direct answers to direct questions; they were allowing the rumors to fly and seemed to be enjoying the game of "guess when and where" as one journalist put it.

Meanwhile, assuming Lindsey would be brought back to Quantico, Lola Scott decided to return to Virginia to be near him and Scott's lawyers while awaiting her husband's fate. "There in

Kentucky, though I was closer to him, I felt I wasn't doing anything to help him," Lola said. "I think it's more important for me to be here, trying to get him out." Lola thought that the Marine Corps would drop its case against Lindsey. If not, then she was confident he would be acquitted at a new trial.

Lori agreed completely with Lola. Both believed the Marines would be unable to get Judy Connors back to testify again at a new court-martial. "I think it would be very, very hard for the Marine Corps to retry the case after all this time," Lori told the *Potomac News*.

(What neither Lola nor Lori knew—what nobody knew until author Cohen discovered the fact much later, was that while all this waiting and gamesmanship was going on, Major Ron McNeil was already in secret contact with Judy Connors. She agreed to return to testify at a second trial. McNeil began to prepare her for her testimony, though no official decision had as yet been announced that there indeed would be a second trial.)

On July 16, Cohen received a phone call from John Leino, who related a strange story to add to all the other strange stories that surrounded the Scott case. He said that Scott had called him and told him that Gunnery Sergeant Nummer (from the Ft. Leavenworth prison) had said that he, Scott, would be given a forty-five-day leave, and asked, "Scott, where do you want to go . . . Louisville, Quantico?"

Leino said he spoke to Nummer and told him this was the first time he had ever heard of a prisoner having a choice of where he could directly go upon his official release or separation from the prison facilities. Nummer was noncommittal, Leino said, but "I think Lindsey will come back to Quantico," he said to Cohen. "There are rumors flying all over the place."

Later that day, Leino called back and said he'd just spoken to Lieutenant Colonel Brehm, of the Quantico judge advocate general's office. Leino said, "Brehm told me the JAG office was waiting for orders to be cut to release Scott." Leino said he pressed him: "When?" Brehm responded. "Sometime later today." Leino said he asked, sarcastically, "To where?" and Brehm said, "Scott will return to Quantico . . . but he doesn't have to go if he doesn't want to. He can go home if he wants to."

By that time, John said, it was too late in the day to do any more, he didn't think anything further would be happening until the next morning. He said to Cohen: "The same confusion—that's happening now—happened all those weeks and months ago that finally led up to Scott's DuBay hearing."

On the morning of July 17, Scott was released from Leavenworth, but not without a continuation of the confusion that was marring the sense of gratification—even euphoria, in some quarters—over the decision by the Court of Military Appeals. It began early on that morning with a call from Lori to Cohen saying she'd just spoken to John Leino, who told her Scott was probably going through his release procedure at that very moment but still with no word about where he was going. Cohen phoned a Mr. Gooch, a civilian clerk at Leavenworth, who confirmed, "Lindsey Scott is currently processing out—and he should be ready to leave here pretty soon."

Cohen next spoke to Lieutenant Colonel John Shotwell, the official public-affairs spokesman at Marine Corps headquarters in Washington, D.C., who read him the newly cut orders stating that Private Lindsey Scott had officially been ordered to leave Ft. Leavenworth. Shotwell went on to say that Scott had been given a thirty-day leave and he could go virtually wherever he wanted during that period. Shotwell said those orders would shortly be released to all the media. "Mr. Cohen," Shotwell said, "there are literally hundreds of interested media requests to know what was next going to happen to Scott. As of this morning, Scott has requested that he wants his exact time of leaving Leavenworth and where he would be going to be kept secret."

Having been promised that he would receive Scott's exclusive "first call," Cohen had a clutch of airline tickets covering all the options: one from his base in Los Angeles to Louisville, one to Washington, D.C., and one even to Kansas City (nearest major airport from the prison)—should Scott decide to stay over there en route to Louisville.

A bit later that morning Leino called Cohen with the latest from the Quantico judge advocate general's office: "They are now saying that Scott will have to sign a pay voucher at Quantico. I argued that if he flies to National Airport, we could meet him and he could sign the voucher there and be on his way—maybe to Louisville." Signing that voucher was important, John explained. It authorized the Corps to start paying Scott again—and as a corporal, since the court's decision automatically restored his rank. As for back pay, it would happen but not until a decision was made one way or the other about a second court-martial.

Then, with a nervous little laugh, Leino told Cohen, "With all this craziness, that shouldn't be, we have another crisis in the works. Gary Myers, with good thoughts intended, spoke to Lieutenant Colonel Brehm at the JAG office and suggested that since he lives in Old Towne [Alexandria, Virginia] and a quick ten-minute drive from National Airport, 'Scott can come to my town house instead of the hour-plus drive to Quantico . . . just to sign a pay voucher.' Brehm liked the idea," Leino continued, "but when Gary tried to call Scott at Leavenworth this morning with his idea, he learned from a Staff Sergeant Fields that Scott said he didn't want to talk to him.

"So Gary called me," Leino continued to Cohen, "and said 'I don't need any of that crap from him,' and said he was withdrawing from the case."

About an hour later, with this disturbing "crisis" still brewing, Gunnery Sergeant Nummer at Leavenworth called Cohen and advised him that "Private Scott wanted you to know that he will be going to Louisville via Kansas City and would arrive at approximately 2200 tonight. Please call his wife and she will tell you where they will be staying."

Quickly Cohen packed his bags, called Lola Scott, then Lori, and asked her to call John Leino and if she planned on flying to Louisville. In a voice filled with sadness, she whispered, "I'm not feeling very well now. It's that darn ol' flu"—her euphemism for what really ailed her. "Please tell Lindsey I'll call him later tonight or first thing tomorrow morning."

At the Louisville airport about fifty people greeted Scott with tears and cries of joy. Some carried signs such as JESUS WAS INNOCENT AND SO WERE YOU; WE LOVE LINDSEY; WELCOME HOME. They crowded around him, everyone talking at once, trying to shake his hand, embrace him, a "homecoming hero" as one local newspaper described him at the scene at the airport.

Scott thanked them all for their support, but said, "A celebration would be a little bit premature at the time because my case is not over yet." He said he planned to "go into seclusion" for several days to be with his wife and daughter, Latavia, who would be four in just two weeks. Many in the crowd wept as he said, "My greatest pleasure will be relaxing and spending the day with my daughter. I missed her first words. I missed her first steps. I missed changing her diapers. There's a lot we have to catch up on now that I'm home."

That same evening, at the motel where Scott and his wife were staying, author Cohen met with him privately, and was surprised to find a far different person from the shy, slightly pudgy Marine he'd seen at the DuBay hearing. His forty-five months of prison had slimmed him down. Weight training at Leavenworth had firmed and muscled his body. This was a self-assured Lindsey Scott, fashionably dressed, with a trim mustache and stylish glasses. During the meeting, John Leino called to welcome him back, and to warn him that he was not free from his legal problems. "Be very, very careful of what you do and what you say," Leino cautioned him. "There is likely to be another court-martial."

"Why?" Scott asked.

"Because the Marines don't like to lose."

Leino took the opportunity to try to clear up whatever problem Scott had with Gary Myers. He reminded Scott how helpful Myers had been, how Myers had volunteered his services from the very beginning, and how important he would be in any future court proceedings. Scott agreed to apologize to Myers for any "misunderstandings."

"Okay, Lindsey, good. Now, if you should talk to the media, whatever you say, don't 'sound off' about the case. Leave that to Lori, Gary, and me. And watch yourself during your leave. The NIS is probably watching your every move, just hoping to catch you in some new problem."

(As Gary Myers later related to coauthor Milton J. Shapiro, to this day he has no explanation for Scott's refusal to take his call to Leavenworth. But to "keep the peace," several days later, as he was leaving for a short vacation in Europe, Myers said he telephoned Scott from Kennedy Airport in New York—and got through. He asked Scott why he refused the first call. "Scott said, 'It was a stupid thing. I'm sorry. Forget it,'" Myers related. "Well, I thought, the kid's been under tremendous pressure—so I said to him, 'Fine, Lindsey, in that case I'll continue marching with you.' And I called him again several times from Europe. I was glad it got straightened out.")

The "seclusion" Scott said he had been hoping for was quickly and rudely shattered—too many friends and family knew where he would be staying and too many, inadvertently or not—had given it away to the press. As he and Cohen were chatting there came a knock at the door and in walked a TV reporter complete with camera crew—unannounced and without an appointment. Scott agreed to a short interview. As soon as they left, a reporter from a Louisville newspaper came in from the hallway where he'd been waiting, and Scott agreed to another short interview. And then the telephone began to ring. . . .

(An exasperated Cohen decided to escape from the media circus and caught a seven A.M. flight back to Los Angeles the following morning.)

All the next day and for many days after, newspaper and television reporters hovered around Scott or telephoned him seeking interviews—preferably on an exclusive basis. Scott granted most requests; however, mindful of John Leino's warning, he carefully walked the minefields laid by some reporters looking for a scoop of some kind, hoping to catch Scott in a slip of the tongue, attempting at times to anger him into a blast at the Marines or Ervan Kuhnke—anything that would give them an edge for a headline or a snippet of "sensational" news.

Scott handled himself well. He said he felt no ill will toward the Marine Corps, and though he blamed Kuhnke for his incarceration, he showed restraint, saying: "Things like that happen." He expressed his confidence in the military justice system and said he was "grateful" to the Marines for granting him leave before he had to report to Quantico.

"You can't blame the whole thing on the Marine Corps," he said. And he wasn't bitter. "I cannot allow myself to be that kind of person," he told *The Washington Times*. "I want to put it behind me and go on with my life. I'm not a quitter. The Corps taught me not to quit. I am a good Marine."

Despite Scott's careful fielding of the questions, Lori was concerned. "I'm worried about Lindsey talking to too many media people," she said in a telephone call to Cohen. "He really should avoid any reporter now, at least until Petersen decides what he'll do next. I told Lindsey that the NIS will be watching him with a magnifying glass. If he screws up just *once,* that report will be rushed right to Petersen at Quantico."

Early in August, Cohen received a phone call from Lee Hockstader of *The Washington Post,* who had been covering the Scott case since the DuBay hearings. According to the reporter, he had spoken to "the new Marine prosecutor, Major Ron McNeil," who said, "I think there will be a new court-martial." Hockstader also gave him the interesting information that he had spoken to Judy Connors's personal attorney, who indicated that his client would be available if she were asked to return to testify. Cohen then called the attorney and asked if he could talk to her sometime in the future. The lawyer told him Judy would not talk to him or anybody else connected with the media.

Several days later, when Scott got a telegram from Lieutenant General Petersen's office granting him an extended ten days' leave, Lori invited the Scotts to stay with her. "I want to keep an eye on him," she confided to Cohen. They were all together, therefore, in Lori's "dream house" when on August 16 the third rerun of the original 1984 *60 Minutes* story on the Scott case was aired. At the end of the original filmed story, Harry Reasoner, substituting for Morley Safer, came on with an update on Scott's current status.

On August 25, Cohen received another phone call from Lee Hockstader. The reporter had a tip: a confidential Marine source had told him that Petersen would definitely order a new court-martial, possibly by the end of the year. Two days later, Scott reported to Quantico, where, after a meeting with Lieutenant General Petersen, he was restored to his rank of corporal and reassigned to his old unit, Security Battalion—but not as an investigator. He also received permission to live off base, was given immediately a year's back pay, with the rest to be paid to him following the final resolution of his case.

With rumors flying about in the press and around Quantico, Gary Myers decided to take advantage of his acquaintance with Lieutenant General Frank Petersen to discover his intentions regarding a second court-martial. "I've known him for twenty years," Myers said to John Leino. "I'm going to see if I can find out which way he's leaning." He did get to see Petersen, and the two men had a cordial, private meeting at Quantico; but it produced nothing. "Unfortunately, Frank kept his thoughts very close to his vest," Myers reported.

(The friendship of Myers and Petersen dated back to 1970. At that time Myers was an Army captain assigned to the Washington, D.C., office of the deputy assistant to the secretary of defense for civil rights. The department covered all four armed services—Army, Air Force, Navy, and Marines. Petersen, a lieutenant colonel of Marines then, had been wounded in Vietnam and reassigned to that same section. With Myers, he began a long tour of U.S. bases in the Far East to investigate racial problems in the military. The two men spent many months together on that tour of duty. Considering the nature of their assignment, Myers found it even more bitterly ironic that Petersen should refuse to drop the charges against Scott and insist on a second court-martial.)

With that avenue of information closed, Myers met with Leino and Lori and the three agreed on drafting an official Petition for Dismissal that Myers would hand-deliver to Petersen. Lori called Cohen (in Los Angeles) to bring him up to date with this news; when he asked her how she was feeling she assured him, "Don't worry, if there's another court-martial I'll be ready, again, to help."

On October 8, Myers met with Petersen again and delivered the petition, which was signed by him, John Leino, and Captain W. Brennan Lynch, the new Marine detailed defense attorney. In essence, the petition made the point that it was now impossible for Scott to get a fair trial: "There can never be a constitutionally fair and impartial retrial which meets due process and equal protection requirements," it said. "A new trial will not sweep away the transgressions of ineffective defense counsel in the first trial.

Forever lost opportunities will elevate the new trial to no higher level of fact finding than the first."

The petition went on to cite witnesses who were "lost forever" due to the passage of the years. Ruby Hills was "compromised by defense counsel's ineffectiveness. . . . She will now be portrayed as being inconsistent and having an 'improved memory.' She could have provided an alibi defense, which if properly developed in the first trial would not have been subject to such assault and innuendo. . . .

"No new evidence can be developed. The taint of the first trial has entombed for all time what can be adduced at a new court-martial.

"We anticipate major problems with chain of custody of evidence which the government has an absolute duty to preserve. Scott's car is gone. The whereabouts of the Negroid hair, the steel pot, clothing and other evidence are unknown to the defense."

The petition excoriated Kuhnke and Major Al Roach for losing "virtually all the exculpatory evidence through their ineffective representation of Scott. . . . Because Major Roach was a government counsel appointed by the government and not the accused, responsibility for his ineffectiveness should be borne by the government and not the accused. The Court of Military Appeals recognized that Scott should not bear the consequences of his counsels' failures."

And, finally, "We respectfully request dismissal of all charges and specifications."

Exactly two weeks later, on October 22, at 2:40 A.M., the Quantico public-affairs office, under the direction of Lieutenant Colonel Bobbi Weinberger, began faxing a press release to the world media: "The charges against Corporal Lindsey Scott were sent to a rehearing before a general court-martial today by Lieutenant General Frank E. Petersen, Commanding General, Marine Corps Development and Education Command, Quantico, VA.

"General Petersen made his decision as the convening authority after considering the evidence and the recommendation of his staff judge advocate, Colonel James P. McHenry. No trial date has been set."

*   *   *

There was a quick, biting response in the press from an incensed Gary Myers, who knew Petersen so well: "General Frank Petersen has spent his career demonstrating that a black man could also be a good Marine. In this case, he has ignored the Constitution and unjustifiably sent a young black man to trial. This . . . undoubtedly qualifies him to move from three stars to commandant. It is an outrageous result, and I expect an acquittal, and subsequent to that acquittal, I expect an apology from the general.

"This is not going to be a pretty trial."

22

It was New Year's day of 1988, a bright, cold winter morning with an ice-blue sky, and Lori was walking through the sprawling woodlands surrounding her dream house with her husband. The air was still, the ground white with frost. She had lost a lot of weight, and was bundled up in wool sweaters and her favorite winter jacket. She loved these moments of peace and quiet, the crispness of the winter morning's air, the frost crunching underfoot. Seriously ill though she now was, Lori rejected rest and confinement in her relentless quest for civil rights and justice for all—not only for Lindsey Scott.

She was in a reflective mood that morning. Perhaps it was because it was the beginning of a new year she felt would not end well. The second court-martial of Lindsey Scott was now set for the twenty-fifth of the month, and she was angry with the military, with Lieutenant General Petersen, for putting Scott and his family through the ordeal of another trial. But now she spoke to Paul about the heavy toll the past several years had exacted on them and on her children. She wanted Paul to know how much she appreciated his patience and his understanding through those difficult years. "You have been such a supportive, such a wonderful person, both as a husband and as my best friend," she said to him. "I want you to know that. I want you to know how I feel about that."

She talked softly about her children, how they had allowed her to be an "absentee mother" over the years, how they had steadfastly stood by her, especially "when we would get all those stupid death threats or when we would come home and those idiots had our trash cans turned upside down."

She spoke of the fact that she still had her mission to complete, and with the next court-martial starting in little more than three weeks, she had things to do. And she said, "Lindsey will walk out a free man *if I have anything to do with it*!"

Two weeks before the trial was to begin, Lori called Cohen with information about the judge named to preside. "John called me last night," she said, "and would you believe it, first we thought it was good news because Quantico went black with Petersen. We now know what that was all about. . . . Well, here's the news. They appointed a new judge for the court-martial, and—are you ready for this—he's black! Now, really! Give me a break. It was bad enough we all had to deal with 'their token' at the first trial"—referring to the prosecutor, Major Thomson. "Now the judge!"

(Lori, who had fought so many civil-rights battles down through the years, had come to view systems—such as the military justice system—with a great deal of skepticism when a high-ranking black was picked to play a crucial role. She was far from being alone in this regard. Scott's father, for one, who also had fought civil-rights battles, felt the same way. "Our worry is," Lori once confided to Cohen, "when one of our own finally made it through the ranks, just how *white* had they become?")

The judge himself, Lieutenant Colonel Eligah D. Clark, then the military circuit judge of the Atlantic Judicial Circuit, dismissed as "ridiculous" questions raised by the media about the Marines choosing him because of his race. "I was chosen from a pool of available judges," he said. "I was just the next up."

On January 13, Leino, Myers, and Captain Lynch came before Judge Clark at a closed session in chambers for pretrial motions. Appearing for the prosecution was Major McNeil as lead counsel and as cocounsel, Captain Steve Hinkle, who was prosecuting his first case. The first defense motion, for a dismissal of all charges, was denied, as counsel knew it would be; but motions by defense counsel to dismiss charges were more or less automatic in criminal cases, as were denial by judges. On the rare occasions such motions were granted, more often than not it was due less to the strength of the defense argument than to the glaring weakness of the prosecution's case.

The defense moved on to its next request, which was for a reasonable delay of the trial, a continuation of a few weeks to give the defense more time to tie up loose ends and prepare witnesses. McNeil objected that the defense was just stalling. Judge Clark denied the motion.

Because this was a closed session before the judge, the curious and interesting subject that arose next was revealed to author Cohen only long after the event, through conversations with John Leino, Gary Myers, and Ron McNeil. Introduced by the defense team as a "proffer," as a possibility of defense evidence that *might* be introduced in open court, was a fifty-page report on the victim, Judy Connors, prepared independently by the local Prince William County Police Department. According to the information he had, Leino said, the report contained many interviews with area people alleging that Connors was a prostitute (allegations Lori had reported hearing during her own investigations at the beginning of the first trial; NIS investigators also had been informed of these allegations at that time).

These allegations raised the possibility of motive for the attack other than a sexual one, and, therefore, not only pointed to a suspect other than Lindsey Scott, but raised the question of why the NIS never bothered to look for any other suspects. Perhaps more important, these allegations brought into question the credibility of the victim's entire story of the night's events.

Leino said to Judge Clark that rather than bring the report forward in open court during the trial, he was introducing it at this closed session for the judge's ruling on whether or not it would be allowed.

McNeil argued vigorously that the report "had no merit." He made a motion to suppress it and any of its findings under the Rape/Shield Law that covered both the civilian and military worlds. (Under this law, the rape victim cannot be attacked by the defense.) Judge Clark agreed: "As a result of this law, motion by the government is granted. The evidence will be suppressed."

In fact, the exercise was never meant to be anything more than "a flyer," allowing the prosecution to win a point on a motion the defense had no intention of introducing before a jury. Said John Leino: "There was no way we would want to drag Judy Connors through the mud on this. That's the ethical part. Tactically, we also had our reservations about the integrity of that report . . . a possibility of mistaken identity. Bringing it out in open court—even if we could have—would only have served to confuse the issue. Scott's defense was always to be an alibi defense. *He wasn't there. He didn't do it.*"

The following evening Cohen had dinner in Washington with Gary Myers. The lawyer expressed his disappointment at being denied the dismissal and continuance motions, but at that time made no mention of the report on Judy Connors. He did tell Cohen, however, that he had received a packet of information from a Florida attorney who had just successfully defended a client charged with rape by using a DNA report as the defense. This became a "precedent case" in the United States, in civilian courts. Myers said he was thinking of testing a DNA defense in the military courts—starting with the Scott case.

(DNA—Deoxyribonucleic acid, is the chief constituent of chromosomes and is responsible for transmitting genetic information from parents to offspring. A person's DNA, or genetic fingerprint, can be extracted from human cells and "mapped" on film. The separated DNA, detected with X-ray film, produces a column of bands that looks similar to the bar coding used for pricing supermarket items, and is unique to each person. The chances of two people having the same genetic fingerprint range from 1 in 200,000 to 1 in 30 billion. This scientific technique was developed at Leicester University in England by geneticist Alec Jeffreys. He was among the first to demonstrate the forensic application of the test, which can be performed on samples of blood, semen, sweat, tissue, and in some cases strands of hair. The test was first used by immigration authorities in England to resolve an immigrant's disputed parentage. Although DNA evidence is widely used today as forensic evidence in criminal cases, such as *People* v. *O.J. Simpson*, each case still becomes controversial.)

At the Cohen–Myers dinner that evening, the two men discussed the fact that the second court-martial had attracted so much national media attention that the Quantico public-affairs office had been forced to make unique arrangements to accommodate everybody. A media building had been set up with closed-circuit television to take the overflow from the courtroom's limited seating capacity. Special credentials had to be obtained by application to the PAO officer, Lieutenant Colonel Bobbi Weinberger, with copies of the application to two other PAO officers, including, in Cohen's case, Lieutenant Colonel David Tomsky in California (where Cohen lived), who was the official Marine liaison with Hollywood movie producers. One application also had to go for approval to Lieutenant General Frank Petersen. Cohen, however, told Myers he wanted a daily pass to sit and observe from inside the courtroom. Myers said, "I'll talk to both Lori and John and we'll figure something out."

During the days leading up to the opening of the second court-martial, Leino, Myers, and Lynch worked nonstop preparing their defense, spending late nights in the extensive Howard & Howard law library reviewing and rereviewing the stacks of transcripts from both the first court-martial and the DuBay hearings. During the day Leino "fine-tuned" some of his witnesses; each day he phoned Lori, who told him that as he had asked, she had invited Ruby Hills and Lola Scott to the house and helped them prepare for their testimony. Gary Myers was researching DNA defense possibilities while Captain Lynch pored over military law books looking for precedents that might prove useful during the trial (Leino related later that Lynch's organization work had been nothing less than "brilliant").

As part of the proposed alibi defense, the defense team hired a private investigator, Morgan Cherry, to prepare a time study of events on the night of the crime according to Judy Connors's account. With a video camera/time clock mounted on his car, Cherry retraced the route allegedly taken by Connors's assailant from the time he picked her up at Spanish Gardens to where he left her in the woods following the attack. The point was to prove that based on the time elapsed and distance covered, Scott could not have committed the crime because he was elsewhere. (Unfortunately for the defense, this exercise proved to be a waste of time. During the trial, the prosecution objected to the videotape's introduction on the grounds that it was unreliable since the actual scene of the attack had never been pinpointed. Judge Clark sustained the objection and the videotape evidence was thrown out.)

One day about a week before the trial, Lori decided it would be a good idea to have a private chat with Scott. She called him at the base, where he was a supply clerk with the Security Battalion, and suggested they get together. Scott agreed, and early that evening they went for a walk into the civilian village called Quantico Town, which seemed to be plastered to the Marine base like an old Band-Aid. They walked across the railroad tracks and strolled slowly along the two short blocks of the town, past the dusty military-surplus store, the small nondescript shops, the small "greasy spoon" café squeezed behind two old-fashioned gas-station pumps.

Scott noticed how much weight Lori had lost; she looked so fragile that it frightened him. He now realized that something was seriously wrong with her: her eyes were sunken and yellowish, ringed with black. Her skin, too, was tinged with yellow. Shocked as he was, he knew Lori well enough to remain silent. She would tell him if she wanted him to know about it.

In a hoarse voice Lori began telling him how incensed she was that the Marines were putting him through another agonizing trial. Scott shrugged and said, "They can do whatever they want to do and whenever . . . you know that." Suddenly she was racked by a spasm of coughing and grabbed his arm for support. Upset, Scott suggested they sit down for a while, perhaps go across the street to the Command Post Pub, a favorite Marine hangout, for a cup of coffee or something. Lori, as ever refusing to show weakness, rebuffed him with an "I'm all right, don't worry. It's just this flu that won't go away."

As she tightened her wool scarf around her neck, Lori abruptly changed the subject, mentioned how Scott's daughter had grown, how pretty she looked. Scott replied that though she wasn't quite five, Latavia seemed to know what the trial was all about. "So Lola and I answer all her questions, letting her know that the Marines are still 'good people,' but that they just made a mistake about me."

For a moment then the old fire returned to Lori's voice and she said, "Lindsey, from the beginning I promised you that if it was the last thing I ever do, I won't quit until you're totally free again. And I still mean that." Scott nodded, and took her arm again as they walked back up the street and recrossed the railroad tracks, which glistened in the bright winter sun. When they reached Lori's car, she stopped and, in a maternal way, took both his hands in hers and said, her voice filled with concern, "Lindsey, don't ever forget . . . trust John. Trust Gary, and please, *please* be careful about the NIS. I know they're still watching you."

"Yes, I know they are," Scott said. "I see them all the time . . . everyplace I go. Even right now they're probably watching us . . . but . . . well, why don't you go home now, Lori, and take care of that flu?"

The tension grew as the time clock ticked down to nine A.M., Monday morning, January 25. The stress was affecting them all—Scott, his family, Leino, Myers, Lori. After an abortive attempt to cut down on his cigarettes, Scott had begun chain-smoking again. In recent weeks, as though suspecting him of some clandestine activity, the Marines had been springing periodic "surprise" urinalysis tests on him. Lori was desperately fighting complete exhaustion. With each passing day she became weaker and weaker; each day she refused all exhortations to check herself into the hospital. "I've still got unfinished business in defending Lindsey," she said stubbornly to author Cohen. "Not till I feel my work is done will I consider going into the hospital."

For Scott's defense team, this second court-martial was the culmination of what Leino began to call a "holy war" and Myers termed the "final conflict." Along with Lori Jackson, Leino and Myers had devoted the better part of four years to the Scott case; there had been secret meetings to avoid NIS scrutiny, late-night strategy sessions, weeks and months of interviewing witnesses and trying to find new witnesses, expert witnesses, searching through the law books for quotable precedent cases. Together they had endured their small wins and their large losses, the endless waiting for decisions on appeals eventually denied. And there were the death threats to "you nigger lovers" that came in the middle of the night.

The grinding work had in particular worn down John Leino, whose devotion to freeing his client had reached an almost religious plane—he was a religious man—and had disrupted his home life. He found himself smoking too much and eating too much, and tried to find some way to take his mind off the case—for a few hours at a time at least. He owned a little beach house on Virginia's eastern shore, and routinely he forced himself to "sneak out there," where he began to build a drystone, freestanding wall, rolling boulders weighing as much as sixty and seventy pounds. It helped, but aggravating the strain now was Lori's condition; John and his wife, Patty, had developed a special closeness with her. To both she was "like a sister."

(Neither knew until just before the second court-martial just how ill Lori really was. They suspected she was suffering from more than what she insisted on calling "the flu." But John was tied up in knots with the case. Patty was a schoolteacher. They had been keeping in touch with Lori daily by telephone and hadn't seen her in weeks. One day in January, however, Patty paid Lori a visit to see her dream house. She returned home in tears. When she told John that Lori had liver cancer, he, too, burst into tears.)

With about a week to go before the court-martial, and after they had lost their pretrial motions, Leino, Myers, and Captain Lynch moved their "command post," as Leino described it, to the basement law library at LeJeune Hall, where once again the trial would take place. It was a drab, soulless, windowless office, about twelve by fifteen feet, with graying linoleum floors, harsh fluorescent lighting, a long, ancient conference table flanked by equally ancient chairs, and walls lined with gray metal shelves. Appropriately, Leino at first sight called it "the bunker," and the bunker it remained throughout the weeks of their siege, their last-ditch battle to win freedom for Lindsey Scott.

23

At precisely 6:30 A.M. on January 25, 1988, author Ellis A. Cohen waited outside his hotel in Old Towne (a historical neighborhood in Alexandria, VA) for the arrival of Gary Myers, who had graciously agreed to transport him the thirty miles to and from Quantico each day. This would give Cohen a unique opportunity to learn about the defense strategy for the coming day, and then later, hear the lawyer's analysis of the day's events. (Equally fortuitous, Cohen became very friendly with the government's lead prosecutor, Major Ron McNeil, who would telephone him nightly with *his* analysis of the day's events on the prosecution side.)

When Cohen and Myers arrived at Quantico's main gate, they got their first taste of the new, heavy security imposed for this second court-martial. An MP stopped the car. Myers had to show satisfactory identification. His name and the license number of the car were then checked against the MP's list, and he was given a bright yellow pass to place on the dashboard above the steering wheel. This would become a daily ritual.

As one of the defense attorneys, Myers was allowed a privileged visitor's parking spot at the rear of LeJeune Hall, where once again the court-martial would take place. This enabled Myers and Cohen to enter the courthouse by the back door, rather than the tightly secured front door to be used by visitors. Once inside the building, Myers attached to his coat one of the Marine-issued photo ID badges—the only credential allowing the wearer free, unescorted access to the entire building. Cohen, as a visitor, though arriving with Myers, was subject to the same restricted access as all other visitors: the walk between the courtroom and the rest rooms—and that was it. Even that necessitated negotiating a gauntlet of armed guards, some in uniform, some in plain clothes.

The atmosphere at Quantico was far different than that of the first court-martial. The case had engendered so much publicity over the preceding years (much of it due to the efforts of Lori Jackson) that it had now become, in the jargon of the media, "big time." On hand were the three national TV networks, CNN, local and regional TV affiliates, the wire services, *The Washington Post, USA Today,* and a number of the smaller local and regional newspapers. Scores of journalists and technicians had been sent to cover the trial—so many that the Marines had set up a special media center, about a hundred yards from LeJeune Hall, and installed a closed-circuit TV with a battery of monitors. With the exception of Cohen (who had obtained his courtroom pass thanks to Leino and Myers), Lee Hockstader of *The Washington Post* (because of his paper's stature), and eight lucky journalists chosen each day by lottery, all other media people had to view the proceedings from the media center. For the convenience of the journalists and technicians, the center had been equipped with soft-drink and snack machines, telephones, photocopiers, and fax machines. All of this was run by the able public-affairs officer, Lieutenant Colonel Bobbi Weinberger and her staff.

Security was unprecedented. Visitors to LeJeune Hall had to step through an airport-type metal detector stationed just inside the front entrance. Once they cleared the detector, male MPs frisked all males, female MPs frisked all women visitors. Then each person was handed a mimeographed sheet of "guidelines applicable to all persons entering this building for the purpose of viewing the Scott trial." These guidelines included the passing through the metal detector and having personal items such as handbags and briefcases inspected. In addition, considered "contraband" and to be left in the visitor's car were "weapons of any kind, tape recorders, and cameras." Smoking was authorized only in designated areas. No eating or drinking was authorized in the building. Visitors were not allowed on either the basement or second floors. "Failure to comply with these instructions," said the guidelines, "will be reason for removal from the building."

Quantico bristled with heavily armed guards. Around LeJeune Hall, armed, uniformed Marines kept a watchful eye on all activity. Their very presence was intimidating; everybody had to pass by them whether they entered by the front or back door. And just for this trial, newly painted signs had been placed on the grassy area, stating in large letters, WALKING ON GRASS IS *NOT* PERMITTED—thus forestalling any adventurous types from trying to avoid the walk along the sole cement path authorized for visitors. Were all that not enough, Marine sharpshooters in camouflage carrying sniper rifles patrolled the woods and hills around LeJeune Hall.

Seasoned journalists, some of whom had covered the world's war zones, were amazed at the security precautions. "Talk about overkill!" one of them exclaimed. Another said laughingly to Cohen, "Hey, Ellis, you're in the know. Am I in the right place? Is this the Scott court-martial or do the Marines have half a dozen terrorists stashed away in the basement!"

The Marines never offered an official explanation for this massive upgrading of security. However, the theory afloat among the media group was that in the wake of the disaster suffered in Lebanon, the Marines were taking no chances on possible disturbances from the left or the right during the course of the trial and after its verdict was announced. Despite the peacefulness of the vigils and picketing outside the Quantico main gate by Lori Jackson and her civil-rights activists following the first court-martial, Lori's success at attracting both local and nationwide publicity had made her something of a legend at Quantico, a veritable thorn in the Marines' side. The resulting concern about civil-rights activists and militants "storming the Bastille" amounted to near paranoia.

Equally, the Marines were aware of the telephoned death threats to Lori and to John Leino, and the appearance in the visitors' waiting line of several tough-looking skinheads—believed by NIS to be part of a neo-Nazi group responsible for the threats—heightened their concern.

Once those with privileged courtroom passes—media people,

NIS security men, Quantico brass, and Scott's family and friends—had been seated, there were few seats left for the public in the small, twenty-four-seat gallery of the courtroom. (Lori was too ill to come to court but told Leino she would be there if she was needed.) Contrary to the lax security arrangements of the first trial, visitors were not allowed to stand either in the courtroom or in the adjacent hallway. Anticipating an overflow crowd of spectators, and worried about possible disturbances, the public-affairs office had arranged for an extra visitors' room in LeJeune Hall, complete with closed-circuit TV monitors and the usual complement of unobtrusive NIS agents backed by several uniformed MPs bearing sidearms.

By 8:30 A.M. the protagonists in this courtroom drama were seated at their respective tables, awaiting the arrival of the judge. At the defense table, Captain Brennan Lynch wore a khaki shirt and tie, dress green wool pants, and well-polished black patent-leather shoes. Gary Myers, as nattily attired as ever, wore a dark suit, "yuppie" suspenders (visible at times), and black shoes—very conservative, very Brooks Brothers. John Leino, as was his style, was more casually dressed in a beige suit over a short-sleeve shirt.

For the government, Major Ron McNeil and Captain Steve Hinkle were dressed like Brennan Lynch, except for the fact that McNeil wore his wool green uniform coat.

Seated between Myers and Leino, Corporal Lindsey Scott was dressed like McNeil, on his coat sleeve a yellow "hash mark" denoting his four years of Marine service. Over the left breast pocket of his uniform coat were two badges: marksman (rifle) and sharpshooter (pistol). He wore new black-framed military-type glasses and sported a fresh, short, Marine haircut.

At 8:45 the lucky eight members of the press filed into the courtroom and took their places in the gallery. At 9:02 came the bailiff's cry of "All rise!" and Judge Clark entered by the back door to the courtroom, carrying along with his briefcase a yellow seat cushion (where the first trial lasted just five days, this one was expected to go two to four weeks). At 9:15 the eleven potential jurors entered by the same door—all selected by Commanding

General Petersen with the assistance of Colonel James McHenry, the staff judge advocate. Of the eleven, seven would be selected as members of the jury following the voir dire—the challenges by prosecution and defense counsel. For a guilty verdict, at least five would have to so vote.

At 9:20 the prosecutors said they were ready. The gallery audience, fidgeting in its seats for the better part of an hour, settled in for the opening round of the battle.

Procedural matters came first. Judge Clark opened with an important instruction to the potential jurors: "If you become a member of this panel, you must decide this case solely on the evidence of *this* proceeding . . . not consider that there was an original trial."

The voir dire was set to begin, but then Major McNeil rose and read off a list of nineteen potential witnesses the government intended to call. When he finished, Judge Clark turned expectantly to the defense bench to hear its list of witnesses. To the surprise of the courtroom, however, Myers said, "Your Honor, with all due respect, the defense wants to maintain confidentiality to the prosecution with our list of defense witnesses."

Judge Clark fired back, "Mr. Myers, the purpose of discovery is to prevent ambush."

Myers and Leino huddled for a moment with Captain Lynch, who advised the two civilian attorneys that they would have to reveal their list of witnesses (Scott was not listed). After Lynch read off the names of the ten potential defense witnesses, he realized—after glancing at McNeil and noting the smirk on the prosecutor's face—that he had misunderstood the judge's remark; the defense was not required to reveal its list. Lynch sat down and apologized quietly to Leino and Myers. "Sorry, I bungled this one," he said.

The challenges and the selection of jurors began, but after fifteen minutes of questioning the judge interrupted and called a twenty-minute recess because his mike wasn't working. Once that was repaired—it was now about 10:30, and the judge was banging his gavel calling the room to order—the gallery settled down again, only to have the proceedings disrupted by the late entrance of Mr. and Mrs. Scott and one of Lindsey's brothers. Mrs. Scott drew a fair share of startled stares, wearing as she did during the first trial one of her trademark flamboyant hats—this one fire-engine red, matching her red sunglasses.

Once again the focus turned back to the potential jury members as one by one they were polled, accepted, or rejected by counsel. The final seven selected were: Colonel Donald Festa (made jury foreman due to his senior rank); Lieutenant Colonel Patricia R. Breeding (one of the two women selected); Lieutenant Colonel Donald F. Bittner; Major David L. Jones (the sole black juror); Major Ronald W. Richards; Captain Leon M. Pappa; Chief Warrant Officer (CWO) Patricia J. Schmoller. They took their seats in the raised jury box, handsome in their winter green uniforms, "fruit salad" (service ribbons and awards) over the left breast pockets, ready for the opening arguments by counsel. It was now 4:05, and though many in the courtroom were beginning to squirm after the long day in court, Judge Clark said he was anxious to get on with the trial and asked the attorneys to present their opening statements. (The weather was perfect for the grim drama about to unfold: as spectators and protagonists tensed for "the opening bell," as one media wit described it, outside the courtroom freezing rain and sleet turning to snow slashed against the windowpanes.)

First to rise and speak was Captain Hinkle. This was his first speech as a military prosecutor, and he could not help but realize that he was making it in the full glare of a national spotlight. He would be addressing not merely the thirty-five or so persons in the courtroom, or even just the scores of visitors and media personnel on the base watching on the TV monitors, but millions of newspaper readers and TV-news watchers. Small wonder that the young captain appeared nervous as he rose to his feet, shuffled the notes he'd placed on the table before him, and began to speak.

His inexperience soon betrayed him in voice, in presentation, in his frequent need to consult his notes. (Major McNeil would later acknowledge his regret at sending his "rookie partner" in to make the opening statement.) Hinkle conceded early in his speech that "Scott knew Judy and her husband, but she had no recollection of knowing him." He said this to impress the jury with the fact that

Scott knew where Judy lived, and probably the whereabouts of her husband that evening (it will be recalled that Scott and Kevin Connors worked and sometimes carpooled together. The other side of that coin, however, was the conundrum over Judy's problem with identifying Scott that began with her first interview by NIS and continued unsolved forever).

Hinkle took the jury through the events of the night of April 20, 1983, recounting in detail the sexual and physical assault on Judy. He brought up the forensic evidence and said the prosecution would bring in FBI experts to talk about that evidence, but acknowledged that it had either proved "negative or inconclusive." He went on about the Identi-Kit questioning of Judy by NIS Agent Lindner, the photo and the physical lineups held by NIS, and spoke of how Judy had identified Scott as the man who had assaulted her. In effect he could add little or nothing to the case the prosecution had presented for the first trial: it still hinged on Judy Connors's identification of Scott and the web of circumstantial evidence NIS investigators had spun about him to support her identification.

"We will prove Corporal Scott is guilty of the charges beyond a reasonable doubt," Hinkle proclaimed.

Gary Myers rose next to argue for the defense. His approach was markedly different from Captain Hinkle's. Myers, after all, was an experienced military trial counsel, a lecturer in military law at Georgetown University, a former member of the Virginia Legislature. Where Hinkle had chosen to speak from behind the prosecution table, Myers, carefully buttoning the middle button of his coat (a Gary Myers ritual), walked to the podium center stage and angled it to face the jury.

Speaking extemporaneously, in well-modulated tones and measured cadence, Myers told the jurors that respecting their educational backgrounds, he could afford "the luxury of being blunt and direct" with them. He wanted to point out, he said, that "from this moment forward you are the embodiment and custodian of the Constitution of the United States, a doctrine grander than any secular document ever drafted in the history of mankind. It is a document about individual rights. . . . I cannot overemphasize the need for you to take a global view of what you do today."

Myers then took an oblique swipe at "command pressure," a

controversial subject whose shadow hung over the Scott case from the start. "The duty you have now, to protect and preserve the Constitution, is a higher duty than that of being a Marine or that of taking orders from any commanding officer," he said. "You owe it not only to yourselves, but to those who have gone before you and those who will come after you."

From this, the "philosophical" side, as he termed it, Myers turned to the "practical." He referred to the fact that the Court of Military Appeals had unanimously declared that the prior trial had been "constitutionally defective," because Scott's lawyer had provided an "ineffective defense." This was analogous, Myers said, to a platoon commander, in combat, jeopardizing the lives of his platoon.

"The first trial will raise its tainted head in this proceeding," said Myers, "and it is necessary for you to recognize . . . why and how the government is attempting to use it to compromise, impeach, or impugn the credibility of defense witnesses."

He then started his attack on the prosecution evidence, both direct and circumstantial, prefacing it, however, with a few words about the victim. "With respect to Mrs. Connors," Myers said, "we do not view her as a fraud, as a liar, as a harlot, as a cheat. What we view her as a woman who was senselessly and brutally beaten by a subhuman member of our human species. We are not here to attack this woman." Myers questioned, however, her identification of Scott, which was the foundation of the government's case. He reminded the jury that she had originally testified—and would testify again—that throughout her ordeal she did not get a good look at her assailant, and initially had described him "generically," as a big black man.

The NIS attempts to get an identification from Judy Connors were flawed, Myers claimed. First, when NIS officer James Lindner built up the Identi-Kit face with her, not only did he know Scott, but he had heard the remark NIS agent Claude Rivers had made the night before—"Sounds like Scotty"—on hearing Judy's vague description of her assailant. That, maintained Myers, compromised the Identi-Kit routine, because, Myers said, although Lindner would testify that it is the victim who controls the

Identi-Kit, he, Lindner, went into her hospital room thinking "Scotty."

Moving on to the photo lineup, Myers pointed out that "Lindner went to Prince William County—not to the Marine Corps, to Prince William County—to get five mug shots. . . . Mrs. Connors described her assailant as one with thick, dark-rimmed glasses. Curiously enough," he continued, "the NIS chose three men with wire-rimmed glasses, one man with a haircut obviously beyond Marine standards . . . and the two men left, the only two men left, Mrs. Connors identified, and the evidence will show categorically that Mrs. Connors did not positively identify Corporal Scott."

Myers described the physical lineup as equally flawed. Each man in the lineup, he said, had been issued dark, thick-rimmed glasses, "and beyond that, the *only* person in the physical lineup who was the same as the men in the photo lineup . . . was Corporal Scott. And once again, the evidence will show that not only did Mrs. Connors not positively identify Corporal Scott, but *could not* positively identify Corporal Scott even in the face of what Agent Lindner will testify was his severe pressure to get a positive ID."

Myers continued, point by point, to challenge the prosecution's evidence. When he came to forensics, Myers said—referring to his own background in engineering—that "one thing about scientific evidence properly done, properly managed, properly executed . . . is that it doesn't lie, it has no motive, its credibility is not an issue. Where are the forensics in this case?" he asked rhetorically. There was nothing to link Scott forensically to the crime, he said.

Toward the end of his statement, Myers turned to the defense posture. And here he introduced the name of Ruby Hills, the former security guard at Zayre's, and the alibi defense she would provide for Scott. Myers talked about her credentials, the top security clearance she held at her current job, her work as a private investigator, the important position she had held at the time of the crime as security supervisor for all the Zayre's stores in the area.

"At 2015 or thereabouts, Corporal Lindsey Scott was in her store," Myers said. "And she remembers. Now . . . the government will use every legitimate means possible to impeach this witness. Please watch the prior trial and what it does to this witness," he said. "But her unshakable testimony will be that this young man was in her store, at that time, on that date.

"An alibi defense is an absolute defense," Myers continued. "One cannot occupy two spacial coordinates at the same time. If you find that this man was at Zayre's . . . he did not commit this crime."

Myers wound up his argument with an eloquent return to the philosophical aspect of the case. Waxing lyrical, he said to the members of the jury, "Your commitment, and your oath is to preserve, protect, and defend the Constitution of the United States against all enemies foreign and domestic. And you are to preserve this magnificent document on behalf of those who have gone before you, and many of whom we both know have given their full measure. For those presently today, who live under that glowing torch of freedom, and perhaps of equal importance, for those yet unborn and unnamed, who can only hope that they will not be born into a world of tyranny, guarding the Constitution is the most certain safeguard against that possibility. Today you are its guardians. . . .

"I say finally to you, that as to those who would clang cymbals and rattle sabers, there is no place for them in the consecrated halls of a constitutionally constructed courtroom. Your duty is clear, as is your mission. We know that you will do it with honor, and dignity, and integrity. So help you God."

On that note, court adjourned for the day.

24

Over their breakfast toast and coffee, followers of the Scott case could read in their morning newspapers about two important incidents that occurred on the first day of the trial, one inside the courtroom, the other outside. The first came during the voir dire of prospective jurors. One of them, Colonel Donald J. Robinson II, a former Petersen chief of staff, admitted to defense attorney Gary Myers that he knew a prosecution witness, Leo Rodriguez, and further admitted he had spoken with a member of the staff judge advocate's office and had inferred from the conversation that the man thought Scott was guilty. Myers therefore stormily challenged Robinson's fitness to serve on the jury, and Judge Clark duly removed him.

Myers told reporters later that he thought it "outrageous" that the staff judge advocate, Colonel James P. McHenry, had included Robinson's name on the list in the first place. In a prepared response, McHenry said he had discussed his "feelings about sufficient evidence" with Robinson, but that Robinson was included on the juror list because "he met all the requirements established by law and the commanding general."

To many observers, this incident smacked of command pressure, an opinion strengthened by the second incident. Dick Harry, the former Lieutenant Colonel Richard Harry, who always claimed he had been "fired" by Lieutenant General Twomey for releasing Scott from confinement because of lack of evidence, showed up at the visitors' entrance to LeJeune Hall with a letter he said he wanted to hand-deliver to Lieutenant General Petersen. Although Harry never got into the building—the MPs had been given orders to keep him out—he did attract the attention of reporters, and made a "grandstand speech" on the LeJeune Hall steps. "Justice in the military is at the whim of the commanding officer," he said, in a prepared statement. "It is time to stop this circus, this persecution, this racial attack on Lindsey Scott."

Nevertheless, the show went on.

Day two of the court-martial saw the beginning of its central drama—the adversarial jousting of lawyers during the direct and the cross-examination of witnesses. It was here that the government expected a stern test; Leino and Myers were aggressive, well-prepared, experienced defense attorneys who could play hardball in anybody's court. This was no Ervan Kuhnke the government prosecutors were facing.

The first prosecution witness of the day was Todd Hamilton, the man who had picked up Judy Connors after the attack and driven her to the emergency medical unit. He related how Judy had staggered up to his car, her face and clothes bloody, crying that she had been raped and stabbed and thought she might be dying. She described her assailant, Hamilton testified, as "a big black man." As he was being cross-examined by John Leino, Scott's mother, Mildred, suddenly broke down weeping and shouting hysterically. While Scott remained seated, looking at her anxiously, friends helped her from the courtroom, and Judge Clark halted the proceedings for a few moments.

Considering that he was a prosecution witness, Hamilton scored better for the defense on an important point. The knife allegedly used to cut Judy Connors, the knife that the government alleged had been the serrated steak knife Scott had borrowed from his landlady, the knife that had never been produced in court—that knife, Hamilton testified, was not the kind of knife that Judy Connors had described to him—and this shortly after the assault. Hamilton said Judy told him she had been stabbed with a folding knife.

The next government witness was NIS Special Agent James Lindner. He was a key prosecution witness, arguably the most important with the exception of the victim herself. As the case agent, the chief investigator for the NIS, Lindner had conducted the Identi-Kit sequence, the photo lineup, and the physical lineup that formed the basis of the victim's identification of her assailant. Now, as Lindner sat in the witness chair, Captain Hinkle, the young government prosecutor, took him through the gamut of evidence the NIS had collected during its investigation. It might have been fresh evidence to the jury—though it is hardly credible that these Quantico-based officers were completely ignorant of the first court-martial and the DuBay hearings—but many in the media and many of the courtroom visitors had heard it all before.

The difference in the two trials soon became evident when John Leino began to cross-examine Lindner—who had been brought back to testify from London, where he was the NIS assistant special agent in charge. His voice often rising when Lindner appeared to be evasive in his answers, Leino probed deeply into the techniques the NIS agents used during their investigation. The information he revealed raised questions among many observers, including the media, about the NIS's integrity in its investigative methods and its results. The effect, if any, on the jury at this point in the trial was moot—although both defense attorneys and author Cohen believed the jurors were not paying close attention, particularly to the matter of Judy Connors's identification of Scott. Time and again during that cross-examination, when Lindner replied "I don't know" to a question, Leino would say, his voice incredulous: "You were in charge of the investigation, and you don't know?"

During his lengthy cross-examination, Leino focused particularly on two things: the NIS's methods of getting Judy Connors to identify her assailant, and the forensic evidence, if any, linking Scott to the crime.

Leino handed Lindner the six photos the agent had shown to Judy following her Identi-Kit interview. Lindner agreed that her description of "a big black man" included the fact that he was wearing dark-rimmed glasses.

Leino: "Has that description changed any in the last four or five years?"

Lindner: "No, sir, it hasn't."

"Isn't it true in the photo array that three of the individuals are wearing civilian-type glasses and two of those sets are wire-framed? Is that a fair statement?"

"Yes, it is."

"And isn't it also true that individual number one has a haircut that doesn't meet the standards of the Marine Corps? He looks like a space cadet, doesn't he?"

"I would say he wouldn't make a good Marine as far as his haircut is concerned."

"Not the commandant's son, at least."

"No, sir."

"She indicated two individuals that looked like the assailant, correct? Neither of those two individuals was wearing the wire frames. Neither of those two individuals was number one, with the haircut. She picked out the remaining two. Out of six."

"She did."

Leino took Lindner to the physical lineup, and Lindner agreed that Judy Connors had picked out two men there, too.

Leino: "Are the individuals in the photo array the same as the individuals present in the lineup?"

Lindner: "No, they're not."

"So in the photo array she picked out two individuals, one of whom was Corporal Scott, and at the physical lineup she picked out two other individuals, one of whom was Corporal Scott. That's three different people she indicated looked like her assailant. . . ."

Referring to Judy Connors's work with Lindner on the Identi-Kit, Leino reminded him that she had wanted to make a change in the lips on the composite picture. "The lips were too big?"

"Too wide," Lindner said.

Judy asked for some adjustments in the chin, in the length of the face, in addition to the lips, Leino remarked, and Lindner agreed.

Leino: "And isn't it true that at no time in the entire investigation did she mention a gold tooth?"

"No, she did not."

"And at no time in the entire investigation did she mention a scar on Scott's lip."

"No, she did not."

"You recognize that he has a scar on his lip, do you not?"

"No, I didn't know about that. I knew about the gold tooth."

"Take a look at Scott's face. Do you see a scar there?"

"From here I don't see it."

"Would you please walk up a little closer to him. See if you can identify the scar. It's on his upper lip."

Lindner walked toward Scott. "Yes, I do."

Leino: "From approximately three or four feet."

(Judy Connors had testified in the first court-martial that from the time she was picked up at Spanish Gardens through the rape, strangulation, and knife attack, she had never been more than perhaps an arm's length away from her attacker; during the rape, mere inches away from his face.)

Leino turned to the report Lindner had filed on May 16, 1983, during the NIS investigation. "What were the forensic tests that were done?" he asked.

"Standard rape examination . . . at the hospital certain items were obtained as evidence from the victim . . . blood, saliva, fingernail scrapings . . . head-hair samples, pubic-hair samples . . . vaginal swabs. Later on we obtained all her clothing. Later on we obtained specimens of body fluids from Corporal Scott . . . blood, saliva, head-hair samples, pubic-hair samples . . . his clothes. We sent it all to the FBI laboratory in Washington, D.C., to look for, basically, cross-transfer of body fluids, fibers, hair . . . anything that might link the suspect to the victim. All the tests came back negative or inconclusive . . . except for one Negroid hair of unknown origin found on the sweater of the victim."

"Why do you do those tests in a rape case?"

"To try to link the suspect with the victim."

"Are these tests reliable, given today's advances in forensic science?"

Captain Hinkle called out an objection. "The government doesn't object to Agent Lindner testifying to what's his knowledge, but when he starts talking about—"

"Excuse me," Judge Clark interrupted. "Are you objecting to the competency of the witness?"

"Yes, Your Honor," said Hinkle.

"Objection overruled," said the judge.

Leino repeated the question: "Based on your experience as an investigator, are the tests reliable? Are the testing procedures reliable?"

"The testing procedures, or the results?"

"The testing procedures, if you know, and the results, if you know."

"I know nothing about the procedures, I'm not a chemist or a laboratory technician, but the results of them are circumstantial evidence."

"And you don't consider circumstantial evidence to be very significant, do you?"

"I do consider it to be significant."

"Well, let me give you an example. Let's say the Negroid hair you found matched Lindsey Scott to a tee . . . would you kind of pooh-pooh it today and say to the panel, 'You can't rely on this stuff'?"

"I wouldn't. If it were identified to a tee."

"If you had a positive result with regard to the Negroid hair, would you anticipate that it would be used in an attempt to prove Corporal Scott's guilt?"

"Yes, I would."

"Why is that?"

"Because of the linkage with the victim."

"Exactly. That's my point. With regard to all these tests, and you enumerated them, you found not one result that linked Corporal Lindsey Scott to Judy Connors."

"Correct."

Leino continued in that vein, questioning Lindner about the inside of Scott's car. "Where did the fellatio occur in the vehicle, if you know?"

"The front seat."

"Which side of the front seat? Did the assailant make her come to him, on the driver's side, or did he crowd over to her on the passenger side?"

"To the best of my knowledge, the fellatio took place close to him, the rapist."

"Near the steering wheel."

"Yes, sir."

"Was she wearing a hat or a scarf?"

"Not to my knowledge."

"And she had long hair, did she not?"

"Yes."

"And as far as you know, the entire car was vacuumed, for fibers. Is that correct?"

"To the best of my knowledge, yes."

"They do the whole thing, don't they? And they do it microscopically, don't they? And we're not talking about patches of clothes here, we're talking about microscopic fibers that oftentimes can be identified. Is that correct?"

"Yes, sir."

"That's why you vacuum, isn't it?"

"Yes, sir."

Leino paused for a moment. "Not one fiber was found. Do you have an explanation for that?"

"No, sir."

Leino paused again, just looking at Lindner, then he said, "Pretty lousy forensics, isn't it? In a serious rape case?"

"Yes, it is," Lindner agreed.

Leino then asked about the search for the crime scene, and ascertained once again that it was never found. He next asked about the so-called blood trail. "And you started your search for the crime scene at what has often been referred to as the blood trail, didn't you? But the fact of the matter is you don't even know if it was blood, do you?"

"No, sir, we do not."

"You didn't take a test, did you?"

"No, sir, we did not."

"Why didn't you?"

"Because at that point in time it didn't seem as crucial as it now is. We thought we'd find the crime scene."

"You were out there that night a couple of hours after the attack looking at that blood trail, weren't you, and you had a tracking dog out there trying to follow the blood trail to the attack scene, didn't you, and the dog looked up at you and said, 'What do you want me to do?'"

What was never fully explained, Leino's questioning brought out, was how the so-called blood trail started on the paved road, at Point A, and ended on the paved road at Point B, yet no blood or signs of blood were ever found on either side of the road, though the victim had said she was knifed in the woods leading off the road. "It's all speculation, isn't it?" Leino said. "You never found a crime scene, you don't know if it was blood."

At the conclusion of his cross-examination, Leino returned to the scene of the physical lineup. Lindner remarked that because the latter took place soon after the attack, and the victim was upset at having to view the men in the lineup, one of whom was possibly her assailant, it was kept quiet and low-key.

Leino: "A fair statement is that it was quiet in that room."

Lindner: "Yes, sir, it was."

"And she turned to you and said, 'I'm sorry. I can't be sure.'"

"Her closing statement, yes, sir."

"Is that your standard for a positive identification in a rape case?"

"No, sir."

"Thank you for your honesty."

(At about 5:40 P.M., after the courtroom had emptied for the day, author Cohen remained in the visitors' gallery and was quietly going over his day's notes when in walked prosecutor Major McNeil with Judy Connors, her mother, the family attorney, and a woman named Roberta Roper. Ms. Roper, who had successfully lobbied the Maryland Legislature for tougher crime penalties and more assistance for victims, was there to give Judy Connors moral support. As Cohen looked on, his presence ignored by the group, McNeil placed Judy on the witness stand and then briefed her on who sat where. Cohen then heard McNeil advise Judy to look constantly, and directly, at the jurors when she responded to both his and defense questions.

Later that evening, as he had promised, Cohen called Lori to give her the day's news—and it was good news for the defense, with Todd Hamilton's testimony about the folding knife and Leino's cross-examination of Lindner both scoring important points. But Lori's husband, Paul, told him that she had suffered an uncomfortable afternoon and was sleeping.)

* * *

Early on the Wednesday morning, January 27, as Gary Myers and his regular passenger Cohen pulled up at the main gate at Quantico to pick up his daily pass, the guards refused to let him through. Myers immediately kicked up a storm. "What are you talking about, I can't go through! I'm the defense lawyer in the Scott case!" he shouted angrily. This went on for some fifteen minutes, Myers becoming enraged. The time was now 8:10. He already was late for the customary daily interviewing of prosecution witnesses, and it was expected that Judy Connors would be called that day. Eventually a senior MP appeared and said, "Sir, sorry for the delay . . . but we have orders not to let you through. Right now we're trying to find the PAO"—Lieutenant Colonel Bobbi Weinberger—"for instructions on what to do."

Finally a phone call came in and the MPs handed Myers his daily pass. No explanation for this incident, which Myers called "harassment, plain and simple" was ever forthcoming. Cohen asked PAO Weinberger about it, but as Cohen described it, she essentially told him to mind his own business. Myers complained to Colonel McHenry, the judge advocate general, and to Judge Clark. Both said his gate delay—they declined to employ the word "harassment"—would not happen again. It didn't.

Before court began Myers asked for an "802 session," a private meeting in judge's chambers with both sets of attorneys present. There he said he was formally requesting a DNA test as part of Scott's defense. He wanted a blood sample taken from Scott (this was done during the lunch break) and sent to a company called Cellmark Diagnostic of Germantown, Maryland (the same lab that performed DNA for *People* v. *O.J. Simpson*), where it would be tested against semen samples from the vaginal swabs of the victim after the attack. Much to Myers's surprise, McNeil not only agreed readily, but said the government would pay for the test.

This request, as Myers later that day announced to the press, was a "bold step." DNA identification in 1988 was a new technology. Myers said he knew of five civilian cases where it had been used. All five cases had been appealed, Myers continued, with no decision yet at the appellate level on the test's validity.

The question here was whether there were enough heavy DNA molecules remaining in the five-year-old semen for the test.

"There is no doubt in my mind," Myers said, "that someday this test will be the norm in all rape and paternity cases."

As expected, Judy Connors was scheduled to testify that morning, but the prosecution first called Gunnery Sergeant Thomas H. Aultman, chief investigator at CID (Criminal Investigation Division) and Scott's immediate superior, to testify about the state of Scott's car. During the investigation immediately following the crime, after Scott had been declared a definite suspect, Aultman led the search of the car for forensic evidence linking Scott with the crime. On the witness stand, Aultman said it appeared to him that the passenger door and the window on the passenger side had been "wiped down." The rest of the car was "dirtier," Aultman said.

On cross-examination, Captain Brennan Lynch, Scott's military defense counsel, showed Aultman photographs of the interior of the car and asked, "Where's the contrast in these photos?"

Aultman: "Sir, these photos do not depict that."

Lynch: "Well, why were no pictures taken that would show a contrast, if there was one?"

Aultman: "I don't know."

As pertinent as Aultman's testimony might have been within the context of circumstantial evidence—though challenged by the defense—it was a mere sideshow to the testimony of Judy Connors. This was the crux of the prosecution's case: Judy Connors's identification of Lindsey Scott as the man who raped her, forced her to perform fellatio, and attempted to murder her.

At 11:15 A.M. Major McNeil called Judy Connors as the government's next witness. Clutching a wad of tissues in her left hand, Judy took the stand and again told her story: the telephone call telling her that her husband had been in an accident, that someone would pick her up in a car and take her to the hospital; her movements leading up to getting into her assailant's car; the sexual assault, the knife attack, and all that happened subsequently. Well rehearsed (and legitimately so), she looked at the jury as she answered the prosecutor's questions. In particular, she seemed to be directing her gaze, and her answers, at Lieutenant Colonel Patricia Breeding.

Again she testified about her first glimpse of the car's driver, that the parking lot where he picked her up was "lit up enough so I could see him and get a description of what he looked like. I noticed he was a black male. He had glasses on. He looked to me to be between the ages of about . . . twenty-four and twenty-eight. That's the best I can do." She reviewed her memory of the car, inside and out, and what she described as a metal bucket or pot on the backseat. Judy got through all of that before the court broke for an hour's lunch at noon.

After the break McNeil led her through the drive in her assailant's car, then into the sexual attack. McNeil wanted a description of the knife used to threaten her. He needed it to counter Todd Hamilton's statement of the previous day that she had described "a folding knife." The prosecution had contended from the first court-martial that Scott had used the serrated steak knife he'd borrowed from his landlady.

McNeil: "Do you recall what the knife looked like, Judy?"

Judy: "Yes, sir."

"Would you describe for us what the knife looked like?"

"To the best of what I saw, it looked like, it wasn't a big, huge knife, but it wasn't a little pocketknife. It was about the size of a steak knife."

"Did you mention to anyone that fact that it could have been a fold-up knife?"

"I said it could have been. I wouldn't stake my life that it was, or that it wasn't . . . but you know, it could have been, but it didn't appear to me to be a fold-up knife."

Apologetically, McNeil asked her a series of detailed questions about the sexual assault. Weeping, dabbing at her eyes with a tissue, Judy said she was "disgusted," but that "I knew if I didn't do exactly what he wanted me to do that he would hurt me. I was afraid for my life. . . ."

"Do you know whether he ejaculated, Judy?"

"I believe he did, sir, yes."

All this detail, of course, was necessary for the record. At the same time, McNeil was also directing her answers toward lending credence to her identification of Scott as her assailant. Thus, as he was questioning her about the act of rape, he asked, "And how far was his face from you, Judy?"

"Not far at all."

"Can you give us an approximation?"

"I don't know, six inches, I guess."

When she described how her assailant was choking her, McNeil asked, "Judy, when he was choking you, how far was his face from you?"

"Not far . . . half a foot, a foot."

Judy then responded to questions about being taken for medical attention, until at last McNeil was ready for his final series of questions.

"I would like to ask you, based again . . . going back to April 1983. At that point in time, can you give as accurate a description as you can of what your attacker looked like? In other words, would you start with his hair?"

"He had a military . . . well, his hair was fairly short. His hair was black. His hair was curly. He was medium built. He wore glasses. He looked to me to be between the ages of about twenty-four to twenty-seven or twenty-eight."

"And he was a black male, wasn't he?"

"Yes, sir."

"Did he have any facial hair?"

"No, sir, he didn't have any facial hair. He was clean-cut."

"Judy, if you ever saw this person again, would you be able to recognize him?"

"Yes, sir."

"And, Judy, I'm about to ask you a very important question. I want you to look around this courtroom and I want you to point to the individual who raped you, who forced you to commit sodomy, who stabbed you and slashed your neck, and left you in the woods to die. Would you point to him?"

Dramatically sobbing, Judy Connors extended her arm and pointed to Corporal Lindsey Scott.

As she did so there were groans and murmurs from Scott's

supporters in the gallery, and Scott himself (who had rehearsed this moment with his attorneys) shook his head slowly and softly uttered, "No."

McNeil allowed Judy Connors to hold her accusing finger on Scott for a heartbeat or two, then announced: "Let the record reflect the witness has properly identified the accused, Corporal Scott."

25

During Major McNeil's direct examination, John Leino watched Judy Connors carefully. He could see how well prepared she was, how professionally McNeil had managed her in the months preceding the trial. Her tears and her moments of emotion had been real enough, but underneath the facade, Leino sensed, she was cool and composed and she had her story ready, a story that was true as far as it went. Perhaps, however, its meaning needed some adjusting by the defense; perhaps, too, her memory of events, of previous testimony, needed closer scrutiny.

Hard questions needed to be asked. Leino knew that without resorting to badgering, he had to try to reach beyond her composure, her self-confidence, and so he resorted to a commonly used courtroom tactic: tiring a difficult witness, even angering her by relentless questioning, particularly in sensitive areas, and by keeping her on the witness stand as long as possible.

(As Leino later related to coauthor Shapiro, "She was so well prepared that if she had ever had any doubts before about Scott being the man, now she was locked into him like a heat-seeking missile. And I knew I had to break through that facade by asking her about her identification of him, over and over. And I did that. I kept going back to it. She had always said, 'I'm ninety-nine percent sure. I'm as sure as I can be.' Well, that's not good enough. That's not good enough to send a man to Leavenworth for thirty years.")

At 3:30 that afternoon, Leino began his cross-examination of Judy Connors, and he kept her on the stand the rest of the day and well into the next. Very much on his mind was the memory of

Lindsey Scott's testimony during the DuBay hearings—that his then–defense attorney, Ervan Kuhnke, "didn't want to ask her about the attack. He said he knew it would disturb her."

Leino knew he couldn't afford—Lindsey Scott couldn't afford—that much courtesy.

He began politely enough, however, as was the customary approach, asking, "Mrs. Connors, you know me, don't you?"

"Yes."

"We met just last night, isn't that correct?"

"Yes, sir."

"Is there any doubt in your mind, ma'am, that everyone here is after the truth, and to do justice in this case?"

"No, sir."

Before long, Leino got to her identification of the assailant. He questioned her closely about her testimony to McNeil regarding events in the parking lot at Spanish Gardens, when she was picked up.

"Do you remember testifying earlier today and saying you got a very good look at the individual?"

"Yes, sir."

"Do you now wish to change that testimony?"

"No, sir."

"Do you remember ever testifying differently?"

"Just to the best of my recollection that I got, you know—"

Leino interrupted: "I would like to refresh your recollection. Do you remember testifying at the previous court-martial?"

"Yes, sir."

Judge Clark interrupted, asked that the jury members leave the courtroom, and remarked that there was a definite procedure for "refreshing recollection" and a "procedure for impeaching with prior inconsistent sworn statements." There followed a technical legal argument, about which way Leino was going with this line of questioning. Leino said he had been trying to give the witness the benefit of the doubt, but now his questioning would be not just for "refreshing recollection" but for "impeachment purposes." Prosecutor McNeil said he had no objection, but was "concerned about the confusion." Finally Judge Clark asked Leino, "Are you indicating that there would be some inconsistency between what she testified to here today and what she previously testified to under oath?"

Leino: "I am, Your Honor."

Judge Clark: "Very well. I'm going to allow this procedure in the presence of the members. Bring the members back, please." (The jury returned. Leino continued.)

Leino: "Just to clarify so there's isn't any confusion about this, you remember testifying earlier here today that, in the parking lot after receiving the third phone call and being instructed to go down and stand by your car, you noticed a car at the other end of the parking lot and that car started to back up?"

"Uh-huh."

"And at that time, because of the circumstances, you testified earlier today, you got a good look at the car and the driver of the car?"

"Yes, sir."

"Is that correct?"

"Yes, sir."

"Now, have you ever testified differently at a previous proceeding under oath?"

"Sir, I think it depends on what you call a good look. What I meant when I answered that question was I got a good enough look at him to know, I got a good enough look at the car to know what the general shape and color the car was, I got a good enough look at him to see he was a black male, he had glasses on, the general look of him. I'm just giving you the best I can, being as honest as I can."

"I understand."

"I wouldn't say I got a fantastic look at him, a great look at him. I'd say, you know, I got a good enough look to see what I just told you I saw."

Leino earlier had handed her part of a transcript of her testimony at the first court-martial (which had prompted Judge Clark's interruption) and now he said, "Could you please read that previous statement?"

"Question: Did you get a pretty good look at the man at that time? Answer: No, not at that time. All I knew was, you know, that he was in there and that he had glasses on, and that he was black. That's about all I noticed at that time."

Leino questioned her a bit further about her movements in the parking lot, getting into the car and talking to the driver. She said that as she was walking toward the car, he said, "Come on, let's get going." and she did look at him then.

When she got in the car, Leino wanted to know, "Did he turn toward you and speak?"

"No, sir."

"He spoke looking out the front?"

"Yes, sir, he did."

"So, aside from this momentary look that you had when he was talking to you, until the time you left the parking lot, that's the only time you saw his full face?"

"Yes, sir, not the only time that night, but the only time at that point."

When she had been testifying for more than an hour, Major McNeil asked for a short recess so that she could relax for a few minutes (and, defense counsel noted, confer with the prosecution). Leino had no objection. He was now operating with an eye on the clock; he did not want the court to recess for the day right in the middle of his cross-examination of Judy on the subject of identification. Thus when Judge Clark asked him, "How much time do you anticipate you will need for the rest of your cross-examination?" Leino replied, "It may go as long as another hour, Your Honor. Maybe longer."

Following his attack on Judy's two contrasting testimonies about how clearly she had seen her assailant in the parking lot, Leino turned to the ride into the woods, the assault, the rescue by Todd Hamilton in the passing car, and Judy's emergency medical treatment. Leino reviewed it with her minute by minute, down to how long her assailant had to wait at a red light before crossing Route 17. Such minutiae were, of course, important in view of Scott's alibi defense of his whereabouts, during those critical minutes. At the same time it drew the cross-examination ever closer to the moment—5:38—when Judge Clark banged his gavel and said, "Okay. Members of the court, we're going to recess at this point for the evening. I anticipate we'll reconvene tomorrow morning at 0900."

(Afterward, Cohen, Leino, and his wife, Patty, met and talked about Lori. All were terribly worried about her deteriorating condition. "She should be in the damn hospital," said Leino, "but no, she tells me, 'I won't check in until I make sure Ruby Hills is fully prepared this time and gives Lindsey his alibi.'")

When court resumed the next morning, January 28, at 9:11 A.M., John Leino was ready to zero in on Judy Connors's identification of Lindsey Scott as her attacker. First, however, he apologized to her for what he called "the tedium of yesterday," but explained that "the times are very important in this case." Judy said she understood. Then he questioned her about the knife used in the attack.

"With regard to your testimony of yesterday, do you recall stating that your recollection would have been clearer four years ago, at the time of the attack?"

"Yes, sir."

"No doubt in your mind about that?"

"No, sir."

"And you testified in your direct testimony that the knife the assailant used may have been a folding knife, is that correct?"

"It could have been. It didn't look to me to be a folding knife."

"It didn't look to you to be a folding knife. However, you utilized the term 'folding knife' in describing the knife on the first occasion that you described the knife. Isn't that correct? That's what's in your testimony."

"That I described it as a folding knife?"

"Yes, ma'am."

"Which testimony?"

"The first statement that you gave to the investigators, the statement that you gave to Mr. Hamilton that he testified to earlier—he described it as a folding knife."

"I don't recall describing it as a folding knife."

"Are you disputing the fact that you called it a folding knife?"

"No, sir. I simply don't remember how I described the knife."

"I see. But you don't dispute that you described it as a folding knife? Is that correct, in your previous statements?"

"I don't recall exactly what I said. I said it could have been a folding knife. I didn't believe it was a folding knife."

"But yet you used the term 'folding knife,' at any rate? Is that a fair statement?"

"Yes, sir."

"And yesterday you used the term 'steak knife'?"

"Yes, sir."

"Isn't it a fact that in the last four and a half years you have never used the term 'steak knife' to describe that knife? Isn't that correct?"

"Not that I remember, sir."

(At this point in the cross-examination Leino was beginning to get under the witness's skin and her composure was beginning to slip. Up to that point she had been sitting demurely in the witness chair, hands folded neatly in her lap; now she had placed one arm over the back of the chair, her legs were crossed, and the top leg was swinging back and forth.)

Leino: "You had a working relationship with Agent Lindner, did you not?"

"I don't understand what you mean."

"Well, he was the chief investigator, you were the victim?"

"Yes, sir."

"You worked together on this case, did you not?"

"Yes, sir."

"You had discussions with him, did you not?"

"Yes, sir."

"Did you have discussions about your identification of the assailant?"

"Yes, sir."

"And isn't it a fact that Agent Lindner told you that you had to make a positive identification of the assailant?"

"Yes, sir."

"Something short of a positive identification of the assailant isn't enough. Isn't that what he indicated to you?"

"Yes, sir."

"However, you stated that you simply couldn't be sure whe
you finished viewing the physical lineup. Isn't that true?"

"That I wasn't positive. Positive to me is 100 percent. I was 99.
percent sure."

"But you didn't use the term '99.9 percent sure' at the lineup
did you?"

"I don't remember, sir."

"You don't remember? Are you disputing the fact that you ma
have turned to Agent Lindner and said, 'I'm sorry, I simply can'
be sure'? Are you disputing the fact that you may have said that?"

"No, sir."

"You're not? So you may have said that?"

"Yes, sir."

"That's a fair statement?"

"Yes, sir."

"Now, with regard to the description of the assailant's automo
bile, you testified that you drove around with Agent Wardman t
look at cars. Isn't that true?"

"Yes, sir."

"You testified at the Article 32 hearing four years ago that yo
don't remember getting out of the car to look at any automobil
when you were driving around. Is that correct?"

"Yes, sir."

"Is that still your testimony here today?"

"Yes, sir. But the more I thought about it, I think I may hav
gotten out and looked inside the car. I am not going to stake m
life on that. I can't remember exactly if I did or not."

"You're not staking your life on that, are you?"

"I wouldn't swear to it, but I could have gotten out and looke
at a car."

"But this man's life is at the stake, isn't it?"

McNeil leaped to his feet. "Objection, Your Honor! Defens
counsel is making argument during examination."

Leino: "I will withdraw the question, Your Honor."

Judge Clark: "Excuse me. Members, will you step out, please?"
(The members of the jury withdrew from the courtroom.)

Judge Clark: "Please be seated, everyone. I'm going to counsel

counsel, just please remain seated, not to use direct examination or cross-examination as an opportunity to make argument."

Leino: "Yes, sir."

Judge Clark: "Once improper evidence comes out before the members, instructions have a very limited ability to erase it from their minds."

Leino: "Yes, sir."

Judge Clark: "Everyone is aware of the significance of this trial, not only for Corporal Scott, military justice, or the public perception of military justice in general, but it's of an immense nature and we must all ensure that it is conducted properly."

(The members of the jury were then recalled, and Leino continued his cross-examination.)

"Isn't it a fact that upon first viewing the lineup, you turned to Agent Lindner in response to his question 'Is the attacker there?' and you said, 'No, he's not'?"

"I don't remember saying that, sir."

Leino questioned Judy about the Identi-Kit, and her identification of Scott's car, sometimes covering ground covered earlier, sometimes repeating questions, but inevitably returning to the focus of his cross-examination: her identification of Scott.

"When you reviewed the photographs of people, do you remember looking at a brown folder and seeing six photographs?"

"Yes, sir."

"You picked out two individuals there, didn't you?"

"Yes, sir."

"And then, at the lineup?"

"Yes, sir."

"That was the first time that you recall having seen a profile of Lindsey Scott, the person that was later identified to you as Lindsey Scott. Isn't that correct?"

"Yes, sir."

"I mean, it's clear in your mind, and you testified previously, that you never saw this individual that attacked you prior to the night of the attack. Isn't that correct?"

"Yes, sir."

"However, you understand that you lived in the same apartment complex?"

"Yes, sir, and if I had seen him, I wouldn't have taken any notice of him because I didn't know who he was. I could have seen him but I wouldn't have known, I wouldn't have remembered him because I didn't know him."

"Well, if you had seen him, let's say more than once at a chance meeting. You understand that it's been represented at previous hearings that you supposedly had bumped into him with your husband?"

McNeil jumped up. "Objection, Your Honor. Assuming facts not in evidence."

Judge Clark sustained this objection and Leino withdrew the question. However, he had a point to get across to the jury: that there was a possibility—nothing more than that, a possibility—that the victim had seen Scott around the apartment complex where they both lived, perhaps even in the company of her husband, since they had worked and carpooled together and therefore, subliminally, on seeing photos of Scott, seeing him in the physical lineup, had selected that vaguely familiar face as the "ninety-nine percent sure" face of her attacker—because it was the only face that "rang a bell" with her.

So Leino rephrased the question but continued hammering at that point: "If you had seen him on more than one occasion, not necessarily on a regular basis, but in an apartment complex sometimes, for instance, people that live next door to each other will bump into one another just going in and out of the door. Is that a fair statement?"

"Yes, sir."

"Are you saying that in that type of casual contact, just within the confines of the apartment complex, you would have recalled him?"

"Yes, sir."

"So, is it a fair statement to say that if you had seen him before it was only on one occasion, and in no way were you introduced or anything like that?"

"If I had seen him before, it could have been on one or two occasions. It could have been on three or four occasions, but if I had ever seen him before, I would have just glanced over him. I wouldn't have remembered him. I don't know how many times

I could have seen him, but I certainly don't remember him. I didn't take any notice of him."

"I understand that . . . what I am trying to elicit from you is, are you saying that you may have run into Lindsey Scott three or four times in the apartment complex, and you wouldn't have been able to recognize him as an individual that you had seen before? Is that correct?"

"Yes, sir."

"Is that your testimony here today?"

"Yes, sir."

Leino left that area of questioning for a time, to ask Judy again about her identification of Scott's car, and asked her detailed questions—with apologies—about the sexual aspects of the attack. But always he returned to identification.

Leino: "At some point, you became aware of the fact that Agent Lindner wanted to be sure about your identification of the individual?"

"That is correct."

"And isn't that why you said, 'I'm sorry, I can't be sure,' because in your own mind you weren't completely sure of the identification?"

"I wasn't one hundred percent, that's correct."

And Leino again, later in the cross-examination: "Isn't it a fact that the positive identifications that you've given in this case, meaning that's him, to the best of your recollection, occurred first when looking at the Smith & Wesson composite and then later at the formal proceedings, after you discussed your case with the government lawyers? Is that a fair statement?"

"No, I was sure. I was 99.9 percent sure all along, sir."

"In fact you said at your preliminary hearing that you were ninety-nine percent sure. Isn't that correct?"

"Yes, sir."

"But you're never absolutely sure?"

"One hundred percent?"

"One hundred percent. Is it a fair statement that you're not absolutely sure here today, meaning between ninety-nine and one hundred percent?"

"No, sir. I'm as sure as anybody could ever be, sir."

"Now. Four and a half years later. Is that right?"

"Yes, sir."

Just before the lunch break, Leino closed out his cross-examination with another, similar exchange, one more time drawing out from Judy Connors her admission that she never had been able to say, with certainty, that she was "one hundred percent sure."

On Friday, January 29, 1988, while in the courtroom at LeJeune Hall in Quantico, Virginia, Lieutenant Commander Ronald L. Schubert, of the Navy Reserve Medical Corps, was describing the knife wounds suffered by Judy Connors, some three thousand miles away, in Richmond, California, an extraordinary event, on the sly, was taking place. Until now, only a handful of people ever knew what occurred. How author Ellis A. Cohen found out is no less extraordinary.

In the late spring of 1988, months after the court-martial, Cohen received a late-night telephone call at his residence in Los Angeles. The caller identified himself and said he would speak on the condition of absolute anonymity. Cohen recognized the name: a senior Marine officer, highly placed within the Quantico-base command structure. The caller said he had a copy of a "confidential" document relevant to the Scott case. It had not come into his hands until recently, and though the case was over, he believed that Cohen would find this document of importance. And, the caller said, he felt duty bound to reveal its contents. He instructed Cohen to fly to Washington and told him what airline and flight to take. He told Cohen to check baggage. At the baggage carousel, he would come by and hand him the document.

That is exactly how it happened; Cohen was standing at the carousel when a man in civilian clothes approached him (Cohen vaguely recognized him but said nothing), handed him a nine-by-twelve manila envelope, shook his hand, said "good luck," then turned and disappeared into the crowd.

That document, marked "CONFIDENTIAL," includes photocopies of photographs. It is dated 5/9/88. It is on the letterhead of Forensic Science Associates of Richmond, California. Parts of it have been summarized (where noted) or excluded, including some technical chemical analyses the authors felt were not necessary to this publication. The document, in letter form, is addressed to Colonel James P. McHenry, Judge Advocate, Quarters 195, Quantico, VA 22134. It begins: "The following information was communicated to me by Colonel James McHenry and Lieutenant General Frank Petersen."

A short summary of the Scott case followed, including the FBI examination of physical evidence in 1983 and again in December of 1987, containing vaginal slides and swabs and the victim's panties. Part of this document is now presented verbatim:

The vaginal swabs (Q4) and panties were reexamined by the FBI Laboratory in December of 1987 (Report dated January 7, 1988). At this examination semen was identified on the vaginal swabs and panties; however, the genetic tests on these items were inconclusive. In January 1988, vaginal slides were submitted to Cellmark Diagnostics for DNA testing. At my suggestion the underpants were also submitted to Cellmark. The Cellmark analysis was initiated by the defendant. The analysis failed to obtain useful DNA from either the slides or the panties (Report dated February 16, 1988).

On January 29, 1988, I met with Colonel McHenry and Lieutenant General Petersen at my office in California. At that time I advised them that the DNA analysis being attempted by Cellmark had virtually no chance of success. They were further advised of the potential value of the underpants evidence. The former evaluation was based on the five-year age of the specimens stored at room temperature. [Authors' note: the victim's panties were kept in a paper bag in a file drawer.] They were advised that the DNA in biological specimens stored for this length of time at room temperature causes severe degradation of the DNA, making the Cellmark analysis virtually impossible. The only mechanism for gaining probative DNA typing information from these specimens was through the use of the PCR amplification strategy described below. It was requested that such DNA typing studies be initiated in order to assist Lieutenant General Petersen in potential postconviction review and to shed whatever light on the identity of——

assailant. [Note: authors have blocked out real name of victim.] The timing of this request for analysis together with the scheduling of the court-martial undermined any potential use of this analysis in the Scott trial itself.

The PCR amplification strategy mentioned above is rather technical. Its results can, however, be summarized by saying that the type of the sperm found in the victim's vaginal swab and panties was of a type (called DQα type 3, 7. in the document) "that occurs in approximately nine percent of the population. Lindsey Scott was determined to be DQα type 3, 7.; therefore, he cannot be eliminated as the semen donor in this case."

This January 29 meeting at Forensic Science Associates between McHenry and Petersen, during the first week of the trial, and the subsequent findings, did not end their involvement, or the events documented.

The following items of physical evidence were received from Gail Papure of Park Ridge Hospital on 2/10/88 via U.S. Express Mail: [Authors' note: the trial was still in progress.]
1. Five vials of blood labeled——[real name of victim's husband deleted by authors] (3 EDT A vials, 2 Clot vials).

The following items of physical evidence were received from the Naval Investigation Service (NIS), Quantico, on 2/9/88 via U.S. Express mail:
2. Vial of blood labeled——EDT A (1/27/88).
3. Vial of blood labeled Lindsey Scott, EDT A (1/27/88).
4. Plastic bag labeled one slide from item C, Log #QV048-83 with a slide mailer containing one unmounted slide labeled——, sperm motile.
5. Bag labeled one acid phosphatase tube with sample [not legible] from victim containing plastic tube labeled——, 4/21/83, acid phosphatase, containing approximately ¼ swab. . . .

The document is signed Edward T. Blake, D. Crim. [Authors' note: This was the chief DNA expert hired by Robert Shapiro, lead defense attorney for O.J. Simpson.]

(There is more to this document, but the authors feel that the above extracts clearly shows its significance. The defense team did not know about this secret meeting. And when author Cohen later questioned Petersen on why he and McHenry made the trip themselves, he refused to comment.)

When the trial resumed after the weekend, most observers reckoned that with the testimony and cross-examination of the victim completed, the prosecution's case was just about complete as well. However, there remained fireworks still to come before the defense called its witnesses.

The February 3 edition of *The Washington Post* reported that:

> In cross-examinations of government witnesses during the first seven days of Scott's court martial . . . the [defense] lawyers have suggested that, at best, the investigation [by NIS] was a bungling display of oversight and incompetence and, at worst, a ham-handed attempt to frame an innocent man. . . . Gary Myers, one of Scott's three attorneys, repeatedly pointed to what he hinted were flaws in the investigation, which he scorned as "a day late and a dollar short."
>
> The thrust of the criticism by Scott's attorneys is that the investigation prematurely fixed on Scott as the assailant and failed to consider the possibility of other suspects. For example, NIS agent David C. Martin testified [on Monday after the break] that there were about 90 blacks in Security Battalion on Quantico. "What other black men . . . were investigated in any depth?" asked Myers. "None that I'm aware of, sir," replied Martin.

From the outset, Scott's attorneys decided to keep him off the witness stand. They felt that his poor performance at his first court-martial indicated that he was too emotionally involved, he angered easily, and when he was angry he became confused and no longer knew what he was saying. "McNeil would make mincemeat of him in front of a jury," Leino said.

However, at the end of the first week of the trial, Scott indicated that he wanted to take the stand to refute some of the things NIS agents had said about him. Leino and Myers strongly rejected this idea—but then an opportunity arose to allow him to testify in a reasonably insulated atmosphere, without the presence of the jury. This occurred when the defense made a motion to suppress the testimony of a prosecution witness—the Quantico Town's police chief, Leo Rodriguez.

An "Article 39(a)" was called for, which meant the jurors were sent from the courtroom. Rodriguez testified—as several investigators had done already—that he noticed the passenger side of Scott's car appeared to have been "wiped down." The prosecution's suggestion was that Scott had done this to eradicate forensic evidence. Rodriguez said he asked Scott, "Why did you only clean this side?" and the officer said that Scott replied, "That's all the time I had."

Scott's attorneys claimed that remark should not be allowed as testimony before the jury because Rodriguez had not advised Scott of his rights before starting the conversation, and because he had terminated his interview with NIS investigators and said he wanted a lawyer. It was here that Leino and Myers decided to let Scott take the stand.

After Myers questioned him briefly about his demand to see a lawyer before he made any more statements to the investigators, McNeil cross-examined. Over the next twenty-nine minutes (as Leino held his head in his hands and Myers and Lynch noticeably winced), Scott wilted, stumbled over his words, and appeared so confused and shaken by McNeil's rapid-fire barrage of questions that his credibility was undoubtedly damaged.

The agonizing twenty-nine minutes were, at least, "damage limitation," since the jurors were not present. And when he returned to his seat, Scott said to his lawyers, "Don't let me do that again." Judge Clark ruled in favor of the prosecution and Rodriguez was allowed to tell his side of the story to the jury.

On Friday, February 5, the prosecution called its twentieth witness, Commander Steven S. Sohn, a Navy forensic pathologist, to the stand. He testified that the victim had suffered an abrasion on her neck, consistent with a wound inflicted by a serrated knife.

With that, the prosecution rested its case.

Scott's lawyers then made a pro forma motion asking Judge

Clark for a summary verdict of not guilty. The judge denied the motion.

The defense, in reality, had only one big gun in its arsenal of witnesses: Ruby Hills. And her alibi for Scott would have to withstand McNeil's inevitable assault on her "improved memory." For whatever it might be worth, Leino, Myers, and Lynch could derive some comfort in the points Leino scored in his cross-examination of NIS Agent Lindner and Judy Connors.

Over the weekend Leino called Lori to bring her up to date on the trial, to ask about her health, and to inquire about the readiness of their star witness. He also spoke to Ruby herself. At the early-Monday-morning meeting in "the Bunker," Leino reported to his colleagues, and to Cohen, that Ruby sounded well prepared—"thanks to Lori's prep"—but, he said, his heart was breaking when he spoke to Lori: "Her voice was hoarse and low. She sounded terrible. I could feel her spirit, but I couldn't hear it. That's something I miss."

An earlier request by author Cohen for an interview with base commander Lieutenant General Petersen was finally granted, and on the morning of February 8, PAO Bobbi Weinberger escorted Cohen upstairs—above the LeJeune courtroom—for a brief but exclusive interview with him. Because the trial was still in progress, Petersen refused all direct questions that pertained to the case. Even so, Cohen asked him a few questions "just so he knew where my interest was":

1. Was there a specific reason you decided to court-martial Scott again?

2. Many supporters of Scott don't think he can get a fair trial at Quantico, that the command has poisoned the base with rhetoric about his guilt. Are you endangering your last month or so (Petersen was due to retire) with the possibility of Scott being found guilty again—and on your watch?

Cohen reports: "In answer to both of these questions and others, Petersen just smiled, but the PAO—Weinberger—stared daggers at me for being so direct with the general. So I realized that maybe I was there for another reason. The general, before I left him, asked some curious questions about my potential TV movie . . .

and to play his type of game, I ducked answering him with any specifics. But to my surprise, Petersen said: 'Mr. Cohen, I have met Bill Cosby and I think he would be an ideal choice to play me in your movie.'

"I could not help but think, as I left Petersen, that Scott might be sentenced to thirty years hard labor again, and Petersen was concerned about who would portray him in a potential movie."

The week began badly. Another 39(a) session was called (members of the jury absent). The defense wanted to introduce testimony from Dr. Gwynne Peirson, an assistant professor of criminology at Howard University, showing that NIS agents had used flawed photographic and physical lineups to obtain identification from the victim of her assailant. Peirson was also prepared to challenge the NIS method of identifying Scott's car.

Peirson said it was improper of the NIS to allow the victim's husband, who worked with Scott, to be in the car with her as they drove around the base with NIS Agent Wardman looking for the attacker's vehicle. There was a chance, he said, that he could help his wife identify Scott's car. "I cannot think of any circumstances where that would be proper," Peirson said. "Either it was done through incompetence or with intent to focus the identification."

The lineups were similarly improper, Peirson claimed. He pointed out that in the six-photo lineup only two of the men bore any similarity to the victim's description of her attacker, and the victim picked out both of them. Afterward, in the physical lineup, Scott was the only person who had also been in the photo lineup. "By including only one person in the photo lineup and the physical lineup," Peirson said, "you are narrowing the focus."

The prosecution presented its own "academic expert" to rebut Peirson. Dr. Michael McCloskey, a psychology professor at Johns Hopkins University, testified that there is "no scientific evidence" beyond "common sense" proving that lineups can be biased. "Common sense," he said, would dictate that a lineup with five white men and one black would be unfair if the suspect was black.

After listening to both academics, Judge Clark decided that Peirson had not proved his expertise in lineup identification and rejected him as an expert witness.

The next day another blow fell: this was the attempt to introduce as evidence the videotape made by private investigator Morgan Cherry (previously alluded to), which, the defense claimed, proved that based on time and distance covered by various events, Scott could not have committed the crime because he was elsewhere. This was intended to complement Ruby Hills's testimony that Scott was at Zayre's when the crime was supposed to have been committed.

Judge Clark refused to allow this as evidence, sustaining the prosecution objection that the eighty-four-minute tape was unreliable, particularly since the scene of the attack had never been found.

The defense put Lola Scott on the stand. There wasn't much hard evidence she could contribute except to support her husband's testimony about that small bucket that had always loomed large in the prosecution's case. Judy Connors remembered a silver metallic bucket on the backseat of her assailant's car, filled with objects that clanked around: investigators had removed from Scott's apartment a metal pot they claimed was filled with cleaning materials. Scott insisted that he would never have used a cooking pot for his cleaning utensils, but had used a green plastic bucket to clean his old apartment. Lola supported this story. Shown a photograph of the green bucket, she said, "I know in my heart that this is the bucket. The way I was brought up, the way my husband was brought up, I know and he knows that you do not use a pot to clean the floors with," she said. "It's to cook food in."

A more useful witness—if the jury was prepared to believe what he had to say—was Marine Sergeant Sammy Lee. Stationed in New Orleans when he heard of the second court-martial, he volunteered to come up and testify for Scott. Lee said he had been at Quantico at the time of the crime and had helped set up the stage for the lineup. According to Lee, when the actual lineup was held, he heard an NIS agent (Lindner) ask the woman (Judy Connors), "Can you identify anyone standing back there?" Lee said he was just four feet away when the woman looked through the peephole for fifteen or twenty seconds. "She looked back at him," Lee testified, "and said no."

Earlier in the trial, Scott's lawyers had protested that the NIS had been harassing Lee ever since they'd discovered that he was going to testify. They questioned him twice and asked him to take a polygraph test. He refused. Asked by reporters if he believed that the NIS had been trying to intimidate him, Lee said, "Yes, they tried to. But it didn't work." (The judge refused to allow any testimony on that subject.)

At this point in the trial, matters seemed to be going the prosecution's way. Judge Clark's recent decisions against the defense had darkened the mood of the defense table. Scott was beginning to worry. During the breaks he was seen pacing back and forth in the hallway. "I'm getting a little nervous," he said to Cohen.

Later that day Scott's father held an impromptu press conference on the LeJeune Hall steps. He said he was not satisfied with the way the judge was running the trial. "It's beginning to look like it's going to be the same old kangaroo court," he said. Mr. Scott got both TV and newspaper coverage with his remarks, and Gary Myers hit the roof. He approached Lindsey and said, "What we *don't* need now is any badgering of the judge. I understand your dad's feelings, but please try to restrain him while we're all trying to get the court convinced that you're the wrong man!"

Thursday, February 11, the fourteenth day of the trial, dawned cold and clear. Myers picked up Cohen at six A.M. so they could get to LeJeune Hall early for a conference with Leino and Lynch. This was the day Ruby Hills was scheduled to testify. Scott would get the alibi he desperately needed. As Myers and Cohen reached LeJeune Hall they had the opportunity to witness the daily ritual of the raising of the colors, which always took place in front of LeJeune Hall because the commanding general was based there. While a bugler stood by, ready to play, three Marines surrounded the flagpole ready to raise the Stars and Stripes. Two officers stood as witnesses behind the bugler. Myers and Cohen watched the ceremony, and for a minute or so forgot about the trial and why they were there. It was a moving moment.

Operational strategy in the Bunker that morning was hushed. The lawyers knew they were in a corner; they had to score big with Ruby Hills. Before Ruby, however, they would put Pam Biller on the stand.

Pam testified between 9:40 and 11:30 that morning. She said she recalled serving Scott a Coke in Zayre's sometime in late April. After checking her time card for that week to refresh her memory, she said she believed it was April 20, but she could not be certain.

The judge called for a lunch break, and Scott's lawyers retired to the Bunker for a meeting and a hasty lunch. Leino was just finishing a sandwich his wife had packed for him and going over some transcripts and notes when there was a knock at the door. A Marine excused himself and said two women were at the front-door security checkpoint looking for him. Leino knew who one of them would be: Ruby Hills. Who the other one was puzzled him. He threw on his suit jacket and raced out to the hallway and up the steps to the main lobby.

There, to his amazement, alongside Ruby Hills was Lori Jackson—a very frail-looking Lori Jackson. She looked awful, shrunken, with her overcoat almost falling off her thinning frame. Her face was yellow with jaundice. She could speak only in a hoarse whisper. "John . . . how are things going? I heard . . . do you need my help?" Leino embraced her. She was shivering slightly in the cold. "Everything is just fine, Lori," he said to her. "But what are you doing here? It's freezing outside! You should be home in bed!"

"I know," she said. "But I just wanted to make sure everything goes all right today with Ruby."

His big, burly arms around her, Leino said, "Bless you. You never quit, do you? Now, I want you to get right back in your daughter's car and get back to your nice warm house. As always I'll call you tonight and tell you about the good results." And with that he gave her a kiss on the cheek, then turned away quickly so she wouldn't see the tears in his eyes.

Ruby Hills did her job that day. She explained why at the first court-martial she could not place Scott in Zayre's on the night of April 20, 1983, but that today she could. She had been given the opportunity to cross-reference her files and could now state unequivocally that she had seen Scott in the store from 8:15 to 8:30 that night. Asked by one of the jurors how she could remember Scott's face months and years later, she said that she remembered that he was very unusual looking. She said he had a face that "reminded me of Howdy Doody, with his squirrelly cheeks and froggy eyes."

Ruby told the judge that she had been harassed and intimidated since she became a witness for the defense in the Scott case. She told of anonymous phone callers threatening her and of accusations that she was romantically involved with Scott and was helping him only because they were both black.

Toward the close of the day's proceedings McNeil laid the groundwork for his assault on Ruby's credibility. "Have you ever stretched the truth in court when you testified?" he asked.

"No," Ruby replied.

Although Ruby was their last witness, Scott's attorneys did not "rest" the defense, but asked for a continuance till Tuesday to await the results of the DNA test from Cellmark Diagnostics (as mentioned previously they had no knowledge of Petersen and McHenry's trip to California, and the opinion of Dr. Edward T. Blake of Forensic Science Associates that the "DNA analysis being attempted by Cellmark had virtually no chance of success)".

Judge Clark granted the extension and adjourned the court till that time.

Ruby's testimony gave a lift to Scott and to the defense attorneys. It was their first "hit" in many days. According to a reporter for the *Free Lance-Star*, "After striking out several times early in the game, Corporal Lindsey Scott's defense team connected for a ninth-inning home run yesterday. But they won't know whether it was a game-winner until next week, when the case is expected to go to the jury."

Gary Myers also weighed in with a baseball analogy. Asked if he thought Ruby Hills's testimony could salvage Scott's defense, Myers told the reporter from *The Washington Post,* "Don't forget Bobby Thomson"—a reference to the pennant-winning ninth-inning home run, "the shot heard round the world," hit by the New York Giants' Bobby Thomson against the Brooklyn Dodgers in 1951.

The next day Cohen received a phone call from Lori at his hotel. She seemed pleased with the newspaper accounts of Ruby Hills's testimony. She told Cohen that it was now time for her to check into the hospital, but first she was going to do an interview with Lee Hockstader of *The Washington Post*. Cohen told her he would stay in touch with her daily.

"Please don't tell anyone where I am," she said to him.

Cohen agreed and told her he'd come to visit her soon. "Just follow everything your doctors tell you to do," he said.

26

It could be said that there was a kind of perverse irony in the fact that Lori Jackson, a woman with so much love to give, and who gave so much love, should enter the hospital on St. Valentine's Day. It was a sunny, but very cold February 14 that saw her leave her dream house in Spotsylvania County. Her husband drove her into Washington, D.C., accompanied by some of her children, where she was admitted to Washington National Hospital. As she was being pushed by wheelchair to her room—followed closely by two of her daughters, one holding a small suitcase, the other carrying a plant—Lori, ever attuned to current events, *her* current events, tugged at Paul's sleeve and said, "Don't forget, I need to have a TV with cable in my room. For CNN. And I want them to deliver *The Washington Post* every morning."

Lee Hockstader's interview with her in *The Washington Post* appeared just two days later. The lengthy page-one story titled CORPORAL SCOTT'S ARDENT PATRON (subtitled *Virginia Civil Rights Activist Is Called "Heart and Soul" Behind Marine's Case*) delved into her background and her childhood "brushes with the Ku Klux Klan" in Alabama, but concentrated on the Scott case—and on the state of her health.

Hockstader described how she had come to know Scott through the letter he'd sent imploring her to help him, and how, once she had decided to take up his cause, "the case . . . was transformed from a line entry on Quantico's judicial docket to her crusade for civil rights and individual justice in the Marine Corps." The journalist said that now, as Scott's second court-martial neared its end, Lori was recognized as "Scott's most ardent patron." He quoted John Leino's paean to her: "the heart and soul behind our case."

Hockstader mentioned that after five years of fighting for Scott, her absence from the gallery had been noted. He wrote of the rumors that she had cancer. (Secretive still about her true condition, Lori denied the rumor to the reporter, insisting on calling it "high blood pressure.") Hockstader quoted her: "I heard a rumor, too. They had me on my deathbed. Do I look like I'm dying?" Nevertheless, the reporter said that she had "lost a tremendous amount of weight. . . . The whites of her eyes are yellow as lemons and her weight loss has drawn the skin tightly over her cheekbones."

That was not the only Hockstader byline in the *Post* that day. In his regular coverage of the Scott trial, he reported (as did many others) that the results of the DNA testing on the semen samples recovered from Judy Connors's panties and from the vaginal smears were "inconclusive." Gary Myers, who had instigated the defense request, now said he would ask Judge Clark for an eight-week continuance so that further tests could be made— perhaps elsewhere than at Cellmark Diagnostics. Myers said he didn't think it likely, however, that the judge would grant the defense request. He was right. Clark turned him down.

When the trial continued, the expected attack on Ruby Hills's credibility continued with a vengeance. STAR WITNESS CALLED A LIAR screamed a headline next day in the *Potomac News*. In fact three area law-enforcement officers came to the witness stand and claimed that Ruby Hills was a liar.

"She's not truthful," said Prince William County Police Captain Charles E. O'Shields. He and polygraph examiner Allan R. Marlett testified that Hills had lied to them in interviews when she applied to become a police officer in 1981. Both said they would not believe her testimony.

The third witness, Fairfax County police officer Terry Lee Maxwell, told the jury that she knew of at least one time that Ruby Hills had lied in a Prince William County court case. It had to do with a shoplifting arrest made by Hills. Asked by prosecutor McNeil if she would believe testimony by Hills under oath, Maxwell said no.

Ruby, in rebuttal, said O'Shields was testifying against her because she once "stepped on his toes" by filing a sex-and-racial discrimination complaint against him after she was denied a job with the Prince William County police. She alleged that the testimony against her was prompted by "bruised egos and a thirst for publicity," her accusers having heard that there might be a TV movie made about the trial. "This case is turning people into demons," she said.

The defense also called in rebuttal a string of witnesses who testified that they knew Ruby Hills to be an honest person. Among them were Charles Walker, her former landlord; Philip Qualls, who worked with her at Zayre's; and Gary Pittman, a Prince William County police officer.

On the morning of February 17, after all rebuttal witnesses had been called and testified for both sides, Gary Myers announced, "The defense rests." It was 10:22 A.M.

Judge Clark called a recess. "Stay by your phones to 1330," he said to the members of the jury. While most visitors in the gallery remained glued to their seats (in order not to lose them) the defense team retired to the Bunker to think—and to avoid thinking. What was done was done. John Leino, however, began mentally rehearsing his closing arguments, which would come after the prosecution, in the person of Major Ron McNeil, stated its case.

At two P.M. Judge Clark returned, a small suitcase slung over his shoulder and carrying four large notebooks. Gunnery Sergeant Gasporatti—the official court recorder—distributed copies, in booklet form, of the court's official instructions to all attorneys. "Do counsel want to add anything at this time?" asked the judge. Both Myers and Leino said that they wanted to take the opportunity, publicly and for the official record, to thank the military counsel, Captain Brennan Lynch, for the superb job he had done.

At 2:17, Judge Clark said, "Now that all evidence has been presented, the government must be able to prove beyond a reasonable doubt that the accused is guilty of all charges." Three minutes later, Major McNeil rose, faced the members of the jury, and began his closing argument.

He pointed out how important this case was—"important to Corporal Scott . . . important to the military justice system . . . important to Judy Connors." McNeil said that he would highlight the evidence given by witnesses so that the jury would understand the government's position. "And the government's position is that we have proven beyond a reasonable doubt that Corporal Scott is the perpetrator of these crimes." He went to explain what reasonable doubt meant, and said he would present his argument in four parts: first, Judy Connors; second, the investigation; three, the accused, Corporal Scott; four, the defense witnesses, "and the attempted production of an alibi defense."

Immediately McNeil brought up Ruby Hills: he reminded the jurors that "two women came into this court and testified that they each saw Corporal Scott on the night of twenty April, 1983. Who do you believe? Judy Connors or Ruby Hills? Who is more credible? Who had the ability to more accurately recall the time and events that took place . . . the time . . . and the date? Who had the greater opportunity to observe Corporal Scott and recall the details of that observation?"

The prosecutor reviewed the movements of Judy Connors on the night of the crime, as she had related them during her testimony. He compared the ability of Judy Connors to tell investigators about what happened, and about her assailant, hours after the event, with the fact that Ruby Hills was called upon to testify in court—at the first court-martial—five months after the event, about what she was doing on the night of the crime. "In the five months between April and when she was called upon to testify she saw thousands of people enter the store," and during that time, said McNeil, there was nothing to direct her attention to Corporal Scott or to cause her to think about him. Yet she claimed she saw him that night at eight o'clock. But she could not recall the date at the first court-martial. McNeil then described how it was—according to Ruby Hills—that during the second court-martial she could recall the date. "We find her testimony incredible," he said.

McNeil said that there were many things that Judy Connors accurately identified: Scott's car, inside and out. She identified his clothes, picked him out with the use of the Identi-Kit, the photo lineup, and the physical lineup. She was with him for forty-five minutes, McNeil said, always close to him. "Her memory was current. Her memory was fresh." McNeil compared that with the fact that Ruby Hills only saw him—according to her own testimony—for perhaps five or ten minutes. "She never walked up to him, she never talked to him," McNeil pointed out. "She observed him from an upstairs vantage point at Zayre's. Through binoculars."

McNeil implied that Ruby Hills might have been influenced by suggestion from Lori Jackson, who showed her photographs of Scott. "Ruby Hills then becomes friends with Lori Jackson. A civil-rights activist." (At the mention of Lori's name, John Leino turned red with anger.)

Returning to Judy Connors's identification of Scott as her attacker, McNeil reminded the jury that she had said, repeatedly, that she was "99.9 percent sure" it was Scott. In the courtroom she pointed to Scott as her attacker, McNeil said. In indicating to the jury that Judy Connors had been very close to Scott during the ride in the car and during the attack, and had ample opportunity to see his face, he indulged in details of the sexual assault.

"We talk about five minutes, we talk about two minutes, we talk about ten minutes very easily in our lives. I'm going to ask you to do something for me when you go back into the deliberation room. I'm going to ask you to time two or three minutes. Sit there for two or three minutes and think of Judy Connors having to pump Corporal Scott's penis, and then evaluate if she had a good opportunity to observe Corporal Scott . . . then I'm going to ask you to time five to eight to ten minutes and visualize Corporal Scott raping Judy Connors and then evaluate if that was sufficient time for Judy Connors to identify Corporal Scott as the person who attacked her."

As for the issue of Scott's gold tooth, McNeil said: "Well, the government contends it's not that obvious. . . ."

The prosecutor continued with an analysis of the investigation. "Consider," he said to the jury, "that NIS is not on trial, CID is not on trial, the Quantico Police Department is not on trial, and the Prince William County Police Department is not on trial. Corporal Scott is . . . Corporal Scott *is* on trial." Contrary to what the defense contends, McNeil said, "There was no pressure put on

NIS to go out and find a suspect . . . you heard Agent Dick Wardman testify—he was the senior agent in charge of NIS at the time—that the commanding general didn't apply any pressure to him, the chief of staff didn't apply any pressure to him, the staff judge advocate didn't apply any pressure to him, and his superiors within NIS didn't apply any pressure."

McNeil contended that the reason investigators concentrated on Security Battalion was that the caller had mentioned CID, and "how many Marines on the base know what CID is? The caller obviously knew." The language of the caller, the prosecutor said, was the language that would be used by a police officer. The caller knew the Connors's phone number, where to park his car, knew Kevin Connors was working that night, McNeil said.

NIS agents wanted to be fair to Corporal Scott, McNeil claimed. "In fairness to NIS, they screened over a hundred Marines in Security Battalion," he said (the defense had always disputed this claim and contended that the prosecution had never been able to provide proof of it).

"Now let's talk about part three of my argument. Let's talk about Corporal Scott," said McNeil. "It's the government's belief that Corporal Scott's actions show a consciousness of killing." His actions on the morning following the crime, said the prosecutor, the fact that—according to investigators—he appeared to be nervous, that he asked questions about semen, about forensic evidence, all point to the fact that he was nervous because he was a suspect, "and the reason he was a suspect in his own mind was because he had committed the crime. . . .

"Corporal Scott appeared to be upset on the morning of the twenty-first of April," said McNeil, "because Corporal Scott never expected Judy Connors to live . . . he never intended her to live . . . that's why he was surprised the next morning when he heard his supervisor talking about what had taken place the night before." When he realized that Judy Connors was still alive, said McNeil, and had described her attacker as having short hair, a Marine Corps haircut, Scott went out to try to cover his tracks. "He washed his car down, he got a haircut."

Toward the conclusion of this part, McNeil turned to the subject of motive: "Why would Corporal Scott do something like this? We don't know why. We do not have to prove a motive in this case. We think the motive in this case·was sex, however . . . and the intent, was murder.

"I'm now prepared to start part four." McNeil began to try to discredit defense witnesses. Pam Biller, he said, "contributed nothing." As for Lola Scott: "The government feels sorry for Mrs. Scott. She's trying to save her husband . . . but there are inaccuracies in her testimony." McNeil got on to Sergeant Lee's testimony about Judy Connors's words at the physical lineup. "Sergeant Lee's testimony is not credible," the prosecutor said. He said that testimony from a number of NIS agents who were at the lineup, and a sergeant who stood guard, pointed to the possibility that Sergeant Lee had not been in the lineup room at the time. For all these years, said McNeil, Lee never said anything to anybody about what he claimed Judy Connors said at the lineup. "The government contends that if he really was there, he would have brought it to somebody's attention immediately. For reasons unknown he came to this court and testified that he was present and he saw these things when in fact he didn't see them.

"Now let's come to the alibi witnesses." First McNeil discussed Pam Biller. He mentioned that when Agent Lindner showed her a mug shot of Scott, she didn't remember seeing him. Then he brought Lori into his argument again, insinuating that she might very well have influenced Pam Biller's thinking by showing her a photo of Scott with his cap on, and talking to her about Scott, "possibly about Scott's situation and the fact that he needed an alibi and that he was in a lot of trouble." (Leino, inflamed at McNeil's implication, furiously started writing notes.)

"It's ridiculous to expect that we should believe the testimony of Pam Biller," said McNeil.

Similarly, McNeil scoffed at the testimony of Ruby Hills, at her "improved memory" between the time of the first trial, when she could not pinpoint the date she said she had seen Scott, and now, when she claimed a further look at records enabled her to name the date as April 20. "Incredible testimony," said McNeil. "Her friendship develops with Lori Jackson. We think she was trying to help Lori Jackson. She goes to Lori Jackson's house for the *60 Minutes* airing [he meant the filming].

"We believe that Lori Jackson and Ruby Hills were so friendly that Lori Jackson helped Ruby Hills testify. The government contends that she is not a truthful person and she should not be believed."

Staring directly at the jury, McNeil concluded, "You have to evaluate the testimony and the credibility of all these witnesses, and I'm certain you will do that. We believe, the government believes, that we have proven the guilt of Corporal Scott beyond a reasonable doubt. As a result of that, we request that you return a verdict of guilty to all the charges and specifications."

Judge Clark called a 39(a) session then (with the jurors absent) for one simple purpose: he said to Scott, "Corporal Scott, you do have a right to testify." Scott replied, "Yes, sir." And that was all.

It was 4:10, the jury was recalled. Judge Clark informed them that Corporal Scott would not be testifying. (Just then Lola Scott entered the courtroom for the first time that day. Her nerves raw, she had wanted to hear John Leino's closing arguments.)

From the moment Leino began speaking, at 4:12, the difference between his style and the prosecutor's was glaring. McNeil, understandably, was cool, dispassionate, efficient, calculating, logical. Leino was fiercely impassioned, his voice full of emotion. It was clear that Leino spoke from the heart—and to the heart . . . to the hearts of the members of the jury, as well as to their minds.

He appeared tired as he stood up to speak, and his voice, hoarse, strained, revealed his weariness as he paced back and forth in front of the jury, saying to them, "You'll have to excuse me a little bit, it's the weight of about four and a half years as counsel on this case." He paused for a moment, then went on, slowly, in measured tones, as was his style: "Most cases, to most lawyers, are important. Some cases, once in the life of an attorney, if he's lucky, reach a point where the Constitution of the United States becomes a real, viable entity in the courtroom. You can touch it, you can feel it, taste it, smell it, as sure as the sunlight that's coming in through the windows of this courtroom."

Leino spoke of his mentor, T. Brooke Howard (then eighty-five), "a living legend," and how he, Leino, "used to kid him that

his first law partner was Thomas Jefferson . . . and if there i
one thing he taught me that stays with me, about the criminal law
and the pit, here, is that the single most powerful entity i
jurisprudence is common sense. The reasoning of the jurors. Th
experience that we talk about that a jury has. It must be over
hundred years here. The document that was celebrated last year, i
two hundred years old. And the basis of that document is reason
Reason cited as ideals, and I would represent to you and I don'
think anyone would dispute it here today, that the most importan
thing about that document in this trial, even after four and a hal
years, is the presumption of innocence." Leino wheeled suddenl
and pointed at Scott. "He is innocent right now. Unequivocally
unrebuttable presumption, *he is innocent.*"

The courtroom was breathlessly silent as Leino spoke. Th
jurors, as expressionless as they had been when McNeil spoke
appeared to be more attentive, however. Several leaned forward
The two women—Breeding and Schmoller—began taking non
stop notes.

"He'll only be guilty, if you decide that he is guilty," Leino
continued. "And how do you do that? You recognize the heav
burden that the *people* have placed upon the government, and tha
is—proof beyond a reasonable doubt. The government can't tak
you to the front steps of the cathedral and make you walk alone u
those steps . . . and get married at the altar. They have to tak
you by the hand . . . and show you, this is what happened, thi
is how it happened . . . and they've got to do it to the exclusio
of the reasonable defense. The defense here is alibi. Everyon
understands that.

"The defense relies on certain testimony to establish that alibi
If you don't believe that alibi . . . he's still innocent. Why
Because they have to establish his guilt . . . beyond a reasonabl
doubt."

Then, in a whisper to the jury, almost as though he were tellin
them a secret: "They can't make you suspect that Scott did this
That he snuck around doing these different things . . . then h
blew it and then he panicked. *That's not it.*" Leino paused, fo
effect, then his voice rose. "They can't sit back and say, 'Yo
know, we think he probably did it.'

"Lest anyone be confused, or uncertain," Leino continued, "this efense team, in this trial, recognizes absolute, positive human orror, the horror that Judy Connors underwent . . . that she's een living with all these years and that she will continue to live vith for the rest of her life. She is the absolute victim . . . but iere are other victims. At this stage, with the presumption of inocence, it may very well be that Corporal Scott is also a ictim."

(At this point, as though on cue—but of course in reaction to ₎eino's words—Lola Scott rushed from the courtroom, crying.)

Leino continued after that brief interruption, moving on to the nore prosaic subjects of the prosecution's case versus that of the efense. Dramatically, his voice rising, then falling, now slowly, ow rushing quickly through a sentence, he attacked the investi- ,ation, the investigators, the prosecution's evidence for failing to rove Scott's guilt "beyond a reasonable doubt. That's their duty," ₎eino said.

"Four and a half years ago, Judy Connors testified that 'I did not et a good look at the car or the driver in the parking lot when he acked up to me.' There's nothing sinister here. I know from her ieart of hearts she was testifying to the best of her recollection. he was committed . . . she was committed to *'my prosecutors.'* The second brace of prosecutors. Why does she say that? Think. Reason it through. Why does she have the attitude that these ¿entlemen are *her* prosecutors? I'm not saying there was some ₎ind of conspiracy . . . the term was used by them . . . but I'm aying through the development of this thing . . . the victim ✸ecomes the victim twice over. My cocounsel, Gary Myers, brings ιp an excellent point. He says, 'In her mind, someone has to pay.' The outrage I've suffered requires that someone has to pay, and 'm relying on my prosecutors, and I'm relying on the investiga- ₎ors to make certain . . . because that's their job.

"So when she comes to the stand four years later, she says, 'I got ₐ good look at the car, I got a good look at the driver.'

"Did you notice the gold tooth? 'No.' 'Why not?' 'Because . . . when he spoke to me, he was looking away.'

"And then later on, under cross-examination, she says: 'When I was standing by the window, he turned to me and said, "Come or Mrs. Connors, we gotta go." '

"You can see the gold tooth. I don't care, frankly, what Claud Rivers [NIS agent Rivers] said. Brooke Howard taught me a lon time ago—and I don't mean to be facetious but I think it i indicative of human nature . . . just because a man carries badge don't make his mouth into a prayer book. This is seriou business and I don't have to tell you that."

Leino next went on to cite a number of things the investigator did not do—because they felt they had enough on Scott and didn' have to look further. They did not bother looking for or siftin evidence that did not fit their conclusion. "I'm not an expert o photography," Leino said, talking about the alleged "wipe-down of the passenger side of Scott's car, "but I believe given the stat of art of photography, you could probably—if there was a clea line of demarcation—you could probably photograph it. An frankly I can't see it in the photos. But that's your decision.

"What I'm saying is . . . if they couldn't photograph it, if thi was the most serious crime committed on this base in decades perhaps the most serious crime of all time, why didn't the impound the car?" Leino pointed out that if Scott was as clever a the prosecution claimed he was, then how was it that he decide "he could get rid of all the hairs, all the fibers, by wiping dow half the car in which an attack took place on both sides of the from seat? That's their case. That's their proof. Beyond a reasonabl doubt."

(By this time, in addition to the two women, other jurors ha begun to take notes: Major Jones, Captain Pappa, the jury forema Colonel Festa.)

As he continued Leino said there were times he did no understand what was so sinister about Scott's moves that day about the cleaning materials he was carrying, about which bucke he was supposedly using—a green plastic one or a metal pot—al things the prosecution had harped on. Did these things "somehov camouflage his moves? Disorient the victim, if she survived th attack? I don't understand it," he said, "but maybe they'll say 'Well, you don't understand the criminal mind.'

"Where's the indication that he's a criminal? What is there in hi background that you can point to? He's nothing but a good Marine. He's nothing but a good person. Married. With a baby on the way. And moving out of his apartment. And I think you're entitled to consider this."

Still pacing up and down in front of the jury box, sweating profusely in the stuffy atmosphere of the small courtroom, overheated by his own exertions, Leino attacked once again the NIS's methods of obtaining a positive identification from Judy Connors: the photo lineup, the Identi-Kit. And he questioned again her identification: "At the first court-martial she said she didn't get a good look at him. At the second court-martial she said she did get a good look at him." And at the photo lineup and the physical lineup, Leino repeated, she picked out two men.

He spoke about the forensics: "Nothing in the car. Nothing on his clothes. Nothing on her clothes . . . and we're talking about microscopic analysis."

After a while, as he continued criticizing the unprofessional handling of the investigation, which focused on Scott too early to the exclusion of any other possible suspects, Leino paused, heaved a deep sigh, and said, "You know, I didn't want to get into this, but I've got to, just so you understand. The prosecutor talked about Lori Jackson . . . Lori Jackson . . . Lori Jackson. Her presence is here and I can feel it. It just so happens that Lori Jackson fought for the truth. From Selma, Alabama, with Dr. Martin Luther King to this very day. Now she's fighting for her life in Washington, in a hospital room."

"Objection, Your Honor," McNeil called. (It was most unusual; objections very rarely occur during final argument, as counsel for both sides are traditionally given wide latitude.)

Judge Clark overruled when, responding to a question from him, Leino said he would not continue with this subject, and apologized.

He returned briefly to the alibi defense. "Ruby Hills came in here and testified. And they had their shot at her. Under cross-examination. And what did she do? She explained how she remembered him. Well, if there's another conspiracy between Lori Jackson and Ruby Hills . . . 'a civil-rights activist.' I don't know what they mean by that. I hope they don't mean what I think they're trying to imply. Let's just avoid that." Lori Jackson showed her some photographs, Leino said, and it jogged Ruby Hills's memory. She checked her records again. . . .

"And I don't care if she's Mata Hari, I don't care if she's Squeaky Fromme"—the former Charles Manson associate who tried to assassinate President Ford—"there are certain things that she knows."

Back to the identification, as he prepared to end his argument: "It looks like the car . . . it looks like the man . . . I'm ninety-nine percent sure . . . and when the chief investigator concludes his testimony after four and a half years . . . the standard-bearer of this investigation . . . and I ask him, 'Is this a positive ID?' . . . he says no. . . . He says no. And is that *proof beyond a reasonable doubt*?

"It is our position that what it all adds up to is . . . reasonable doubt."

In closing, Leino said, "The burden is heavy . . . because the impact is profound.

"I'm just going to leave you with one thought. One of the best things that I've done in my life—besides marrying my wife, Patty—was to take the oath on the parade deck of Quantico . . . allow me this. I realized then as I realize now that that oath—an oath I considered then to be a blood oath to this country, and to this Corps—meant one thing, and that was the protection and the defense of the Constitution. You know what that means to this defense . . . two hundred years of self-determination and free- dom . . . two hundred years of justice.

"During your deliberations, you are the embodiment of that Constitution. And that is what I touch and feel and taste in this case. Godspeed with your deliberations."

It was now 5:24 on a darkening February evening, and the judge called another 39(a) session. After thinking a moment, he admon- ished Leino for several of his arguments. "Some did cross the line," he said, referring in particular to Leino's mention of Lori Jackson from "twenty-three years ago." When the members of the jury returned to the courtroom, Judge Clark said to them, "In regards to counsel's mention of Lori Jackson, ignore the mention of Selma, Alabama, and Martin Luther King."

The judge allowed the prosecution to do a rebuttal of Leino's closing argument that lasted half an hour; at 6:15, he began some final instructions to the jury. One of these, significantly, was "Eyewitness Instruction," a paper handed to each juror, but read aloud, too, by the judge, to give either counsel an opportunity to object to any part of it. Following are several of the important parts of that instruction:

One of the most important issues in this case is the identification of the defendant as the perpetrator of the offense. The government has the burden of proving identity beyond a reasonable doubt. It's not essential that the witness herself be free from doubt as to the correctness of her statement. However, you, the members of the court, must be satisfied beyond a reasonable doubt of the accuracy of the identification of the accused before you may convict him. If you are not convinced beyond a reasonable doubt that the accused was the person who committed the offense, you must find the accused not guilty.

Identification testimony is an expression of belief or impression by the witness. Its value depends on the opportunity the witness had to observe the offender at the time of the offense and to make a reliable identification later.

In appraising the identification testimony of a witness, you should consider the following:

Are you satisfied that the identification made by the witness subsequent to the offense was the product of her own recollection? You may take into account both the strength of the identification, and the circumstances under which the identification was made.

In this case, the identifying witness is of a different race than the accused. In the experience of many, it is more difficult to identify members of a different race than members of one's own. If this is also your own experience, you may consider it in evaluating the witness's testimony. You must also consider, of course, whether there are other factors present in this case which overcome any such difficulty of identification. For

example, you may consider that, if the witness has had
sufficient contacts with members of the accused's race that she
would not have greater difficulty in making reliable identification.

The judge closed the day's proceedings with a reminder to the
members of the jury that the burden of proof lay with the
government, and any statement he (the judge) had made during
the trial that might tend to influence them either way should be
"disregarded." At 6:47, he excused the members and told them to
report at nine the next morning.

On the way home from that long, grueling, exhausting day, John
Leino and his wife (who had come to court to hear her husband's
closing arguments) stopped by Washington National Hospital to
visit Lori. She was half-asleep, hooked to a slow-drip IV bottle.
She smiled up at them. They gave her the best wishes from Gary
Myers, and from Lola and Lindsey Scott. She asked them how
things were going. Leino put on a brave face; at that moment he
was not brimming with confidence. "Things could work out in our
favor," he said to Lori. "We're all keeping our fingers crossed. The
jury gets the case tomorrow." Lori began to doze off. They bent
over the bed, gave her a peck on the cheek, and left.

The following morning, when the jury entered, Judge Clark
began by reviewing some of the instructions he had given them the
evening before. (And author Cohen was "bumped" from his usual
seat. Throughout the trial he had taken the same corner seat by the
visitors' entrance at the back of the room. This morning a NIS
agent, in business suit and concealed handgun, usurped his place.)

Judge Clark added to his review a weighty thought for the
members of the jury: "Influence of superiority and rank should not
bear on any decision." Before announcing "Court is closed," at
9:47 A.M., he reminded everyone that there would be "secret
balloting," and that two thirds of the members—five of seven—
"must concur for a guilty verdict." The members then left to begin
deliberations.

27

As soon as the members of the jury retired for their deliberations, Leino, Myers, and Lynch moved downstairs to the Bunker, accompanied by Lindsey and Lola Scott and author Cohen. There they would await the verdict. Understandably, the tension was palpable. Quickly the room became blue with cigarette smoke (only Cohen was a nonsmoker). Attempts at idle conversation quickly sputtered to a halt.

At 11:40—seven minutes less than two hours since the jury began deliberations—Colonel Festa, the jury foreman, asked the bailiff (stationed outside the security-guarded jury room) to call the courtroom together in ten minutes.

Quickly the bailiff sped to the judge's chambers, to the prosecution team in the JAG office next to the courtroom, and to the defense team in the basement. There was near panic as everybody rushed pell-mell to the courtroom, including the eight media people chosen for the day and visitors with passes stuck to their blouses or jackets. Everyone, however, had first to go through a physical search with a handheld "wong" that scanned the entire body. Both sides of the hallway outside the courtroom were lined with security people, uniformed and in plain clothes.

At 11:50—incredibly—everyone was back and seated; expectant, tense, ready. Judge Clark entered the courtroom as the bailiff bellowed, "All rise." The jury members next filed in through the back entrance. The judge ordered everyone to be seated and asked for quiet, then addressed the foreman. "Do you have a verdict?"

To everyone's surprise—and some chagrin, especially among the media—Festa replied, "No. We request a one-hour recess to have our noon meal." The judge agreed and said, "We will be in recess till 1300."

Back in the Bunker, the original group had been joined by Laurie Myers (Gary's wife), Patty Leino, a Scott family priest, and private investigator Morgan Cherry—the man who had done the time-study video disallowed by the judge, now retained by Leino and Myers for posttrial security. Cherry advised the lawyers that he had three armed plainclothes guards standing by to handle a swift exit for Scott (this on the assumption, or hope, that he would be acquitted; the defense team reckoned his chances at fifty-fifty). Also with hope of good news, the Scotts had their bags packed and told Cherry that they wanted to go to Lola's parents' house in a small Kentucky town, about a two-hour drive from Louisville.

About 3:55, all heard the bugler sounding taps as the flag was lowered to half-mast in memory of a retired general who had died. At 4:35 Scott began to pace nervously. "What if they find me guilty again . . . will there be MPs all around me?" he asked.

Leino quickly attempted to calm him. "Lindsey," he said, "if they find you guilty, the MPs will lock you up. But if they acquit you, the MPs will line up to shake your hand." With that remark most in the room began to laugh, breaking the tension.

At around five P.M. Captain Lynch came down to the Bunker to tell Leino and Myers that he'd literally evicted Ruby Hills from the building and sent her home after he'd discovered that she had been seen crying in the ladies' room near a jury member, Lieutenant Colonel Patricia Breeding. Myers, in utter shock, bolted from the room and raced upstairs to make sure she was gone. Such an incident, the defense team realized, could send an uncomfortable signal to the jury—via Breeding, who the defense believed could be a "swing voter." When Myers returned to say, with relief, that Ruby was gone, he also reported that the court would reconvene at six P.M.

Everyone returned at six, more calmly this time, to hear that the jury wanted to recess for the night and return the next morning at eight. Judge Clark suggested that "due to logistical reasons [morning traffic], I want you back at 0900." The judge then adjourned the court.

* * *

The Washington Post played it big in its February 19 edition. "Outside Quantico Court-Martial Room, it's Theatre," the story began.

> A jury of seven officers deliberated for 6½ hours but did not reach a verdict yesterday in the court-martial of Corporal Lindsey Scott—the gripping Quantico marine base whodunit that has ignited debate about racism and justice in the corps. . . . All week as the climax has neared . . . the stage has grown more crowded with colorful characters . . . a sometimes uneasy mix of people, including civil rights activists, victims' rights advocates and spit-and-polish marines.
>
> They have formed the backdrop for one of the most closely watched military cases in recent memory, a case tinged with suggestions of racism. Scott is black; the victim is white. . . .

At home that night, John Leino worried. He was not optimistic about Scott's chances. A religious man, he remembered a Finnish custom. At moments of personal crisis, religious Finns take the Bible and allow the pages to fall open where they may; then they search on those two pages for some sign, some inspiration.

John Leino went to his Bible and did just that; he placed it on the desk in front of him and allowed the book to fall open. And there, before his eyes, was John II:1, and the words seemed to leap at him off the page: "Lazarus come forth!" (Lazarus was the Biblical figure, the brother of Mary and Martha, raised from the dead by Jesus.)

For the first time, John Leino believed that Lindsey Scott would go free.

The morning of February 19 was gray, chilly, and drizzly. At Quantico one of the reporters remarked to Myers and Cohen that he recalled the skies having that same bleak, hopeless look on October 10, 1983, the day on which Lindsey Scott had been found guilty and sentenced to thirty years hard labor at Leavenworth. Only John Leino expressed guarded optimism. He did not share with the others his reading of the Bible and discovery of the

Lazarus quote. At 9:07, Judge Clark ordered the court closed to start the second day of deliberations.

That same morning, at about that same time, Lori Jackson was being taken into the operating room at the Washington National Hospital for a procedure. Her husband took a chair in her room, to wait. Paul knew, and Lori had been told the night before, that the jury probably would come to a decision that day. (Later, some of Lori's children joined in his vigil at her bedside.)

Once again the members of the jury asked for their noontime lunch break, and once again it was granted and the court recessed for an hour. This time, however, at 2:05, there came a loud knock on the door of the Bunker. Every heart in the room skipped a beat. The bailiff, Sergeant McFeeter, poked his head in the door and said that he had just been handed a note by the jury foreman Colonel Festa; everyone had to be back in court within ten minutes.

As they all rushed out to the hallway Myers said to Leino "Well, John, it's showtime!" And with a nervous little laugh, Leino said, "Yeah."

The little courtroom was now packed with extra Marine MPs with holster flaps unbuttoned, hands resting on pistol butts. Extra men in dark suits were on hand, too, shoulder holsters visible beneath their suit coats—ready for any disturbance, any verdict. At the defense table, Myers, Leino, and Lynch stood at attention. Leino leaned over to Scott and said, "Lindsey, you got to believe."

Judge Clark entered. The members of the jury entered. Everyone then sat down except for Colonel Festa, who stood facing the judge.

Judge Clark: "Has the court reached its findings?"

Colonel Festa: "Yes, it has, Your Honor." He handed an envelope to the bailiff, who in turn handed it to the judge.

Judge Clark: "Proceed."

A stern-faced Colonel Festa looked directly at Scott, who was standing to hear the verdict: "Corporal Lindsey Scott, United States Marine Corps, this court-martial now finds you—of all specifications and charges—NOT GUILTY!"

A moment of silence—then pandemonium in the courtroom. Scott's knees buckled. John Leino grabbed him in a big bear hug.

In the gallery, Scott's mother shouted out, "Thank you, Jesus!" and was led from the courtroom by a friend, as the court was still in session. Scott, freed from Leino's embrace, took a few steps and stretched out his arm for a handshake with McNeil and Hinkle, saying to them: "I didn't do it. I'm innocent."

While shouts and cries of joy echoed in the courtroom and Judge Clark banged his gavel in vain for silence, at Washington National Hospital, in Lori Jackson's room, her husband was watching the news on CNN, passing the time, trying to keep his mind occupied, deeply worried about his wife, terminally ill with liver cancer. By now, he knew, she would be in the recovery room. As he watched the TV a breaking-story slide appeared behind the late-afternoon CNN anchorman, Bernard Shaw, who said: "This just in . . ."

Paul leaped to his feet and raced down the hallway to the recovery room, a beaming smile on his face.

In the hallway, coming toward him on a hospital gurney, was Lori, several IVs hooked to her frail arms. When she saw Paul approaching, saw his face, she reached for his hand.

"CNN just broke in about the case," he said to her. "Bernie Shaw just announced the verdict."

Lori squeezed his hand. Her lips moved. Paul leaned over her, his ear to her lips. "I know," Lori whispered. "I know."

Nine months later, on November 25, 1988, one day after Thanksgiving, at 5:30 A.M., Lori Jackson died peacefully in her sleep.

The law says he's [Scott] "not guilty." It doesn't say we have to find him innocent.

—RICHARD COHEN, "Critic at Large"
The Washington Post Magazine

POSTSCRIPT

Because we take longer, the military system [of justice] is actually fairer than the civilian system.

—Lieutenant Colonel John Shotwell
Head, Media Branch
Division of Public Affairs.
Headquarters,
U.S. Marine Corps,
Washington, D.C.

It looked, by the size of the participants and the number of television cameras, that there was going to be a presidential press conference. By my count, there were at least fifteen electronic media teams representing the American networks and tabloid news shows plus other countries throughout the world, in addition to scores of newspaper, magazine, and radio reporters. But this was not for lame-duck President Reagan, instead this major coverage awaited "free man" Corporal Lindsey Scott and his victorious defense attorneys, John Leino, Gary Myers, and Captain Brennan Lynch, at the Quantico Media Center.

(Funny thing: As we all drove from LeJeune Hall in an unmarked white van, the kind with those darkened windows, the entourage included four NIS, gun-toting agents, dressed in those dark, nondescript suits, all now assigned by the command to *protect* Scott. Hmm, just wondering: "If Scott was found guilty on all charges, would this same security group have been assigned to 'safeguard' Scott down the road, the other way, and back to the Quantico brig?)

During the five years of this case, Lori Jackson had pushed to get the press to cover it. One of the best examples of her success was the tremendous coverage *The Washington Post* gave this story, starting from the days before Scott's first court-martial. Back then, the Scott story was lucky if it was found on page 37. But to herald Scott's acquittal, the *Post* ran, under their page-one banner headline CORPORAL SCOTT NOT GUILTY IN 2ND COURT-MARTIAL, a four-column wrap-up story.

Lee Hockstader, the writer of this story, reported that: "In the news conferences [two separate: one for the government and one for the defense], Marine prosecutors and defense lawyers agreed that questions surrounding the victim's identification of Scott as her attacker were probably the key factor in the jury's decision. On the second day of the trial, the chief military investigator in the case [NIS agent Lindner] testified that the woman told him five days after the attack that she 'didn't get a good enough look' at her assailant to identify him positively."

When Corporal Lindsey Scott had his moment to speak to the throng of media, his tone was very understated. He said: "I maintained my innocence from the beginning. It was proven today by a jury of my peers that I was innocent. . . . I'm innocent. I'm free."

He said further, "My feelings about the Marine Corps have never changed. They're the best fighting force," and he said he received a "very fair trial" under the military justice system (which his family and backers had roundly denounced as racist and inept).

Both Scott's civilian attorneys, Myers and Leino, added their comments to the reporters. Myers: "I think [the jury] just came to the conclusion that it was a toss-up—and a toss-up is not a guilty verdict." And Leino, who delivered an emotional closing argument to the jury, concluded the defense team's press conference with those now familiar words: "Lazarus, come forth!"

When Major Ron McNeil, the government's lead prosecutor, had his chance to speak, he said the investigation into the attack on the young wife of a military policeman on April 20, 1983, would *not* be reopened. "The issue is *definitely* dead," McNeil concluded. But was it really?

*   *   *

In an exclusive story in *The Washington Post,* on Sunday February 21, 1988, two days after the not guilty verdict, Lee Hockstader reported that according to a source close to the proceedings, the Scott jury fell one vote short of convicting the Marine for a second time. "Under military law," Hockstader wrote, "a defendant may be convicted by a vote of two-thirds of the 'members of the court,' as military juries are known. In the Scott case, that meant a 5-to-2 vote would have convicted him, while a 4-to-3 vote equaled acquittal.

"Such a split is considered fairly unusual, though it is not unheard of. Unlike civilian courts, there was no possibility of a hung jury.

"Scott cannot be retried on the same charges."

Hockstader said as many as five sources confirmed to him what prosecution and defense attorneys said Friday (at the press conference)—that the key to Scott's acquittal was that several jurors were *not* convinced by the uncertain identification of Scott given by the victim in the days after the attack.

When Myers was asked about the jury's vote, he responded: "I don't think it means anything to me. It was a close case; you get a close result."

Within twenty-four hours after the final press conferences, Marine Corporal Lindsey Scott arrived in Louisville to a hero's welcome. Family and friends crowded in front of his parents' apartment holding signs heralding his return.

Talking with local reporters, Scott said he had decided that his future life did not include the Marine Corps. He said he would "muster out" of the Corps within the next three weeks. "I've been to hell three times—two courts-martial and four years in prison. . . . I was really set on being a career Marine, but now I think it is best for the Corps and me to go separate ways." (Note: The Department of the Navy gave Scott this option to take an early retirement, which would include an honorable discharge at the rank of sergeant (a promotion he was given after his acquittal) and all benefits. Since Scott's service with the Marine Corps technically expired on October 1, 1984, while he was in Leavenworth

Prison, he was not bound by a legal enlistment contract and had been on a "legal hold" ever since.)

Scott was able to collect about $29,000 in back pay and allowances that would cover the thirty-three months between the expiration of service on October 1, 1984, and July 16, 1987, when he returned to full pay status (following the Court of Military Appeals' decision).

Initially, Scott thought about joining either the Louisville police or fire department. But he did neither. After a few years battling his former attorney, Ervan Kuhnke, in civil court, Scott finally settled a $1.5 million malpractice suit. Both Scott and Kuhnke agreed, as part of their settlement, not to discuss the terms of the settlement. But sources told *The Washington Post* that Scott received somewhat less than $100,000, the maximum amount covered by Kuhnke's malpractice insurance.

Scott finally decided to move away from his birthplace of Louisville to a smaller community, where he would go into business for himself. Along with his wife, Lola, he just wanted to enjoy watching his daughter, Latavia, grow up.

In a stunning announcement, on May 9, 1988, less than three months after Scott's military acquittal, Prince William County's chief prosecutor, Paul B. Ebert (who later became the now famous prosecutor in the John and Lorena Bobbit case), said that he hoped to retry "civilian" Lindsey Scott on the same four charges that had led to Scott's five-year ordeal.

Even though the Fifth Amendment bars double jeopardy, Ebert believed that it did not apply to Scott because, as he said: "The Commonwealth of Virginia's legal system and the military judicial system are separate."

Ebert, who commented to reporters at a press conference that he thought Scott was guilty and "an injustice was done," said he wrote a letter to state Attorney General Mary Sue Terry to seek her opinion on his legal standing to prosecute.

Immediately, both John Leino and Gary Myers commented to the media. Leino: "Apparently, they're going for the best two out of three. Here we are [three] months after the trial and the state prosecutor of Prince William County wants to take a shot at him.

Who's next, Manhattan South?" And Myers: "In Mr. Ebert's case, sometimes what a man is thunders so loudly you cannot hear what he says he is."

According to a story by the Associated Press, attorney Paul Ebert said that his interest in the case was stimulated by reports that the Marines had continued to pursue tests of genetic material after Scott's acquittal. The tests sought to determine whether DNA from Scott's blood matched that of semen from the victim's panties after the April 1983 assault. (According to a very reliable Marine officer, who spoke on the condition of anonymity, disgruntled members of the NIS filtered confidential information to Mr. Ebert regarding the third DNA test that was *personally* ordered, in California, by Quantico's commanding general, Lieutenant General Frank Petersen and Staff Judge Advocate Colonel James McHenry.)

But four days after Ebert's press conference, Virginia Attorney General Mary Sue Terry sent him a four-page letter and informed him that one cannot be tried by the state of Virginia if one previously faced the same charges in federal court.

Remarking to press inquiries, attorney Gary Myers said: "I think it's over. It was over for all reasonable people when the verdict came out."

And Ebert released a statement: "From my interpretation . . . the state has prohibited any further prosecution. I have always intended to be guided by her [Terry's] opinion."

After their resounding success, Scott's two civilian attorneys advanced, in separate ways, their legal careers. John Leino became a full partner in his prestigious Alexandria, Virginia, law firm, now named: Howard, Leino & Howard. Gary Myers opened his own law firm, Gary Myers & Associates, specializing in military law, and operating out of his Washington, D.C., office.

Finally, and sadly, one day after Thanksgiving 1988, I was visiting with my family in the east when I received a phone call informing me that my friend Lori Jackson had died peacefully at her oldest son's home in Lorton, Virginia. Her children honored me with the request that I deliver a eulogy at her Tuesday funeral. Of course, I accepted.

As I had my dad (he and my mom knew and loved Lori as well) drive me to the Mountcastle Funeral Home in Dale City, Virginia, I jotted some notes that I wanted to refer to when I spoke to the gathered friends and family.

It was a beautiful, very bright, late-fall day, a day that Lori would have chosen herself. The one P.M. service began on schedule with the overflow crowd assembling in the chapel. John and Patty Leino sat some rows behind us. Officiating were the Reverend Helice Greene and the Reverend Ambrose Perry, with Martha King playing appropriate interludes. Standing to the right of Lori's opened coffin, I asked everyone to quietly pray for peace in eternity for our dear friend Lori. Then I said:

"She was a very special friend of mine. She always gave . . . she always cared . . . she always made a difference . . . and never asked for anything in return.

"Just eight weeks ago, I was invited to a dinner the equivalent of a Thanksgiving meal—a dinner that Lori prepared, with some help from her daughters. This was the last time I saw Lori before her passing. After the dishes had been put away, Lori discussed with me what these last five years had meant to her. And why she gave up so much of her time with her family. And she answered me with the same word both times: *rights!* That was what our friend Lori was all about. All she wanted to do was make this world of ours a little more equal . . . *and she did*.

"If I have my way, God willing, Lori will always be remembered by millions of people."

At the last dinner with Lori and her family, I asked her how she wanted to be remembered, and she replied: *"As a loving person!"*

—Ellis A. Cohen

EPILOGUE

After covering *United States* v. *Corporal Scott*—almost every step of the way—I often thought about something that Lori Jackson shared with me when we first met in 1984: "Ellis, there's something wrong about what Judy said on the record. She knew Lindsey, but never mentioned his name. And the day she says she was raped and almost murdered was also the day that she suddenly quit her job at Hardee's restaurant. Something about that bothers me." Her comment has always left me curious.

Following Lori's passing in late 1988, I was more determined than ever to find some connection between the afternoon of April 20, 1983, when Judy quit, and that near-fatal evening. After I reread the transcripts of the first court-martial, one question and answer stood out in my mind: Scott's civilian attorney Kuhnke, while cross-examining Judy, asked her if she had "Negro friends," and she responded: "I used to when I was working at Hardee's. I knew a couple guys that worked there, friends of mine. . . ."

Over the five years of the Scott case, Judy, more than anyone else, was the most evasive principal to all media. I tried repeatedly to speak at length to her—even approaching her family attorney—all to no avail. In late 1988, I asked Major Ron McNeil, the lead prosecutor in the second court-martial, if he could try to persuade Judy to speak with me. I indicated that I wanted her comments in order to do full narrative justice to the story. McNeil wrote her a letter on my behalf, asking her to speak or write to me.

Here's some of what Judy wrote to McNeil (I only received the portion of her response from McNeil that pertained to my inquiry):

She expressed ambivalence speaking to me. "On one hand, I'd *like* to talk to him and let him get a little *truth* about this case for a change." But she went on to talk herself out of any interview. She concluded with:

"The only one thing in this whole world that enables me to deal with the fact that Lindsey Scott is a free man is the fact that I *know* that a time *will come* when, like all the rest of us, Lindsey Scott, too, will face his Maker."

Even though I never got to do a lengthy interview with Judy, her few comments indicate her continuing belief that Scott was her assailant. But, I wondered, was there something that the government knew and never revealed? This, by the way, was the scuttlebutt among the media mavens that covered the case.

The military case was now long over, but maybe, if I pursued some of the key government players, someone might shed some new light. So I made a short list of who might know something that had never been revealed before:

Major Ron McNeil, the person on the prosecution side with whom I became the friendliest, swore that he was not privy to any "secrets" about the original incident, investigation, or trial proceedings. In fact, he jokingly said: "If you discover anything juicy, please let me know."

Lieutenant General David Twomey, the original Quantico commanding general who was ultimately responsible for Scott's first court-martial, never spoke to anyone, at any time, in the media. I tried through the proper procedures; that is, I requested an interview from the Marine public-affairs office. I tried at least five different times over the years either to reach the general on the phone or by letter; each time I was sent a neatly typed answer that said: "I spoke with Lieutenant General David Twomey, USMC. I asked him if he would be willing to talk with you about the circumstances surrounding Corporal Scott. General Twomey declined to be interviewed or comment on the subject."

Lieutenant General Frank E. Petersen, the Quantico commanding general who was ultimately responsible for Scott's second court-martial, did grant me a meeting during the trial and left the door open for further inquiries (I thought). In fact, he gave me his private phone number at his LeJeune Hall office. I exchanged a few telephone calls with Petersen after Scott's acquittal. Then I received the first of a few letters from Petersen, on his official three-star letterhead. The first, dated April 11, 1988, in response to my posttrial inquiry, he characterized the information I had requested as "both complicated and lengthy," and invited me to meet in person. But Petersen later backed down.

Major Donald Thomson, the original lead prosecutor, was the hardest person to locate. He left the Scott case in 1985 after the DuBay hearings. (And in March 1987 he left the Marine Corps.) But late in 1990—through a fortuitous conversation with one of the media people who covered some of the Scott case—I got a clue where to find him. He was employed as a public defender in a small community in the heartland of America. I contacted him and convinced him to meet with me.

On a very cold, snowy morning, three days before Christmas 1990, I traveled to meet with him. (To protect his privacy, the location remains secret.) Thomson and I sat down for breakfast. I showed him my tape recorder and he agreed to allow me to tape our conversation—which lasted three hours. And to my utter surprise, what Thomson revealed was a bombshell. (After my hearing Lori's curiosity about Judy Connors and Hardee's restaurant over and over again, what the retired Marine major told me not only confirmed certain rumors, but revealed information that would have, most likely, changed the entire government case of *United States* v. *Corporal Scott.*)

"The NIS bungled the case against him (Scott)," Thomson began. "I believe he could be innocent." (I was shocked at this startling revelation. As I didn't want to show any outward emotions—I wanted to hear everything the former prosecutor wanted to reveal—I just continued to question him in no special order.)

The following are some of the more sensational comments that Thomson made to me over the three hours, all *on the record:*

Cohen: "Did you think that Judy Connors might have been lying and did you check on her background?"

Thomson: "Yes. NIS checked on her background. Lindner was the one who did it. It wasn't a part of the NIS investigation. He checked around. He interviewed some of the individuals she worked with. I was aware that Judy was very close with some blacks where she worked."

Cohen: "If you had to do everything over again, would you pursue these blacks as suspects?"

Thomson: "I think I would. . . ."

(At this point, Thomson said that he erred in not telling Mr. Kuhnke about the two black individuals. "If I knew, he should have known," Thomson admitted. He further stated that he confronted Judy with this information, saying, "The evidence indicated that you had been close, promiscuous with two black guys who worked with you." But he then added that she denied that this was the case.)

Cohen: "Lori Jackson's assertion that one of the high-ranking officers at the base hated blacks and was systematically getting rid of all the blacks in Scott's Security Battalion—do you have any knowledge of this?"

Thomson: "That's an opinion that I share. I do believe this."

Cohen: "Lori Jackson said the NIS had a vendetta against Scott. Once Judy was wheeled into Camp Upshur, one of the NIS agents said: 'Sounds like Scotty!' Do you now believe that the NIS was biased against Scott?"

Thomson: "Yes. But not just the NIS, the prosecution as well . . . Everybody's bound by that [the notion of innocent until proven guilty] because we're all agents of the government."

Cohen: "You seem to have some trouble now believing that Scott was the guilty person?"

Thomson: "I can tell you the reasons why I have some discomfort about his conviction. One . . . because I've seen another individual who looks just like him, and two . . . I know that direct evidence [meaning Judy's eyewitness identification] was probably the most compelling evidence at his trial, and it shouldn't have been. I think that if I was the defense counselor, and had the case, I would rip the prosecution to shreds."

Cohen: "With what?"

Thomson: "The lack of identification."

In conclusion . . . the vast majority of court-martials never attract public attention.

Men and women in the armed forces are charged, convicted, and sentenced all within the closed world of the military court-room.

The system of military justice is, by its very design, intended to help enforce discipline and is clearly biased against the rights of the defendant.

One can only theorize about how many innocent people, who are honorably serving their country, are trapped like Lindsey Scott—without a Lori Jackson and the means to hire a first-class defense—and suffer insurmountable injustices.

—Ellis A. Cohen

ABOUT THE AUTHORS

ELLIS A. COHEN is a producer and author who resides in Los Angeles. He has developed a number of award-winning television and feature films starring such television luminaries as Jean Stapleton and Judd Hirsch, and has written one previous book. Cohen is currently CEO of a media production company and is working on ideas for his next book.

MILTON J. SHAPIRO is an American author currently living in England. In a career as a journalist and author on both sides of the Atlantic spanning some forty years, he has published more than thirty books.

TRUE CRIME
AT ITS SHOCKING BEST

__CROSSING THE LINE: The True Story of Long Island
  Serial Killer Joel Rifkin
Lisa Beth Pulitzer and Joan Swirsky   0-425-14441-0/$5.99
The riveting account of the notorious Long Island serial
killer. Includes exclusive interviews, photos, and
psychological evaluations.

__WHEN RABBIT HOWLS The Troops for
  Truddi Chase   0-515-10329-2/$6.50
The #1 New York Times bestseller, as seen on Oprah.
A woman journeys back to the unspeakable crimes she
suffered, seeking the origin of the 92 voices that live
within her.

__FROM CRADLE TO GRAVE Joyce Egginton
                                       0-515-10301-2/$5.99
One by one, Marybeth Tinning's nine children died of
mysterious causes. This startling New York Times
bestseller takes you into the mind of a mother who
committed the unspeakable crime.

__ZODIAC Robert Graysmith   0-425-09808-7/$5.99
The terrifying story of the nation's most bizarre mass
murderer. He claimed 37 dead, but the real toll may
have reached 50. He was never caught.